TIM

"Who are _____ _____ ___ __g in my cabin?" Abby asked, ___ eyes fixed on the width of the strange man's shoulders.

"I am called Elan, " he replied softly. "I do not know how I came to this place. I was hunting elk when suddenly I found myself here."

"Look, I don't know what you're doing on my ranch hunting elk out of season, but I think you had better leave!"

Elan puzzled over her words. She was speaking English, but making little sense. He wondered if living in the wilderness had addled her brain.

A deep uneasiness began to steal across his mind as he looked the woman over. Her attire was most unusual. Was it possible? No, it could not be possible.

"Can you tell me the date?" he finally asked. "I have been on this expedition for a long time."

Instantly she looked up to meet his gaze. "It's July 6, 1995."

Elan could not believe it, but somehow he had been catapulted almost two hundred years into the future. It was the only explanation he could muster.

Either that or the woman had been catapulted two hundred years into the past.

✧ ✧ ✧

THE BOOKWORM
14, 140 Athabascan Ave.
Sherwood Park, AB 464-5522

Yesterday's
Tomorrows

✦MARGARET LANE✦

HarperPaperbacks
A Division of HarperCollins*Publishers*

This is a work of fiction. The characters, incidents, and dialogues are products of the author's imagination and are not to be construed as real. Any resemblance to actual events or persons, living or dead, is entirely coincidental.

HarperPaperbacks   *A Division of* HarperCollins*Publishers*
10 East 53rd Street, New York, N.Y. 10022

Cover illustration by Vittorio

First printing: October 1995

Printed in the United States of America

HarperPaperbacks, HarperMonogram, and colophon are trademarks of HarperCollins*Publishers*

❖ 10 9 8 7 6 5 4 3 2 1

Yesterday's Tomorrows

1

Elan stealthily made his way through the dense pine thicket, never taking his eyes from the enormous bull elk he stalked. Grayish brown with a dark chestnut mane and a straw-colored patch on his rump, the elk must have been at least a thousand pounds and carried a rack that spread five feet or more. It was a mystery to Elan how the large animal made its way so effortlessly through the forest without entangling itself in the low, drooping branches.

The elk paused in its unhurried climb and majestically swung its head around. Elan lifted his long rifle and closed his left eye, sighting along the bore. Muttering a curse under his breath, he brought the rifle down. The beast was just out of range. It had steadily kept two hundred yards or more ahead of him all afternoon.

The elk raised its head to sniff the air, then in a sudden panic thundered over the ridge and was gone in a flash of hooves. Elan froze, feeling the fine hairs on the nape of his neck rise. He was downwind from the elk. It had not been his scent that spooked it.

Indians? Bear? Without moving his head, Elan carefully shifted his rifle from his right hand to his left, and slowly, ever so slowly, slid his free hand down his buckskin-clad leg until his fingers closed around his bone-handled hunting knife. He eased the blade from its leather sheath and gripped it tightly as his eyes searched unsuccessfully along the ridge. He too sniffed the air, but failed to detect anything but his own very ripe scent.

If he didn't return from his hunting trip, Captain Lewis would shake his fine head, and might, if the notion struck him, record Elan's passing in one of the journals he frequently scribbled in. Elan was not even an official member of the expedition that had laboriously made its trek to the great ocean to the west and was now returning to share its findings with the rest of the world.

Hearing of Lewis and Clark's commission to travel to the headwaters of the Missouri River and across the Shining Mountains to find a waterway to the ocean, Elan had intercepted the expedition's overloaded keelboat as it made its ponderous way up the treacherous Missouri. He had argued at length, finally convincing the two men to allow him to come along. They drove a hard bargain: He would not be paid, but his expertise in hunting and his strong back insured his inclusion. Those two things and his knowledge of Indians and their languages were what had gotten him where he was now.

Eyes bored into his back. Elan knew it with the certainty born of nearly twenty years of wilderness hunting and trapping. These Shining Mountains he traversed just might be his final resting place, and he longed suddenly for the familiar terrain of the upper Mississippi and that she-devil, the muddy Missouri.

Elan cocked his head, straining his ears, but heard only the wind as it whispered through the trees and the faint gurgle of a nearby stream. Sweat dried on his face, and his scalp prickled once again, a sign of heightened awareness.

In one fluid movement he whirled and flung himself face down behind an uprooted half-rotted pine. He forced himself to breathe slowly and evenly, but nothing could have prepared him for what he saw. Nothing.

"Mon Dieu," Elan said, reverting to the boyhood French he rarely used unless he was translating for French-speaking tribes unfamiliar with the English language.

He was American, and damned proud of it. His father had followed George Rogers Clark, freezing and starving on the two-hundred-mile march to Vincennes in 1779, and had waded for days through icy floodwaters to see the surrender and capture of the hair-buyer Hamilton. English was the language of the Americans, and his father had made sure Elan spoke it, even going so far as to force him to be educated at the mission schools.

"My God," Elan repeated in English, getting to his feet and sheathing his knife. He bounded over the deadfall in a graceful leap and advanced into the small clearing just to the east of the downed tree.

The Indian sat cross-legged on the ground, his withered arms stretched out palms up in front of his emaciated body. He was entirely naked except for the breechclout covering his pitiful loins. His gray hair, unbound, flowed past his thin shoulders and waved lightly in the breeze, and his clouded eyes stared vacantly in death. He was as dried up as a piece of jerky that had been long smoked over a fire, and just about the same color. Deep lines crisscrossed his face, and he looked, Elan thought, as old as the snow-capped mountains surrounding him.

"What is it that you hold, old one?" Elan asked softly. He stood over the ancient Indian and leaned forward to study the leather medicine bag strung on a thong. The bag, unlike the Indian who held it, appeared new and was finely made and decorated with colorful quills. Elan knew whatever the bag held was powerful medicine. At least it had been to the Indian.

The prominent decoration on the bag consisted of two jagged lightning bolts, one black and the other red, intersecting in a field of white. There were also other Indian symbols on it with which Elan was more familiar, but it was the lightning bolts and the energy they represented that drew his interest.

Had Elan found the Indian stretched out on a burial platform with his weapons and accouterments, nothing on earth could have induced him to venture close enough to touch even the ground the platform shaded. Though he was not superstitious in the least, he held great respect for religion, any religion, and that included the religion of the red man.

But this Indian held out his hands in the classic gesture of gift giving, and Elan was by his very nature inquisitive. He reached for the bag.

July 6, 1995

Sara Abigail De Coux drove as if the demons of hell pursued the ancient hay truck she pushed—by sheer willpower, it seemed—over Stemple Pass. The gears of the worn-out truck ground audibly, but not loudly enough to drown the frequent stream of profanity that escaped Abby's clenched teeth.

"Eminent domain!" she railed for perhaps the tenth time since she had left the courthouse in Helena after suffering the latest and what was probably the last of her humiliating defeats. She removed her hand from the steering wheel to ball it into a fist and pound the hard plastic seat cover in impotent rage. "They killed Daddy," she said, speaking aloud again, even though there was no one to hear her.

The government's determination to annex the De Coux ranch to the national forest surrounding it had, Abby was sure, brought on the fatal stroke her father had suffered. For three of the five years since the government had started its quest, Abby alone had been left to fight, and fight she had. Using every dime she could put her hands on and all the grit of a fifth-generation Montanian who had lost her mother at the tender age of five, Abby fought.

She had concentrated so fiercely on her fight that she had ignored everything else in the process, alienating both long-standing friends and the man who loved her, the latter by refusing to marry him until she had the ranch safe. Bitterness welled up in her as she thought of the wedding invitation she had received six months ago from Paul Koehler and the enclosed note expressing his desire to remain friends.

Well, it was of no matter. If Paul didn't have the gumption to stand by her, then she was well rid of him. But it still hurt. It hurt a lot.

By the time Abby braked to cross the rough cattle guard and drove through the open gate of the ranch, she had decided what to do about her immediate future. Although she had never considered herself a procrastinator, she wasn't quite ready to face closing the ranch and dismissing the hired help. It could wait a week, and she was determined to have that week. She deserved it.

"One of you saddle Little Sister," Abby called across the yard after she parked the truck under a shed and climbed out with her shoes and hat in her hands, her white summer dress swishing around her legs. Several of the ranch hands were idly propped or sitting on the fence, taking a break from inoculating the spring calves. Waiting, she imagined, for her to return and share with them the morning's results. Well, she didn't feel like talking about it just yet. "I'm riding up to the old cabin for a few days." Even though she owed them no explanation as to her comings and goings, she wanted somebody to know where to find her in case her attorney happened on a miracle. Not that it was very likely.

The cabin, nestled in the foothills of the mountains surrounding the ranch, was on the original De Coux homestead and was still used by the hands as a line shack and a hunting cabin. Abby and her father had frequently used it for the same purposes, but she hadn't been up there since his death. She hadn't been able to face being there without him. But now she thought it fitting somehow, since her heritage had begun there, to pay a last visit and say good-bye.

Abby rode Little Sister with practiced ease, one leg out of the stirrup and thrown over the pommel. It was a glorious summer afternoon, and she was determined to enjoy it to the fullest.

How long had it been since she had taken the time to fully appreciate the big blue sky over her head, the rich, intoxicating fragrance of the pine forest, the cool mountain breeze on her face? She studied the ripening huckleberries that grew in profusion along the trail and decided to pick some from the patch she knew grew near the cabin. Wildflowers, white, yellow, blue and purple, colored the underbrush and announced their presence, basking under the warm summer sun before they were covered again, all too quickly, by winter's snow.

"What in the . . ." Abby said, startled out of her reverie by the unexpected violent tossing of Little Sister's head. She quickly changed her position and managed to get her foot back in the stirrup before the little mare reared, but just barely. Little Sister came down on all fours, backing up, ears flattened, snorting and shaking her head.

Abby allowed the mare to back while she worriedly scanned the ridge. Bear was the first thing that came to mind. The bears loved the huckleberries as much as she did, and this was the time of year when they were hungrily foraging. She searched the clear-cut, a deep and lasting scar on the lush landscape, but failed to detect any movement.

She soothed the horse, stroking her neck and talking quietly until Little Sister stopped backing and stood trembling in the middle of the trail. Then Abby opened her mouth and started singing. If there was a bear in the area, she wanted to alert it, and with any luck it would amble away.

As Abby sang she gently urged Little Sister forward, and the mare went, unwillingly at first, then with less resistance. "See, Little Sister?" Abby said during a pause from her singing. "My singing can scare off any beast!"

Abby rode more alertly now, rather than dreamily gliding through familiar territory. It was a welcome relief when she rode into the clearing and spotted the cabin. She rested for a moment in the saddle and thought of the many happy nights she and her father had spent within its rough log walls. In all of her twenty-five years, this would be the first night she had spent in the cabin without him.

She fingered the solid gold chain that encircled her neck. The necklace and the heavy gold nugget that hung from it had belonged to him. She had removed it from his neck the day he died and placed it around her own. It was a yoke she'd worn proudly, but now its weight seemed to drag her down. She'd depleted every ounce of her strength, and now felt overburdened, defeated, helpless as only a woman in a man's world could feel.

"Easy, girl," Abby said softly, abandoning her song in midrefrain in reaction to Little Sister's renewed skittishness. "Take it easy." She nudged the mare into resuming an unhurried pace. The cabin was never locked and was always well stocked for emergencies. Abby was suddenly eager to get inside. But first things first. Little Sister took priority.

After unsaddling the mare, Abby gave her a quick rubdown with a handful of grass and then turned her out to graze in the meadow. She had no fear of Little Sister wandering far. The little sorrel mare, raised from a foal, was as devoted to Abby as a faithful dog.

She picked up the saddlebags and slung them over her shoulder. Then, hefting the heavy saddle, she lugged it to the small porch of the cabin and dropped it with a thud and jangle of the metal trimmings.

Abby brushed her hands off on the legs of her dress and opened the cabin's door. She advanced into the gloom, pausing to allow her eyes to adjust. *What was that smell*? She reached for the curtains separating the main room from the bedroom and threw them back, expecting to find a dead pack rat at the most. She recoiled instinctively in shock as motes of dust flew through the air and her eyes focused on the form of a man sprawled across the double bed.

Was he dead? He certainly looked it, Abby thought as

she relaxed her grip on the curtains. And who in the world was he? She edged closer, feeling her pulse slow after the initial jolt, but it was still racing. Then she got another whiff.

"Whew!" Abby said, wrinkling her nose and breathing through her mouth. If he wasn't dead, then he surely ought to be!

She studied the huge man sprawled across the bed that was ridiculously small for him. He looked like something out of a history book. Some of these modern-day mountain men took things a little too far, in her estimation. He was dressed in leather, old leather, from the look and smell of it. The fringed hip-length close-fitting jacket he wore was laced to the throat and was stretched across a set of the widest shoulders she'd ever seen. Powerful arms rested at his sides. One hand fell across the stock of an antique rifle, or the replica of one, she supposed, and the other hand clutched some sort of bag decorated Indian fashion. Another, larger bag was slung over one shoulder.

Abby noted the steady rise and fall of the man's chest, so he wasn't dead after all. Drunk, more than likely, although she failed to detect the odor of alcohol. Not that *any* odor could be detected over the rank smell of the man himself, she thought in disgust.

Abby let her gaze travel downward from the muscled thighs, also clad in leather, to the moccasins and leggings that reached his knees. He was well armed, that was for sure. The knife in his leg sheath looked big enough to skin a grizzly, and some sort of hatchet was tucked into his wide belt.

The man's features were nearly indiscernible under a mat of black curly facial hair, but Abby noted that his nose was long and narrow. His hair, the same color and texture as his beard, was pulled back from his face and tied with a strip of leather.

Anger replaced curiosity as she studied the man. He was intruding, trespassing in her cabin. And it was still *her cabin on her land* even though it would soon be public domain. Before the government had begun its thievery, the De Coux family had taken a lenient attitude toward hunters and fishermen who inadvertently or sometimes deliberately encroached upon the boundaries of their property. But no more. No Trespassing signs were clearly posted all over the ranch. This drunken fool had deliberately ignored the warnings.

"Wake up!" Abby said, punctuating her sentence by jabbing the man sharply in the side with her fist. She would have kicked him had she been able to get her foot up high enough to do so without losing her balance. He didn't so much as grunt. "Get up!" she repeated, putting more effort into it and giving him another swift jab.

Abby rocked back on her bootheels and planted her fists at her waist, resisting the urge to pound his nose. It was only his size that stayed her. She breathed deeply, realizing that her heart was racing, and she could feel the blood flow to her face as anger and frustration mounted.

There was nothing to do but return to the ranch house and summon help. She glanced at her watch. By the time she got back to the ranch and rounded up the hands, he could be long gone; and she wanted him caught. He had ruined her day by staking claim to her cabin. She might not be able to fight the government, but she could damn well fight this drunk!

Surely he had some identification. Leaning over him for a closer look, she couldn't find any pockets in his clothing. She decided to open the pouch he held tightly in his hand. It was likely where he carried his wallet.

YESTERDAY'S TOMORROWS   11 ✧

Suddenly his strong arms came up to capture her around the waist and hurl her across the bed. She landed with a resounding thud against the chinked log wall. Pure terror washed over her as she struggled against the steely arms that pinned her.

She felt some measure of satisfaction as her kicking hit home, and she screamed, even with the knowledge that there was no one to hear her. Then she clamped her jaws to the hand that covered her mouth and tasted blood before it was hastily withdrawn. But she was no match for the huge man who issued only a grunt now and then as he managed to subdue her by straddling her and holding her arms above her head.

Bested and held fast, Abby stopped screaming and squirming long enough to draw several ragged breaths. She glared furiously at the man who was now studying her carefully, a puzzled frown narrowing the heavy brows over his glittering black eyes. He pulled her arms together so that he could hold both wrists with one hand, and with the other he slowly, tentatively touched her breast, moving his fingers across it until he encountered her nipple.

"Merde!" Elan exclaimed in wonder, his explorations confirming his growing suspicions. A woman! She wore her dark hair cropped short around a heart-shaped face. Had he examined her face more closely through his slitted eyes as he pretended to sleep, he would have surely recognized it as being totally feminine. Her cheekbones were high and well defined. A pair of raven's-wing brows arched above sooty black lashes and framed a pair of startling blue eyes that were also unmistakably feminine. Those eyes were glaring at him murderously.

He shook his head to clear his vision, but understood it would take more than that to put him to rights. He had regained consciousness only a few seconds before he heard the footsteps approaching the bed upon which he found himself. He realized he was in a cabin, but he did not know why he had come to be there or how. His last memory was of the clearing and of reaching for the medicine bag.

And his attacker had turned out to be a woman dressed in strange male clothing. It was indeed a puzzlement, as were the strange objects of furniture in the cabin.

"Take your dirty paw off my breast and let me go!" Abby said, spitting the words out with as much bravado as she could muster, dismayed that her voice squeaked despite her best effort to sound stern. She was having great difficulty controlling her frantic heartbeat and could feel her entire body trembling, much as her voice wavered. To her surprise and immense relief, the man jerked his hand away from her breast and released her arms. He shifted his body weight just a fraction, and she took advantage of his movement to bring her knee up and jab him in the groin as she scrambled to her knees and flung herself across the bed. In her mad scuffle to get away, her hand brushed across the bag decorated with Indian designs.

"Nooooo!" The word echoed and thundered in Abby's ears as her fingers grazed the quilled pouch, and she felt herself falling into a blackened void, swirling in a vortex, feeling as if she were being torn limb from limb as flesh separated from bone and rejoined, only to separate and rejoin again and again.

2

"What happened?" Abby asked groggily as she gradually became aware of her surroundings and found herself face down and sprawled flat on the dusty floor. She painfully pushed herself upright into a sitting position and looked around. Her left arm was asleep, and she rubbed it absently. She must have fallen on it when she tumbled from the bed.

She swung her head around, remembering her fight with the strange man. He too was on the floor, leaning against the wall across the small room from her. His long legs were stretched out and crossed at the ankles, and his arms were folded across his massive chest as he watched her with calculated interest. His face was illuminated by a weak shaft of sunlight that fell through the small window.

"I do not know," Elan said, unable to deliver a satisfactory explanation to either himself or the woman. That the strange happenings were linked to the Indian medicine bag, he was sure. He had used his hunting knife to lift it and hang it on a peg on the wall, for he feared touching it again until he could better understand his situation. He had heard stories of mystical events associated with Indian medicine, but had never before experienced it himself.

At the deep resonance of his voice Abby scrambled backward until she encountered the unyielding wall at her back.

Elan had awakened some time before the woman, and had taken advantage of her unconscious state to study her quite thoroughly. Her short hair proved to be the greatest enigma, although there were many others, to be sure. Had she been ill and lost her hair? He had heard of such things, but she seemed perfectly healthy now. She had fought with the strength of a wildcat when he threw her across the bed. Her determination overcame her tiny size, and he had the uncomfortable feeling that she would not hesitate to attack him again if she felt the need.

Her faded blue trousers were of a style and material he had never seen on any man and certainly not on any woman, and they fit much too snugly to be comfortable, he thought, outlining every curve of her very womanly limbs. To the touch, the trousers reminded him of tent canvas or sailcloth. He wondered briefly at her wanton disregard for propriety. Had she filched the trousers from some young boy? And if so, where was the boy now?

The short brown coat she wore over her man's shirt, though leather, had sawtooth metal sewn into the front of it and a bewildering creature painted on its back. When he first examined the silver-colored drawing he had thought it some species of bird, but its mouth gaped open, showing teeth shaped like Indian arrowheads, and he finally concluded it must be some flesh-eating sea monster with fins shaped like wings.

They eyed each other, Elan with grave curiosity, Abby with quaking fear, until he took it upon himself to offer her some reassurance.

"You have no cause to fear me," he said gently. "I will not harm you."

Whatever he was, he was not a man to hurt a woman. Truth be known, he wasn't quite sure how to act around women. His only experience with them in his adult years had been with squaws or with the women who plied their trade in the waterfront cribs in St. Louis. This woman seemed to fit neither mold, but neither was she like the fine ladies he had seen shopping in St. Louis. He was at a loss as to what to do with her until he could find Captain Lewis and turn her over to him.

"Who are you and what are you doing in my cabin?" Abby asked, keeping her guard but reverting to the authoritarian tone she used in running her ranch. The man's casual repose did little to alleviate her fear. She didn't believe him for a minute, and felt certain he must have beaten her senseless, because she ached clear down to her bones. She was feeling strangely disembodied, and though she thought of jumping up and running from the cabin, she knew that with the weakness that overpowered her she would never make it. And he had her blocked in, having positioned himself between her and the only door.

"I am called Elan," the man said softly. "I do not know how I came to this place. I was hunting elk and found myself here. I did not know there were whites in the area. Captain Lewis will be greatly surprised when I bring him this information."

Abby drew a deep, calming breath and released it slowly. The man was making no sense, and she wondered in dread if he was insane. She noted his trace of French

accent and, calling upon her high-school French, dredged
up *élan* as "moose." Well, he was certainly big enough to
fit the description. Once again her eyes fixed on the
width of his shoulders, then on the bulging muscles of his
upper arms beneath the tightly fitting leather.

"Captain Lewis?" she asked cautiously.

"Yes," Elan said, nodding in the general direction of
the door. "He is camped down in the valley on the west
bank of the creek. It will be dark soon, but we will go
and meet him in the morning. He will be much interested
in talking with you."

"Look, buster," Abby said, "I don't know what you're
doing on my ranch hunting elk out of season, but I think
you had better leave, and the sooner the better!"

Elan's brows knitted as he puzzled over her words.
She was speaking English, but making little sense. He
wondered if living in the wilderness had addled her
brain. Perhaps so. He got to his feet and crossed the
room to offer to help her up off the floor. She was his
responsibility now, and he would take care of her until
Captain Lewis could be found.

She studied him for a long moment, then hesitantly
held out her hand. He noticed the red paint on her nails
and wondered about it as he effortlessly pulled her to her
feet.

Abby swayed, and her knees would have buckled had
Elan not gathered her to him. She found herself leaning
against his rock-hard chest, and regained her balance if
not her composure. Her legs had no more strength than
overdone noodles.

"You are weak," Elan said with concern. He too had
experienced such a feeling each time he regained consciousness after encountering the Indian medicine bag, but he
seemed to have recovered more quickly than the woman.

"I feel like I've been run over by a Mack truck," Abby admitted. "What did you do to me?" He led her to a chair, and she dropped gratefully into the hard wooden seat, giving it a cursory glance and wondering when the ranch hands had replaced the plastic-and-chrome dinette set that had been in the cabin for as long as she could remember.

She was confused by his gentleness and the apparent concern expressed in the man's dark eyes. How could he beat her senseless one minute and handle her so gently the next? As soon as she regained her strength she would nail him with something and make her escape. He was definitely not to be trusted.

"I believe we have fallen under some powerful spell," Elan said, watching the woman for her reaction. "It is the medicine bag that has put this evil upon us," he continued, looking at the bag hanging on the wall.

Abby followed his gaze and frowned. It was true that touching the bag was the last thing she remembered before coming to, but she didn't believe in such superstitious nonsense.

Elan then looked around at the odd contents of the cabin. He had never seen anything like it, even east of the Mississippi, and paned glass windows were a rarity even in St. Louis. The log poles carried the sharp smell of pine sap, a smell he had not noticed when he awakened the first time and found the woman punching him. Then too, the furnishings of the cabin seemed different. There was a rag rug on the floor by the bed that he did not remember, and the bed was now covered with a worn quilt rather than the brightly printed cloth he was sure had been there before. He had not noticed the heavy wooden shutters on the windows, either, and was almost certain they had not been there when he had first awakened and tussled with the woman on the bed. Had time passed while he slept? Enough time for someone to change the cabin and its contents?

A deep uneasiness began to steal across his mind as he directed his attention once more to the woman. Her attire was most unusual, and yet she seemed entirely comfortable wearing it. She watched him carefully out of the corner of her eye, and she appeared equally troubled as her eyes alighted on certain objects. Was it possible? No, it could not be possible. Then the simplest thing to do would be to ask her. She probably thought him touched as it was; he could tell from the apprehensive glances she kept darting his way when she thought he was not looking.

"Can you tell me the date?" he finally asked. "I have been in the wilderness for a long time."

Instantly she looked up to meet his gaze, then stared at him mutely for several long seconds. She moistened her lips with the tiny pink tip of her tongue before she spoke. "It's July sixth, 1995."

Elan covered the space between them in two swift strides and, taking her by the upper arms, hauled her to her feet. "You must tell me the truth!" he said, giving her a shake. "I must know the truth!" Even daring to think he might have traveled through some slight time change with the medicine bag, he was unable to believe it could have carried him almost two hundred years into the future. He was sorry now that he had asked such a question. The woman had taken full advantage of his unspoken fear and was now tormenting him with it.

"I am telling you the truth, you raving lunatic!" Abby screamed, scared silly by the frantic glint in his eyes. After a few moments he seemed to come to himself, and he released her at once, muttering in French. She couldn't follow his words, probably couldn't have under the best of circumstances, but certainly not when he had scared her half out of her mind.

"I am sorry," Elan said as she rubbed her hands up and down her arms. Sometimes he failed to realize his own strength, and he could only hope he had not bruised her. He would have to try harder to keep his head clear and his temper in check.

Abby stared at him silently, her heart pounding wildly against the wall of her chest as she fought for control of her breathing, feeling as if she would hyperventilate any second. She was determined not to pass out. She needed all her wits to deal with the insanity that faced her. And he was insane. There was no other explanation.

"Please forgive me," Elan said softly, angry with himself for losing his composure and frightening the woman. He did not think he'd lost his wits—addled though he felt—but somehow he had been catapulted almost two hundred years into the future. It was the only explanation he could muster, but he was at a loss to understand it.

"Don't touch me again," Abby warned, finding her voice, though it shook uncontrollably. She had to get out of the cabin, to distance herself from this unstable man. She could feel the gradual return of her strength, but she knew she would be no match for his huge size. She had to remain calm, and by doing so maybe she could settle him down.

"I know you think me crazy, but I am not," Elan said, his mouth curving into a wry smile as he folded his arms over his buckskin-clad chest, leaving Abby to wonder if he was clairvoyant too. "For me the year is 1806," he continued in a singsong voice, as though reciting a story. "I joined the great expedition of Captain Lewis and Captain Clark and went with them to the ocean to the west. We traveled across the Shining Mountains and found many strange plants and animals. We found great numbers of Indians as well, and I remained with Captain Lewis when the two men split our party on the way back to the Missouri. That is how I came to be in this place. Now, will you tell me your name and how you came to be here?"

Abby stared at Elan in slack-jawed amazement, deeply disturbed by his revelation. Whether or not he was insane, his story and its delivery had the ring of truth. She slowly sank into the chair she had vacated only minutes before and tried to collect her thoughts. He really believed he had traveled with Lewis and Clark, and had outfitted himself to the teeth to play the part. She decided that, under the circumstances, it might be best to humor him.

"Why did you join the expedition?" Abby asked, twisting her fingers together in her lap in an effort to still the shaking of her hands.

"It was a great opportunity," Elan answered, eager to explain himself. "I wanted to see the richness of the land, to be one of the first to discover where the traps could best be placed. I have saved my money and have it safely put away in a bank in St. Louis. By learning about this land and the Indians who hunt here, I can grow rich, perhaps rich enough to start my own fur-buying company. The trapping is playing out in the East, and there is a great need for the furs I can trap in this land. Now," he concluded, flashing her a grin that revealed even white teeth that contrasted sharply with his black beard and served to soften his features, "I have answered your question, but you have not answered mine."

"What question?" Abby asked distractedly, trying to absorb what he had told her and make some kind of sense of it when there was none.

"Who you are and how you came to be here," Elan said patiently, not surprised in the least that she had forgotten his question. She seemed dazed, and probably did not believe a word he had just said.

"My name is Abby, and I rode up to the cabin on my horse, Little Sister," Abby said, suddenly remembering the mare. If she could get to Little Sister, maybe she could get away. "I'd better see about her," she added, struggling to her feet. Her dizziness had passed for the most part and she felt a little stronger, though she was still sore from head to foot.

"I will go with you," Elan said, obligingly stepping aside as Abby brushed past him and opened the door. She swallowed her disappointment, determined to keep her composure. She should have known getting away wouldn't be so easy.

Abby had already stepped out onto the porch when she remembered that her saddlebags were still on the bed where they had fallen as she fought with the man who called himself Elan. He was right behind her, blocking the door. If she could catch Little Sister before he realized what she intended, she could still get away. She shaded her eyes against the sun and looked in vain for the little mare. Impatiently she left the porch to round the cabin. It was possible Little Sister had decided to find a drink at the creek. It was then that she realized the saddle she had left on the porch was no longer there. What had happened to it?

She stood rooted to the ground, staring in stunned silence at the pole corral and small three-sided shed behind the cabin. She searched for the outhouse, and she finally spotted it several yards farther from the cabin than it should have been. An antique buckboard that she had never seen before was parked between the corral and shed, which should have been falling down in disrepair.

And in the corral was a roan gelding she hadn't noticed when she arrived.

Abby turned to face Elan, a questioning look on her face. She was speechless.

"What is it?" he asked cautiously. She looked as if she might topple over any second.

"Where did this come from?" Abby swung her arm in an arc that encompassed the corral and outbuildings. She hadn't been to the cabin in almost three years, but she couldn't imagine why the hands would have mended the pole corral instead of stringing some barbed wire, if indeed the hands had done it. Where had the buckboard come from? And the horse? Did they belong to the man? And why was the outhouse so far from the cabin? How long had this strange man been at the cabin, and for what purpose?

Thick willows lined the creek that flowed behind the property, obscuring the water that gurgled over the rocky ground. What had before been open creek bank was now hidden by the dense growth except for one cleared area at the end of a path leading from the cabin. Abby's stomach did a flip-flop. She refused to accept what she saw. It couldn't be true; it just couldn't be true. All of Elan's insane ravings about traveling through time had her spooked, that was all. There had to be some very reasonable explanation, and Abby was determined to discover it.

Elan observed the conflicting emotions course across the soft features of her pale face and wanted to comfort her, but was at a loss as to how to do so. Somehow, and for some reason he did not understand, she had made him feel responsible for her. It was an unwelcome feeling, and one he was not at all comfortable with. He would just as soon not have her to look after when he was not at all certain of his own predicament.

"Everything is different," Abby said, musing aloud. She cut her eyes questioningly to Elan.

He moved away from her and spent several minutes examining the outbuildings before returning to her side. In spite of herself, Abby found that she couldn't help but wonder what he looked like under the dirt and heavy beard. She was still staring at him when he came back to stand next to her.

"Different how?" Elan asked with a growing sense of unease as he saw Abby's confidence disappear. If Abby was also lost in time, then they could really be in trouble.

"The corral, the shed, the creek, everything. I don't understand how it all happened without my knowing."

"What happened? Tell me how it is different."

"Don't you see?" Abby asked, impatiently flinging out her arms even as she realized that of course he didn't see what had once been and was no more. "The corral and shed were falling down, and I've never seen the buckboard or the horse before. And the willows have grown up around the creek and the . . . " Abby's voice trailed off uncertainly as she noticed a far ridge of thickly timbered pine. "The c- . . . clear-cut . . . the clear-cut," she stammered, her eyes widening.

Elan followed Abby's pointing finger and studied the ridge for several seconds, finding nothing but more of the tall pines that grew tall and thick as far as the eye could see. None of the timber had been felled. At least, none he could see. "The timber has not been cut," Elan said reasonably.

"But it was. The timber was cut on that ridge before I was born. I remember looking at it on my ride up from the ranch and thinking again what terrible destruction clear-cutting does to the land."

"Then we are not in your time either," Elan said heavily, voicing Abby's worst imaginings. He had somehow drawn her into his insanity, unhinged her mind so that the ground shifted beneath her feet and her world as she knew it disappeared. She felt her control slipping, that fragile thread of sanity stretching to its limit as her brain madly assimilated and discarded information, searching desperately for rationalization and finding none.

"No," Abby said as she drew her leather flight jacket closer around her and hugged herself with her arms. "I don't think we are in my time." But even as the words left her mouth she could not believe them. Of course they were in her time. There had to be another explanation.

As she retraced her steps to continue her search for Little Sister, another buckboard approached. Lifting her hand to shade her eyes, she noticed that it was pulled by a sway-backed nag and driven by a tired-looking middle-aged woman. A teenage boy with light brown hair sat beside the woman, and a young girl rode in the back.

"Hello!" Abby said, striding forward to meet them. She sensed rather than saw Elan following her. At last! Some other people who could put an end to the insanity of the afternoon. But what were they doing in such old-fashioned clothing? They looked like actors from some film about the Old West, and instead of reassuring her, their appearance only caused her more distress.

"How do," the woman said, pulling the reins to stop the horse, then setting the brake. "We didn't know anyone was here." She wore a faded yellow calico dress that was much worn and patched. Her matching sunbonnet, tied under her chin with a faded yellow ribbon, was devoid of any adornment. A few wisps of graying brown hair drooped around her tired face. The boy and girl with her were also poorly dressed and carried the same gaunt look as the woman.

"My name's Abby," Abby said, stopping beside the buckboard and extending her hand to the woman. She was thankful to see someone, anyone. "Who are you?" The woman looked at Abby's hand for a long moment, then wiped her hand on her skirt and offered it for a brief shake before returning it to her lap to clutch her skirt. The boy and girl stared wide-eyed, first at Abby, then at Elan behind her.

"We're the Johnsons," the woman said hesitantly. "My boy, Frank," she said, patting the boy on the leg, "and my girl, Sally. Don't suppose you was expecting us?"

"No," Abby said, glancing at Elan, who seemed content to allow her to do the talking. He seemed more interested in the woman and the children than Abby, taking in every detail of their appearance.

"Well, we just came to fetch a few things," Mrs. Johnson said. "We'll just get them and be on our way."

"What things?" Abby asked slowly, turning her head to follow Mrs. Johnson's gaze to the three-sided shed. She had no intention of allowing the woman to haul off anything, and wondered at her nerve. "I'm afraid I don't understand, Mrs. Johnson."

"Did you know the Spooners?" Mrs. Johnson asked as she reluctantly redirected her attention to Abby.

"No," Abby replied. "Who were the Spooners?" She smiled at Sally, who was peeping shyly over her mother's shoulder. The little towheaded girl ducked her head and popped her thumb in her mouth.

"The folks that lived here," Mrs. Johnson said. "They just up and disappeared. Some say the Indians got 'em. Some say different."

That got Abby's attention. The woman was talking as if Indian raids were commonplace. Just as quickly as it appeared, Abby shoved the thought from her mind. She was going to find a reasonable, rational explanation for the afternoon's events. She was!

"What do you know about it, Mrs. Johnson?" Abby was careful to keep her tone neutral, but she did note Elan edging closer to her as he began to scan the tree line.

"Must have been a couple of weeks ago old Stump came by our place." Mrs. Johnson glanced at Frank for confirmation, and he nodded solemnly. "Old Stump does some prospecting up the mountain." Abby smiled encouragingly, just wanting her to get on with it. "Stump said he'd been through nigh on to a month before and saw Mrs. Spooner. We missed seeing him that time, I reckon." Frank again nodded his agreement.

"Yes," Abby said, hoping the woman would finally get it out.

"Old Stump said Mrs. Spooner was in quite a state, running around and acting like a crazy woman and muttering all the time about some Indian medicine man taking away her husband." Mrs. Johnson shifted on the seat of the buckboard.

Elan swung his head around and gave Mrs. Johnson his undivided attention, the tree line forgotten at the mention of the medicine man. Could it be the same one he had found with the medicine bag?

"Old Stump speculated she might have killed her man," Mrs. Johnson continued. "Everybody in the gulch knew he beat her something terrible."

"That's awful," Abby said. "But then what happened to Mrs. Spooner?"

"That's the thing," Mrs. Johnson said, leaning forward for better delivery of the news. "Old Stump said she wouldn't come with him, and when he came back through the day before yesterday, she was nowhere to be found. He couldn't find no sign of her anywhere. It was like she vanished into thin air."

"My goodness," Abby said, "what a story!" But that still didn't explain what the Johnsons were doing on her place. Or what the Spooners had been doing there, either. Nothing was making any sense, but Abby did know with absolute certainty that the Johnsons were not going to be hauling anything off. Anything there was on the place belonged to her, and she intended to keep it. "Now, Mrs. Johnson. What was it you came for?"

"My girl and me came over after talking with Old Stump. We packed up all the Spooners' things and put them in the shed. I was waiting for Frank to get loose so's he could load them on the buckboard. The trunks was too heavy for me and Sally." Mrs. Johnson was beginning to look more worried by the minute, and it was apparent she regretted finding someone she had to explain her actions to.

"Well, this is my property, and I'll be keeping anything found on it," Abby said. "If the Spooners happen to return, then I'll work something out with them, but in the meantime, whatever is here is mine. But tell me, Mrs. Johnson," Abby said as she tossed a triumphant look at Elan, "would you be willing to answer a few questions for me?"

"What kind of questions?" Mrs. Johnson asked suspiciously, her gaze nervously dancing over Abby to rest on Elan.

Abby smiled, hoping the woman would think her scatterbrained rather than insane. "Could you possibly tell me the date? You see," she went on, sliding her eyes once more to Elan to gauge his reaction, "we've completely lost track of the time."

"Why, it's July," Mrs. Johnson answered with a frown. "The sixth, I believe," she added. "We celebrated the Fourth at the settlement just two days ago."

"The year, Mrs. Johnson," Abby persisted somewhat desperately, determined that Elan hear it from some other source. And then she could put her fears to rest also. It was July 6, 1995. She was certain of it. Mrs. Johnson would confirm it, then tell her she and her children were on their way to a pioneer parade or some such. It would all make perfect sense.

"The year is 1875," Mrs. Johnson said, gripping her dress more tightly in her fist.

Abby took a stumbling step back, as if to distance herself from the woman and the words she didn't want to hear. Elan reached out a steadying hand and caught her elbow in a tight grip. Abby glanced at him in confusion. So it was true after all, and he was not insane, as she had first thought. They had somehow traveled through time and were now in the year 1875. The confirmation made her head spin and her heart beat like a trip-hammer.

She listened dully as Elan questioned Mrs. Johnson thoroughly, asking about the nearby settlement and the people of the area. She could hardly keep her thoughts straight, and she was more than a little surprised by his composure. When at last the woman insisted she must return home to prepare the evening meal, Abby watched the departure with mixed emotions. Certainly she could not throw herself on the buckboard and demand to go with the Johnsons, but she wasn't at all certain she wished to be left in the hands of the strange man who still kept a possessive grip on her arm. Then an idea began to take shape in her mind.

As the buckboard departed Elan looked down at Abby's face, relieved to see her color gradually returning, and with it Abby's sense of confidence. But when she lifted her head to meet his eyes, he realized she had a new sense of purpose. Where before he had seen confusion and doubt, he now saw anticipation, and if anything, that worried him even more. The only thing he wanted to do at the moment was get the Indian medicine bag and see if he could return to his time. He dropped her arm and left her standing alone in the waist-high grass.

"Where are you going?" Abby asked as she hurried after Elan. "Wait a minute. I want to talk to you! Don't you dare touch that medicine bag!"

3

Abby plowed headlong into Elan's unbelievably hard back as he halted just inside the doorway of the cabin, his abrupt stop giving her no time to control her momentum. "Did you hear me?" she asked breathlessly as he spun to face her. "I want to talk to you about something."

"I am taking the medicine bag," Elan said. "You may come with me or stay here. It is all the same to me. I must try to find Captain Lewis before the expedition moves east without me."

"No," Abby said, clutching at his arm, then dropping her hand. He was as hard as a brick wall, warm, solid flesh beneath the soft buckskins. Entirely male. She dismissed that thought and concentrated on the matter at hand. She had no intention of taking a little side trip to 1806 with Elan and the medicine bag before she returned to her time. But Mrs. Johnson had said the year was 1875, and if she was right, then there was something Abby wanted to do before she went back to her own time. She was just desperate enough to try anything if it meant saving her ranch, even if it was illogical and irrational.

Eighteen seventy-five happened to be the year Abby's great-great-grandfather had founded the homestead upon which she now stood, and in the last hundred some-odd years her family had increased the original 320-acre site to a ranch many times that size. How many times had her father opened the family Bible and proudly shown her the record of the De Coux family, starting with the first entry recording the marriage of André and Sara Abigail?

Curiously, there was no record of her great-great-grandparents before that cryptic entry of 1876. No one knew whence they came or how they came to be in Montana Territory. Abby had traced her mother's family, the Blakes, to the Carolinas in pre-Revolutionary days, but had found nothing when she'd tried to do the same for the De Coux line.

All she knew of her father's family was that André had supposedly been French-Canadian. There was some indication, too, that he might have had some Indian blood, but she did not know much about that. No one knew squat about Sara Abigail except the rumor that she could foretell the future, and Abby had her doubts about that. Sara Abigail, the great-great-grandmother for whom Abby was named, had never foretold the losing of the De Coux ranch!

"No?" Elan asked. "You wish to remain? Do you realize that if I take the medicine bag with me, you may never find your time again? You may be forever lost. You can come with me now and perhaps then find your way back to your time."

Abby caught her bottom lip in her teeth and tried to think of a reasonable argument she could use with him. Could this primitive woodsman possibly understand the overwhelming urge she felt to try to find her great-great-grandparents and save her land? She would have to try appealing to reason.

She refused to let Elan or anyone else stop her! Surely she had been sent back to 1875 for a purpose. Perhaps her destination had been the time of the homestead because losing the ranch was so much on her mind. And now that she was here, she wanted an opportunity to fix things. Maybe she could keep the government from stealing her ranch after all. If she could actually find her great-great-grandparents and straighten out the mix-up with the Sparne name on the land deeds, she could return home and thumb her nose at the government.

"Will you just listen to what I have to say?" Abby asked. "Then you can decide what to do."

Elan crossed his arms over his chest and stared at her darkly as she gathered her courage and began her argument.

"This homestead was founded sometime around 1875 by my great-great-grandfather. The government is trying to steal my land because of some name discrepancy on the original land deeds. They want to make my ranch part of the national forest that surrounds it. I've been fighting them for five years, and it looks as if I'm getting nowhere fast. If I could just find my great-great-grandparents, maybe, just maybe, I could straighten out the mess, and the government will have no grounds to steal what has been in my family for over a hundred years. I don't think I could stand it if they take my land. It's a part of me, like my arm or my leg. They've already taken my daddy. He died fighting them. I can't let him down. I have to stop them from stealing our land."

Elan looked from the woman to the medicine bag as he thought about her plea, and against his better judgment he found himself actually considering her request. His father's approval had been very important to him, and he had spent the better part of his life living to please him.

And he had to admit that he was more than a little curious about the time in which he found himself as well as curious about the woman herself. It would be interesting to explore this new territory, and to return to his time with knowledge of the future would work in his favor. It was well worth considering.

"How long do you think this will take?" Elan asked. If the expedition left him, then he supposed it was really of no great importance. He would be able to find his way back to the Missouri, and as long as the medicine bag hung on the wall, it was possible that they could return to their times whenever they pleased. It was also entirely possible that they could not, for the time leaping seemed entirely unpredictable to him.

What if they could get back to her time, but not his? Or get to his time and not hers? Then he would really have his hands full trying to drag her with him to the Missouri, for he could not leave her alone in the wilderness. Another thing also worried him: He was not sure how they would live. But more than that, he was not completely certain he trusted the woman to wait for him if she suddenly decided to return to her own time. She could very well leave him stranded in this unfamiliar place.

"I don't know how long it will take," Abby said, moving into the kitchen area and eyeing the cast-iron stove with trepidation. "A few weeks, perhaps. Or maybe a few months. I want to go to the settlement and ask around. We're going to need supplies, too. It's a good thing my saddlebags came with us. I have some emergency rations in them, but"—she glanced over her shoulder at the huge man studying her—"they won't last long."

"If I agree to this, do I have your word that you will not trick me?" Elan asked. "We must make a vow to touch the medicine bag only if we are together."

"Agreed," Abby said. She held out her hand, and Elan realized she expected him to shake it to seal the agreement. He took it with some amusement, marveling at the small hand that was engulfed so completely within his own.

"Ayeee! Ayeee!" The shrill cries rent the air, so startling Abby that she tripped over a small stone and would have lost her balance if Elan hadn't countered her movement by dropping the buckets of water he carried and jerking her in the opposite direction. Elan clamped his long fingers around Abby's wrist and dragged her behind the shed before she could even think to issue a protest.

"Stay out of sight," he said in a voice that brooked no argument. Then he was gone, slipping around the shed without a backward glance.

Abby listened to Elan's exchange with the Indians for several minutes before working up the courage to defy his directive and peep around the shed. He spoke in a low but firm voice, his guttural speech a vivid contrast to the high-pitched shrieks issued by the braves.

Elan held his ground, unmoving and seemingly unafraid as he faced three obviously very agitated Indians. They were bareback on Indian ponies and thrust their arms about wildly, threatening Elan with their bows and lances. The oldest of the painted braves was doing most of the talking. The other two, hardly more than boys, were backing him with youthful bravado. All three were clad only in breechclouts and moccasins and they all wore necklaces of bear claws around their necks.

Several earrings hung from the lobes of the apparent leader, the one who seemed to be working himself into quite a fury. Quivers of arrows were slung across their backs.

Things didn't look as if they were going so well to Abby, and this was something she had not expected when she made her decision to stay for a while. She thought longingly of the medicine bag hanging on the wall of the cabin. But of course she couldn't leave Elan to face the music alone even if she could get to it. After all, she had promised. Then too, she was determined to find her ancestors and wasn't about to be thwarted before she really got started. She peered around the shed again, focusing on the weapons wielded by the trio. Some kind of decoration dangled from their lances and waved in the breeze. It looked like . . . hair?

Oh, my God! Abby thought as her stomach gave a sickening lurch. *Scalp locks!* Her hand crept up to touch her own close-cropped hair as she stared in horrified fascination at the fluttering tresses. She had to do something! She'd be damned if she'd let them kill Elan and have a go at her!

She fumbled with the buckle on the saddlebags slung over her shoulder, thankful she had insisted on washing up at the creek before she started supper. She'd slung her saddlebags over her shoulder and carried them with her rather than rummage through them in the cabin for the soap and washcloth she needed. Since Elan had insisted on accompanying her, she'd asked him to bring the buckets for water. They'd been returning to the cabin when the Indians arrived.

Elan's gun, such as it was, was still on the bed in the cabin. She didn't have the faintest idea how to shoot it, but her own nine-millimeter Beretta automatic was what she was after. She never went anywhere without it. She unfastened the buckle and opened the saddlebags with hands that trembled. She had to get herself under control if she was going to be any help. Her fingers closed around the cool metal, and she pulled the gun out before she could change her mind.

She held the pistol tightly and eased out from behind the shed. She knew from their increased agitation the exact second the Indians spotted her, but she refused to acknowledge them. Let them think she was a humble female and posed no threat. She kept her eyes trained on the toes of her boots and moved slowly but steadily. She held the gun behind her leg as she walked through the high grass and halted just behind Elan.

"I have a gun," Abby whispered. She wasn't sure if the Indians spoke any English, but she wasn't taking any chances. Elan's posture didn't change one iota after Abby made her announcement, and she realized he'd been perfectly aware of her presence before she opened her mouth. Ignoring her, he spoke heatedly to the Indians and used his hands to sign.

"Can you shoot?" Elan's soft question would have amused Abby under any other circumstances. She was a crack shot and had trophies to prove it.

"Yes."

"If it comes to it, kill the one doing the talking," Elan said. He knew he could take the other two with his knife and his hatchet.

"I can kill all three before you can blink," Abby said. She pulled the pistol from behind her and planted herself firmly in a shooter's stance as she brought the pistol up and pointed it. The Indians stopped their screeching threats and were silent as Abby trained her eyes on them.

Elan risked glancing at Abby out of the corner of his

eye and satisfied himself that she knew what she was doing. He was eager to examine the gun, but that could wait until later.

"Tell them," Abby said, "that if they don't get off my land, I'll blow their ugly heads right off their shoulders." And she would, she thought angrily as she stared at the scalp locks. Elan made more deep guttural sounds and moved his hands rapidly.

The Indian doing the talking made another threatening thrust with his lance. Abby released the safety and met his furious stare as she took aim for the spot between his eyes.

She'd never seen such hate as that directed at her by the harsh, glittering black eyes, and coldness washed over her as she contemplated killing the man, but she refused to lower her gaze, knowing she couldn't show any sign of weakness.

They studied each other for several minutes. Abby ignored the sweat trickling between her breasts and popping out on her forehead. Her arms were leaden with the weight of the gun, and she was afraid they'd start to wobble if she gave in to her fatigue. She clenched her teeth and wondered if her hammering heart could pound through the wall of her chest. Aiming at a living being was much different from aiming at a cardboard cutout.

Just when she thought she'd have to make good her threat, the Indians whirled their horses in unison and rode hard across the meadow, leaving a cloud of dust in their wake. It was not until they entered the trees and disappeared from sight that she dared to relax.

Abby released a shuddering sigh, not realizing she had been holding her breath. She engaged the safety, then dropped the gun to her side. Elan spun to face her, his face dark with anger.

"I told you to stay out of sight," he said. Now that the Indians knew he had a female, he worried they might come back and try to take her. Captives fared poorly with them, and white captives even worse. "That was a very foolish thing you did."

"I thought they were going to kill you," Abby said, tipping her head to meet his eyes. "What did they want?" He could at least be grateful she'd come to his rescue. But no, she had a classic male chauvinist on her hands. She could see she had her work cut out for her.

"They wanted us to leave this place," Elan replied. "They claim this land is sacred ground for the Great Spirit who leads them on their hunts. They said the Great Spirit did away with the man and woman who built the cabin and he would do away with us also."

"Malarkey," Abby said. So that's what had happened to the Spooners. The Indians indeed had gotten them. Well, they weren't going to run her off her land. She'd shoot the next one on sight! "What did you tell them?"

"I told them I had much respect for the Great Spirit and I would take their words under consideration," Elan said. "Then you appeared and made them lose face. They will not forget it."

"Better for them to lose face than for us to lose our hair. Didn't you see those scalps on their lances?"

"Yes. But you have little to worry about." He grinned as his hand came up to finger her hair. "Your hair is hardly worth the taking."

Abby laughed at the humorous twinkle that had replaced the anger in his dark eyes and deftly stepped out of his reach, refusing to acknowledge the little thrill that coursed through her at his gentle touch. "The man has a sense of humor," she said. "Let's see how he likes what I have in mind next."

"And what is that?" Elan asked suspiciously, his brows shooting together as he took a deliberate step back, fighting the urge to move closer and comb all ten of his fingers through the silky hair he had briefly touched.

"A bath," Abby replied.

"You are going to bathe?" Elan asked, remembering the large wooden tub he had seen in the shed.

"Oh, no," Abby said as she shook her head and wrinkled her nose. "You are."

4

Elan held the bar of yellow soap to his nose and sniffed, unable to identify its scent. "Are you in yet?" Abby called from the cabin.

"No!" Elan answered sharply. The woman had insisted that he bathe, and he had to admit that he did indeed need to clean the grime from his body. He couldn't remember the last time he had bathed, but it had been at least two weeks, if not more. Icy mountain streams invited nothing more than a cursory dip, and that was all he and the other members of the expedition had done for longer than he cared to remember.

Abby had demanded that he present a more favorable appearance if he expected to come back into the cabin to eat. Whatever she was cooking smelled delicious, and a plaintive growl from his stomach prompted action. He hurriedly stripped off his buckskins and discarded them beside the tub before gingerly lowering himself into the steaming water.

Abby had built a fire in the stove with the wood he had hauled from the well-stocked woodpile next to the shed. Bucket after bucket of water had been heated and now filled the tub except for two steaming buckets left on the porch for rinsing.

"Ready or not, here I come," Abby said, throwing open the door as she issued her warning. Elan had just enough time to snatch up a linen towel and drape it across his lap before Abby appeared carrying a lantern and dragging one of the wooden kitchen chairs behind her. It was dusk, with shadows deepening around the cabin as the sun sank lower behind the mountains, bringing a chill to the air.

"What a picture," Abby teased, amused as much by Elan's injured air as by his arms and legs hanging awkwardly over the sides of the tub.

"Go back inside," Elan demanded. "It is not proper for you to watch my bath."

"Proper or not," Abby said as she deposited the lantern on the chair, "I'm going to see that you're scrubbed clean." She rolled up her sleeves and pulled a washcloth from the pile of linens and clothing she had handed him earlier. Then she knelt by the tub.

The clothes had been found in a trunk in the shed. Some of the Spooners' belongings, she assumed. After critical examination, she'd determined they could be of use. Of course, the pants would be too big in the waist and too short to reach Elan's ankles, but they could be tucked into his over-the-calf moccasins. The shirt would stretch tight over his wide shoulders. However, the outfit would do in a pinch, and it beat the buckskins hands down. She'd mentioned burning the buckskins but had been forced to withdraw that idea. Maybe they would prove salvageable after a good scrubbing.

Elan reached for the washcloth and took it from Abby's hand. "I can bathe myself," he said. Surely this female didn't mean to scrub him as if he were a child! He shifted uncomfortably at the thought of her hands and the private places they might reach.

"Well," Abby said, sitting back on her heels to study him, "you needn't get huffy. I was just going to scrub your back. Besides, I took care of my father after he got sick, so I know what I'm doing."

"I'm not your father, and I'm not ill," Elan said firmly, putting the soap to the cloth.

"Okay," Abby said, getting to her feet. "I'll see if I can find a pair of scissors and a razor. Hurry up and get clean. I'll come back and help you wash your hair. Then we'll get rid of that beard and give you a haircut."

Elan thoughtfully fingered his beard, not at all certain he wanted it shaved. He had become quite attached to it. *Merde,* but she was a bossy little thing! Well, she could boss all she wanted. He would do as he pleased and she would have to learn to accept the rest. He went to work with the washcloth and soap.

"I found them!" Abby said when she returned to the porch. "There were scissors in the sewing box I found in one of the trunks, and I remembered to pack my razor; so we're in luck!"

She tossed the items on the chair beside the lantern and struggled to lift one of the heavy wooden buckets of water. She managed to get it high enough to dump over his head and laughed as he spluttered and coughed under the deluge.

Elan mopped the water from his face and bit back the curse that came to his lips. Then he felt Abby's hands in his hair, loosening the leather strip and freeing his long locks. She poured some liquid in his hair that smelled of apples and worked up a lather. He gradually relaxed as Abby's fingers scrubbed and massaged. He grudgingly admitted to himself that her able fingers on his scalp felt good, and it seemed the most natural thing in the world for those same fingers to move down his neck and across his shoulders.

Abby knelt behind Elan and hummed under her breath as she worked, concentrating on her task. It wasn't until she began massaging his thick neck and broad shoulders that she actually became aware of what she was doing. Elan's tense neck muscles had relaxed under her fingers, as had the tautness in his shoulders, but he was hard and muscular, very much the virile male. She began to wonder how his body would feel against hers . . . then shook herself out of her reverie.

Surprised by her intense reaction to Elan's solid flesh under her fingers, Abby abruptly snatched her hands away and reached for the bucket. With a grunt, she lifted it and dumped the remaining water over his head. She really knew nothing about him, and she didn't want to give him any ideas!

Elan sat straight up, shaking his head violently at the shock of the now cooling water as it cascaded over his head and shoulders. "*Merde!*" he spluttered. "Are you determined to drown me, woman?"

"Only if you keep complaining," Abby answered lightly, feeling decidedly better as she picked up the scissors and crawled around the tub on her knees. She reached for a rung of the chair and pulled it closer. She needed a better vantage point to see how to trim his hair. "Let's see," she said, running her hands through his thick wet hair and tilting her head. "I think I'll just trim it around your face a little."

As Abby worked Elan allowed his gaze to wander over her face and down her neck. He discovered that she had neglected to close the top two buttons of her shirt. His eyes widened as Abby reached to snip a lock of hair and a bit of cleavage was revealed by her movement. His loins immediately tightened and he knew he should avert his gaze, but she held him transfixed. He concentrated on the white scrap of lace that bound her breasts but failed to conceal her rosy nipples, and he wondered what kind of garment it was and why she would want to wear something that looked so uncomfortable.

"Much better," Abby said under her breath. Elan forced his gaze away and up to her face when she spoke. She held the tip of her tongue between her teeth as she concentrated, and he suddenly was tempted to taste her lips, to slant his mouth across hers. He was thankful for the darkness and shadows that hid his mounting desire. He had no wish to frighten her, and truth to tell, he could not understand his intense reaction to the tiny woman.

"Now," Abby said, putting down the scissors and picking up her disposable razor, "the beard."

Elan reached for the razor and took it from Abby's hand. What did a woman need with a razor? Besides, the object resembled nothing he had ever seen. "This is a razor?" he asked.

"Yes, it's a plastic disposable razor. You use it until it's dull, then you throw it away."

"Why?" Elan asked, holding it up to the light and examining it more closely. "Can it not be sharpened?"

"It was made that way. You just buy a new one when it gets dull." Then she remembered: She wouldn't be replacing this razor. At least, not in this time. It would have to last until she returned home.

"It makes no sense," Elan said with a frown. "Why make something to be thrown away after only a little use?"

"It would take too long to explain," Abby said, again picking up the scissors. She would need to trim his beard anyway before she could use the razor.

"What need do you have for a razor?" Elan asked, turning the pink plastic handle first one way and then the other in his hands. A razor was not a feminine article, though the small pink object he held appeared more feminine than masculine. And he wondered at the material it was fashioned from. It was neither wood nor metal. Nor was it bone. What was this plastic?

"To shave my legs," Abby answered absently, snipping away at his beard.

"What?" Elan asked incredulously, not sure he had heard her correctly. He lost all interest in the razor as his wide eyes examined the face hovering so near his own.

"To shave my legs," Abby repeated, grinning at his shocked expression. "It makes them nice and smooth. In my time, most women do it. Men seem to like them that way."

Elan tightened his grip on her razor, stunned by her words. He cast his eyes to the shapely curves outlined by her trousers. If she was trying to shock him, then she had succeeded. He was speechless.

"I learned to shave my daddy when I was a little girl," Abby said, putting down the scissors, then working up a lather and soaping his face. She rinsed her hands and reached for the razor, which Elan relinquished without protest. "He used to let me sit on the bathroom sink and shave him. When he got sick and couldn't take care of himself, I was able to tend him. I had a sitter for him during the day so I could run the ranch, but I took care of most of his personal needs."

Abby stroked Elan's soapy face with the razor, removing the thick beard. She then dipped the razor in the tub water, accidentally brushing against Elan's hard, hairy thigh with her hand before bringing the razor up again to his face. She tried not to think about her contact with his bare flesh and willed her hand not to tremble.

Elan forced himself to breathe deeply and calmly. Abby's innocent touch to his thigh had sent his blood surging through his veins, forcing his heart to pound painfully in his chest. He lowered his eyes, once again taking in the soft curves of her breasts. As each stroke of the razor on his face created more and more sensual thoughts, he wondered how her smoothly shaven legs would feel to his touch.

"Are you done?" Elan asked thickly when Abby at last rinsed the razor in the tub water and placed it on the chair.

"Just about." Abby gazed at his clean-shaven face, then lifted her hands to run her fingers lightly over his jaw and across his chin. "Talk about a diamond in the rough," she murmured. He was younger than she'd first thought, probably not much older than thirty. The lips that had been partially hidden under his facial hair were full and beautifully shaped. The dimples were a pleasant surprise, as was the distinctive cleft in his chin. Cleaned up and dressed properly, he would be a devastatingly handsome man.

Elan's passion rose as Abby continued her appraisal, and the cooling waters of the tub did nothing to cool his growing desire. The small fingers that danced across his face stoked the fires burning within him, quickening his breath and his need. What manner of woman was she really? Surely no true lady would attend his bath.

Abby flinched, taken unaware when Elan's hands flew like quicksilver, one capturing her wrist in what felt like a band of steel, the other seizing her chin to tip her face. She could only stare at him blankly.

"What is it that you want, woman?" Elan asked through his teeth. "Look at me, Abby," he said, tightening his hold on her chin and forcing her startled eyes to meet his. "I am not an old man, helpless and needing assistance in the bath. I am a strong man, and you are not a little girl tending her father. You are a woman full grown."

His long fingers gradually loosened their hold, and he released her to stroke her hair tenderly with his huge hand, regretting his momentary loss of control. He had no wish to harm or frighten her. "Go, Abby," he said softly. "Go now!"

Abby struggled to her feet and raced across the porch and through the cabin's door. She slammed the door shut behind her and leaned against it, fighting for control, gasping for breath, the deep resonance of Elan's voice lingering in her ears.

Elan lounged on the floor, his back against the rough log walls as he sharpened his hunting knife on the whetstone. He frequently let his eyes wander from his task to settle on Abby, who sat in a small rocker near the stove.

He and Abby had plundered the trunks in the shed and had found many useful items, including the ill-fitting, unfamiliar clothing he was wearing. After his bath, he had scrubbed his buckskins clean and hung them across the pole corral. The pants and shirt he was wearing would do until the buckskins were dry. Abby was altering one of the three dresses she had discovered, humming a tune as she worked.

He watched her cut and snip and sew, fascinated by the dexterity of her small fingers, and he wondered how the dress that had been made for a larger, taller woman would look when she was done. Of the three dresses unpacked from the trunks, the one she was working on had the prettiest color, and he thought the sky blue would suit Abby well. It would complement her eyes.

Elan contemplated his situation and wondered if he had been wise to let the woman convince him to stay. He still had no idea how long she planned to remain in this time and was not sure she knew herself. Hunting and trapping were the only things he knew, and if they were planning on spending any length of time in this place, he had to find some way to outfit himself. His money, so carefully saved and in a bank in St. Louis, was of no use to him in this time. Perhaps some person in the settlement would be willing to outfit him, or maybe the Bay Company was still in operation.

Before, he had had only himself to worry about, but now he had Abby. Though she insisted on maintaining her claim on the cabin and the land, he felt the need to protect her. For what could a woman alone do in this wild, unforgiving country? Whether she realized it or not, he knew she needed him. And he had given his word that he would help her.

Abby looked up from her sewing and saw that Elan was watching her. She smiled uncertainly and went back to her task, finishing the seam before she stood and put the dress down on the rocker. She thought of the argument she'd had years ago with her father over her taking a cooking and sewing class. He had insisted she take at least one year of home economics in high school. It was one of the many things they had butted heads over. Abby had wanted nothing to do with cooking or sewing, but her father had been determined to at least try to make a lady of her. It hadn't worked very well at the time, but at least she could thread a needle and take a stitch. The dresses she'd found in the trunks had been of the same style Mrs. Johnson had worn, and Abby was fairly sure she could alter them to fit. The seams might be crooked and the hems lopsided, but at least they would be passable. If she was going into the settlement, then she needed clothing suitable to the times, and they were the closest things she had. "It's late," she said, stifling a yawn. "I'll finish this tomorrow."

Elan sheathed his knife and put it to one side with the sharpening stone. Then he got to his feet and crossed the room to stand over Abby. "What?" she asked, tilting her head to look up at him. He gazed at her for a long moment, then strode past her to the door.

"I will check the horse," Elan said, opening the door and walking out into the darkness and the evening chill. He inhaled the sharp, clean scent of the mountain air, seeking to clear his head and cool his blood. Watching Abby work in the faint lamplight had brought a fierce and desperate longing to his heart and to his soul, a feeling totally alien to him. He had never known the intimacy of home and hearth. Since leaving the mission school, his home had always been the forest, his hearth a campfire.

He walked to the corral and stroked the nose of the roan while he stood under the brilliant starlight and waited for Abby to prepare for bed. It would be more seemly for him to sleep in the shed, but Abby had insisted that he should share the warmth of the cabin. Also, he knew he should remain near her in case the Indians returned.

"Come on in," Abby called in response to the hesitant knock on the cabin's door. Elan stepped into the room, seeming to fill the small cabin with his presence and giving Abby second thoughts about insisting that he sleep in the cabin with her.

Abby had made his pallet on the floor in front of the stove and then had undressed and donned her nightgown.

She was suddenly thankful she had packed the high-necked flannel gown that covered her from her earlobes to her toes. She burrowed deeper under the covers, realizing she had neglected to pull the blankets she had strung up for curtains.

Elan removed his moccasins, then stripped off his shirt, leaving Abby somewhat breathless as she watched his rippling muscles in the lamplight. When his hands fell to his waist to fumble with the buttons of his trousers, Abby sharply sucked in her breath, and his head snapped back at the sound. She briefly met his inquisitive eyes, then quickly lowered her lids, feeling the blush creep to her face.

Elan hesitated, his hands at the waist of the ill-fitting trousers. The lamp afforded just enough light to see Abby's wide-eyed stare before she shuttered her eyes. The woman who had so unabashedly scrubbed him in his bath was now flustered by his half-dressed state. He took a step and reached for the blankets, then changed his mind and instead allowed his hand to once again seek the buttons of his pants. If he closed the curtains, little of the stove's warmth would reach her. He leaned to cup the glass lamp chimney and blew out the flame before the trousers fell from his hips.

5

Abby *settled herself* on the seat of the buckboard and nervously smoothed her skirt as Elan stowed their guns under a quilt tossed behind the seat. She was excited at the prospect of going to the settlement, but she was apprehensive too. She decided to look upon the trip as an adventure and tried to calm her nerves, telling herself that she was a grown woman and perfectly capable of handling any situation that arose.

"I think one of the first things we should do is find someone who might know where to find my ancestors," Abby said as Elan climbed up and settled himself beside her on the narrow seat of the buckboard. His hard leg pressed into hers, and she quickly shifted to give him more room as he released the brake. The unexpected contact did little for her already jangled nerves, and she found herself suddenly thrown off balance as the buckboard shot forward. She grabbed Elan's arm for support and just as quickly released it when he chuckled at her discomposure. Taking a deep breath, she determinedly continued her train of thought, hoping she wasn't babbling. "And if they haven't arrived yet in the valley, then I guess I should find someone who might be willing to sell me a few head of cattle to get the ranch going. I might as well make myself useful until I can find them."

"I have no interest in playing nursemaid to a herd of cattle," Elan said as they bounced along the rocky ground. "I must find someone to outfit me so that I can hunt and trap. We will live off the land. We have no need for cattle." He was not interested in learning to farm. He had always been successful with his hunting and trapping and saw no need to change. He wanted nothing to keep him from the forest when it called him forth, and Abby could not possibly mean to tend a herd.

"You can't be serious!" Abby exclaimed. "The hunters and trappers nearly devastated this part of the country. I mean to have the cattle. This is my land, and I'll do as I damn well please."

"You must learn to curb your tongue, Abby. It is not proper for you to speak as you do." He knew what was best, and she would soon learn to accept his judgment. He was prepared for another argument, but Abby surprised him by lifting her chin and staring straight ahead. The remainder of the long ride was spent in silence as he concentrated on following the directions given by the Johnsons. Finally he spotted the outskirts of the small mining settlement.

When Elan encircled Abby's small waist with his hands and swung her down from the buckboard to set her in the dusty street, his hands lingered on her for a moment. Noticing that he seemed reluctant to release her, she eyed him questioningly. She was wearing the blue dress she had altered and a matching bonnet fashioned from some of the excess material. She was sure she'd done a pretty good job on the dress and the hat, even if the brim of the sunbonnet refused to stand up as well as it should. She thought she looked quite smart, but as Elan's eyes swept her up and down she wondered if perhaps she had neglected something vitally important. But then, how would he know if she had?

"Will I do?" Abby asked, offering a shy smile. She didn't usually fish for compliments, but she sought to ease her own concerns as well as to break the strained silence between them. It was essential that they fit in with the other settlers of the area, that they draw no undue attention to themselves. That they were homesteading on the Spooner place and had the Spooners' horse would raise questions enough.

"You will," Elan said abruptly, releasing her to take a look around.

Abby surveyed the street, which was devoid of anyone but two Indian men squatting on the rough plank sidewalk outside the trading post. They were dressed in cast-off clothing and wrapped in red trade blankets, their heads covered with battered black hats that concealed all but the lower portions of their faces. Remembering the long history of the Indian's fall into the white man's quagmire of whiskey, she wondered if they were drunk. She looked to Elan for his reaction, but his face was like a stony mask.

The settlement consisted of a total of six crude timber buildings, three on each side of the street. Abby and Elan stood on the north side before the trading post. Flanked to the east by a blacksmith's shop and stable, and to the west by a saloon, the trading post was the largest structure in the small settlement. Directly across the street from the trading post was another saloon, then a two-storied building with a sign proclaiming it to be a hotel and eatery, and a smaller building with Claims written in foot-high black letters across its door.

Elan opened the door to the trading post and ushered Abby inside. The short, plump man behind the counter looked up and closed his ledger at the tinkle of the bell hanging on the door. Dressed in a yellow shirt and brown trousers held up by suspenders, he leaned his elbows on the counter and greeted them cheerfully. "Morning, folks, what can I do for you?"

Elan advanced to the counter and reached across it to offer his hand. The proprietor took it with a chuckle and wrung it thoroughly. "You folks must be new to the valley. Ain't seen you around before. New folks coming in all the time. Got the Indians all riled up, by golly. Yes, sir, all riled up. You see any signs of Indians on the trail? Where you folks from? Got any news?"

Elan shot Abby a frustrated look, taken aback by the barrage of questions. But as the trader continued in the same vein he soon realized that answers were not necessary.

"Name's Roberts," the trader said without seeming to pause for breath. "You need it, I got it. Whiskey, tobacco, yard goods." The last was directed at Abby, who had wandered over to inspect a table covered with several bolts of material and spools of ribbon and lace.

"I am called Elan," Elan said quickly before the trader could find breath to start up again. "I need someone to stake my hunting and trapping." As he spoke Abby fingered a bolt of red satin. She loved red, loved the flash and fire of the color.

"Don't give no credit," Roberts said, shaking his head. "Cash on the barrelhead. That's the only way to do business. Why, if I staked every trapper and miner coming in my place, I'd be broke before the first snow fell. Got anything for trade?"

"I have nothing to trade but my hunting and trapping," Elan said. "But I am an honest man and I would not cheat you." Elan looked around the establishment, noting the barrels of goods. He and Abby needed staples. He could provide them with meat, but they would need other supplies as well. He had to have the traps in order to take the beaver and other small animals whose pelts were so valued in the East. For how else could he and Abby live until she was ready to return home?

"Don't 'spect you would, Elan," Roberts said with a brief shake of his balding head. "But the trapping's just about played out around these parts. You could probably still scare up a little gold, though most of the miners hereabouts have pulled up stakes and headed for the Black Hills over in the Dakota Territory. Most folks around here now are ranching, raising beef for the mining camps and the railroad crews."

"Mr. Roberts?" Abby asked, strolling to the counter to stand beside Elan. She had an idea. Elan might not have anything to trade, but she felt certain she did. It would be hard to part with her father's necklace, but she firmly felt she had to see this through. Daddy would have certainly approved if it meant saving the ranch. She would somehow be able to fix whatever had gone wrong if she could just find André and Sara Abigail.

"Yes, ma'am?" The rotund trader stood straighter, and Abby smiled into his small gray eyes. Before she could change her mind she quickly unbuttoned the first three buttons of her high-necked dress.

"I have something you may be interested in," Abby said, pulling out the gold necklace and nugget. The trader swallowed, somewhat at a loss for words, as Abby's fingers closed around the necklace and she held it out for his perusal.

"Abby!" Elan said. "It is not necessary!" She had told him of the sentimental value of the necklace, and he was deeply ashamed that he could not prevent her having to give it up. And he was very sure he did not like the way the trader was looking down her dress. Her action was innocent, but the trader's was not.

But it was necessary and she knew it, even if Elan refused to accept it. The necklace was worth a lot of money, even in 1875 dollars. Desperate times called for desperate measures. She could think of nothing else of any real value that either of them had. It was her idea to stay and therefore her responsibility to provide for their necessities while they waited for her to straighten out the land deeds.

"Perhaps we can come to some agreement?" Abby asked, ignoring Elan's angry glare even as she wondered if it was directed at her or at the trader. She favored Roberts with her best smile. The trader's head bobbed up and down while his Adam's apple worked frantically.

"I'm sure we can, Mrs. Elan," Roberts said eagerly. Abby lifted her arms and reached behind her neck to unfasten the clasp. She laid the necklace on the counter. Roberts scooped it up and hastened to place it on his gold scales. Elan turned on his heel and strode from the store, shutting the door behind him.

Impulsively Abby removed the watch from her wrist and placed it on the counter. Roberts would be intrigued by its quartz movement, and she felt certain that when she explained that it was the latest in technology from the East, he would have to have it. The greedy gleam in his eyes bespoke his true nature. She had replaced the battery only last month, so it was sure to work for a year or more. Besides, what need did she have for the watch? She could easily replace it when she returned home.

Elan paused outside the trading post and scanned the street while he reined in his temper. Frustrated by his lack of bargaining power, he was forced to admit his dependence on her. It was an unfamiliar feeling, not being in control of his life. Never before had he been refused credit. Traders up and down the Mississippi and the explored sections of the Missouri knew Elan was a man of his word.

The building across the street with the door reading Claims caught his eye. After a moment's hesitation, he stepped off the sidewalk. Abby probably had not considered filing a claim, since she thought of the Spooner homestead as hers in the first place. He would take the trader's advice and file a mining claim as well. He knew nothing about mining, but he was willing to learn. At least he could be of some use while she bargained with the trader for the supplies they had to have.

"Elan!" Abby's excited voice stopped him as he took his first step. "Keep this," she said, thrusting a fistful of money at him. "I don't have any pockets!" Elan reached for the strange-looking green paper money and shoved it into his pocket, totally ignorant of its worth. Maybe Abby knew.

"Don't you want to help me pick out the supplies?" Abby asked hesitantly when he turned to leave.

"Get what you want," Elan said without looking back. Abby watched him cross the street in the direction of the saloon, then reentered the trading post, regretting already her impulsive need to include him. If he got drunk with her money, she'd cheerfully murder him.

Elan was back in time to help Roberts load the supplies, and Abby was glad to see he seemed to be over his snit. She was somewhat disappointed that the trader had not heard of her great-great-grandparents, but Roberts assured her he was well acquainted with everybody in the valley and that sooner or later all newcomers showed up at his trading post. He promised to send word as soon as they arrived. She had told Roberts that the De Couxs were friends of her family and that she had heard they were headed for the valley.

Abby supervised the loading, keeping a mental tally of the barrels of flour, the half-bushels of dried beans and cornmeal, the sacks of sugar, coffee, and salt, and the boxes of powder and lead for shot, as well as some cooking utensils and oil for the lamps. She'd also included several patent medicines she had grave doubts about, but considered them better than nothing, and a bottle of whiskey, which she told herself was also for medicinal purposes. She worried that she'd overdone it with the supplies, but decided she'd rather have more than she needed than not enough.

When the last item was safely loaded Abby took Elan's arm and smiled up at him, playing the dutiful wife the trader thought her. "You had better go get what you need to run your traps, dear. We still have quite a bit left on our line of credit, and Mr. Roberts will be more than happy to help you." If she was going to keep Elan from absconding with the medicine bag, then she had to keep him happy. And if hunting and trapping would keep him happy, then that's what he needed to do.

Elan nodded. As much as it galled him to rely on her charity, he had little choice in the matter. "First I will help you to the buckboard," he said, softening under Abby's beseeching smile.

"Take your time, dear. I'm heading for the saloon," Abby said, patting Elan's arm in a show of wifely affection. "Mr. Roberts told me I could find a man there to talk cattle with." The trader blanched and stumbled backward, nearly tripping over one of the Indians squatting on the sidewalk.

"I . . . uh . . ." Roberts said, certain the cold stare sent him meant that he was about to be severely throttled for directing Mrs. Elan to the saloon. "I didn't tell her to go there! I just told her that's where John Winston could sometimes be found. He's got the largest cattle spread in the valley and could sell you a few head if you need them. That's all I said. I swear. Tell him, Mrs. Elan," Roberts pleaded, swiping a hand over his bald head and throwing Abby a look of pure desperation.

"Of course, Mr. Roberts." Abby could almost feel sorry for the terrified little man. She well remembered her first impression of Elan and his immense size and strength. But she had come to the conclusion he was really just a big teddy bear. Her smugness was abruptly curtailed, however, when Elan snatched her off her feet and plunked her down in the seat of the buckboard. She was too shocked to mount a protest before her bottom hit the hard, unforgiving board.

"Stay put," Elan said, then turned to follow Roberts back to the trading post. Abby opened her mouth to reply. "I mean it," he added, turning to fix her with a hard stare before he closed the door. Abby shut her mouth and stayed put.

"How 'bout some whiskey and tobacco?" Roberts asked in an effort to appease Elan. "Women don't never think about the small comforts a man needs." He scurried around the counter to put some space between himself and the deceptively calm trapper following him. "Why, Mrs. Elan only picked up one small bottle, hardly enough to take the chill off an evening, I'd say." He reached behind the counter and produced a bottle and a shot glass. "Have a drink on the house," he invited.

Elan slouched down and propped an elbow on the counter, raking his eyes first over the whiskey, then over the trader. Roberts fidgeted, then swept up the bottle and replaced it with another. "Finest in the place. It's what I meant to get the first time," he hurriedly added.

Elan could feel his anger rising, the slow boiling rage he always experienced when cheating traders plied trappers with rotgut whiskey. He had seen men trap all winter only to drink up their profits in a matter of weeks and go into debt again outfitting for the next year's trip.

He had been powerless to stop his own father from falling into that unending cycle, until he was a hopeless, useless drunk who froze to death one winter night while Elan was running their trap line.

"Whiskey steals a man's soul," he said quietly, gently pushing away the bottle and glass. "And tobacco rots the teeth and fouls the breath. I have no need for such things. Now, where are my traps?"

Abby became aware of the sudden tensing of Elan's body as he brought the buckboard to an abrupt halt. She'd resisted touching him as they made the long ride to the settlement, sitting stiffly at his side and avoiding as much contact as possible in the narrow seat of the buckboard. However, during the ride back to the cabin, she'd dozed off with her head leaning against his side. He had lifted his arm to encircle her shoulders and pull her to him.

Now Elan wordlessly handed Abby the reins, then reached behind her to pull his rifle from under the quilt covering it and Abby's pistol. She opened her mouth to speak, but he held up a warning hand as he leapt to the ground and scanned the terrain. He threw back the quilt and picked up the pistol, then thrust it in Abby's lap. She scooted over to set the brake on the buckboard before taking the pistol in her hand.

Abby's stomach knotted, and she discovered that her mouth was uncomfortably dry. She released the safety on the gun and tossed aside the reins to grip it with both hands. The Indians had returned and left a calling card, a lance planted in front of the cabin, its feathers waving a grim welcome.

Elan advanced, cautiously entering the open door of the cabin. He was out of sight for several minutes, leaving Abby to imagine painted faces behind every tree as she turned her head in first one direction and then the other.

She wondered why the Indians hadn't burned the cabin and the outbuildings, but was immensely grateful they had not. What they had done, however, was smash every pane in every window and strew the contents of the cabin and the shed all over the yard. She shuddered as she thought of what might have happened had she and Elan been home when they came calling.

Elan soon emerged from the cabin and continued his inspection, closely examining the ground, kneeling at times as he made his way around the cabin and then to the edge of the pines. He returned after several minutes and propped his rifle on the wheel of the buckboard. Then he reached to help Abby down.

Abby reset the safety, then put the gun down on the seat before reaching for Elan. She placed her hands on his arms and felt the controlled strength of his flexing biceps as he swept her from the seat. He lowered her to the ground, but did not release her. For several long seconds they remained as they were, his hands on her waist, hers resting on his arms. She raised her face to look at him, noting how the sun touched the ebony curls of his hair and made them gleam. He wore it pulled tightly back from his face and tied with the leather strip, and for some reason she couldn't understand, she wanted nothing more than to loosen it, to toss the binding aside and run her hands through the thick locks.

But of course she didn't. Her eyes fell to his throat, to the straining material that he had not been able to button past the middle of his chest. Dark curly hair spilled from the neck of his shirt. She wondered how he had become so strong. But then, if he really had walked across the continent and back, living off the land, that would explain his strength, if not his size.

Elan realized as he held Abby around the waist that she was so tiny his fingers touched. She was standing and looking up at him with a question in her deep blue eyes, patiently waiting for him to release her. If he did not do so soon, she would begin to fear him, would suspect the effect she had on his concentration. He reluctantly dropped his hands to his sides. Hers slid down the length of his arms before she removed them to clasp them in front of her. He dreaded what he must tell her. It would not be an easy thing for him to do.

She stepped away from him and turned to survey the mess scattered about the yard.

"Abby?" She glanced back over her shoulder to find Elan regarding her soberly. "There is something I need to tell you," he said.

"What is it?" Abby asked, feeling the butterflies dancing in her stomach. She had already had all the nasty surprises she wanted for one day, but the uneasy frown on Elan's face told her she was about to get another one.

"The medicine bag is gone."

"No!" Abby said. "It can't be!" She whirled and ran, stumbling over the unfamiliar and hampering long skirt of her dress, impatiently snatching it up over the tops of her boots. She raced across the small porch and through the open door of the cabin, tripping on an overturned chair and bruising her shin. She dropped to her knees and began a mad search, tossing aside pots and pans, linens and clothing, and ruined food.

It was too much. The medicine bag couldn't be gone. It had to be somewhere in the jumbled mess! It was her only link to the past . . . or was it the future?

As long as the medicine bag had hung on the wall, she had been confident that she could return to her ranch. It was impossible to believe she had lost her life as she knew it. She wanted to go home! She had skated through the last couple of days as though playing a part, acting a role that would soon end with an Academy Award she could tuck into a niche on her bookshelf, then get on with her life. She couldn't possibly be stuck in this time warp forever and ever!

Why had she been so foolish as to believe she could fix whatever had gone wrong? She was strong, but she wasn't strong enough to deal with this. This wasn't the place for her. What if she never found her ancestors? Where were they? They should be here. At least they should be in the area, and Roberts had never heard of them!

And Elan. Elan, who had agreed to stay so she could stay. Now he was stuck, too. He was going to hate her— if he didn't already.

Elan found Abby crawling around on the floor and muttering to herself about things he did not understand as she sifted through the disarray left by the intruder. There had been only one. At least, only one had been anywhere near the cabin. He had found the tracks of one unshod Indian pony and the moccasin tracks of one brave.

Elan reached down and pulled Abby to her feet. He pried an iron frying pan from her cold fingers and tossed it aside. "Come, Abby," he said. "We will clean this later." She resisted, still mumbling and searching with her frantic eyes. He scooped her into his arms and made his way across the room to the rocker. Using one hand, he turned it upright. He sank into the chair and cradled her in his arms. Then he untied the strings of her bonnet and pulled it from her head. After tossing it across the room, he slowly began to rock, clumsily stroking her hair with his huge hand, and as he did Abby quieted and closed her eyes.

Elan was puzzled. Something nagged at him, something he could not quite grasp. He contemplated the mess made of the cabin. Everything in the cabin had been pawed, torn out, or emptied, but not destroyed. The medicine bag had hung in plain sight on the wall. True, it was gone, but somehow he felt that it had not been the purpose of the visit. Then what?

What had the Indian seen or heard about that he wanted so badly? It had to be Abby's gun. And if he wanted it so badly that he would take the time to go through everything in the cabin, he would surely be back. The gun was now in the buckboard, unguarded. He should get it and his rifle safely inside. He stopped the rocking motion of the chair, and Abby's eyes sprang open.

"Thank you, Elan," she said, her mouth curving into a weak smile that touched his heart. "I think I needed that." She was going to be all right. Her eyes were free of the panic he had seen when she was scrambling around on the floor. Her slight weight was so pleasing in his lap that he was loath to release her, and she seemed in no hurry to be released.

"It is nothing," Elan said, smiling down at her. "For in truth, I like holding you in my arms."

Abby smiled lazily, a smile that culminated with a definite sparkle in her blue eyes, a sparkle Elan had longed to see. She lifted her hand and touched his cheek, feeling her heart give a funny little lurch. "As much as I like being lazy, I'd better get up and see about this mess, and you need to get the wagon unloaded."

Elan stood with Abby in his arms and swung her around before setting her on her feet with a flourish. "I just remembered. I have a surprise for you."

"What is it?" Abby asked, wondering what small trinket he'd picked out for her at the trading post, and desperate for any diversion to keep her occupied until she had time to think things through.

"You must wait until tonight," Elan said, striding out the door. "Waiting makes it much better."

6

She found him over an hour later, sprawled in the grass in the meadow, flat on his back and watching a pair of bald eagles soaring and diving. As she approached he turned his head to watch her progress through the high grass. She was shocked at the flood of feeling that shot through her, warming her all the way down to her toes. She spread her skirt and made herself comfortable as she settled down next to him. It was warm in the sunshine, but the cool mountain breeze kept it from being uncomfortably hot.

Elan pointed across the meadow. "The eagles have a nest in that tall tree," he said. "Do you see it?"

Abby shaded her eyes and followed the direction of his finger. She scanned the trees unsuccessfully for perhaps half a minute. "No, I can't find it," she said.

Elan sat up in one lithe movement. "Come. Sit here and I will show you." Abby scooted over, and Elan moved to position her between his long legs. When he had her settled correctly, he cupped his arm around her and lifted her right arm. "Put your arm along mine. Yes, like that."

Abby extended her arm along Elan's, her fingers falling far short of his wrist. As she studied the sprinkling of dark hairs along the fingers of his hand, he dipped his head to rest his cheek against hers, and she could feel the slight stubble on his face. That realization, along with her awareness of his hard body settled protectively around her, sent her heart into a Kentucky Derby sprint. "Now," he said softly, "close your left eye to sight along my arm, and follow my finger."

"What?" Abby asked as warmth spread through her lethargic limbs. She realized she hadn't heard a word he'd said. What was wrong with her? She was beginning to feel like a teenager in heat, and all he was trying to do was show her an eagle's nest. From his painful sigh, she realized he was rapidly losing patience with her, and she struggled to corral her wandering thoughts.

"Close your left eye to sight along my arm, and follow my finger," Elan repeated. *Merde,* but she was destroying his concentration. He had left the cabin and sought the peacefulness of the meadow to escape the turmoil she had unleashed in him as he held her in his arms and rocked her like a babe. Then when she sought him out, he could not help but draw her into his arms again. As long as he did not touch her, he could control himself, but the slightest touch of her small hand, even the brush of her breath against his skin, was enough to send his blood drumming through his veins.

Abby did as Elan told her and found the nest immediately. "I see it!" she said. "High in the tree!" Elan grinned, caught up in her girlish exuberance, relieved to direct his attention to the nature around them.

"Now, follow my finger and I will show you something else." He lowered their arms and slowly moved them to the west. "What do you see?" he asked.

"Deer," Abby said. "There must be dozens of them. But how did you know?" The deer were grazing in the tall grass near a stand of aspen. They blended perfectly with the landscape. She would never have spotted them without his help.

"It is what I know," Elan said. "I have spent my life learning the habits of the animals of the forest." He took her hand and placed it in her lap, cradling her in his arms, pleased that she made no objection. He would be content just to hold her, to breathe her sweet feminine scent, to enjoy the softness that was Abby, for he understood he could do nothing else and in reality should not even be touching her in any way. She was not for him. He was "a half-breed," as her people would say, and he knew his place.

"Can you track?" Abby asked, breaking into his thoughts. "I've read that mountain men can track."

"Is that what I am, Abby?" he asked, inhaling the clean scent of her hair and finding his pulse suddenly leaping. He had been called many things in his life, but never a mountain man. Sometimes he was called Frenchy. Sometimes he was called a breed. Other times he had been called worse names, but never had he been called a mountain man. It was a name he liked, he decided, and one he would not object to. "Am I a mountain man?"

"In the early eighteen hundreds the men who hunted and trapped in these mountains became known as mountain men," Abby said. "So I guess that's what you are."

"Then I am a mountain man," he said, his warm breath caressing her cheek and sending a shiver down her spine. "And yes, I can track."

"Then why didn't you go after the Indians who took the medicine bag? If you can track, why didn't you try to get it back?" Abby shifted in his arms to find a more comfortable spot and dropped her head into the hollow between his neck and shoulder, fighting the urge to purr like a well-stroked cat.

Elan considered her question, and it was several long minutes before he answered. "It was only one Indian, Abby," he said. "He spent the night down by the creek and raided the cabin as soon as we left this morning. He has a day's head start. He will meet with the hunting party he left and they will return to their village. I am only one man. I cannot take on an Indian village."

She would accept his explanation without question because it was reasonable, but Elan knew in his heart that it was not the only reason he had not pursued the brave, nor was it the most important one. And that knowledge left him with overwhelming guilt.

Somewhere, tucked into a tiny corner of his heart, in a place he had never discovered before, was the desire—no, not the desire, but instead the need, the chest-crushing need—to keep Abby close, to prolong the time they shared. In her initial fright after discovering the ransacked cabin, she might have insisted that they try to return to their times. That he was not ready to do. Not yet. He made a solemn vow to keep her safe, and he tightened his arms around her.

"I really got us into a fine mess, didn't I?" Abby asked. "How will we ever get out of it?" As Elan's arms held her closer Abby realized she could feel the steady beating of his heart against her back. Somehow, having his arms around her gave her reassurance, comfort. It was as if nothing could harm her as long as she had his protection. She'd been afraid he would be angry with her, and she was relieved to find that he was not.

"I am a man, Abby. I made the decision to stay. You must not blame yourself for something you cannot help," he said. "Do not lose hope. We will find a way home when the time comes for us to go." Abby could only hope he was right, but she had her doubts.

They remained in the meadow watching the eagles soar and hunt until hunger forced them to consider the evening meal. Together they strolled back to the cabin, both reluctant to lose the closeness they had shared sitting amid the sweet grass and colorful wildflowers.

Abby flopped down in her rocker with a tired groan and picked up her sewing basket. She finally had the cabin back in order and had even succeeded in placing a light meal on the supper table. She threaded her needle and went to work on the drawstring purse she was making with leftover material from her blue dress and bonnet. She glanced at Elan out of the corner of her eye and noted he was hard at work on a project of his own.

She couldn't imagine why he preferred the hard wooden floor to one of the chairs, but he rarely sat anywhere besides the floor. He would come to the table to eat, but complained about the table legs being too short to accommodate his legs. He was doing a bit of sewing of his own, using deerskin from a hide he had found in the shed, and seemed absorbed in his task.

Elan's long fingers moved nimbly, and while she would have thought him inept with a needle because of the size of his hands, he was surprisingly skillful. But then again, his every movement was so gracefully executed that she often felt clumsy in comparison. It was no wonder he was an excellent woodsman and hunter. He moved with the same unaffected dignity and grace as did the creatures he stalked. He seemed as one with them.

Elan sensed Abby's eyes on him and looked up, finding her engrossed in his sewing rather than her own. "A man must learn to sew when he spends months in the wilderness and depends on the hides of animals to clothe himself," Elan explained.

"I thought that's one of the reasons why trappers kept squaws," Abby said, immediately regretting her teasing when Elan's face darkened.

"And what is it you know of trappers and their squaws, Abby?" Elan asked, returning his attention to the deerskin. Abby dropped her eyes to her lap, feeling the flush creep up her neck to stain her face.

"Only what I've read in books," she replied, concentrating on her sewing.

"Come here, Abby," Elan said as he held up his finished work. "This is for you."

She put aside her sewing basket and walked across the room to him. He remained seated on the floor and held up his finished product. "What is it?" she asked, leaning over and peering closely.

"It is a holster for your gun. You should wear it. Having the gun nearby is no longer safe enough. You must keep it within instant reach," Elan replied.

"Where should I wear it?" Abby asked, taking the soft leather pouch from his outstretched hand and turning it over to examine it. She didn't want to wear it on her hip. It would constantly be in the way. Not only that, but she would feel foolish running around like Annie Oakley.

Elan shrugged his wide shoulders. "Wear it where it will be most comfortable." Abby immediately planted her foot on a nearby chair and hiked up her skirt. She strapped the holster to her thigh, just above her knee.

"What about here?" she asked, pulling her skirt higher and straightening the holster on her leg. "I think this will do fine."

Elan's eyes locked on Abby's bare leg, and he found himself unable to tear them away. She had been serious about shaving her legs, he realized. He was only able to get his breathing under control when Abby dropped her skirt and took a few steps to test the feel of the holster on her leg.

"Thank you, Elan," Abby said sincerely. "I'll feel much safer now. Was this my surprise?"

Elan rose and walked over to stand near her. "No, I still have your surprise," he said.

"What is it, then?" Abby asked, favoring him with a smile that reached her eyes and made them twinkle expectantly.

"I filed a homestead claim while we were in the settlement today."

Abby blanched, feeling her heart skip a beat. "You did what?" she asked, her throat tightening painfully.

Elan's smile broadened as he dug in his pocket and pulled out a slip of paper. "I used part of the money you gave me to file on this abandoned claim. The land will no longer belong to the Spooners."

"Nor to me," Abby said in a broken whisper as the full import of his words struck home. She had been unable to vent her anger on something as enigmatic and intangible as the government's bureaucracy as it labored to steal her land, but here was Elan, flesh and blood, sinew and bone, and no less a thief. She welcomed the fury that flooded her, the blinding rage that had been pent up by five years of frustration, and before she realized what she was doing, she swung at him, catching him unaware with her swift and sudden movement.

Elan's head rocked back as he was blindsided by Abby's unexpected blow. Abby unclenched her fist and flexed her bruised fingers, shaking with rage and fear for what she had done. She had struck him, something she had never before done to another living being, and he was strong enough to kill her with a single blow. When Elan did nothing more than peer quizzically at her, she wanted to throttle him again for not even realizing what he had done to her and her family when he filed the claim. Instead, much to her horror, she did something she had not done since childhood. She burst into tears.

"Abby?" Elan took a hesitant step toward her and awkwardly touched her shoulder. "What is wrong?" She jerked away from his touch, and he dropped his hand, uncomfortably aware that he had somehow caused her distress and unsure what to do about it.

Abby dashed her hands across her tear-streaked face and glared at him. "You've stolen my land," she said. "How could you? You know what it means to me!"

"I have not stolen your land, Abby," Elan said. "I filed the claim to keep someone from stealing it from you. I am the man and it was my place to do so. Now, let us go to bed. You are tired. You will feel better after a good night's sleep."

"A good night's sleep won't change a damn thing, Elan," Abby said as she reached to draw the blankets closed. "I don't think I can ever forgive you for what you have done."

It was midmorning before Abby was ready for her expedition. She swung her pail, her mouth watering as she thought of the cobbler she would attempt if she found a plentiful supply of huckleberries. As she entered the shade of the pines a hundred yards or so behind the cabin, she was delighted to find a patch of the small purple berries. She was glad she had decided to wear her jeans rather than the blue dress. Jeans were much better suited for tromping through the brush.

She wandered among the trees, gathering the ripe berries, pausing to eat a few as she picked, and soon her hands and mouth were stained with purple juice. She had hoped the berry picking would relieve her of some of her restless energy and would give her time to think as well.

She realized she had little insight into the male psyche, and even less insight into that of a man from the early nineteenth century, but she just couldn't for the life of her understand Elan and his motives. He seemed to have absolutely no concept of what he had done by claiming her land, and maintained instead that he was keeping it safe for her. But the fact remained that the homestead was now in his name. Things were even more complicated than before. Instead of making things better, she seemed only to be making them worse.

She had been hard at work for perhaps an hour when she straightened to swat at a buzzing mosquito. A small sound drew her attention, and she looked behind her, expecting to find Elan returning from his early-morning hunting trip. The sight of the small brown bear cub not ten yards away greedily consuming huckleberries froze her to the spot.

She had broken the cardinal rule. Deep in her musings, she had forgotten to make noise, and had instead been picking berries without making her presence known. If baby bear was here, then mama bear wasn't far away. Fearfully turning in the direction of the rustling brush, Abby saw what she dreaded most. She slowly took a backward step, fighting every instinct that screamed

Run! Run! Run! when she saw mama bear with another cub. The huge brown silver-tipped grizzly swung her massive head back and forth as she issued a series of grunting snorts and pawed at the ground.

She should scream, wave her arms, make loud noises, Abby thought as the huge bear rocked from side to side, baring her yellowed teeth, her fur rippling in fury. But Abby could do nothing. She was paralyzed with fright. The pistol strapped to her leg was useless. Wounding the monster would only make matters worse. She needed a cannon, or quite possibly a SCUD missile. She had lived in Montana all of her life and knew the danger of bears, but she had never before faced one in the wild. It was a terrifying sight.

Now was the time her life was supposed to flash before her eyes, Abby thought as she failed to get even a small squeak past her inoperative vocal cords. But she couldn't dredge up a single happy moment. Several hundred pounds of growling, slobbering, grunting, maddened bear was all she saw.

"Get behind me, Abby," Elan said loudly, breaking her trance. She flinched at the sound of his deep, commanding voice, but it shook her loose from her paralysis. She cautiously eased behind his bulk on legs that threatened to give way.

"Bear! Bear! Bear!" he shouted, waving his arms, shaking his rifle as he yelled. "Go, bear! Go!" The grizzly continued to paw the ground, but her cubs fled. For several anxious seconds Abby was afraid the bear would charge, and it took all of her willpower not to turn tail and run, even knowing the bear would give chase.

"Go!" Elan shouted. "Go! Go! Go!" The grizzly abruptly turned and loped away in the direction her cubs had taken. Abby sagged against Elan's back, suddenly too weak to move. Elan watched the bear until she disappeared over the ridge, then he spun to face Abby, relief turning to anger over the scare she had given him.

Anger rapidly gave way to concern as he gazed into a pair of enormous blue eyes framed by lush ebony lashes. The ashen pallor of Abby's face served to give her wide eyes an even deeper hue than the sky overhead and to make her silky lashes seem darker than midnight. Only the purple smears around her mouth gave color to her face. And it was those smudges that calmed him, for they gave her the appearance of a wayward child.

"You should not wander so far from the cabin," Elan said gruffly, taking her by the hand and pulling her along with him as he made for the clearing. "It is dangerous."

"You're not kidding," Abby muttered ungraciously as she struggled to keep pace with his long strides. She stumbled over a root and came perilously close to losing her hold on the bucket of berries. She pulled loose from Elan's grip and tightened her hold on her pail. All she needed to cap off the morning was to lose her hard-won berries.

She was suddenly seized with hysterical laughter. She laughed until her sides ached, bending forward at the waist and wrapping her arm around her middle while she carefully cradled her pail. Elan's astonished look only intensified her amusement, and soon she was gasping for breath as tears streamed from her eyes and splashed down her cheeks.

She had somehow traveled back to the year 1875 and had lost the way home. There was no telling how long she'd be stuck in a place totally alien to her. A place where she had to cook on a wood-burning stove. A place with no running water, no flush toilet. A place with no telephones, no television, and no automobiles. She had faced down marauding Indians and a crazed grizzly. Her family homestead had been stolen by a man she hardly knew, a man to whom her fate was inexplicably linked, a man who understood her no more than she understood him. *And she was worried about spilling a bucket of huckleberries!*

When Abby finally caught her breath and managed to get herself under some semblance of control, she found Elan propped against a pine, worriedly studying her. She bit back another fit of giggles and hastened to assure him she had not plunged over the edge.

"I'm okay, Elan," Abby said somewhat breathlessly. "I was just struck by how absolutely funny and horrible things really are. Here I am trying to salvage my family homestead, and you and everything else seem to be working against me at every turn. I can't even pick a damn bucket of huckleberries for a pie without worrying about being eaten by a bear. I think I need a drink, and something tells me that you will strongly disapprove of my having one."

"Ladies do not drink, Abby," Elan said quietly with a disapproving frown.

"I know, Elan," Abby said, nodding at his expected response. "But you know, I think I'll have one anyway, and I don't intend to ask your permission. I just don't feel much like a lady today." And with that she stomped through the brush, leaving him to contemplate her outburst.

Elan watched Abby's departure, unable to concentrate on anything beyond the entrancing sway of her hips as she made her way out of the trees. Although she wore her man's trousers they took nothing from her femininity, and if anything, only served to enhance it. He was finding it more and more difficult to keep a respectful distance between himself and Abby. He realized that Abby in her innocence only added to his problem. She seemed completely unaware of the effect she had on him.

7

The invitation came unexpectedly, sending Abby's excitement soaring as she thought of the possibilities awaiting her at the Winston ranch. Frank Johnson, riding a fine black mount, had delivered the missive and was rewarded with a dish of huckleberry cobbler and a cup of coffee. Abby's later exploits picking berries had gone decidedly better than her first one had.

"Good-bye, Frank," Abby said now as he left. "Congratulations again on your job. I know you'll work hard for Mr. Winston."

"Yes, ma'am," Frank said as he settled his hat on his head. "I like working for Mr. Winston."

"And don't forget to tell him we're looking forward to the party," Abby added as Frank swung his horse around. The young man tipped his hat in acknowledgment as he rode away.

Well, she *was* looking forward to the party. How Elan would feel about it was anybody's guess. Her outburst had really shaken him, and they had hardly exchanged two words in the last three weeks. He was away as much as he was around, preferring solitude to her company. He was always up and gone before dawn and rarely spent any time in the cabin until it was time to retire for the night.

Elan's filing the homestead claim on Abby's cabin had thrown her completely off course. His going behind her back hurt as much as anything, and she imagined he felt pretty smug about it. While she was busy trying to figure out what they needed for basic survival, and trading her jewelry to get it, he had been establishing claim to her land. She refused to consider that the idea to remain in this time for a while had been hers, and she was certain he had taken the action deliberately against her. She was convinced he had stayed for his own selfish purposes, not to be of any help to her.

She was also convinced his pretense of kindness and gentleness had been just that, a sham, a way to get what he wanted. And what he wanted was a roof over his head and the means to trap and pan for gold. He had put to good use the mining implements he had found in the shed, and spent as much time panning the creek as he did hunting. His mining efforts had been surprisingly successful, for he had accumulated quite a few good-sized nuggets and several ounces of dust.

He probably missed his squaw, and she was certain he'd had one. Why else would he have looked so guilty when she mentioned trappers and their squaws? Well, she wasn't going to be his squaw. They were in the same boat, both of them out of their natural environment, but that didn't mean they had to stay together. There was always the chance the medicine bag would turn up again. She would figure out something as soon as she could get her cattle operation going and prosperous. Surely he'd be ready to move on by that time anyway. From what she had read about mountain men, they rarely stayed in one place long.

She would have to wait until spring to buy her cattle. She knew that. She had no way to feed them during the winter if the snow fell too heavily for them to forage on their own. She looked out over the beautiful natural meadow, with its waist-high grass, and longed for the means to cut the hay. Well, there was no use wishing for the impossible. Somehow, she would find a way to get it cut next summer. Surely by then her great-great-grandparents would have arrived and she would have some help. But in the meantime, she'd have to build her herd slowly. Her lack of money was as frustrating as her inactivity.

Elan checked his fish net, wading into the icy stream and pulling it from the rocks where he had it anchored. He found it brimming with cutthroat trout, and his mouth watered at the thought of fresh fish for the evening meal. It would be an agreeable change from the venison he and Abby had eaten for the last few days. Perhaps it would improve her disposition.

In truth, he was as dumbfounded by Abby's reaction to his filing the homestead claim as he was by her emotional outburst the day she happened on the bear. He was the man of the house, and it was not only his place to file the claim but also his right to do so. Unless life had changed more than he could possibly imagine, a woman would be laughed out of any government claims office if she tried such a preposterous act.

Abby eventually would come to realize the prudence of his actions and would appreciate his efforts on her behalf, for truly, how could she manage without him? He hoped she would soon see her mistake. He was growing weary of her stony silences and her injured sniffs.

Elan unsheathed his hunting knife and selected a flat rock on which to clean his catch. It was a warm afternoon in late August, but he thought of the coming winter as he stood in the shade of the willows, gutting and rinsing the fish.

Soon the snow and ice would come and he would begin the harvest of furs. It was of some concern that there did not seem to be as many beaver as there should have been in the area, but it just meant he would have to travel farther in his search. It would be good to find a warm cabin waiting and a woman for companionship when he ran his trap lines during the freezing winter. He ignored the familiar tightening in his loins when he thought of Abby, and quickly turned his attention to the fish. Abby needed gentle handling. She was not to be rushed. He was a patient man.

Abby scrawled a note to Elan on the back of the Winston invitation and hurriedly changed into her jeans and shirt. She knew she should take the buckboard, like a proper lady of the times, but she was in too much of a hurry to get to the settlement and back before dark. She could ride the distance in half the time. Her only concern was her pistol. She tossed it into her pack and carried it with her out the door. She'd feel foolish strapping it to her leg in plain sight over her jeans.

She had nearly reached the settlement when she was jolted by a horrible thought. What if Elan couldn't read? Would he think she'd been abducted by the Indians and try to find her? Not likely, she thought grimly. If anything, he'd probably be relieved to have her out of his hair.

Abby tied the horse to the rail in front of the trading post and hurried into the establishment. She smiled and nodded at a middle-aged woman who looked her up and down quite thoroughly on her way out the door. Abby made for the table of yard goods. If she was going to a party, then she was determined to have a party dress.

"Howdy, Mrs. Elan," Roberts said, also looking her up and down and frowning worriedly. "What can I do for you? Ain't seen you in a spell. Shore did enjoy that venison loin Elan brought in last week. Elan with you?"

"Not this trip, Mr. Roberts," Abby replied distractedly as she tried to do a mental tally of the yards of material and lace she needed for what she had in mind. She was troubled too by her lack of sewing skills. She'd never attempted to design a garment herself, and had been surprised when she'd managed the hat and drawstring purse from the leftover material of the blue dress. Altering the other two dresses had been easier than the first, her skills improving with practice. But making an entire dress from scratch was something else altogether.

Roberts made his way to Abby's side, feeling it safe to do so since Elan was not in the vicinity. He was eager for a better look at Abby's form-fitting pants and shirt. He edged closer, allowing his arm to accidentally brush hers.

Abby turned to Roberts and gave him a cold stare. "I shall tell Elan you were most enthusiastic to please me, Mr. Roberts." He scurried to the other side of the table and gave Abby a weak smile.

"Ah, what can I do for you?" Roberts asked, trying to keep his eyes focused on Abby's face rather than her bust. The very thought of Elan's taking offense at his behavior had him sweating profusely, and he was suddenly rather eager for Abby to finish her business and go.

"I need a price on the red satin and the black lace,"

Abby said, fingering the glossy material as she unrolled several yards off the bolt.

Roberts ran his finger under his collar and licked his lips. Elan would surely kill him if he let Abby leave with what he'd bought with the saloon girls in mind. No respectable woman in the territory would think of wearing such a thing!

"Well?" Abby asked impatiently, picking up the spool of black lace.

Roberts desperately took the plunge. "Mrs. Elan, I don't believe red is the color for you."

"Nonsense!" Abby snapped. "I've been told all my life I look wonderful in red. Now, what is the price?"

Roberts paused for several moments. "Take what you need. I'll just put it on your account."

After several minutes of careful consideration, Abby followed Roberts to the counter and spread the bolt of material and spool of black lace across its smooth surface. She returned to the notions table, picking out threads and buttons. "Do you know of a seamstress I can hire?" Abby asked Roberts as he busily snipped the yards of material and lace Abby had unrolled. He folded them neatly before answering.

"Well . . ." Roberts hesitated, not wanting to help her but afraid she would go looking on her own if he didn't. He really couldn't afford to allow her to go into the saloon, not if he wanted to live and do well, and she was just ornery enough to do it if she went around making inquiries about a seamstress and heard about Annie.

"Well, what?" Abby snapped impatiently, plunking down the notions with the material.

"I'll be right back," Roberts promised. He rushed around the counter and out the door as fast as his stumpy legs would carry him.

Soon he returned, dragging behind him a young woman who appeared to have been yanked from her sleep. Although she was decently dressed, her disheveled appearance reminded Abby of an unmade bed. Her honey-blond hair flowed wildly around her shoulders, and she was barefoot. Not only that, but she was protesting loudly, using more profanity than Abby had realized was around in 1875. Her lively green eyes snapped fire with each curse she threw at Roberts. When she spotted Abby she clamped her mouth closed, but not before shooting Roberts a look of pure venom.

"Mrs. Elan, meet Montana Annie. She makes all her clothes, and most of the other girls', too."

"I'm Abby," Abby said, offering her hand. Annie hesitantly shook it. "Come sit with me a few minutes," Abby said encouragingly, leading Annie to a couple of straight-backed chairs near the wood-burning stove in the corner of the store. Annie appeared to be in her late teens or early twenties, but the girl had a hard look about her, as if she had lived a lifetime in those few years. It wasn't difficult for Abby to guess Annie's occupation.

"Did Roberts tell you why I wanted to talk to you?" Annie shook her head and continued to study Abby, her thoughtful green eyes taking in every detail of Abby's clothing.

"I want you to make a party dress for me." Abby smiled when Annie's eyes widened. "Will you do it?"

"You mean for pay?" Annie asked suspiciously, gripping her hands tightly together in her lap. She placed one bare foot atop the other, then slid both self-consciously under her skirts.

"Yes, for pay," Abby said. "I want it made from the red satin on the counter. I plan to wear it to John Winston's party in two weeks. Can you have it ready by then?"

Annie's interest in her hands fled, and she stared at Abby open-mouthed before she found the sense to speak. "Are you sure you want a red dress to wear to the party?" Annie asked, whirling her head to locate Roberts. Why, the man had taken leave of his senses, selling red satin to a respectable woman! And if John Winston had invited Abby to a party, Annie was sure Abby was respectable despite her apparel. Roberts shrugged and proceeded to wrap Abby's purchases in brown paper, then tied the parcel with a string.

"Yes, I am," Abby said. "Red is my favorite color, and I refuse to have another. I can do a little sewing but I've never made a dress by myself. I really need your help."

"I can make the dress," Annie said, wishing she could be at the party to view the results.

"Then we are agreed? I really want it in time for the party."

"I'll make the dress," Annie said, her generous mouth curving into a wide smile. "And you will have it in time for the party!"

Abby dashed breathlessly into the cabin after unsaddling the roan and turning him out to graze. Elan was nowhere in sight. She tossed her pistol on the bed, then kicked off her boots and tore off her clothing, intent on changing before Elan returned and discovered she'd been to the settlement in her jeans. Not that she gave a damn what he thought, but it would be easier not to provoke him. She paused indecisively, clad only in her white lace bra and matching bikini panties. Should she put the blue dress back on, or choose one of the others?

The blue one could use a good washing. She would wear the black one. As much as she hated what she had dubbed "the widow's weeds," it was her only other dress suitable for everyday wear. The emerald-green wool trimmed in ivory lace looked more like a dressy dress to Abby. She wasn't about to cook in it.

Elan stepped through the open door of the cabin and tossed his stringer of cleaned fish on the table. His jaw tightened as he viewed Abby's undressed state. The little fool! Leaving the blankets open was simply careless, but leaving the door unlatched and wide open was asking for trouble. He had cautioned her repeatedly about keeping the door latched and the shutters closed when she was home alone. This time it was he who surprised her. Next time it could be anyone.

Abby spun around at the sound of the fish being flopped on the table. "Oh, it's you!" she said, relieved to see Elan and not some Indian after her hair. "You might have said something instead of sneaking up like that!"

Elan could not force himself to avert his eyes from Abby, and heard only vaguely what she said. The white lace undergarments she wore did more to enhance her shapely curves than to hide them, and he was more than a little taken aback by her complete lack of modesty. She watched him curiously, but seemed not the least bit uncomfortable with her *déshabillé*.

In three quick strides, he covered the space to the blankets and jerked them closed. He was still gripping the coarse woolen material in his hands when Abby emerged under them some minutes later.

Abby's eyes settled on Elan's hands, hands that could fit hers in the palms, and she studied them, bemused by his ability to exercise such restraint when weaker, smaller men would not. He had the strength to take anything he wanted, yet he always acted the perfect gentleman. He had startled her, but after she got over her initial fright she found she could only stare at the expression on his face until he pulled the blankets closed. He was embarrassed at catching her in her underclothing!

Growing up on a ranch and taking the place of the son her father never had, Abby had given little thought to feminine modesty. The ranch hands always treated her like one of the boys, and Abby had never considered herself feminine in any respect. Her brief affair with Paul had been her sole excursion into exploring that aspect of herself, and it had only left her wishing she had left well enough alone. She was sure that had she been enticing and sexy, Paul would have never left her for someone else. Since meeting Elan, she was learning about an entirely different facet of herself. Elan found her desirable, desirable as a woman. It was a heady thought.

Elan released the blankets and tipped her face toward his with his fingers. She met his eyes, glittering dark pools that seemed to drink her in, and she waited for the kiss he was sure to give. A muscle twitched in his jaw, and Abby reached up to touch his face, as if she could brush away his rigid control with her fingertips. Instead of accepting the invitation she offered, he drew a sharp breath. Then he dropped his hand and was gone, leaving her to her own thoughts.

Supper was a sorry affair. Abby had been unable to concentrate on her cooking, finding her thoughts dominated by Elan. She had never experienced such unbridled passion as that which he unleashed each time he raked her with his probing black eyes or came near enough for her to touch the rock-hard strength of his powerful body.

He had stolen her land, although he denied that was his intent. He frowned at the idea of her buying a herd. He disliked her occasional use of profanity. He expected her to dress and act like a lady. It was little consolation that he expected her to act like a proper lady from his time or that she expected him to behave like a man from her time. More often than not, she wanted to scream and stamp her foot at his outdated views. And yet she wanted him. She wanted his arms around her, wanted to rest her head on that solid chest, wanted him to tell her everything was going to be all right, that they would find the medicine bag and return home. She missed the closeness they had once shared, and she didn't know how to get it back.

She wasn't sure she could accept a life of deprivation in the wilderness, as he seemed more than willing to do. In the back of her mind she knew that somehow, somewhere, she would find the medicine bag, and when she did, she would take her chances with it and try to return to her time. But in the meantime, she knew that she desired Elan as she had no other man.

Abby's culinary skills were minimal. Seth, one of the ranch hands, had done the cooking at the ranch for as long as Abby could remember. Her activity in the kitchen had been limited to heating up leftovers and nuking food in the microwave. Learning to cook on a wood-burning stove was just about enough to do her in. She had scorched the beans and would have done the same to the trout if Elan hadn't intervened. That the cobbler she'd baked earlier had been edible had been nothing short of a miracle. She hurled the wooden spoon across the cabin and ran out the door, desperate to escape.

"It is not important, Abby." Elan silently appeared at her side as she stood in the pale moonlight drawing deep, calming breaths. "Only the beans on the bottom of the pot were ruined. The rest can be eaten."

Abby started guiltily at his silent approach, unaware of his presence until he spoke. She sniffed disdainfully.

"Well, I've always had more important things to do than cook. Seth did the cooking at the ranch. I was too busy with the cattle and hands to worry about such commonplace things." But cooking was suddenly of vital importance, and Abby regretted not having learned more about it. She could admit it to herself, but she would never admit it to Elan.

Elan made no comment but wondered about a world in which a woman would not master even the most rudimentary domestic skills. Of course, Abby spoke of having a cook and other servants, those who worked the ranch, which he had come to understand was like a large farm. But why would a woman undertake the responsibility of such an operation without a man at her side? Running a large farm was man's work, after all. Abby should have been content to supervise the running of the household.

Elan guessed her to be somewhere in her mid-twenties, certainly past the age when most women were married. She was attractive, more than attractive, he mused as he studied her profile in the soft moonlight. Perhaps it was her sharp tongue that frightened men away. That and her possessiveness of her land.

Another thought struck Elan with the speed and velocity of a lightning bolt. Why had he assumed Abby unwed? Her advanced age and her familiarity with intimacy certainly indicated she was more than comfortable around men.

Could it be he was coveting another man's wife? And covet he did. When he was near her, he had difficulty keeping his thoughts from straying to her soft curves, her sweet lips. His need for her was a dull hunger, always there, never sated.

"Shall we try it?" Abby's voice interrupted his thoughts, pulled him back from his musings.

"What?" Try as he might, Elan could not get his thoughts past the need to know more about Abby's other life. It was suddenly important that he know if someone awaited her return. As for himself, there was no one. He had been on his own too long, seeking adventure and wealth in a new and promising land.

"The burned beans and crisp trout," Abby replied. "Maybe you're right and they are salvageable." Elan gallantly offered his arm, and she took it with a smile, lightly placing her small hand through the crook of his elbow, allowing him to lead her into the cabin and seat her at the table.

Elan filled their plates with the beans and fish and placed them on the table. He returned to the stove and was soon back with the pot of steaming coffee and two cups. Abby gradually relaxed, allowing Elan to wait on her, pleased by his attention, knowing he was trying to soothe her feelings, for he was not fond of what he considered women's work.

He had established that right off. His first hunting expedition had yielded two plump geese that he had tossed on the table and instructed her to clean. She remembered with amusement his reaction to her horror, and his less-than-patient instructions on cleaning the birds and cooking them. He had eaten the birds, pinfeathers and all, but he had not done so graciously, and thereafter made sure he cleaned any varmint, fish, or fowl he dragged in. But he generally left all the cooking and cleaning up to her.

That is, all the cleaning up but the cleaning of himself. He kept himself clean, washing in the creek, she supposed, for he had steadfastly refused another scrubbing in the tub. She had no complaints, and often noticed the absence of the bar of soap prior to his disappearances. He would return smelling clean, hair damp, clothing changed. She would civilize him yet. Abby smiled and held her cup up.

"A toast, Elan!" she said as he sat and carefully slid his legs beneath the too-short table. He laughed, caught up in her exuberance, enjoying the way the lamplight picked up the sheen of her glossy hair and deepened the blue of her eyes.

"And what is it we toast?" he inquired pleasantly, raising his cup and lifting a brow.

"Why, this excellent meal, of course!" Abby pretended to pout, but the sparkle in her eye gave her away. He touched his cup to hers. Elan was caught in her game and set down his cup to pick up one of the overdone trout. He made a great show of eating it, smacking his lips with gusto as he nibbled around the small bones, then bit the tail with a resounding crunch.

"Truly delicious," he pronounced, dabbing a cloth napkin to the corners of his mouth in mock delicacy, then reaching across the table to do the same for Abby.

"Ah, you spoil me, kind sir." Abby giggled, touching the tip of her tongue to the corner of her mouth to catch a stray crumb he had missed. "But your aim needs improving." She leaned toward him to give him better access just as his hand advanced to correct his error. His fingers lightly brushed across her breast. Abby jerked away from the unexpected contact

Turbulent thoughts filled her mind. Thoughts of Elan's hands pulling her close against his muscular chest, of him stripping away her clothing, of him tossing her across the bed and making love to her with his hands, his mouth, his body. She trembled, flooded with desire, yet ashamed, too, of her violent reaction to his innocent touch. She smiled weakly at his strangled apology. He regarded her with troubled eyes.

Elan glanced at his hand, almost expecting to see it smolder, so acutely did it burn. He smoothed the napkin absently and looked up at Abby's face. Two blazing spots of red stained her cheeks. It was as if she could read the desire in his eyes, he thought.

The meal was finished quickly in constrained silence after both of them made feeble attempts to recapture the lost mood. It was only later, while Abby cleared the remains of the meal and Elan settled into his customary position on the floor to sew a pair of buckskin trousers, that he worked up the courage to question Abby about her past life.

"Abby?" Elan drew her attention as she wiped the table, then turned up the lamp to give him better light for his task.

"Yes?" Abby smoothed her skirt and sank into the rocker. She picked up the sewing basket and reached for her needle and thread. She still had bonnets and drawstring purses to make to match the green dress and the awful black one.

"How is it that you are an old maid?" Elan put aside his buckskin to await her answer, enjoying the sight of her in the shadowed lamplight.

"I'm not an old maid!" Abby said, feeling the blood surge to her face at his use of the chauvinistic term. She longed to slap him senseless, but that would be difficult, she thought as she seethed. He couldn't possibly have any sense to lose!

Elan's face fell. It was just as he expected. No woman as attractive as Abby would be unwed at her age, even with her sharp tongue and demanding temperament. He did covet another man's wife, and since that was the case, he wanted to know whom he faced.

"Why have you not spoken of your husband?" Elan asked. "Will he not be worried about you?"

"I don't have a husband," Abby said, remembering Paul's heartless abandonment. "I'm not married and never have been."

"Then you are an old maid." Elan grinned, relieved to have his fears vanquished. He went back to his sewing. He looked up a few minutes later to find Abby standing over him, her hands on her hips, her mouth drawn into a tight line, her eyes shooting sparks.

"Unmarried women from my time do not appreciate being called old maids," Abby said. "We prefer to call ourselves career women."

"I do not understand," Elan said with a slight frown as he put aside his sewing and rose.

"No," Abby said, "I don't imagine you do." She turned to walk away, certain any explanation would be a waste of breath. How could she possibly explain the place women held in the work force in the 1990s? He would never understand it.

Elan reached out and captured Abby by the elbow, spinning her around and pulling her to him. Her eyes widened in shock as she collided with his powerful body. Her lips parted to issue a protest. She never got it out.

8

Elan released Abby's arm to place both of his hands at her waist. Then he effortlessly lifted her off her feet until they were facing each other. Abby gripped his shoulders, speechless at his action. "If I never call you an old maid again, will you consider forgiving me?" Elan asked, his lips so close she could taste his breath. Abby nodded, unable to make a single sound, able only to look deeply into his eyes as every bone in her body melted.

"Put your arms around my neck," Elan said, his voice growing husky as his accent deepened. Abby uncurled her fingers and cautiously slid her hands around his neck, combing her fingers through his silky hair.

"Do you think a kiss might be as binding as a handshake?" Elan asked, drawing her closer until she could feel his lips moving against her own.

"Yes," Abby murmured as Elan's mouth slanted across hers. He was gentle, exquisitely gentle as he traced her lips with the tip of his tongue, then slipped it between her teeth and explored the recesses of her mouth. She gave herself over to him, allowed him complete possession, and when he withdrew, she released a long shuddering sigh and opened her eyes, finding it difficult to focus, difficult to think of anything but the liquid warmth flowing through her.

He lowered her then, sliding her down the length of his hard body until her feet touched the floor. Her breasts swelled and ached for his touch as they rubbed against his buckskin-clad chest, but they received no relief as his hands left her waist to disengage hers from around his neck.

He had molded her to him, and she was acutely aware of every muscle, every sinew, every contour of his magnificent maleness. He was man and she was woman. Never had she been so intensely aware of her own fragile femininity or so overwhelmingly acquainted with another's blatant masculinity.

Elan brought her hands down and took each in turn to his mouth to lightly kiss each palm before regretfully releasing her. "Good night, Abby," he said softly. "I am glad we are friends again."

"Yes," Abby said as her fingers fluttered across her swollen lips. "Friends."

"Ouch!" Abby said, flinching as the pin pricked her flesh and was hastily withdrawn by an apologetic Annie, who busily muttered to herself through a mouthful of the offending objects as she took in the excess material at Abby's waist. It was the last fitting, and with only a day left before the party, both Abby and Annie were understandably nervous about their combined results.

Abby balanced on a straight-backed chair in Annie's

tiny room behind the saloon. It was simply furnished with an iron bedstead, potbellied stove, wooden bedside washstand, and the chair upon which Abby stood, and barely large enough to contain these pieces. The room's only saving grace was its private entrance through the saloon's back alley.

The bright yellow muslin curtains on the one small window and a quilted bedspread and matching rag rug were evidence of Annie's efforts to give the cramped room a homey touch. Abby heaved a sigh as she thought of the young woman's efforts for normalcy in her hard life.

They had gradually become friends in the two weeks Abby had visited for her fittings, and Annie had slowly opened up and revealed a delightful, bubbly personality and a dry wit as she came to know and trust Abby.

How Annie could maintain such a cheerful outlook in view of what she had faced in her short life was beyond Abby's imagination. She vowed to do everything she could to help Annie out of the degrading profession into which she'd fallen.

It was on Abby's third visit, and over a piece of Abby's huckleberry cobbler and a cup of Annie's strong coffee, that Annie had told Abby her story.

Annie's father, Lester Dent, had been an overseer on a large Mississippi plantation before the War Between the States. After the war, there was no longer a plantation to oversee, and the Dents—Annie, her mother, father, and two older brothers—had headed west. They joined a wagon train in St. Louis bound for Oregon Territory. Somewhere in Wyoming Territory, Annie wasn't sure where, her father was accused of stealing from another man. He and his family were banished from the train.

Less than a week later, the Dent family had been set upon by a Cheyenne war party. Annie's entire family was massacred and she was taken captive. She lived as a slave to the Cheyenne for almost five years, until the trader Roberts swapped a rifle and various trade trinkets for her.

Roberts brought her to Montana Territory and set her up in his saloon. To Annie, who was about twenty years old at the time, it was paradise compared to the life of slavery with the Indians who'd so brutally beaten and ravaged her.

"Be still!" Annie said as she jabbed the dress with another pin, bringing Abby's mind back to the present. "I'm almost done!"

Abby stiffened her spine and held out her satin-clad arms while Annie slowly made her way around the chair, nodding her approval as she walked. Abby glanced downward, past the daring décolletage lined with black lace, to the draped folds beginning at her waist and falling softly to midthigh before falling in a straight line to her ankle. She felt Annie tug on the bustle, and Abby craned her neck for a look at her backside. Annie completed her circle and stood once again in front of Abby, lovingly fingering the red satin.

"I still think you should have a corset," Annie said, a tiny frown marring her otherwise pretty features.

"Well, you can forget it," Abby said, taking Annie's extended hand as she stepped carefully down from the chair and onto the rag rug. "I just wish I had some matching shoes," she said, lifting her skirts to reveal her western boots.

"I have an idea." Annie scurried to the bed and, reaching under the covers, pulled a small wooden box from under the frame. "See if you can wear these," she said, pulling out a pair of black heeled slippers and holding them up for Abby's consideration.

The slippers fit reasonably well after Annie ingeniously stuffed the toes with some scraps of cloth. Abby whirled happily around the small room, certain she'd be the belle of the ball. She stopped suddenly and threw her arms around Annie, giving her a fierce hug. Annie's face glowed with pleasure.

"I wish you could come, too, Annie," Abby said wistfully as the other woman helped her out of the red dress and laid it across the foot of the bed. Abby donned her bra, then reached for her blue dress and pulled it over her head. She had explained on a previous visit that her undergarments were something new from back East. Annie had been very curious about them the first time Abby had to undress for a fitting.

"Where John Winston wants to see me ain't in his front parlor," Annie said with a short laugh as she picked up her needle and threaded it. She perched on the bed beside the dress to make the last-minute alterations.

"Annie!" Abby said, smoothing her dress and buttoning the bodice. "You don't mean . . . ?" Her cheeks flamed as she stared at Annie.

"I do mean." Annie nodded, her lips curving into a self-satisfied smile. "One of my best customers. Every Friday night, regular as clockwork. That's why I've got to get this dress finished and get you out of here. He'll be here soon."

"Oh, Annie, how do you stand it?" Abby asked.

"It ain't a matter of standing it with John Winston," Annie said matter-of-factly. "He's a fine man. Knows how to treat a woman. Real gentle, he is, when he needs to be gentle, rough-and-tumble when he don't."

"Good lord, Annie," Abby said. "How can I ever look the man in the face after what you've told me?"

Annie giggled and bent her head, picking up her sewing. "Same way you look anybody in the face knowing what wonderful things your man does to you under the covers. And a fine man he is, too!"

"Annie!" Abby exclaimed, thoroughly rattled by Annie's frankness.

"Not that I know what *your* man does," Annie said, stricken by the thought that Abby might have misunderstood. Abby had been so reserved in her confidences that Annie had the uncomfortable feeling all wasn't well at the Elan cabin, and she didn't want to do anything to add to the problem, if indeed there was a problem.

"Well, that's a relief," Abby muttered, not really knowing why it was such a comfort to hear Annie deny intimacy with Elan. After all, she had no claim on his affections, and she supposed it was only natural that a man would dally somewhere. It was the first time she'd considered that Elan might be engaged in such activities, and it annoyed her to realize she didn't like the thought one little bit.

"Now, don't you go buying trouble," Annie said as Abby sank onto the bed and heaved a deep sigh. "I ain't heard none of the girls mention being with your man. Heard a lot of speculating about what he'd be like, though," she said mischievously as the other woman shot her a grateful look. "You just keep him busy and happy at home and you won't have a thing to worry about."

"Have the girls really been talking about him?" Abby asked, intrigued in spite of her earlier denial to herself that she cared where Elan spent his affections.

Annie nodded, then giggled again as she plied the needle. "I'd say he's been the main topic of conversation among the girls since y'all got here."

"What have they been saying?" It would almost be reassuring to know it wasn't only her, that there were others just as powerless under his spell.

"I don't have to tell you," Annie said. "You know how you feel when he's with you? You get that nervous, jumpy feeling in the pit of your stomach, and your fingers just itch to touch him?"

Abby nodded miserably and met Annie's cool green eyes. "Honey," Annie said, sighing dramatically, "any real woman who ever looks at that man is going to feel the same way!"

Abby eased into the hot water, bracing her hands on the sides of the wooden tub and lowering herself slowly down. Much later, after scrubbing herself clean and washing her hair, she drew her legs up to her chest and encircled them with her arms. Then, leaning forward, she dropped her head and rested her chin on her knees.

Elan would be furious, but she didn't care. She had neither the energy nor the inclination to drag the tub into the cabin and then to mop the floor after her bath. It was effort aplenty just to haul and heat the water and fill the tub on the porch. She was tired, too, of hiding behind a barred door and shuttered windows. She refused to live any longer in dread, fearing each unfamiliar sound. Plenty of women had survived life in the wilderness, and she could, too.

Abby let her eyes drift over the meadow that fanned out in front of the cabin, imagining the herd of cattle that would graze there come spring. It would be the beginning of putting her ranch back together. It was the only purpose she had, the only future she could envision. Let Elan roam the mountains and rape the land. Her dream was a lasting one, a dream of renewal, for each spring hereafter, new calves would be born to graze amid the tall grasses, and Montana would meet the call to feed the Northwest.

Abby absently squeezed the washcloth, letting warm water trickle between her breasts and over her stomach. She felt renewed, refreshed, from the top of her freshly scrubbed head to the tips of her toes, but she was restless, unfulfilled, weak with longing.

Damn the man! As much as she wanted to deny it, as much as she fought against it, he dominated her every waking thought and most of her dreams too! Was she falling in love with him? No, of course not. It wasn't possible. They had just been thrown together, been too much in each other's company.

They were two completely different people who could never resolve their divergent lives. Abby considered herself a thoroughly modern woman, and she realized Elan wanted her to be someone else. He wanted a woman subservient and unquestioning, a woman he could depend on to cook, clean, and generally take care of him. She didn't have time for all of that. She had a ranch to build. At least she did until that darn medicine bag reappeared and she could return home. She dropped her head back against the rim of the tub as she slid deeper into the water. Closing her eyes, she drifted into a daydream.

Elan paused in midstride when he spotted Abby in her bath, his breath catching painfully in his throat, his mouth suddenly dry. He carried his rifle in one hand, a plump rabbit in the other. Though he leaned casually against a pine, the skinned rabbit slipped unnoticed from his fingers and fell to the pine-needle carpet at his feet, betraying his true state of mind. He tightened his grip on his rifle, then very deliberately propped it against the rough pine bark.

Abby rose from her bath, still in a dreamlike state. She reached for the towel thrown across the back of the chair where her gun and bath articles sat. Dabbing her face, she shivered as the soft breeze cooled the drops of moisture on her skin, leaving her tingling with something akin to anticipation.

When Elan's hands covered hers to take possession of the towel, Abby thought for a moment that her desire for him was so urgent that she had conjured him up, seemingly from nowhere.

Abby uttered no protest as Elan used the linen to blot away the dampness on her body, nor did she object when he wrapped the cloth around her, scooped her up in his arms, and strode through the open door of the cabin. Instead, she looped her arms around his neck and rested her cheek against his buckskin shirt, closing her eyes while she drew courage from the steady beat of his heart.

When he placed Abby on the bed, Elan stood back, raking her with his brash stare until he finally wrested his eyes from her exposed limbs to gaze into her eyes. Abby met his bold stare, searching his fathomless black eyes, and then daringly tossed aside the towel and reached her arms out to him.

Elan's hesitation was brief. He wanted to be gentle and bring Abby to no harm, and yet he had struggled so long against taking her to bed that his passion raged almost beyond his ability to curb it. He forced himself to find some measure of restraint as his eyes hungrily devoured what he had dreamed of for so long.

Unable to wait any longer, he quickly unlaced his shirt and pulled it over his head. He then divested himself of his trousers and moccasins. Abby's sharp intake of breath was her only response other than the widening of her eyes as he knelt on the edge of the bed and cupped her face with his hand. The spark of fear that flashed through her eyes was a look he had seen before, and he sought to reassure her.

"I will be gentle, Abby," he said past the tightness in his throat, struggling to restrain his growing need and live up to his promise. She rubbed her face against his palm, giving him the encouragement he needed. He lifted himself over her, balancing on arms that trembled. He fought for some measure of control as he willed himself to remember her virginity and the difference in their sizes.

When Abby lifted her hands to stroke his face, then tangled her fingers in his hair and tugged his face down to hers, Elan realized she had captured his very soul. He kissed her, crushing her parted lips, thrusting his tongue to plunder and conquer until she moaned his name. He abandoned her mouth to trace the hollow of her throat, the curve of her breast, the rosy peak of her nipple.

Abby hungrily met his lips, breathlessly accepting his kisses as they trailed down her neck to pause at her breast. She slid her hands down his broad shoulders and gripped his quivering arms as he first suckled her nipple, then teased with his tongue and teeth. He balanced his weight on his powerful arms to keep from crushing her, and she recognized his self-imposed restraint.

Wave after wave of pleasure rippled through her at the gentleness of his exploration, and she found herself unable to keep still as she writhed and moaned beneath him. She couldn't get enough of him and marveled at the control he exercised.

A low groan from Elan shot a tremor of pure desire flooding through her. She ran her hands down his arms and across the hard planes of his chest, then raked them across his back, urging him closer as her hands made their way to his firm, muscled buttocks.

Elan strove to temper his flaming need, knowing if he took Abby in the midst of raging passion he could do irreparable harm. He eased himself down and lay at her side, tenderly stroking her legs apart, gently exploring her very feminine contours. He dropped his head to touch her lips with his and to whisper against her parted lips.

"It will be painful the first time, Abby, but I will try to be gentle."

"Painful?" Abby murmured, trying to concentrate on his words and not his touch and failing miserably. She knew she would shatter into a million pieces if he didn't fulfill the promise he gave.

Elan heard the question in Abby's faltering voice. Of course she was afraid—terrified, he realized as he became more aware of her trembling and less attuned to his own relentless desire. "After the first time, it will not hurt anymore, I promise." He kissed her eyes and shifted to move over her, relieved when she trustingly opened her legs in response to the gentle pressure from his knee.

"You won't hurt me, Elan," Abby said with more confidence than she actually felt. Although she'd not been a virgin for several years, her sexual experience was limited, and Elan was a much larger man than Paul.

"It cannot be helped," Elan said as her hands tightened on his hips.

Abby's eyes, half closed in languid passion, shot open. *He thought she was a virgin!* Of course he did. Hadn't he questioned her about her marital status and come to the conclusion she was an old maid? And to him, from his time, that meant *virgin!*

She had to tell him the truth. She didn't know why she felt so strongly about it, but she just knew she had to tell him. Somehow he would feel betrayed if she didn't. His tender concern was touching, and he'd feel a fool if she continued to let him harbor a false belief.

"Elan." Abby planted her hands firmly against his chest. "Listen to me!" He dipped his head to nibble at her lower lip, and she almost lost her nerve, so desperately did she want to trace his lips with her tongue and his dimples with her fingers. She wanted him with every fiber of her being, but she had to play straight with him.

"What is it, Abby?" he said, groaning as she surrendered somewhat to her desire and gently traced his lips with her fingers before cupping his face in her hands.

"I am not a virgin." Abby whispered the words, unable to project her voice. She wanted him to tell her it was unimportant, that he didn't care, that holding her in his arms at this moment in time was the only thing that mattered. But, of course, he could not, would not, did not offer her any of the assurances she hungered for.

Elan felt the color drain from his face as surely as he felt the passion desert his body. It was as if someone had dashed him with a bucket of icy creek water. Abby's confession echoed through his brain as he tried to assimilate and decipher her words. She was not married, had never been married. That left only one reasonable explanation.

He was falling in love with a woman who had been with other men. The white-hot anger of betrayal coursed through him as he envisioned Abby lying supine beneath another man. Was she bedding him as casually as she had bedded others? He turned his face from her, unable to look at her another minute.

Elan bounded from the bed, coldly brushing away Abby's hand as she reached to touch his arm. He gathered up his clothing and, without giving her another glance or uttering another word, dressed and left the cabin.

Elan relentlessly pushed the roan, riding as fast as he dared under the light of the full moon. Even though the trail was well lighted from the wash of moonbeams, Elan knew better than to ride as he wished, to ride faster than the wind, to ride fast enough to exorcise the demons taunting his soul.

It was late when he rode into the settlement and down the alley behind the saloon. Though the saloons were still doing business, evidenced by the faint light spilling into the dusty street, there were few people about. Sunday, not Friday, was the day most miners came into the settlement to raise a ruckus.

Elan dismounted, looping the roan's reins around a pole holding up a small awning over Annie's door. He had been told about Annie by Roberts. The trader had slyly indicated that Elan might be interested in Annie's services. At the time, Elan had largely ignored Roberts' glowing descriptions of the sporting girl, but tonight he wished he had paid more attention. He pounded on the door, then stepped back instinctively when it was opened almost immediately.

"What?" Annie said, looking at Elan blankly. John Winston had been gone only a few minutes, and Annie, upon hearing the knock, thought he'd forgotten something and returned for it. Instead of finding her longtime lover, she stared into the maddened eyes of Elan, and all she could imagine was that he was looking for Abby.

Elan roughly pushed past her into the small room, then swung around to face her when she closed the door behind him. He wanted to get it over with as quickly as possible, wanted no lingering sentiments, wanted only the quickness of relief. He did not even want to remember what the whore looked like.

"Abby's not here," Annie said worriedly as Elan's eyes slid from her face to scan the room. "She left hours ago. Isn't she home yet?"

Annie's words hit Elan like the kick of a mule. Abby had been with the whore? Why? The reason was too terrible to imagine. Abby told him constantly she was determined to get her cattle from John Winston and at any cost. Was this the price?

"How long?" Elan managed to get the strangled words past his clenched teeth. He dreaded knowing, but like a man facing the gallows, he was compelled to test the rope. How long had Abby been whoring to get her money?

"I told you," Annie said, twisting her hands together. "She left hours ago. Something terrible must have happened to her!"

"Abby is home!" Elan said. "I want to know how long she has been coming to you!" He eyed the whore suspiciously and took a step toward her, noting that her panic was soon replaced by wariness. He would get the truth from her if he had to shake it loose!

"A . . . couple . . . of weeks," Annie said, scurrying behind the straight-backed chair in a feeble effort to distance herself from Elan. She should have known Abby couldn't keep secret her comings and goings in the settlement. There were too many loose tongues, too many people who loved to stir up scandal. She wasn't at all surprised Elan had discovered his wife had befriended a common whore. And she was even less surprised he was enraged about it.

"She tried to be discreet," Annie said, desperately trying to defend Abby, the only friend she had, the only woman who treated her like a human being. "Today was her last time. She won't be back."

Elan kicked aside the chair that stood between them, then flung it across the room. Annie instinctively covered her face and backed into the corner, sliding down the rough wall to her knees, certain he was going to beat her. Instead, he strode to the door and threw it open. He was mounted on his horse and out of the alley before Annie found the strength to stand and stagger the few steps necessary to close the door. Tears ran unchecked down her face, and she prayed fervently the beating she had escaped wouldn't be suffered by Abby.

The return ride to the cabin was one of the longest Elan had ever made, but still it ended much too soon. He led the horse to the shed and, after unsaddling and rubbing him down, turned him loose to graze the pasture. The cabin was dark, the windows firmly shuttered. He did not bother to try the door, knowing it would be securely latched. Instead, he took the horse blanket, still damp from the roan's sweat, and made for the pines.

Settling down for the remainder of the night, Elan laced his fingers behind his head and contemplated the stars through the overhead canopy of pine boughs. They were the same stars he had studied in what he had come to think of as his other life, and he drew encouragement and strength from their constant presence. At least something was the same as it had been, even if it was nothing more than the unreachable stars.

Elan's thoughts, unbidden, turned to Abby, and try as he might, he could not dismiss her. She was as much a part of him as one of his limbs, and he knew he could never be complete without possessing her. But how could he ever get past her confession and his knowledge of her actions?

He had been a fool to leave her bed, to leave her without giving her a chance to explain. But what could mere words change? Besides, he did not care to hear her explanations, did not think he could simply listen and then dismiss and forget her engagements with other men.

The dull, unrelieved ache in his loins was overshadowed only by the anguish that crushed his chest, that gripped his heart in an unrelenting fist. How had he, Elan, allowed himself to become so enamored by a mere slip of a girl, a woman who appeared so innocent, yet could practice the oldest profession without so much as blinking an eye simply because she wanted money to buy cattle? *Merde!* If he had known what she was up to, he would have gladly turned over everything he possessed to stop her. Now it was too late.

And knowing what he knew, why could he not become another of her customers and use her as they did, paying her with the gold he took from the creek? What stopped him from taking her as dispassionately as he had taken the whores of St. Louis and the willing squaws of the Indian villages? What made his feelings for her so different from anything he had ever before experienced?

9

Winston's party was in full swing when Abby and Elan arrived in midafternoon, Elan driving the buckboard, Abby perched stiffly at his side. Abby wore the green dress and matching bonnet and carried in her lap the red dress wrapped in brown paper. She would change when the promised dance began later in the evening. She had tried to get Elan to wear trousers and a shirt, but he had stubbornly ignored her pleas and wore instead the new fringed buckskins and knee-high moccasins he had recently sewn and in which he seemed so comfortable.

Abby had to admit, albeit grudgingly, that he had never looked more handsome or formidable, for he also had strapped his bone-handled hunting knife to his leg and carried his hatchet in his wide belt. She couldn't be sure of his intentions, but he was certainly ready for any contingency.

His long rifle was safely stowed under a quilt in the back of the buckboard, and her own pistol was strapped to her right thigh. She felt a little foolish wearing it to a party, but Elan had insisted.

Elan was clean-shaven and wore his thick black locks loose around his shoulders, refusing to allow her to trim his hair or to tie it back. His face was a careful mask, expressing neither pleasure nor displeasure, and any acknowledgment of her was minimal, a harsh grunt issued occasionally when she relentlessly pursued some subject.

When they arrived he climbed down and spent several minutes returning greetings from Roberts and the various men he had met on his trips to the settlement. Abby waited impatiently for his assistance as she scanned the large group of people, noting the women busily placing food on the long planks set up on sawhorses and the men gathered around the half beef Frank Johnson slowly turned on a spit over an open fire. Children played games of tag, laughing and shouting above the happy hum of adult voices. She picked Sally Johnson out of the lively swarm, but failed to catch the child's eye.

Abby wondered belatedly if she should have brought a dish. The invitation hadn't mentioned doing so, but she wasn't sure of the local custom. At any rate, there looked to be enough food to feed an army.

Spying Mrs. Johnson, Abby lifted her hand and called a greeting. When Mrs. Johnson recognized Abby, she acknowledged her with a shy smile and a quick nod before turning to a tall redhead at her side.

"Mrs. Elan?" The question caught Abby off guard, so intent was she on the goings-on around her, and so excited at actually attending an old-fashioned shindig. She started when she saw the man standing expectantly beside the buckboard.

He was history come to life, Abby thought as she studied him, casting her eyes over his lanky frame, and from the descriptions Annie had shared with her she knew immediately he must be John Winston. But Annie hadn't done him justice, Abby mused, biting her lip and feeling the color surge to her face as she remembered Annie's descriptions of Winston's exploits in bed.

John Winston was a tall man, not as tall as Elan, but an inch or so over six feet. Whereas Elan was powerfully built, Winston was lean and lanky, but no less dangerous, Abby imagined, her attention immediately captured by the matching pearl-handled pistols resting in the holsters hugging his hips.

John Winston lifted his wide-brimmed black hat from his head, revealing short, straight brown hair the same color as his handlebar mustache. His lips curved gently into a smile that served to soften the harsh planes of his face.

"Mr. Winston," Abby said, returning his smile with a dip of her head. "How very nice of you to include two strangers. Elan and I are pleased by your thoughtfulness."

"The pleasure is mine, I assure you, madam. May I help you down?" Winston asked, settling his hat on his head and reaching out his hands. Abby cast a nervous eye in Elan's direction, but found he still preferred to ignore her, as he was talking with several men and drinking something from a tin cup.

"Thank you, yes." Abby put aside her package and started to stand, then found herself airborne by firm hands that had a solid grip on her waist. Winston settled her on her feet and offered her his arm.

"Roberts tells me you want to go into the cattle business," Winston said as Abby lightly placed her hand on his arm and walked by his side, stealing glances at him from the corner of her eye, admiring the way he looked in his collarless tan shirt and the blue trousers that were tucked into his hand-tooled leather boots complete with silver spurs.

Winston paused as they met other guests and introduced her, but lingered only momentarily with each one. They discussed the cattle operation at length as he led her on a tour of the ranch, pointing out the various outbuildings and describing their functions as well as answering her numerous questions concerning market prices and the size of his herd.

Winston soon steered Abby under a lofty pine and seated her on a beautifully carved, cushioned bench well away from the other guests. He stood looking down at her as she made small talk, complimenting him on his ranch and inquiring about the various people he had introduced her to. Abby was so caught up in the moment she didn't notice Winston reaching into his pocket and pulling out an object until he held it out to her. It was her watch.

Winston's eyes, warm and brown, and to Abby's immense dismay intelligent, coolly appraised her face, searching, she imagined, for any flicker of surprise or discomposure. Her glib explanation to Roberts would not suffice here, she warranted. There was no point in denying the watch had been hers. It would only add to the suspicions she was sure he had, for why else would he steer her so adroitly into such a secluded spot to make his presentation? She mentally kicked herself for being so naive as to trade the watch in the first place.

"I see that you have purchased my watch from Roberts." Abby forced herself to remain calm under Winston's scrutiny as she reached for the watch. "Is it a gift for your wife?" she asked. Winston seemed to be playing the part of a gentleman very well, but the fact remained that he was keeping company with Annie. And as much as Abby liked her, Annie was, by her very own admission, a whore. Abby could not respect any man who would so deceive his wife.

Winston's harsh chuckle was not what she expected. "My wife died in childbirth nine years ago." The blunt statement left Abby at a loss for words.

"I'm so sorry," Abby said after an uncomfortable silence. "A present for a lady friend, perhaps?" She was not to be deterred. She couldn't dare to hope he was returning the watch to her, and even if that was the case, she would be hard pressed to accept such an offering from a virtual stranger, as much as she would like to take the watch and forever hide it before anyone else discovered its workings.

"My daughter," he answered dryly. He placed a booted foot beside her on the bench and leaned over to prop an arm on his thigh. "Perhaps you would be so kind as to explain where you came by the timepiece and how it works? You see," he continued lazily, "neither I nor any watchmaker or jeweler in Helena can quite decipher its mechanism."

Abby swallowed past the sudden lump in her throat and unconsciously licked her painfully dry lips. She looked around, but Elan was nowhere to be found. She commanded her lips to smile, but realized they probably formed more of a grimace than the disarming smile she needed as she tried to play the helpless female. "The watch was a gift from my father, and as to its workings, I'm afraid those things are beyond my understanding." She thrust the watch back into his hands and made to rise.

"Don't go!" Winston's voice was sharp and so commanding that Abby sank back into the soft cushions, momentarily addled. "Please," he added in a softer tone as he tucked the watch back into his pocket, then unexpectedly dropped beside her on the bench.

"I really should be getting back to my husband," Abby murmured, so rattled by Winston's behavior that she actually referred to Elan in a way she had sworn she would never do. But, she admitted to herself, even though she had never verbally acknowledged Elan as her husband, everyone assumed he was, so what was the difference, really? The fact was, nothing had changed his status; she was just calling on Winston's perception of it to remind him of her position.

"Ah, yes, Elan," Winston said, not without a hint of sarcasm. He stretched out his long, lean legs and crossed them at the ankles. "He appears a bit uncivilized in his buckskins, don't you think? But then again, they seem to suit him well."

"Elan is very much attuned to the wilderness, Mr. Winston. He claims buckskins are more suited to his hunting and trapping than conventional clothing. He is happiest when he is traipsing through the woods."

"Then he does not share your interest in cattle?" Winston asked. "I had assumed your husband sent his pretty wife to turn my head in hopes of lowering my price."

"Then I must assure you that you have seriously misjudged Elan," Abby said, deliberately ignoring his backhanded compliment. "He cares not one whit for ranching. I must confess, I am the one who wants the cattle. Elan only seeks to indulge me." She was saved further comment by the approach of a young girl carrying a bouquet of colorful wildflowers. She sensed rather than saw Winston straighten as the child neared.

"Hello, love," Winston said when the child dumped her flowers unceremoniously into his lap and flung her arms around his neck to plant kisses on his cheek.

Abby observed the affection between the man and the child, feeling somewhat left out until Winston placed the wildflowers in her lap and pulled his daughter into his arms. "We'll give the flowers to Mrs. Elan," Winston said, smoothing the spotless white pinafore over the child's green-sprigged muslin dress as she made herself comfortable in his lap. "She's our guest, and we want to make her welcome, don't we?"

"Yes, Papa," the child said happily, turning her attention from the father she so obviously adored to study Abby.

"My daughter, Loraine," Winston said. "Lori, say hello to Mrs. Elan."

"Hello, Mrs. Elan," Lori chimed. "I'm very pleased to make your acquaintance." Abby was immediately impressed with the child and her impeccable manners. Though she was motherless, someone had taken the time to make a little lady of her, and Abby felt a sudden kinship with the girl, for she knew what it was like to grow up without a mother in a man's world. Perhaps if her own mother had lived, or if her father had remarried, Abby would have learned more about feminine traits. For the first time in her life, she found herself wishing she knew more about how to act like a woman.

Lori's emerald eyes, flecked with gold, sparkled with intelligence and mischief, illuminating her dimpled face with a soft glow. Her coppery curls fell midway down her back and were caught away from her face with a green satin ribbon, exactly the color of the green shoots printed on her dress. She was almost too pretty to be real, and Abby couldn't imagine how she could have been playing with the other children and not mussed her hair or her clothing.

"I'm pleased to meet you too, Lori," Abby said, offering the child her hand. Lori took it with a giggle, then, planting one more kiss on her father's cheek, squirmed off his lap and curtsied before skipping away.

"What a charming child," Abby said, watching Lori catch up to her friends. "You must be very proud of her."

"She is my life," Winston said simply. "She goes off to school in Helena next month, and I cannot stand the thought of parting with her. I know it's for the best, but when I think of her leaving me, I wonder how I will survive."

His revelation touched Abby's heart and gave her new respect for the man. That this self-assured cattle baron would admit to such a human failing took her completely by surprise. John Winston was proving to be a most complicated personality, but she liked him.

"Perhaps you could find a governess for her," Abby said, though she realized as soon as the words left her lips what an impossible task that might be, and that surely Winston had considered the idea and discarded it.

Winston reached and plucked one of the wildflowers from Abby's lap, idly twirling it between his fingers. "What about you?" he asked. "Could I interest you in the position?"

Abby stared at Winston, frankly astonished by his offer. She couldn't imagine why Winston would make such a proposal to a virtual stranger. She had never envisioned herself a teacher, and wasn't sure she wanted to be one. However, her hoard from the sale of her necklace and watch was sorely depleted and would be even more so after Roberts deducted the cost of the red satin. If she was going to purchase cattle, she needed funds. It might be something to consider after all.

"I am interested in your offer, Mr. Winston," Abby said truthfully, "but I'm not sure I would make a very good teacher."

"But you are educated, Mrs. Elan." It was not a question, but rather a statement.

Abby conceded the point. "Yes, I am educated." If a degree in business meant anything in 1875, then she was educated. At her father's insistence, she had commuted to Missoula for four years and earned her degree. The traveling had been difficult, but she had steadfastly refused to live on campus. It would have taken her away from the ranch when she could least afford to be gone.

"We should discuss terms," Winston said, throwing the ball into Abby's court.

"I must have time to think this over, Mr. Winston," she said firmly as she brought her thoughts back to the present. "And I must warn you that if I do decide to take the position, I'll want my pay on the hoof. And I'll give you fair warning, I drive a hard bargain."

Winston roared with laughter and got to his feet, offering her his hand. Abby took it and stood, tilting her head to meet his laughing eyes as he tucked her hand into the crook of his arm.

"You want your pay on the hoof. You want it in cattle!" Winston laughed again. "I know you need time to discuss this with your husband, Mrs. Elan. I'll eagerly await your answer. We're going to get on just fine, you and me," Winston said as he unhurriedly led her to the trestle tables heavily laden with food.

Abby tugged again at the scooped neckline of her red satin dress, her courage rapidly flagging as she peered into the full-length oval mirror. The dress was even more shockingly revealing than she had imagined. Its neckline plunged so low as to bare nearly all but her nipples, certainly too low for her to wear her bra. She nervously fingered the satin rose set in the V of the bodice, noting that it called even more attention to that spot. The matching satin rose she wore over her ear was a vivid splash of red in her short dark hair, but wouldn't, she suspected, draw much attention in view of the placement of its twin.

Annie had done a marvelous job, Abby thought as she smoothed her damp hands over the draped skirt and turned to check the wide bow set at the top of the bustle. The numerous tiny buttons down the back of the dress had proved a challenge, but she had managed to fasten them all with Lori's assistance. She was grateful for the child's help and for the loan of her room, and smiled at the young girl who perched on her bed and watched with interest.

"I want to go to the dance," Lori said wistfully as the first strains of music filtered into the upstairs bedroom. "I think it would be lots of fun."

"I know, honey." Abby reached to touch the silky, coppery locks tumbling from the now lopsided ribbon and falling in disarray around the young, innocent face of the child. Lori's frock, so pristine in the afternoon, was rumpled and mussed from her play, and she looked like any other child after hours of romping. "But your papa was quite adamant that you should not. I suspect he thinks you need your rest after playing so hard all day."

"Papa can be so stubborn," Lori said with an exaggerated sigh. "He treats me like a baby sometimes." She plucked idly at her skirt and looked ready to cry.

Abby sat on the bed next to the child and took her hand. "I know just how you feel, darling. My own father was much the same way when I was a little girl. But he only did what he thought was best for me."

"Papa says you are going to be my teacher and I won't have to go off to school in Helena next month. Is it true? Will you live with us and teach me my lessons?"

Abby squeezed the small hand. "It's true that I'm thinking about being your teacher, but even if I take the position, I couldn't live with you. I would probably come two or three days a week for your lessons. Would you like that?"

"I'd much rather you lived with us," Lori said. "Mrs. Johnson lives with us now and keeps the house, but she's no fun. I think you would be lots of fun."

"But you have Sally to play with, and she's fun, isn't she?" Abby asked. "Your papa was very kind to hire Mrs. Johnson and Frank. I think they were having a very hard time before they came to live here."

Lori nodded. "Papa said they were. Mr. Johnson died in a mining accident last year. You don't think Papa is going to marry Mrs. Johnson, do you?" Lori chewed her lip and screwed her face into a worried frown.

"Heavens, no!" Abby said. "Where did you get such an idea?" Mrs. Johnson was forty-five if she was a day. Winston would probably have heart failure at the thought!

Lori leaned over to whisper conspiratorially in Abby's ear. "Papa said he was looking for a wife. He thinks I need a mother."

"Well, I don't think Mrs. Johnson is whom he has in mind." Abby put her arm around Lori and gave her a quick hug. "Don't worry about it another minute."

A light rap at the door interrupted their conversation, prompting Abby's heart to flutter as the moment of truth arrived. Lori returned Abby's hug as they both rose at the sound.

"Yes?" Abby asked, ignoring the butterflies that had taken up residence in her stomach. She had put off going downstairs as long as possible, but realized her reprieve was now over.

"Mrs. Elan?" It was John Winston's commanding voice. "May I escort you downstairs?"

"Of course, Mr. Winston." Abby advanced to the door, stepping aside as it was flung open.

John Winston stood in the doorway taking in every inch of her appearance, allowing his appraising eyes to travel from the top of her head to the tips of her slippers and back again to her face. Abby lifted her chin and returned his gaze, noting the appreciative smile on his lips. He offered her his arm. "Shall we?"

Abby placed her fingers lightly on the proffered arm and squared her shoulders. "Thank you, Mr. Winston. It will be a pleasure."

"Call me John," Winston said as he winked at Lori and closed the door softly behind them.

"I couldn't possibly," Abby protested as they made their way down the narrow hall and to the top of the stairs. She paused to look down at the crowd, searching for Elan. He was near the punch table talking with several of the men. Winston followed her gaze past the dancing couples to find the object of her attention.

"Elan is a lucky man. Tell me, Mrs. Elan, how did you two meet?" The question was innocent enough, but Abby realized with growing dread that John Winston had more than an innocent interest in her. She had aroused his suspicions with her damnable watch, and Winston was not the type to give up when he wanted something. She had the uncanny feeling that he wanted to know everything about her. Was it because he intended to employ her as his daughter's teacher, or for some other reason?

"That's a personal question, Mr. Winston, and one I'd prefer not to answer," Abby replied blithely, lifting her skirt to descend the stairs, more than a little disconcerted by his directness.

"I received much the same answer from your husband, Mrs. Elan," Winston said as they reached the bottom stair. Then, before she could utter another syllable, he swept her onto the dance floor—the wide front room of the sprawling two-storied house—which had been cleared of furniture for the event.

As Abby concentrated on following his complicated steps, she noted alarmingly that he pressed close, pulling her against his lean frame, expertly moving her with him across the floor. She was so intent on not missing a step that she didn't notice Elan's approach, nor did she notice the admiring looks of the men or the hard, set faces of the women until Elan tapped Winston on the shoulder.

They stood, the three of them, in the center of the room as the other couples swirled around them, and for Abby everything seemed to happen in slow motion. Even the music seemed to stop, although later she was certain that it had not. Elan's glittering black eyes were narrowed like those of a feral cat, and they bored into Winston, ignoring Abby altogether, it seemed, as the two men faced each other.

How long they stood there, Abby didn't know. It couldn't have been more than a few seconds, but it seemed to go on forever. With a slight nod to Elan and an almost indiscernible bow to Abby, Winston abruptly turned and strode from the floor.

Elan pulled her into his arms and led her into the dance. If Winston had pressed close, Elan pressed even closer, molding her to him as he whirled her across the floor, confidently leading her through the steps. She tipped her head and stole a glimpse of Elan's face, able only to see the muscle working in his jaw. He did not look down at her, but instead stared over her head as he held her in his firm grip, his iron legs fitted against hers, his groin moving against her belly. And when the music mercifully ended, he encircled her wrist in his powerful grip and, placing his hand possessively in the small of her back, urged her none too gently through the open door and onto the wide verandah-style porch.

"How dare you make a scene!" Abby said when Elan pulled her into a dark corner of the porch and pinned her with his gaze. She was breathless from the physically demanding dance and from the rage welling up at his behavior. Her chest heaved as she panted for breath. The dress was tight enough to restrict her air, and she fought for dominance of her racing heart.

Elan towered over her, propping his arm against the log wall over her head, his mouth scant inches from hers, his cider-sweetened breath brushing her cheek. "It was not I who made a scene, Abby." His tone was deceptively calm, and it sent a shiver down her spine. How well did she truly know him? Was he capable of violence just because she had danced with John Winston? Winston was their host, and she saw nothing untoward about dancing with him. It wasn't as if she had thrown herself into his arms. And besides, Elan had no real claim on her. She was very much her own woman and owed no explanation to anyone for her behavior. But then, why did she want to please Elan? And she discovered, much to her dismay, that she wanted very much to do just that.

Elan traced a deliberate path down her neck with one finger, lingering at the satin rose, then languidly circling a satin-covered nipple. Abby moaned, feeling the tears spring to her eyes at the exquisite longing his touch evoked, and she sagged against him, forgiving him instantly any indiscretion as her arms moved of their own accord to wind around his neck. She rested her face against his chest, inhaling the rich scent of the buckskin, of the man himself, and listening to the comforting beat of his heart.

"It is not enough that you must act the whore, but now you dress like one, too. Can you not see what you have done?"

Abby stiffened at his accusation, and her arms fell to her sides as she shrank from him. "I have not acted like a whore! How can you say such things? In my time, this dress might be considered a little daring, but certainly not inappropriate for a party. I will go change clothes if that will please you."

She had known he was angry over her admission that she wasn't a virgin, but not being a virgin certainly was a far cry from being a whore. Then again, in his eyes, considering the time he was from, she supposed the two things were interchangeable. Were they so far apart in their thinking that they would never be able to communicate?

"You have been with men." The pain in his voice as he made this simple statement wounded her deeply, but angered her, too. He seemed determined to have it out with her. She reached to touch him, but he turned away, as if he couldn't bear to look at her another minute.

The light touch of Abby's small hand on Elan's shoulder robbed him of his breath, and when she moved to encircle his waist with her arms and rested her cheek against his back, her physical nearness was almost more than he could take. Her voice was a caress in the velvety night, much like the caress of her hands as they slid up to his chest. "I have been with one man, and it was a long time ago. I am not a whore. I thought I was in love with that man. He eventually left me, though. When I had to devote my time to trying to save my ranch, he found someone else."

"What were you doing at Annie's?"

Abby frowned at the question, and her hands stilled. How did he know? Had he been following her? Elan slowly turned to face her, to search her eyes.

"Annie made my dress."

"That is the only reason you visited with her?"

"Yes, why else?" Abby's eyes widened at the implication as she stared into the darkness of the black eyes searching her face. Elan's swift movement was unexpected and took her completely by surprise.

It was not until she felt the rough boards at her back that she realized he had indeed moved, and in so doing had pushed her to the wall. His muscular legs pressed into hers, and his chest crushed her breasts. But it was the forcefulness of his lips and hands that would relentlessly return in her dreams.

Demanding, probing, plundering, he took fierce possession of her mouth, then left her still wanting more as his lips moved down her neck and across her breast to nuzzle aside the cool satin and suckle a nipple. At the same time his lips branded her fevered flesh, his hands searched beneath the yards of material to slide up her thighs and find the moistness between her legs. As his long fingers impatiently breached the flimsy material, she wondered vaguely, uncaringly, if he would rip her panties off.

10

"*Ahem!*"

At the sound, Abby snatched frantically at her clothing, pulling at her bodice and tugging down her skirt. Elan's half turn effectively shielded her from view, but she realized ruefully that his attempt to allow her to restore her disheveled appearance had probably come too late to protect her modesty. She peered around him to find John Winston striking a match to light a cheroot. The brief flare of the match provided a bright flash of light on the dark porch, just the amount of light needed to show the amused curve of Winston's lips and the devilment in his eyes.

"Enjoying the night air?" Winston's dry wit made Abby ache to slap the man. She peered around Elan, feeling the flush creep unbidden and unwanted to her cheeks, thankful the moon conveniently chose that moment to hide behind one of the clouds skittering across the star-studded sky.

Winston ambled across the porch to prop his lean hips on the railing, his progress marked by the jingle of his spurs. Diffused light filtered through a curtained window and threw a beam across his booted feet as he made his way. His face remained in the shadows, unreadable. The glowing red tip of the cheroot clenched in his teeth provided the only clue to his presence as he made himself comfortable.

"Never have I found the air to be more agreeable," Elan said pleasantly as his arm encircled Abby's waist, drawing her to his side when she moved around him.

"You did not enjoy the dancing?" Winston's voice carried the barest hint of irony. Abby ground her teeth. Winston was baiting Elan, and not being very subtle about it, either.

"I am afraid that I am a little out of practice with the social graces," Elan said. "It has been a long time since the last party I attended."

"Oh?" Winston's question was quickly followed by another. "And where was that, Elan?" Abby held her breath, unconsciously clutching the folds of her dress in her damp hands.

"St. Louis," Elan answered easily. "But it was many years ago."

"I didn't realize you hailed from St. Louis," Winston said. "What prompted your move to Montana Territory?"

"Mr. Winston," Abby said as she advanced from Elan's side to step into the faint light from the window, "I find that I am quite thirsty. Would you be so kind as to accompany me to the punch bowl? I believe Elan wishes to check our rig and prepare for our journey home." She was improvising and could only hope Elan would pick up on her cue.

Winston tossed his cheroot into the yard and rose to his full height. "With your permission?" Winston asked Elan as he offered Abby his arm. She took it at Elan's nod, more than a little relieved her ploy had accomplished its purpose.

"I shall be happy to accompany you, Mrs. Elan," Winston said agreeably, "but the hour grows late and I must insist that you and Elan remain as my guests. I will have Mrs. Johnson prepare Lori's room for you and your husband. Most of my guests will be staying overnight, and those who cannot be accommodated in the main house will find room in the bunkhouse or will camp down by the creek."

"Whatever Elan thinks best," Abby murmured, lifting a brow as she turned to Elan. She was willing to do almost anything to steer Winston away from questioning Elan about his past. Damn the man and his suspicions!

"I will get our things." Elan strode quickly past them and down the steps into the yard.

"I'll send Frank to help you." Winston led Abby through the doorway and into the crowded room, pausing just inside to gain Frank's attention and speak to him. Upon Winston's directions, Frank immediately departed to assist Elan and to find his mother.

The musicians, two guitar players and a fiddler, were taking a break, leaving people to gather in small groups as they talked and sipped punch. Abby found it interesting to see that times hadn't changed so much after all. Older married women were visiting together on one side of the long room while their husbands grouped around the punch table on the other. Several young couples took advantage of the pause in the music to seek the cool night air, away from the watchful eyes of their parents.

"Nice move," Winston said quietly into Abby's ear as he handed her a crystal cup of punch. She sipped the strong brew, realizing belatedly that someone had spiked it. Well, she didn't care. She felt just reckless enough to down the punch in a single gulp, and did exactly that as she stalled for time so she could search for a proper comeback.

Winston was more astute than she'd imagined. Of course, he probably believed she and Elan had some unsavory incident in their past they wished to hide, that was all. He couldn't possibly suspect the truth, even with her watch in his possession.

She should have realized someone would eventually question the sudden appearance of a couple on a homestead that had been vacated under mysterious circumstances. She wished fervently that she had thought to conspire some story with Elan. If she told Winston some tale, and he questioned Elan separately and was told something different entirely, then he would only be suspicious all the more.

Abby thrust her cup at Winston. "I believe I'll have another." She tapped her foot as Winston complied with her request and refilled her cup. Where was Elan? They needed to talk before things went from bad to worse. Winston was not the type to back off once he became interested, and Abby was more than a little concerned.

"Something has to be done about these bloodthirsty savages. Don't you agree, John?" The question was posed by a neighboring rancher, a stocky, florid-faced man Abby had been introduced to earlier in the day. His wife was the tall redhead she'd seen with Mrs. Johnson. She searched her memory for his name but drew a blank. He was joined by several other men, who voiced agreement. It was plain to see they were all well into their cups. They had all been freely sampling Winston's generous hospitality for several hours.

Winston delivered the refilled cup into Abby's hands before addressing the men, who were heatedly discussing the Indian problem. "This has been the quietest year we've had in some time, gentlemen, and I have hope that we can continue to live in peace with the Indians."

Abby sipped her punch, thinking about her encounter with the small band of Indians. She surmised that telling Winston about it would only serve to fuel his curiosity, and she listened with avid interest as the animated conversation flowed around her. She was reminded of the weight of her pistol strapped to her leg when Winston stepped away from the punch table and brushed against her. She stepped back a pace, wondering briefly if Elan had mentioned the incident to some of the men.

"Well, I say we need to rid ourselves of the problem once and for all! Too many of the savages are slipping off the reservations to hunt. Why, I heard you say the other day you seemed to be missing some beef after your fall roundup. Who knows what might happen if they catch settlers unaware?" The rancher glanced around, gathering support for his views. Most appeared to be in agreement with him. Abby noted Elan's entry as he trailed Frank up the stairs, and she followed him with her eyes until he disappeared on the upstairs landing.

Roberts elbowed his way into the conversation. "I heard those government commissioners treating with Red Cloud and Spotted Tail barely escaped with their lives last week." He hooked his thumbs in his suspenders and settled back importantly on his heels.

"It's no wonder," Winston said mildly. "The Black Hills are sacred to the Sioux and the Cheyenne, and it's ludicrous for President Grant to expect them to cede those lands to the gold prospectors."

"What Grant ought to do is stop feeding the stupid

savages until they give up," the rancher said bitterly. "Then the lazy devils wouldn't be able to get rid of those lands fast enough." Spencer, that was it, Abby thought. The rancher was Luke Spencer and his wife was Mary. Abby now only half listened to the conversation flowing around her as she sipped her punch, putting names to faces.

"The Indians are neither lazy nor slow of mind," Winston said. "And if the government insists on keeping them confined to a reservation, it must continue to feed them. Anything less would push them into a corner from which they would have no recourse but to fight."

"They're no match against the army and they know it!" Spencer said. "Why, Custer marched through the Black Hills last summer and met no resistance, and I'm told he had two prospectors with him. The savages are terrified of 'Yellow Hair'!"

Abby turned to the punch bowl and refilled her empty cup, eager for more of the fiery liquid that was rapidly soothing her jangled nerves. She disliked all the talk of bloodthirsty savages and wanted nothing more than to forget the unpleasantness she had experienced at the hands of the small band of braves who had paid a visit to her place.

"But this past April, Custer was ordered to remove all gold prospectors from the Black Hills," Winston reminded the rancher. "I fear if the prospectors don't comply with government orders to leave, you will indeed have your war, Spencer."

"Oh! The Battle of the Little Bighorn," Abby muttered to herself, remembering her history. She lifted her cup to her lips, but found it deftly removed from her hand as John Winston took it and set it on the snowy tablecloth. "If you will excuse us, gentlemen," Winston said politely as he took a firm grip on Abby's arm, "Mrs. Elan wishes to retire, and I must escort her to my daughter's room."

"But I . . ." Abby's protest was cut short as Winston placed a guiding arm around her shoulders and moved her with him across the cleared floor. She had difficulty keeping pace with his long strides, and her fury grew with each elongated step. The musicians resumed their post and another dance began. Abby balked at the foot of the stairs, enraged by Winston's impropriety. That Elan would manhandle her was bad enough. She certainly had no intention of allowing Winston to get away with it, too!

"Just what do you think you are doing, Mr. Winston?" Abby asked, planting her feet and refusing to take another step. She swayed dizzily, realizing with some remorse that she must have overdone it at the punch bowl. She had hardly touched her food earlier in the afternoon, so unsettled had she been after Winston had questioned her about her watch, and the punch was now rolling around in her empty stomach. She shook off Winston's arm and glared at him, wanting suddenly to slug him but was forced to cling to the newel post to maintain her balance.

"I'm escorting you to your room," Winston said. "I thought I heard you say you were tired."

"I said no such thing!" Abby said. "I said . . ." She bit her lip, realizing with sudden horror that she must have spoken aloud at the punch table. Just what exactly had Winston heard? And what could it possibly mean to him? She really had overdone it. She eyed Winston suspiciously, but his face betrayed nothing more than courteous concern as he arched a brow and awaited her pleasure.

"Good night, Mr. Winston," Abby said, reluctantly relinquishing her grip on the newel post and praying she could navigate the stairs without serious mishap. She lifted her skirts to ascend the stairs. "I can find my own way. Please return to your guests."

"As you wish," Winston replied, but he stood at the foot of the stairs and watched Abby's careful progress until she topped the landing and disappeared from his sight.

Abby paused before the half-open door to Lori's room and leaned wearily against the doorjamb. What had been in that damn punch? Whatever it was certainly packed a wallop. She hadn't felt so disjointed since her date had dumped a full bottle of tequila into the punch at her senior prom.

She could hear Elan's deep, resonant voice crooning a song. The words were French, and although she couldn't follow many of them she guessed correctly that he was singing a lullaby, for she soon heard Lori's lilting voice beg for another as the song ended.

When she pushed open the door, Abby found the incongruous sight of Elan seated in the nursery rocker with the child cradled tenderly in his lap. The cool night air blew in the open window and ruffled his long hair. His cheek rested atop Lori's coppery curls, and his eyes were hooded as he lost himself in the haunting melody.

Mrs. Johnson put the finishing touches to the newly made bed. She gathered up the linens she had stripped from Lori's bed and with a brief acknowledgment of Abby bade the child to come with her. Lori reluctantly obeyed, climbing down from Elan's lap and allowing Mrs. Johnson to take her hand and lead her from the room.

Abby softly closed the door behind her and carefully advanced across the hardwood floor to stand unsteadily before Elan. He cocked his head and regarded her with troubled eyes.

Elan took in Abby's appearance, noting with concern her flushed face and the faint odor of alcohol. It was readily apparent that she'd been drinking, and he was more than a little shocked at her behavior.

Elan made as if to rise, but Abby waved her hand to indicate he should remain seated. "I have neglected you, Abby," Elan said, wondering just how much liquor she had consumed in his absence and what, if anything, Winston had done to encourage Abby's behavior. "I will escort you back to the party."

He knew how much Abby had been looking forward to the party, and the dancing had only just begun. Although he was unfamiliar with most of the dance steps, he had the ability to pick them up quickly, and he wanted Abby to enjoy herself. Perhaps Mrs. Johnson would lend her a shawl so that she could be decently covered.

"I'm tired." Abby swayed, and Elan was immediately on his feet, taking her in his arms. She rested her face against the familiar solidness of his chest, grateful for his presence.

"You're drunk," Elan said as he got another whiff of alcohol. No wonder she swayed so alarmingly, he thought as he scooped her up and took the few steps to place her gently on the bed. Abby sank back into the welcome softness of the feather mattress and closed her eyes, trying to think. It was not an easy task in her current state.

"We need to talk, Elan," Abby said as she struggled to a sitting position against the carved bedstead. "John Winston has offered me employment as a governess to his daughter, and I've been seriously considering it."

"What? Why would you want to do that?"

"Well, for one thing, I could earn enough to buy my herd. And for another, I'm bored. You're off hunting or fishing every day, and I don't have enough to do to keep me busy."

"I am not sure I trust John Winston," Elan said. "I do not like the way he looks at you or the questions he asks."

"I think he just has a natural curiosity about two strangers who appeared in the valley. He seems the type to be interested in anything going on around him. And he's not interested in me. He has someone else."

"Who?" Elan crossed his arms over his chest and waited for Abby's answer. She seemed to know quite a bit about John Winston. The man had dominated Abby's time from the moment they arrived at the ranch. Elan had been acutely aware of every minute she had spent in Winston's company, and finding her in Winston's arms on the dance floor had been the final straw. He had been guilty of neglecting Abby, but he was not prepared to have her turn to Winston for company.

"Annie," Abby said. "He goes to see her every week."

"Annie the whore?" Elan asked, his eyes narrowing as his posture stiffened.

Abby flinched at Elan's frankness, but she nodded. She didn't really like to think of Annie as a whore; nevertheless, she certainly couldn't defend the girl there.

"I do not think it wise for you to spend time with John Winston, but I cannot see the harm in your spending some time with his daughter. Now I will go downstairs to thank our host while you prepare for bed." He turned and reached the door in two strides.

"Take your time," Abby said as Elan opened the door. "Take your time." She put her hands to her flushed face, wondering how she was going to gracefully manage the upcoming situation.

John Winston, not realizing their true circumstances, had put her and Elan into the same room. If Elan and she failed to share the room and the bed, Winston's already suspicious mind would start working overtime. They would have to sleep together. There was no way around it, for there were no extra bed linens left in the room. That meant she could not make Elan a pallet on the floor, and she felt too guilty to demand he sleep there without some comforts.

What was even worse, she had not planned to spend the night, so she had not brought her nightgown. If she slept in the clothes she had worn for travel, they would not be wearable tomorrow. She couldn't possibly sleep in the red dress. It constricted her breathing as it was, and it would be next to impossible to get any rest in it at all.

Half an hour later Elan rapped at the closed door and opened it at Abby's invitation. He found the room bathed in soft shadows. Abby had lowered the lamp and stood beside the turned-down bed fumbling with the buttons of her gown. She had managed to undo most of them, but she had missed a few.

"I guess you'll have to help me," Abby said over her shoulder. "Come in and close the door." She watched Elan's approach in the mirror, transfixed by his movements as he made his way silently to her.

His fingers lightly brushed the bare skin of her back as he quickly freed the last of the buttons, and she fleetingly wondered about his adroit handling of the tiny fasteners. She stared into the mirror, breathing deeply as his callused hands moved across her shoulders and slowly guided the satin down her arms, freeing her from the all-too-restricting material. He dipped his head to drop a kiss on her bare shoulder, and his dark hair fell forward, obstructing her view. She shivered expectantly, wanting desperately to see his face.

Then she stepped from the dress and petticoat as Elan impatiently tugged them off, and she stood only in her

panties. Then they were gone, too, as he slipped his hands
inside them and slid them past her hips and down her
thighs. She stepped out of them and balanced on shaky
legs, watching in the mirror as one of his hands tossed the
scrap of material aside while his other cupped her breast,
his thumb lazily stroking its nipple. She threw back her
head as his mouth grazed her neck, and she lifted her
arms to tangle her fingers in his thick black hair. His
buckskin clothing felt soft against the bare skin of her
back, her buttocks, and the backs of her thighs, but she
ached to rid him of it, to feel his hot flesh against hers.

Elan lifted his head to meet Abby's gaze in the looking
glass. Her arms, uplifted to clutch his hair, served to arch
her back and thrust forward her breasts. He took in the
sight of her displayed in the looking glass and raked his
gaze down the length of her body, taking in her flat belly,
the curly thatch of dark hair hiding the soft mound of her
womanhood, her shapely legs, the same legs he had
longed to feel around his hips.

Abby's gaze delved into Elan's hooded black eyes and
her breath caught in her throat at the passion she saw
mirrored in them. She slowly turned, and as she did his
hands moved from her breasts, then made their way
down the curve of her back to grip her bottom.

Elan pulled Abby close against him, grinding his hips
into her belly, groaning deeply as he lowered his head to
search her lips demandingly. She stood on tiptoe, her
hands gliding up his chest as he leaned down to capture a
rosy nipple, to gently suckle, then to tease with his lips
and teeth.

He scooped her up and carried her to the bed. While
she watched, he unhurriedly unlaced the ties of his
fringed buckskin shirt and pulled it over his head to drop
it on the floor. Then he removed the hatchet from his

wide belt and placed it on a nearby trunk. Next he removed the sheathed knife, taking his time with the laces that bound it to his leg. Then it too went the way of the hatchet.

All the while Abby watched, reveling in the play of corded muscles making up Elan's sinewy arms, the bunched muscles of his broad chest, the knotted muscles of his flat stomach, his curved profile as he bent at the waist to remove his moccasins. When he straightened, he unlaced and removed his trousers. And then he was before her, gloriously naked, standing on the balls of his feet, waiting, it seemed, for her to make the next move, his dark eyes questioning.

She reached out to him, and he pushed her down on the bed, almost rough in his haste. He covered her with his body, holding himself up by the strength of his arms. For one long moment their eyes met, smoldering blue and midnight black. Abby opened her legs and reached to guide him. He plunged when Abby lifted her hips to meet him, became aware of the little whimpers issuing from her throat as her hands clutched his buttocks, pulling him to her. She closed tightly around him as he entered her, drawing him into her silky passage, capturing him, making him hers.

He dipped his head, meeting her mouth, joining with her there also. He could taste the alcohol on her warm, sweet breath, and instead of repulsing him, as it normally would have, it served only to intensify his desire. It was at that moment she wrenched her lips from his and turned her head. He followed her gaze to view their reflections, to see the two of them together, watching as though a stranger might, the coming together of uncontrolled passion, the coupling of a petite dark-haired woman and her much larger long-haired lover.

It was over too soon, as he knew it would be, so long had he been without a woman, and he shuddered, feeling his strength drain away when he surrendered and spilled his seed. Using his last ounce of strength, he rolled to his side, drawing her with him. She rested her head on his chest, panting slightly while he drew in deep, ragged breaths.

Elan stared at the ceiling while he waited for his heart rate to return to normal. In the weeks he and Abby had been together, he had wanted to take her on many occasions, but had successfully resisted the urge. So badly did he want her that the day before he had finally tossed aside the fragile thread of decency that kept him from her bed. Then had come her confession, and his long-held passion had become instead white-hot fury. That she was experienced in relationships with men had been a blow to his pride, one he still had difficulty accepting.

Even knowing Abby had been with another man, tonight he had not thought of her as anything but virginal until he watched her in the looking glass and found himself a voyeur to his own bed. In watching her, it had been as if he had seen her in the arms of another, and that had been as profoundly disturbing as the depth of passion the reflected image had aroused in him.

Elan gradually became aware of Abby's fingers teasing his chest, and suddenly she was atop him, splayed along his body, rubbing catlike, nuzzling the hollow of his neck, making little moaning sounds. He responded to her touch, exploring the soft hollows of her body, inhaling the rich sent of passion spent, and he realized he wanted her again, just as desperately as he had wanted her before.

Abby shivered as a blast of cold air penetrated the bedroom, and Elan, feeling the gooseflesh on her arms, rolled her over and got up to close the window. She stared at him unabashed as he quickly strode across the small room and slammed shut the window. But his next movement took her completely by surprise. In one swift motion he seized the embroidered counterpane and flung it over the mirror.

"I will share you with no one, not even the reflection in a looking glass," he said as he roughly took her in his arms and sought possession of her body once again.

11

As the first faint rays of dawn brightened the sky
and filtered through the cracks of the shuttered windows,
Abby scrambled from the warmth of the bed and hastily
wrapped herself in a quilt before walking in her bare feet
across the cold wooden floor to huddle next to the stove.
Elan was already dressed and downing his second cup of
scalding coffee. He eyed her speculatively. She had slept little during the night and had tossed and turned until nearly
daybreak. Something was on her mind, and he imagined
she was determined to confront him with it before he left
on his hunt. Today was not one of her scheduled times to
tutor Lori and there was no other reason for her to be up so
early. He set his cup down and poured her a cup of coffee.
She took it with one hand, her other holding together the
bulky quilt as she warmed one bare foot with the other.

He thought her beautiful, her eyes still heavy with
sleep, her hair slightly mussed. He could hardly believe he
had lived so long without her. Now that she was a part of

his life, he was happier than he had ever been. Every day with Abby was a new beginning. He needed nothing else.

He leaned against the log wall, a slow grin spreading across his face. She impishly stuck her tongue out at him, and he laughed. She laughed with him and blew into the steaming cup.

"You are up early," Elan said as Abby tested the coffee with a tiny sip, grimacing when she discovered he had neglected to add sugar. She yawned widely, making her way to the rocking chair and tucking one leg under her as she cautiously sat, balancing the cup against the movement.

"I didn't sleep much last night," Abby said. "I have an idea about how to get the medicine bag." She took another sip of her coffee and waited for Elan's response. When he said nothing, she continued. "When we were at Winston's party a couple of months ago, some of the men were talking about General Custer and the Indian problem. I've been thinking about it ever since and I think I have an idea that might work."

"Who is General Custer?" Elan asked. "And what does he have to do with the medicine bag?"

"General Custer is one of the most famous Indian fighters in the West. Next summer there's going to be a big battle down along the Little Bighorn River. General Custer and his cavalry troops are going to be massacred by the Indians. I studied it in my history class. There will be thousands of Indians there, probably every Indian from the territory. The medicine bag is sure to be there, too."

"I do not understand how you plan to get the medicine bag," Elan said, crossing his arms over his chest and frowning worriedly. If thousands of Indians were going to war with the army, that was the last place he wanted to be. He could not imagine taking Abby into that kind of danger even if she happened to be right.

"It's all very simple, really," Abby said, knowing there was nothing simple in the least about what she wanted to do, but hoping she could convince Elan that it could be done. She had really thought a lot about it, and it seemed to be the best bet for finding the medicine bag. Otherwise they could wait years for it to turn up or for them to happen upon it. Having all the territory's Indians in one place at one time improved their odds considerably. She wanted that medicine bag. She had to know that she could return home when she was ready to leave this time. She and Elan had grown so close, she was sure she could convince him to go with her to her time.

"If we can ride down there and get to Custer before the battle, we can warn him about the Indians. Then Custer can win the battle. He'll be so grateful to us for telling him where to find the Indian camp that he'll be glad to help us find the medicine bag."

"I do not think we should interfere with history, Abby," Elan said gravely as he considered her idea. "I will have to think about it. It would be a dangerous trip." Deep in thought, he removed his snowshoes from the nails on the wall and knelt to strap them on. He should have realized Abby would not be content to remain in the wilderness with him forever, but it had been so easy to imagine that she would. At the soft touch on his shoulder, Elan looked up to find Abby hovering over him, her small hand restlessly smoothing the coarse buckskin.

"Promise me you really will consider it," Abby said. He nodded, and she leaned over to kiss the top of his head. "Be careful, Elan," she said as she straightened and walked over to throw open the door, bracing herself against the stinging bite of the cold air invading the warmth of the cabin. "It looks like more snow today."

"I will," Elan said as he bundled up in the bearskin coat he had sewn from the hide of the small black bear he had shot before it found its winter den. "And I will be back before dark."

Elan tracked the huge elk, following its prints in the deep snow. The day was raw and windy, and the darkening clouds overhead foretold more snow to come. It grew dark early during the winter months, and he realized with some trepidation that he had only an hour or so of daylight left. If he did not find the elk in the next few minutes, he would have to abandon the trail and make for the cabin. He could not risk being caught out unprepared when the darkness and coming snow fell.

He realized as he plodded along in his snowshoes that his heart really was not in the hunt. He had a good supply of meat in the cache behind the cabin, and he had only struck out because he needed to get away from the close confines of the cabin. Then too, he seemed better able to think when he could distance himself from Abby. And she had given him quite a bit to think about today.

Elan stopped his measured tread and lifted the rifle. The elk stood on a far ridge, clearly outlined against the horizon. As he took aim an unsettled feeling crept over him, and he lowered the rifle to look around quickly. He saw nothing unusual, and laughed at himself when the elk disappeared over the ridge.

He had hunted elk many times since that fateful day when he had taken the Indian medicine bag and been sent forward in time. So, he wondered, what made this day any different than the others? Perhaps because of the conversation he and Abby had had before he left her standing in the open door of the cabin, he admitted to himself as he changed direction and made for the home-stead.

Abby wanted to search for the medicine bag so that she could return to her home. It was just that simple. However, finding the bag would not be at all simple. In the first place, he had no desire to travel such a long distance through hostile territory, and in the second place, he was not at all sure he wanted to find it, even if they could.

Abby had told him of the wondrous things of the future, things such as horseless carriages and machines that flew in the air, like the one on her jacket. She was convinced he should see these things, that they could both be transported to the future and live amid the comforts of a modern world. But he could not see himself in her world. He was having difficulty enough fitting into the place in which he now found himself, a place where the game was almost trapped out, a place where men tamed the land and stayed in one spot and raised cattle instead of living off the land around them.

As for returning to the world he had left, Elan was not sure that was what he wanted, either. It would be difficult to return to the past when he had seen the future. And there was Abby. She would never consider going back to his time with him, where life was even more primitive than it was now. If he wanted to stay with her, and he could not now imagine life without her, then he had to either go with her to her time or convince her to stay with him where they were.

A huge snowflake hit his windburned cheek, and Elan quickened his steps. Soon snow was swirling around him, engulfing him in a blanket of white, and he was hard-pressed to keep his bearings. After several long minutes he spotted the faint outline of the darkened cabin in the distance. No light escaped the tiny cracks of the shuttered windows and no smoke rose from the metal stovepipe in the roof. Where was Abby?

Elan stepped up his pace, stumbling through the large drifts, crossing a set of blurred sled tracks that were rapidly filling with fresh snow. He made his way to the cabin and threw open the door. It was cold and dark inside. He slammed the door behind him, shutting out the fierce wind and blowing snow. He fumbled around and managed to light the lantern that hung just inside the door. Lifting the lantern and adjusting the light, Elan saw a scrap of paper anchored to the table with a small stone, one of the many Abby had collected from the stream behind the cabin.

Elan held the note up to the light. *Have gone to see about Lori. Frank brought word she is seriously ill. Abby.*

Elan crumpled the note and used it with the kindling to build a fire. Much later, when the cabin was warm and his coffee boiled, Elan settled down on the floor with his cup to contemplate Abby's flight. Of course she would feel compelled to tend the child. Abby had grown very close to Lori during the last two months, but the thought of her staying overnight at Winston's ranch was more than a little disturbing.

Elan liked Winston, but he had reservations about Abby spending too much time in his company. Elan got to his feet and strapped his snowshoes back on. Taking the lantern, he threw open the door and walked out into the swirling whiteness. He felt his way blindly toward the corral, and walked into it before he realized he was there. The gelding stuck his cold nose to Elan's face and nickered. Elan led him out of the corral and into the shed, where he poured him a bucket of feed. Then he closed the makeshift doors he had built in anticipation of the storm that was upon him. There was nothing more to be done but to return to the cabin and wait it out.

The blizzard raged for three days, effectively confining Elan to the cabin. On the one occasion he did venture forth it was only to feed the gelding, and that was a dangerous undertaking, for the snow blew so thickly he became lost instantly and wandered around for the better part of an hour before he stumbled into the cabin's east wall and managed to feel his way to the door. Half frozen and furious at his stupidity, Elan hunkered down and rode out the storm.

On the morning of the fourth day, Elan opened the door and found bright sunshine. Although eager for word of Abby, he delayed his departure until he ran his trap lines. It was early afternoon before he was ready to make the trek to the Winston ranch. The drifts were too high to ride the horse, so he strapped on his snowshoes and set out on foot, determined to walk the five miles across the valley before night fell.

Abby gratefully accepted the bowl of stew from Mrs. Johnson, but refused to leave her post by Lori's bed. After eating a few bites she placed the bowl on the lamp table and rose from the rocker to smooth the child's hair from her face. Lori's forehead was burning hot, and she whimpered in her sleep at Abby's touch. Lori's labored breathing concerned her, and Abby propped another pillow under her head.

"You have to eat, Mrs. Elan. We can't have you getting sick, too," Winston said, entering the room, standing to one side of the door to allow Mrs. Johnson to leave, then depositing a load of wood next to the stove in the corner of the room. Abby looked up, noting the strain on his face. "I'll stay with her while you eat and get some rest," he said.

"Has the doctor gone?" Abby asked wearily, tucking the covers more tightly around the fevered child. Abby had little faith in the bleary-eyed old quack she had found tending Lori when she arrived. His bumbling efforts had afforded little relief to Lori's suffering.

"Frank left at daybreak to take him back to Helena," Winston said as he walked slowly to the bed to stand at Abby's side.

"I don't think the medicine he brought is doing any good," Abby said worriedly. "Lori's fever hasn't broken. All she does is sleep, and her joints are still swollen. She must be in a lot of pain." Abby picked up the brown bottle and opened it, sniffing its contents. "I wish I knew what was in this stuff."

Winston took the bottle from her hands and recorked it. "Laudanum, I suspect," he replied, setting it down. "It's what he prescribed for my wife as she lay dying."

"But that's opium!" Abby cried, whirling to face him. "It won't break the fever! It will only keep her in a stupor! She needs something to break the fever and reduce the swelling. I'm afraid her lungs are filling with fluid. Can't you hear her labored breathing?"

"He claims rheumatic fever is fatal at her age, and that all we can do is keep her comfortable." Winston's voice broke, and he turned his face away.

"I won't accept that, and you can't either!" Abby hurried across the room to snatch up her saddlebags. They lay across the small bed that had been moved into Lori's room so that Abby might grab a few hours of sleep whenever she could, for she had steadfastly refused to leave Lori's side once she arrived at the ranch and found her young charge so ill.

"I have something that may help," Abby muttered, dropping to her knees, pushing aside all thought of protecting her past from Winston's probing. All that mattered now was helping Lori. She dug through the contents of the bag and tossed them carelessly to the floor. She finally found the clear plastic bottle of aspirin and eagerly fumbled with the childproof cap, mentally cursing as she failed to open it.

"What is it?"

Abby looked up to see Winston standing over her, a frown creasing his brow. What could she tell him? She searched for the right words.

"Trust me," she implored when he took the bottle from her hands to study its contents. She caught her bottom lip with her teeth and waited for him to read the label. He carefully aligned the two arrows and popped off the lid. Then he shook one of the white tablets into his hand.

"We will have to crush it," was all he said. Abby pushed herself upright and took the tablet with a trembling hand. She placed it in the soup spoon and carefully used the spoon for Lori's medicine to crush the aspirin. Then, mixing a little water with it, she poured the concoction down Lori's throat while Winston held up her head.

Winston crossed the room and threw back the window curtains, allowing bright sunlight to stream into the sickroom, the first sun Abby had seen since she had arrived. How many days had she been at the ranch? Was it three or four? She worried briefly about Elan, then dismissed him. He was fully capable of taking care of himself. Surely he'd had the good sense not to be out in the blizzard.

Abby wished she knew more about Lori's illness and had more to rely on than the word of the so-called doctor

Winston had brought in. Doc Collins was convinced
Lori's heart was affected. Could he be right? Would Lori
ever run and play again, as she loved to do? Would Lori
ever leave her bed?

"Lori's fever has broken, and she's asking for something
to eat," Abby exclaimed as she rushed headlong into
Winston's small office. Winston closed the ledger in
which he'd been writing and rose to meet her as she
reached his desk.

"Thank God," he said, arresting Abby's mad dash by
encircling her waist and whirling her around the room.
They were both breathless with laughter by the time he
released her. She swayed dizzily, and before she could
escape, Winston had wrapped her in his arms, hugging
her tightly. "Thank you," he murmured into her ear.

"Mr. Elan is here to see you," Mrs. Johnson
announced disapprovingly from her position just inside
the open doorway. Abby jerked out of Winston's arms
and turned to meet not only Mrs. Johnson's grim face but
Elan's as well. She stepped back guiltily as Winston
dropped his arms to his sides.

Elan seemed to fill the doorway, as big as the bear he
had skinned for the heavy coat he wore, and Abby
instinctively shrank back under his penetrating stare. He
had not shaved for several days, and the dark stubble
covering his face gave him the appearance of a wild man.
His lips were drawn into a tight line. His hands were
planted firmly at his waist and his right hand fingered his
hatchet.

She watched mutely, her heart in her throat as the two
men locked gazes, and wondered wildly what, if anything, she could do to ease the tension permeating the

small room. She nearly sagged with relief when Winston spoke in a congenial tone.

"Elan!" Winston advanced to offer his hand. "How good to see you." After several long moments, Elan released the hatchet at his belt and took the other man's outstretched hand, but it was obvious he did so grudgingly.

"I have come to fetch my wife," Elan said. "How is the child?"

"Much better," Winston said. "Mrs. Johnson was just about to take her some broth." Mrs. Johnson nodded, then slowly made her way past Elan and out the door, clearly reluctant to leave the scene she had helped to set.

"Her fever has broken, but she is not recovered yet," Abby interjected, edging away from Winston's desk and glancing longingly at the open door. She wanted nothing more than to escape. Although Elan's tone had been civil, Abby realized he was keeping a check on his anger. She deeply regretted her impulsive dash into Winston's office, and regretted even more Elan's finding her in such a compromising position. She didn't have to guess what he must be thinking, and as much as she wanted to defend her action, she refused to do so in Winston's presence. It would have to wait.

"Will you join me?" Winston asked, stepping to the desk and pouring a snifter of brandy from a crystal decanter. He held it out to Elan.

"Thank you, no," Elan replied. "As soon as Abby can collect her things, we must go." Elan knew he was acting unreasonably in his determination to take Abby on a five-mile trek through deep snow, but he would carry her every step of the way if he had to before he would allow her to spend one more night under Winston's roof.

It wasn't as if he didn't trust Abby, he told himself. It was Winston who bore watching. The man wanted Abby.

Elan was sure he did, and his belief kept him from fully trusting him. What made matters worse, he otherwise liked Winston. He admired the man's fairness in dealing with his employees and he respected his ability to run his spread.

"You can't be serious!" Winston said, setting the untouched brandy on the desk and facing Elan. "You can't possibly mean that you intend to drag your wife through those drifts in this bitter cold. And it's almost dark. At least wait until Frank returns with the sled tomorrow!"

"Collect your things," Elan said, ignoring Winston's protest and addressing Abby for the first time since he had entered the room. She fingered her dress, nervously clutching the folds of blue material, and glanced from Winston's agitated face to Elan's set features.

"Mr. Winston, I'd like to speak with Elan alone," Abby said. She had to make Elan see reason. She had no desire to trudge five miles after dark through snow that must be higher than her head in some places, and her fear that the two men would fight was rapidly turning into anger as they discussed her as if she weren't there, as if her wishes were unimportant.

"Of course," Winston said. Ever the gentleman, he quickly excused himself, leaving Abby to deal with Elan. Abby suddenly regretted his departure because it meant she had to face Elan's anger alone. And he was angry. Not that she really feared him, she hastily assured herself, but she regretted immensely the hurt he must feel.

"I'd like to explain," Abby began, only to be interrupted by Elan's clipped words.

"Get your things!" Elan turned on his heel and was at the door in two strides.

"No!" Abby yelled, thoroughly fed up with his superior-male attitude. Elan turned to face her, and she took an instinctive step back at the dangerous glint she saw in his black eyes. She lifted her chin, determined not to be bullied. She had done nothing wrong. Maybe she shouldn't have dashed into Winston's office, and she certainly should not have allowed him to embrace her, but it was only because they were both so relieved at Lori's improvement. There was nothing more to it than that.

"I will not allow you to spend another night under Winston's roof," Elan said in a carefully controlled tone. "Your behavior does not befit a proper married woman." Did Abby not see that to remain was dangerous? Did she not understand Winston's desire for her? Or perhaps she understood only too well, Elan thought, his blood beginning to boil.

"You will not allow me?" Abby exclaimed in disbelief at Elan's barbaric attitude. "How dare you presume to tell me what I can and cannot do! And another thing," she added as her anger peaked and made her reckless, "you are not my husband! And even if you were, you could not dictate to me!"

Elan flinched as though she had dealt him a physical blow, and Abby wanted immediately to recall her hard words, wanted to hurl herself into his arms. She realized he was only trying to protect her, to keep her from compromising herself. But there was no danger in that. She didn't want Winston, and she didn't think Winston wanted her. She wanted Elan!

The strain of the last few days had nearly been unbearable, and she had missed Elan terribly. The only reason she had come was to tend Lori, and she could not in good conscience abandon the child until she was out of danger. Why couldn't Elan understand that?

Instead of taking her into his strong arms and comforting her, as she wished him to do after her verbal assault,

Elan quickly strode out of the room. She followed him to the front door and braced herself against the biting cold as he strapped on his snowshoes. "At least stay the night," Abby said. "You are being completely unreasonable in leaving like this." Elan glanced at her only briefly before striking out across the yard. "I'll be home when Lori is well enough for me to leave her," Abby called after him. He neither answered nor acknowledged her comment in any way. Abby dragged herself up the stairs, completely drained and defeated. She found Winston dosing Lori with another aspirin and sent up a silent prayer of thanks that he had not questioned the medicine, but she realized the questions would come later, when he could think of something other than Lori's illness.

"Abby?" Lori's pitifully weak voice was barely a whisper. Lori struggled to lift her head, then dropped it weakly on the pillows that propped her up to aid her breathing. She was reclining almost upright, but was breathless with the small exertion. Abby hurried to her side and perched on the edge of the bed to take Lori's hand.

"I'm here, honey," Abby said, noting that the swelling in Lori's wrists seemed to be lessening. Her fever now broken, she was pale and sweaty. "What do you need?"

"Don't leave me," Lori gasped, weakly folding her fingers around Abby's hand. "Please?"

"I'm not going anywhere, sweetheart," Abby assured her, blinking back tears. Tears for Lori and tears for herself. Elan would just have to understand. When he calmed down and could think reasonably, he would realize she could not leave Lori. She stroked Lori's face, then leaned over to kiss her brow gently.

"But . . . Papa said . . ." Lori's weak voice trailed off and her eyes fluttered closed. A small tear slipped down her cheek, tugging at Abby's heart.

"Papa was wrong," Abby said lightly, determined to brighten Lori's spirits. "I won't leave until you're well. I promise." A little smile played across Lori's mouth, and Abby patted her hand before placing it under the covers and drawing them up around Lori's chin. Just the effort to talk had been enough to exhaust the child, and she soon slept.

Abby started when she felt Winston's hands on her shoulders, and she looked up questioningly. She had all but forgotten he was in the room. She found him staring down at her face, his expression unreadable. As their eyes locked his fingers began to move, massaging her sore muscles, draining the tension away.

"Abby, aren't you ever lonely for someone who understands you? Someone who knows what you've been through?" Winston asked. Abby's eyes widened at the familiar use of her given name. And what could he possibly mean by his questions? *Someone who understood her? Someone who knew what she'd been through?* He could not possibly know what she had been through, and consequently he could not possibly understand her. Her heart began to pound as the blood rushed to her face. What did he expect of her? She leapt to her feet, shrugging off Winston's hands, flight the only thing on her mind as she pushed past him and all but ran out the door.

She made it halfway down the hall before he caught her by the elbow and spun her around. "I didn't mean to frighten you, Abby," Winston said, quickly releasing her when he saw the panic in her blue eyes. "I only sought to offer friendship to a fellow soul. You can talk to me, Abby. Why pretend to be someone you are not?" Abby stared at him in disbelief, and she backed up a pace.

"I'm afraid I don't know what you mean," Abby said, growing more worried by the minute and wishing she had left with Elan after all.

"I overheard your exchange with Elan," Winston said. "You were quite vocal in your denial. I couldn't help but overhear. Eavesdropping is not an admirable trait, I'll admit, but it is useful at times." Winston's mouth curved under his handlebar mustache as he smiled affectionately at her.

"You're mistaken," Abby said, regaining some measure of control despite her confusion. "You must have misunderstood."

"Elan is not your husband." Winston said. "Those very words came from your own lips. You cannot take them back."

Abby gaped at Winston, speechless. He was right in that she could not take back what was already said, but she could not imagine he would use it against her. If she wanted to claim Elan as her husband, then it was of no concern to him.

"What time will you be wanting supper?" Abby went weak with relief when Mrs. Johnson made her presence known. Winston stepped back, a flash of annoyance crossing his face as his housekeeper topped the landing carrying a napkin-covered tray.

"Let me help you, Mrs. Johnson," Abby said, eagerly taking the tray and turning toward Lori's door, anxious to put as much distance as possible between herself and her host.

"We will eat in an hour, Mrs. Johnson," Winston said. "You will sit with Lori, and Mrs. Elan will join me." He bounded down the stairs, taking them two at a time, leaving Abby to wonder if he would break his neck in his descent. She noted somewhat resentfully that he made it safely to the first floor. Mrs. Johnson followed Winston at a somewhat more sedate pace.

Abby saw that Lori still slept, so she placed the covered tray on a chest near the bed. She walked across the room and drew the curtains. The sun had long since disappeared behind the mountains, leaving only the faint lamplight to illuminate the room.

She could hear Lori's shallow breathing, and wondered if the child would indeed recover, if her presence would actually make a difference. It was of no matter. She could not leave Lori. She had promised, and even if she had not, she would never forgive herself if she left and something dreadful happened.

And what of John Winston? What had he been trying to say to her? Abby rubbed her temples, feeling the stirrings of a headache. She was too tired to think clearly. Perhaps some nourishing food and a good night's rest would help her put things into better perspective. She slowly made her way to the small cot and collapsed fully dressed on the lumpy mattress. She was asleep as soon as her head touched the feather pillow.

12

November gave way to December, with Lori showing a little improvement. The aspirin was long used up, and Abby was helpless to ease Lori's pain when her joints swelled and became inflamed. Thankfully, the girl's high fevers had abated, and Abby believed she was well on the way to recovery.

To pass the dragging hours, Abby begged Mrs. Johnson to teach her to knit, and she was busily working on a scarf for Elan one sunny afternoon when Winston stuck his head in Lori's door and interrupted.

"I'm going to the settlement. Can I bring you anything?" Abby looked up, remembering it was Friday. In spite of Lori's illness, Winston still made his weekly visits to the settlement, and Abby understood he continued his liaison with Annie.

"No, nothing," Abby answered distractedly, dropping a stitch. It would be nothing short of a miracle if she managed to complete the scarf in time for Christmas and have it recognizable. She put aside the bright red yarn and glanced at Lori, who was sleeping. Lori seemed to spend most of her time asleep, having little energy for any activity beyond swallowing the few bites Abby managed to get her to eat.

Abby studied Lori's thin face and reached to smooth her lusterless hair. It had been coming out in great handfuls, and Abby had cut it short, hoping somehow that would help. Although it was easier to keep clean, strands still fell out every time Abby brushed it.

"How is she today?" Winston asked, entering the room to stand beside Abby. Abby moved away, crossing the room to put the bed between them, making a pretense of straightening the covers.

"About the same," Abby replied. "She seems to wake more often, though, and this morning she asked for a story." Abby smiled, remembering Lori's demand. "But she fell asleep before I finished."

Winston left Lori's bedside to squat on his haunches and toss a large chunk of firewood into the potbellied stove. "What do you think Lori would like for Christmas?" he asked, slamming closed the metal door and getting to his feet.

Abby considered the question. Christmas was only a little over a week away, but Lori had shown no interest in it or much of anything else since her illness. She had offered no opinion when Abby had asked her the same question only a few days before. But all little girls loved baby dolls, didn't they?

"Do you think Roberts has a baby doll?" Abby whispered. Winston grinned at Abby's concerned frown and gestured for her to follow him out of the room. He closed Lori's door behind them.

"I think Roberts may have just the thing," Winston

whispered, leaning close to Abby. She laughed at the twinkle in his eye. It felt good to laugh, Abby realized, trying to remember the last time she had truly felt light-hearted.

"Then get the doll, and some sweets and fruit if he has them," Abby replied. "And ask Frank to cut a small spruce and some pine boughs. I want to decorate Lori's room. She might not feel like going downstairs, so if we have to, we'll bring Christmas upstairs to her. Maybe it will lighten her spirits."

"I'll do that," he replied. "What would you like for Christmas?" Winston's tone turned serious, and Abby stepped away, putting her hand on the brass doorknob.

"Don't worry about me," she quipped, opening the door. "I can't think of a thing I need." Winston reached out and took her arm before she could escape through the door. He pulled her toward him and whispered in her ear. "I didn't ask what you needed, Abby. I asked what you would like to have." Winston had not touched her since the afternoon she and Elan had argued in his office, and he had not taken up the conversation that had so thoroughly rattled her.

Since the argument, Elan had not returned to Winston's ranch, but at Abby's request Frank had delivered an invitation to him last week. The invitation to Christmas dinner had been well received, and Frank soon returned with Elan's acceptance. Abby was looking forward to seeing Elan and hoped she could convince him to continue to visit until Lori recovered and she could return to the cabin.

Abby tried to step away from Winston, but he held her fast. She looked up into his eyes, which were warm with affection, and took a deep breath. "I only want the company of my husband."

"Elan is not your husband," Winston said.

"I have told you," Abby said staunchly. "That is of no concern to you." He continued to search her eyes. "Please release me," she said softly.

Winston dropped her arm but blocked her way, placing his hand on the doorjamb. "You are my concern, Abby," he said. "Are you certain you want a life with Elan in that primitive cabin up the mountain? Is that really the place where you belong? Do you love him enough to stay in such deprivation?" Winston's questions caught Abby off guard. Did she love Elan? She wasn't sure. She loved being with him, and she loved the way he looked at her, and she loved his gentleness when they were together. Abby took a deep breath and lowered her eyes. Elan had never told her he loved her, and somehow Winston's questions brought that omission into sharp focus. Had she just assumed Elan cared for her?

No, that couldn't be true. He had always held himself back, determined to respect her, even when she would have thrown respectability out the window for five minutes in his embrace. Abby didn't regret telling him about her relationship with Paul even though it drove a wedge between them. Elan would eventually come to terms with it. Abby needed the comfort of Elan's strong arms, his steadfast strength, his courage in a strange world. Modern woman that she was, she realized she was woefully inadequate in the 1870s. Elan was her anchor in a tempestuous sea, and she would cling to that anchor with all her strength.

Abby turned her face away, unwilling to allow Winston to see the indecision she felt. Winston was about to visit a prostitute, just as he did every Friday night, and here he was questioning her relationship with Elan. Would he ever realize how much Annie loved him?

Couldn't he love her in return? Surely he felt some affection for Annie. After all, there were other girls with whom he could spend his time and money.

"How can you speak to me of love between a man and a woman when you are on your way to see Annie?"

Winston flinched, dropping his hand and taking a step back, staring at Abby in utter amazement.

"What do you know about Annie?" he asked, his face darkening.

Abby took the plunge. "Annie is my friend. She made the dress I wore to your party, and we became friends during the fittings. I know Annie loves you. You could give her a good life here with you and Lori. She's smart and talented. All she needs is a chance."

"Annie is a whore," Winston said, his voice turning as cold as the winter's chill. "I could never allow her around Lori."

"What about me?" Abby demanded. "You know I've been living with Elan, yet you're willing for me to be with Lori. You seem to have no qualms about my virtue or lack of it!"

"That's different," Winston said stiffly. Abby noted the muscles working in his jaw as he struggled to contain his anger, and she wondered briefly if she had pushed him too far. But she was in too deep to back off.

"It's not different," Abby challenged. "Annie did the only thing she could to survive. It doesn't make her any less a person! If I had been in her shoes, I might have done the same thing. You can't judge her by any other standards. Not only that, but you should be trying to help her instead of taking advantage of her like all the other men do. You're in a position to get her out of the situation she's in!"

"By marrying her?" Winston asked dryly.

"Is that such a horrible thought?" Abby threw up her hands and began to pace the narrow hall. "Actually, I thought you might be willing to set her up in a small shop. She's an excellent seamstress, and if she had a shop, she could support herself in a respectable manner." Abby turned when she reached the stair landing, and hurried back to Winston's side. "You asked what I wanted for Christmas. If you would get Annie established, it would be the best Christmas present I could ever hope to have!"

Elan pulled the gelding to a halt and leapt from the sled. He stood in front of Winston's house for a moment, admiring his handiwork. The sled was small, measuring only four feet across and six feet long. It sported a seat about halfway along its length, leaving the remainder of the space for cargo. Elan had been to the settlement to trade with Roberts and on a whim headed for the Winston ranch instead of returning to the cabin. He had passed John Winston on the way, and had stopped briefly to exchange stilted pleasantries.

He found Winston somewhat distracted, but Winston had assured him he was welcome at the ranch and had invited him to stay the night if he wished. Elan regretted his behavior on his last visit and had stewed over it for weeks before receiving the invitation from Abby. It was just the encouragement he needed to pay her a visit. Until the invitation came, he had not thought anything about Christmas, for in truth, he had not celebrated the occasion since he was a boy in the mission school.

Elan brushed the snow from his bearskin coat as he jauntily made his way up the steps and knocked. Much to his astonishment, Abby threw open the door and flew into his arms.

Instinctively he lifted her and whirled her around before carefully setting her on her feet. "Elan!" she exclaimed. "Where did you come from? I'm so glad to see you!" She entangled her fingers in the thick beard he'd allowed to grow, tugging playfully at the curly black hair.

"Stop, woman!" Elan grumbled in mock anger, his twinkling eyes betraying him. He took Abby's cold hands from his face and held them fast. "You will have me on my knees begging for mercy!"

"Now that's a thought!" Abby laughed. She breathed deeply, enjoying the sharp, icy air as it filled her lungs. Then she spotted the horse and the sled. Seeing the longing in her eyes, Elan scooped her up and carried her to the sled, gently lowering her to the fur-covered backless seat. He wrapped her in more furs and tucked a quilt around her feet and legs. Then he climbed in beside her.

"Where are we going?" Abby asked, resting her head on Elan's shoulder, not caring where he took her, just happy to be with him. She had been confined to Lori's sickroom too long and desperately needed a break.

"I want to take you home," Elan replied, "but I will be content to take you for a ride." Having Abby by his side made him forget all the long, lonely nights she had been away. He had missed her acutely, miserably imagining her with Winston and longing for the evenings they had spent together at the cabin.

Had Abby missed him as much as he had missed her? From the way she came into his arms, it would seem so. His spirits soared as the sled flew across the packed snow. Abby snuggled closer, resting her hand on his thigh, and he marveled at the effect her small hand had on his concentration. Abruptly he changed direction, and in a few minutes they were deep into the pines, sheltered from view of anyone who might pass by.

Abby lifted her head when the sled stopped. Elan turned to take her in his arms, kissing her hungrily until she was breathless. She laughed shakily when he released her mouth to nuzzle her neck. "We're going to freeze to death," she warned. "We've got to be insane to do this."

"I will keep you warm," Elan breathed into her ear, sending tingles clear down to her toes, causing them to curl inside her boots. His hands delved under the furs, sliding up her ribs and cupping her breasts, making her ache to expose them to his mouth as his thumbs and fingers gently tortured her nipples.

Abby fumbled with the laces of his buckskin pants until he impatiently abandoned her breasts to render assistance. She moaned softly when he sprang free, and heard his quick intake of breath when she reached for him.

The quilt and most of the furs had fallen to the floor of the sled as Abby and Elan gave in to the raging passion that drove them. Elan reached under her skirt to remove her underwear and tossed the garment to one side.

"Come here, woman!" he growled. Abby went. He wrapped her in his open coat, molding her to him as she lowered herself over him.

His lips found hers as she squirmed against his thighs, and his tongue explored her mouth. She wrapped her arms around him beneath the heavy coat and rocked in his lap. Elan's deep groans excited her further, causing her to quicken her movements against him. She dug her nails into his buckskin-clad back, and she threw back her head when he released her lips. She gasped, drawing in great gulps of frigid air when he unfastened the buttons at her bodice and freed her breasts to the biting cold.

Then he rubbed his bearded face against her rigid nipples, and she moaned at the sensations the soft, curly hair evoked. He took one taut nipple in his mouth, gently sucking while he warmed her other breast with his huge hand. Abby buried her face in his long hair, inhaling its clean scent.

Elan shifted his hips, thrusting deeper. He felt her grasp him, tighten around him, and he struggled for control. He longed to strip her naked, to roll with her for hours, but the intense cold forbade any such action.

"Please," Abby moaned. Elan responded to her plea and forcefully thrust his hips upward, releasing her breast to place his hands at her hips and pull her down hard against him. He repeated the action, filling her completely until they both found shattering release. Finally Abby slumped against him, resting her head on his chest.

Elan cradled Abby in his arms, wrapping her more tightly in his coat, realizing he was a damn fool for bringing her out on such a day, for exposing her to the elements. They would both be lucky not to come down with pneumonia after such a foolish act. He dropped a kiss on the top of her head. "You are cold, Abby. I must get you back to the ranch before you get sick."

"No, I want to stay here for a while," Abby said, tilting her face to nuzzle his neck. "Just hold me, please."

She felt so safe in his arms. When he held her, she could shut out the world. She could rest in his embrace without worry. It was as if there were just the two of them, as if the rest of the world didn't matter. It was wonderful not to have to think, not to have to move, just to be as one with him.

"I will hold you for as long as you want, Abby," Elan replied, knowing this woman had captured his heart. He seemed powerless to deny her anything.

*　　*　　*

Mrs. Johnson met them on the porch when they returned, her face clearly reflecting her anguish. "You'd better hurry," she said, twisting her hands together. "Lori's taken a turn for the worse. Her fever is up again, and she's crying for you."

Abby raced up the stairs as fast as she dared in her long skirt. She found Lori shaking violently with chills and fever. She was covered only with one quilt and moaned pitifully when Abby tucked another around her. Sally stood in the corner by the window, watching attentively as Abby poured water from a pitcher into a bowl, then wet a cloth to put on Lori's head.

"Is Lori going to die?" Sally asked, bursting into tears. Abby paused. In the weeks she had been at the ranch, she had hardly noticed Sally in her concern for Lori. The child rarely spoke, creeping silently around the house, usually keeping to herself. She seldom visited the sickroom, and then only when her mother sent her for some purpose.

"No, Sally," Abby said, fear sharpening her tone. "We aren't going to let her die. Don't speak of it again."

"Mama says she will." Sally sobbed louder, burying her face in her hands.

"Well, Mama is wrong." Abby moved around Lori's bed to take Sally in her arms. The girl's thin shoulders trembled, and she dropped her hands from her face to clutch at Abby's skirt.

"Can I do something to help?" Sally's voice was muffled by Abby's skirt as the child pressed her face against the folds of material.

"Of course you can, Sally. You can say your prayers every night for Lori. And when she's feeling better you can come visit. But right now Lori needs to rest. Could you go ask Frank to bring up some more wood for the stove?"

"Mama sent Frank to get Mr. Winston," Sally said. She took a deep breath and rubbed her hands across her face. "I could get the wood."

"Go find Elan and ask him to bring it," Abby said, propelling Sally toward the door. "The wood is too heavy for you."

The room was already stifling hot, but Abby didn't know how else to get Lori's fever down since she no longer had aspirin to give her. Lori would have to sweat it off. Abby hurried to her bedside, jerking up another quilt and throwing it across the two already there.

When Elan arrived with the wood, he found Abby holding Lori as if she could transfer some of her warmth to the sick child. He dumped the wood by the stove and knelt at the other side of the bed. Tears streamed down Abby's face, and she held her trembling lip with her teeth. Elan felt each teardrop sear his heart, his concern for Abby as great as his concern for the helpless child.

Abby was letting Lori's illness tear her apart. She took each of Lori's aches and pains as a personal affront to her abilities as a nurse. Abby had spent most of their afternoon together telling him of Lori's progress, proudly relating each triumph. And now Lori was much worse. He knew Abby would blame herself for leaving her, even for the few hours she had been away.

"She's burning up again. We have to break her fever," Abby muttered.

"How did you break her fever before?"

"I used medicine I had in my saddlebags, but it's all gone. I don't have any more."

"Medicine from your time?" he asked. She nodded, increasing Elan's unease. He placed a hand on Abby's shoulder. "Abby, look at me. Does John Winston know about the medicine?" Again she nodded. "Does Winston know the medicine is from another time?"

"I don't know," Abby admitted, sitting up. "We never discussed it. He didn't ask any questions. We just gave it to Lori."

"Papa," Lori moaned. "Papa."

"Hush, darling, Papa's coming," Abby crooned. "Everything's going to be all right."

"Think, Abby," Elan commanded, drawing her attention from Lori's whimpering. "There must be some other way." Abby stared at Elan, noting somewhat hysterically as she caved in and sobbed loudly that she was drenched in perspiration and that Elan's clothes clung damply to him. They were both soaking wet, and still Lori shook with chills.

"We could try putting her in tepid water, I guess," Abby said uncertainly as she stood and paced the room. "That's the only other thing I can think of."

Elan studied her for a long moment, then glanced worriedly at Lori. He was afraid the shock of the water would kill the child, but in truth, she was probably dying anyway. If Abby thought the water would help, then they should try it, though if they failed, John Winston would likely want to kill them both for such an action.

"I will get the tub and tell Mrs. Johnson to heat the water," Elan said, rising from his kneeling position and making for the door.

"Tell her not to get it too hot," Abby instructed. "Tell her just to take the chill off."

"I will come for Lori when the tub is ready," Elan said as he closed the door behind him.

Abby returned to Lori's bed and, falling to her knees, began to pray. Elan found her there when he returned some time later. He helped Abby to her feet, then reached for Lori. He scooped the little girl out of the bed, covers and all, and slowly, carefully made his way down the stairs and through the main room and dining room into the kitchen, where Mrs. Johnson had prepared the tub.

Mrs. Johnson and Sally stood to one side, Mrs. Johnson with a look of strong disapproval upon her face, Sally staring with avid curiosity. "Mr. Winston won't like this," Mrs. Johnson said as Elan knelt and Abby removed the quilts.

"I don't care," Abby said through clenched teeth, knowing Mrs. Johnson was right for once. "If you can't help, at least don't hinder!" She unbuttoned Lori's gown and pulled it over her head, ignoring her feeble protests.

"Well, I never," Mrs. Johnson huffed, folding her arms across her breasts, her mouth turned down in the perpetual frown she wore. Sally edged closer to the tub, and Mrs. Johnson reached out to haul her back. Tears began to run down Sally's cheeks.

"Take Sally out," Abby ordered, neither needing nor wanting any distraction from the task at hand. She nodded to Elan, who gently lowered Lori into the water. Mrs. Johnson did as Abby bade and ushered Sally ahead of her as she made her way out of the kitchen.

Lori began to cry, low moaning sobs that tore at Abby's heart. Elan held the girl in the water, her thin arms flailing until he managed to secure them too. Abby took a cloth and bathed Lori, dripping the water across her shoulders and wiping her face. The water was only waist deep, and Abby wanted her wet all over. She worked diligently, determined to lower the child's fever. She was soon soaked up to her shoulders, but she ignored her own discomfort as she concentrated on Lori.

"What the hell is going on here?" Winston's angry voice startled Abby, and she looked up to find him striding into the kitchen, Mrs. Johnson and Sally hot on his heels.

"We're trying to lower Lori's temperature," Abby said, bracing herself for the confrontation. She had to keep Lori in the tub until her fever broke, or she might die.

"I'm taking her out now," Winston said, his face choleric as he struggled to contain his temper.

Abby stared into Elan's eyes, silently pleading. Elan stood and stepped between Winston and the tub.

"Come, Winston," Elan said quietly. "We will leave Abby to tend Lori. Men know nothing of these things." Winston made to push past Elan. It was a fruitless effort. Elan moved so quickly, Abby wasn't sure he had moved at all until she saw Winston draped over Elan's shoulder. In a split second, he had taken Winston out with one blow to the chin and caught the man as he fell. Mrs. Johnson screamed and grabbed Sally by the arm, hurriedly propelling her out ahead of Elan and his lanky burden.

"Thank you," Abby said shakily.

"My pleasure," Elan replied solemnly. Abby smiled weakly, realizing Elan meant exactly what he said. But she knew they'd both have hell to pay when Winston came around.

13

Elan shifted in his cowhide chair and waited for Winston to become fully conscious, unsure how Winston would react to his taking control of the situation. Elan would have preferred a more peaceful solution to the problem of Lori's bath, but the angry flash in her father's eye had forestalled any thought in that direction. Elan had acted instinctively, and though he regretted having to go to such an extreme, he would do it again unhesitatingly if he felt Abby was threatened even slightly.

Winston sat up cautiously and dropped his hands to his hips as he swung his legs over the edge of the bed. Elan had removed Winston's guns, and they now waited for him in the drawer of his desk in the office downstairs.

"Welcome back," Elan said calmly. Winston looked up, noticing Elan for the first time and finding him seated in a chair blocking the door, his face in shadow. Winston impotently flexed his fingers, then clenched them into fists.

"Lori?" he asked thickly. "How is Lori?"

"Your girl is asleep in her bed. Her fever has broken," Elan replied mildly, as if Winston could possibly think otherwise. "My wife has saved your daughter, no thanks to you or your housekeeper. You are a fortunate man, John Winston."

Winston shoved all ten fingers through his hair. He eyed Elan suspiciously. "How long have I been out?"

"I have no clock," Elan replied with a slight shrug of his enormous shoulders. "Maybe an hour. Maybe less." Elan relaxed in his chair, giving no sign of rising.

"How long do you think you can keep me here?" Winston asked.

Elan grinned. "As long as it takes for you to show some sense," he answered cheerfully. "You seemed to lose your judgment downstairs."

"Damn it, man," Winston growled. "I was worried about Lori!"

"You have trusted your daughter to my wife's care for almost two months, and tonight you questioned her wisdom. That is not good sense."

"She's not your wife," Winston said. Elan raised a brow, but otherwise his expression remained unchanged. He did, however, lean forward.

"This time I will forget your insult to Abby," Elan warned, "but if you ever repeat it in my presence again, I will not be responsible for my actions."

"I guess we know where we stand," Winston replied.

"I think we do," Elan said regretfully. "Now go and visit your daughter." He stood and removed the chair. Winston propelled himself to his feet, and with a curt nod strode past the other man to the door.

"I won't forget this, Elan. But as long as Abby remains at the ranch, I will not pursue it."

Elan made no reply as Winston hurried from the room. He picked up the cowhide chair and carried it with him to place it outside the sickroom. If Abby needed any assistance in dealing with Winston, he intended to be within earshot.

Within minutes Winston reappeared, flicking a cold glance at Elan, who was nonchalantly sprawled in the chair he had set by Lori's door. Winston stepped over Elan's long legs and strode briskly down the narrow hall to take the stairs two at a time.

Christmas Day dawned bright and clear, the sun dancing across the snow-covered landscape, which appeared to be encrusted with tiny diamonds. Abby paced the front porch of Winston's ranch house awaiting Elan's arrival, feeling as excited as a child on this sparkling Christmas morning.

Lori seemed better, and her spirits were much improved. Winston had sent for Frank to help him move the small cot from Lori's bedroom to the front room of the house before Frank took himself off to the settlement. Lori was downstairs now, happily being entertained by Sally. Abby couldn't imagine why Frank should be sent to the settlement in the midst of the holiday preparations, but her questions had remained unanswered. All she could get from Winston was an amused grin whenever she broached the subject.

Delicious smells wafted from the kitchen, adding to the festive atmosphere, and Abby's mouth watered appreciatively as she remembered the plump goose Elan had delivered only days before. Mrs. Johnson had outdone herself, baking several pies and cakes in addition to roasting the goose and stuffing it with sage dressing.

Pulling her jacket closer in the penetrating cold, Abby decided to finish her wait inside. It could be several hours before Elan made his appearance. Dinner was scheduled for late afternoon. Perhaps she could beg a snack from Mrs. Johnson. It was Christmas, after all, and surely even the grumpiest of the grumps would be in a benevolent frame of mind on this of all days.

"Abby?" Lori lifted her head slightly before allowing it to fall back to her pillow. Abby went quickly to Lori's cot, abandoning her plans to raid the kitchen. She was instantly alert, carefully scanning Lori's face for any sign of fever. Finding none, she allowed herself to relax.

"Yes?" Abby perched on the edge of Lori's cot and, without thinking, smoothed the child's now short hair from her face. Sally, who was playing near the fireplace with a corn husk doll, rose and edged nearer the cot.

"Do you think Sally and I have been good enough for Santa to bring us something?" Lori's small face was drawn into a worried frown, and Abby would have burst into laughter if the girl hadn't seemed so serious.

"Of course you have, sweetheart." Abby patted Lori's small hand. It rested outside the coverlet, frail and blue-veined against the rose-pink counterpane. "I couldn't think of two girls more deserving of surprises than you and Sally. Why, I'll bet that's where Frank has gone right now. Seems I heard something about him going to meet some portly gentleman dressed in red."

Lori giggled and snuggled deeper under her covers. "I'm not really worried about me," she confessed, "but Sally would be very disappointed if she didn't get something."

"Well, I don't think either of you has a thing to worry about," Abby said. She leaned over to whisper in Lori's ear. "I have it on the best authority that Santa is very pleased with both you girls. Now, you rest and I'll see if I can help Mrs. Johnson in the kitchen."

Elan stamped the snow from his feet and walked across the porch, his arms piled with gifts. He was hesitant to rap on the door; he had been to the ranch only once since his confrontation with Winston, and on that occasion Winston had been absent. Elan was a little worried at the reception he would receive in view of his last conversation with the man.

Mrs. Johnson had seemed pleased with the Canadian goose he had presented her and told him she would prepare it for Christmas dinner. His mouth watered as delicious smells tantalized his nose. He could almost taste the succulent bird and eagerly anticipated eating someone's cooking other than his own.

Unknown to Elan, John Winston was watching for Elan's arrival. He threw open the door when Elan failed to knock. The two men studied each other for several moments. "Merry Christmas, Elan," Winston finally greeted him warmly. "Let me help you with those." He took several of the packages and led the way to the large, fragrant spruce taking up one end of the room. Its branches were gaily decorated with bits of colored paper and pinecones hanging by red and green ribbons.

"Abby and Sally did the decorating," Winston explained. "Lori directed the placement of the ribbons and recommended the pinecones. Both girls wanted lighted candles, but Abby refused. She was afraid of fire."

"It is a beautiful tree," Elan said as he dumped the remainder of his burden and looked around. He was not familiar with the custom, but thought the decorated tree added much to the festive atmosphere. He grinned at Lori and Sally, who sat cross-legged on Lori's cot, but he failed to see Abby.

"Would you join me in my office for a few minutes?" Winston asked, leading the way. Elan followed, wondering what the man had on his mind.

When they were comfortably settled, Winston behind his oak desk, Elan in an overstuffed chair, Winston began. "I'd like to apologize for my behavior the last time we met." Elan lifted a brow and studied the rancher, who sat with his hands flat on the desktop and leaned slightly forward in his chair.

Elan waited impassively. It would be so much simpler to hate the man if he were not such a decent person. And Elan wanted very much to hate John Winston. He seemed determined to keep Abby with him at his ranch, and though Elan knew the man had nothing to do with his daughter's illness, he had accomplished much of his goal through it.

There was nothing to do but to accept Winston's apology. Anything less would compromise Elan's integrity. And truth to tell, Elan could not afford that. He was a man of principle, and he admitted, at least to himself, that where the rancher was concerned, he had at times done things he later regretted.

"I hope you can understand how a father suffers when he believes his child is in danger." Winston's fatherly concern touched Elan, for although he had no point of reference as far as children were concerned, he well remembered his blind anger whenever his father had been threatened. The alcoholism from which his father had suffered had torn at Elan's heart in much the same way Lori's illness must tear at Winston.

Winston paused, giving Elan time to consider his apology, and he visibly relaxed when he heard Elan's response. "I accept your apology and offer one of my own," Elan said quietly. "Words spoken in anger benefit no one." Winston stood and Elan followed suit, offering his hand to his host.

Winston and Elan were relaxing by the fire, enjoying Mrs. Johnson's hot spiced cider, when Abby rushed into the office. "Frank has arrived and he has Annie with him!" Abby exclaimed, her face flushed with excitement and her eyes dancing. "Oh! Elan!" she added breathlessly upon noticing him, "I didn't know you were here! Mrs. Johnson didn't say a word! Merry Christmas!"

Both men came to their feet instantly upon Abby's entrance. Elan caught his breath as he drank in the sight of Abby. She wore the dark green wool dress with the lace trim. Her hair, grown longer over the last several months, was pulled back from her face with a matching satin ribbon. Two rosy spots graced her high cheekbones, and her eyes fairly glowed. Elan thought he had never seen her so lovely.

"Merry Christmas, Abby," he said, longing to take her in his arms. He physically ached, his need was so great, and he silently cursed the fact that they weren't alone.

"Merry Christmas, Abby," Winston said, a lopsided grin spreading across his face. "I hope you like your Christmas present."

"You don't mean . . . ," Abby faltered, clasping her hands together, her eyes widening, resisting the impulse to dance around the room.

Winston nodded. "I've made arrangements to establish Annie in a shop of her own. She will soon be a respectable dressmaker. I've already commissioned dresses for you and Lori, and for Sally and Mrs. Johnson as well."

"Thank you, Mr. Winston," Abby breathed shakily, hardly able to contain her joy. "You won't regret it, I promise!" And with that, she was gone to find Annie and catch up on their visiting.

"Well, Elan," Winston said dryly as he set his cup on the desk. "Shall we find our way to the dining room? I suspect Abby was sent to fetch us now that my last guest has arrived."

"With pleasure," Elan replied, eager to sample the Christmas fare.

Dinner was a grand success. Even Lori ate heartily after insisting on being seated at the table. Now the two little girls were happily ensconced on Lori's cot enjoying their gifts. There had been dolls for them both as well as the fruit and candy Abby had requested. Elan had presented them each with carved animals that Abby thought showed remarkable skill. For Lori, there was a doe and her fawn. Sally's gift had been two bear cubs.

Annie sat with Abby on the horsehair sofa, timidly whispering to Abby as Elan and Winston made a great show of handing out gifts to the adults.

For Abby, Elan had brought a beautiful beaver muff. She caught his eye when he presented it, and held the muff to her face, enjoying the soft brush of the fur. He was so very handsome, she thought. Although he wore his usual buckskins, the red scarf she had knitted was thrown around his neck and offered a vivid contrast to his dark skin and black hair. He had shaved and looked decidedly more civilized than he had on the occasion of their last meeting. Her fingers itched to release his long hair from its leather tie and pull his mouth to hers.

As if reading her mind, Elan gave her a lazy grin, and

she recognized the unmistakable flicker of desire in his eyes. But as the evening progressed and they had no opportunity to be alone, they both realized it was not to be. At Winston's suggestion, he and Elan took themselves off to the bunkhouse for the night, leaving Abby and Annie to share Winston's room.

"This is the best Christmas I've ever had," Annie confessed as she and Abby piled into Winston's bed and burrowed beneath the covers. It had been decided that Mrs. Johnson and Sally would occupy Lori's bed and Lori would sleep on Abby's cot. Lori had held up well throughout the day, but Abby felt she still needed someone with her during the night. When Mrs. Johnson volunteered, Abby was quick to accept, wanting to spend some time alone with Annie.

"I can't remember a better one," Abby agreed. "Tell me about your shop. I want to hear all the details." She stretched, unkinking her joints, and folded her hands together across her chest.

"I still can't believe it," Annie said, squirming deeper under the quilt. "Mr. Winston made all the arrangements. He rented a section of the trading post the other day when he came to the settlement. Roberts was putting up a partition when Frank came to fetch me today." Annie turned her head to face Abby. "Do you think I can do it?"

"Of course you can!" Abby reached for Annie's hand and gave it a squeeze. "You're a wonderful seamstress."

"But what if the ladies don't come? Mr. Winston will be out a lot of money."

"Listen to me," Abby said firmly. "John Winston is the wealthiest man in this valley. If he's backing you, the ladies will come. It may take a while, but they will come."

"But I don't know if I can be respectable."

"What do you mean?" Abby sat up, propping herself on her elbows. "You know very well you can be respectable. You'll soon put your past behind you. You have Winston's patronage—nobody would dare insult you."

"That's not what I mean," Annie said miserably.

"What do you mean?" Abby asked. "Surely you don't mean you enjoyed what you were doing?"

"I did with John Winston," Annie admitted. Abby laughed, prompting a giggle from Annie.

"Has he been around again?" Abby asked. "I mean, does he expect you to continue your relationship with him?" She knew she was prying where she had no business, but her curiosity was killing her.

Annie nodded. "Yes."

"And?" Abby probed.

"I said no," Annie said.

"You didn't!" Abby gasped, her eyes widening.

"I told him if he wanted to make a lady out of me, then a lady I'd be." Annie sighed dramatically.

Abby burst into a fit of giggles and flopped back down on the bed. Annie was smarter than Abby had realized, and her admiration for the plucky young woman increased tenfold.

"What did he say to that?" Abby asked when she got herself under control. She would vouch it wasn't something pleasant, if she knew Winston as well as she thought she did.

"Something about wringing your neck," Annie admitted, frowning when Abby went into another fit of giggles.

"Stick to your guns, Annie. You'll soon have him where you want him!"

"But I want him in my bed," Annie said playfully.

Abby sobered. "That's where he'll be if you play it right. Don't you see, Annie? He cares about you. If he didn't, you wouldn't be here now. John Winston wants a respectable woman for his wife and Lori's mother. You can be that woman. I just know it!"

Long after she turned down the lamp, Abby lay awake listening to Annie's gentle breathing. She just hoped she was right in believing Winston really cared for Annie. Surely that care could be the foundation of love if Winston would allow it to be. Abby was somewhat confused about Winston's strange behavior toward her. She could only hope it was simply friendship that he had for her and not something more.

And the crisis with Lori's health appeared to be over. In another few weeks, Lori probably would be strong enough for Abby to feel comfortable returning to the cabin with Elan. She could still come twice a week for Lori's lessons, which had fallen by the wayside in light of her illness.

Abby thought of Annie's remarkable courage. Knowing how she desired Elan's strong arms around her, she realized what Annie must be going through. Annie surely desired Winston as much; yet she had taken her stand, determined to make Winston recognize the lady she could be.

And what of Elan? Soon Abby would return to the cabin with him. They had not had the opportunity to discuss further her idea of searching for the medicine bag. Would he take her to the Little Bighorn? Could they manage to change history and save Custer and his men? Would they be able to convince Custer to help them find the medicine bag?

The most burning question in her mind was: If they found the medicine bag, would Elan be willing to go to her time with her? As much as she hated to admit it, Abby had her own concerns about Elan in the 1990s. He seemed to have adapted fairly well to the 1870s, but if he advanced another hundred years or so he would be completely lost amid modern technology. Not that he wasn't intelligent enough to learn what would be required, but he was a man of the land, and in the late twentieth century land was scarce even in the sparsely populated state of Montana. More and more tourists arrived yearly. The state was rapidly becoming the new Mecca of the movie-star crowd, and the wealthy were buying up large chunks of land. No, Elan certainly would never be happy in such a place.

Could she be content to remain with him in this time? Was she willing to give up everything she'd ever known for him? And what was happening at her ranch, the ranch she had fought so hard to keep? Had the government already taken possession? If she could somehow manage to return to her own time, how could she explain her absence?

Abby plumped her pillow and rolled over on her side, conflicting emotions keeping her awake. She finally gave up on sleep and got out of bed to walk to the window, shivering in the cool night air. Faint moonlight allowed her a view of the bunkhouse. She could see lights through the shuttered windows and realized the men were still up. She wondered briefly what they were talking about before the cold drove her back to the refuge of the warm bed.

Annie mumbled something unintelligible in her sleep when Abby eased in beside her, eagerly seeking warmth. Abby drifted off to sleep and dreamed of home.

After breakfast the next morning, Winston excused himself to take Annie back to the settlement. Annie impulsively hugged Abby before their departure and whispered into her ear, "Thank you for being my friend." Abby returned her hug and stood beside Elan until Winston and Annie were out of sight.

"I must go also," Elan said, taking Abby by the hand and leading her back into the warmth of the house when he noticed her shivering. He was already dressed for his cold ride, wearing his bearskin coat and the red wool muffler around his neck. Abby reached inside the coat to wrap her arms around him. She rested her face against his chest, wishing she could go with him.

"I dreamed of home last night," Abby murmured.

Elan wrapped his arms around her, holding her close. "Was I there?" he asked. His chin rested on the top of her head. He felt her deep sigh and knew the answer.

"You could be there." Abby tilted her face and stuck her cold nose against the warmth of his neck. "We could both be there if we could find the medicine bag. It took you there once, and it could again."

Elan dipped his head, absently rubbing his face against Abby's smooth cheek. It was rough with stubble, for he had not shaved, but she didn't care. She moved closer, pressing herself to his hard body, molding herself to him.

"Your world is not the place for me." Elan's words were gentle but determined, and Abby realized with a sinking heart that he was right. "And my world is not the place for you," he continued.

"Would you go back to your world if you could?" Abby asked. It was something they had not discussed, and Abby suddenly realized she had selfishly taken it for granted Elan would either someday return with her to her time or would remain in the time in which they now found themselves. He had never expressed his feelings on the matter.

He considered her question seriously. Did he want to return to 1806? Could he return to his time and forget what he had seen in the future? And more important, could he go without Abby?

"Would you go if you could?" Abby persisted when Elan failed to reply. She was determined to have an answer. It was too important to let it go. What were his feelings about the future? Did he intend to keep her with him and make a life for them together, or was she just a convenience while she was around?

Elan chose his words carefully. "If you were not here with me, then it would not matter. Possibly I would want to return to my time. But in truth, it would be hard to go back when I know so much of the future."

His admission was what Abby longed to hear, but instead of comforting her, as she thought it would, it left her strangely unfulfilled. Elan had spoken directly and honestly, as she knew he would, and each word had come straight from his heart. But he had not told her he loved her. He moved his head slightly and softly touched her lips with his. His kiss was a caress, a gentle outpouring of his very soul.

Abby stretched on tiptoe, pressing herself along his entire length, accepting the gradual demands his lips made as she allowed him possession of her mouth. Her arms tightened around him while his fingers caressed her back. He drew away and left her aching for him as he quickly strode from the house. She watched him from the window until he was out of sight. Then she slowly made her way upstairs to Lori's room, her thoughts in turmoil.

There was no use worrying about it now, she decided. It would be June before she could even think about putting her plans into action. Maybe by then she and

Elan would have come to some agreement on their future, though for the life of her she couldn't imagine what it might be.

14

It was a sunny spring morning in late April when Abby, hearing the low bawling and the unmistakable sound of a herd on the move, threw open the door of the cabin to rush outside. She had been back at the cabin several months, visiting Winston's ranch only to give Lori lessons, and on most of those occasions Winston had been noticeably absent. From Mrs. Johnson's usually tight lips, and from Annie's charming loose ones, Abby had managed to elicit just enough information to hope Winston's absence from the ranch signaled his growing interest in Annie.

She pulled on her jacket as she ran through the dew-dampened grass, eagerly anticipating Elan's arrival. He had been gone better than a week helping with Winston's spring roundup. Over fifteen hundred head had been left in the valley for the drive to the Whoop-Up Trail, and what she saw now was the remainder of the herd being driven to the high country for summer grazing.

Winston sharply cut away from the herd and rode to meet Abby, pulling his big bay gelding to a halt just a yard short of her. He leapt to the ground, leaving the reins to trail as his horse took advantage of his departure to lower its head and graze in the waist-high grass. Winston swept his hat from his head, a broad grin splitting his face. "Would you like to select your herd, or would you prefer I do it for you?"

Abby laughed delightedly and looked around Winston's lanky frame to find Elan riding the roan gelding in their direction. When Winston had asked Elan to join the roundup, he had been quick to accept. Abby was surprised but pleased Elan had shown an interest in the cattle operation. Perhaps, just perhaps, Elan was coming around.

"Why don't we do it together?" Abby suggested as Elan rode up and dismounted.

Winston nodded. "We'll cut your herd, then return for the branding after I drive the rest up to the high country. There's still a lot of snow on the ground, but the grazing should be good. We're starting a little early this year, but then we've got a long drive ahead of us."

"Are you driving them all the way into Canada?" Abby asked. She shifted her eyes to Elan, resisting the urge to fling herself into his arms. He'd been gone too long!

"Not this trip," Winston replied, slapping his hat against his thigh and dislodging a good amount of dust. "I've made arrangements to meet Ford's herd. He'll take them on up. I'll be losing some money, but I don't want to be away from Lori any longer than I have to. As it is, I'll be gone three or four weeks."

Abby nodded, then strolled over to Elan, ostensibly to pet the roan but really to get closer to the man she had missed so much the last week. She brushed against him playfully, enjoying the hard feel of his muscular thigh almost as much as his grin at her boldness. "I'll look in on Lori every day, so you don't have to worry about her." Abby's words were directed to Winston, but Elan clearly had her attention.

"I'd appreciate it," Winston said with a quick nod as he settled his hat on his head and remounted his horse.

"Let me change clothes and I'll be right back." Abby hiked up her skirt and dashed back to the cabin. She would be much more comfortable astride a horse in her jeans, and she intended to make sure she picked the best of the shorthorn cattle. Not that she thought Winston would cheat her, but the very idea of picking the herd got her adrenaline flowing. She could hardly contain her excitement as she slammed the cabin door and began to strip off her ugly black dress.

In a matter of minutes she was on the roan cutting her herd. Elan had mounted one of Winston's horses, but his mind was not on the herd. He stuck close to Abby. She rode expertly, weaving the roan through the herd that numbered better than a thousand head. Most of the cattle were shorthorn, but interspersed among them were numerous longhorn cattle from a place called Texas. Elan was given to understand these cattle were the descendants of Spanish cattle brought up from Mexico.

Abby had explained that the shorthorn cattle were what she wanted. The railroads were drawing nearer, and it would be easier to ship the beef in the cattle cars if they did not have the long horns. Elan thought he would really like to see the rails and the train that traveled them. It was remarkable to think of a huge machine powered by steam that could travel long distances in a matter of hours or cross half the continent in a few days.

"Watch it! Watch it!" Abby cried, turning the roan

and cutting around a bellowing cow who lowered her
head and solidly planted all four feet when Winston tried
to separate her from the herd. "She thinks you're trying
to take her calf!" Abby used her horse to clear a path and
the calf was soon reunited with its reticent mother.

"You're taking all my best beef!" Winston teased,
bringing his bay alongside Abby's mount.

Abby laughed delightedly and made for a heifer.
"Remember," she called over her shoulder, "the calves
don't count!"

Winston groaned and shook his head. "She meant it
when she said she drove a hard bargain," he complained
good-naturedly. His remark was directed to Elan, who
acknowledged it with a grunt before he urged his horse
deeper into the herd. He was not sure he liked Abby darting in and out of the cattle, seemingly without any
thought of danger. He still did not believe it was any
place for a woman, no matter how comfortable Abby
seemed.

"The woman is stubborn," Elan muttered to himself as
he tried to maneuver near her. The other hands, Frank
included, appeared to be watching Abby work instead of
keeping their minds on the milling herd, and Elan was
concerned by their lack of attention.

Later, when he had time to think about it, Elan still
was unable to understand exactly what happened. One
minute Abby was in complete control; the next the herd
was on the move, taking the roan and Abby with it as it
pounded across the open meadow. He lost her in the
thundering sea of dust, feeling panic cinch his gut and
sweat pop out on his brow as he searched frantically
while desperately fighting to keep his seat as his mount
tore out at breakneck speed.

Abby screamed when her horse reared and came

down on all fours, ears flattened, eyes rolling. The roan was carried with the herd, and all Abby could do was hang on for dear life. She lay low in the saddle, unable to see a path in the choking dust. The roan stumbled, and Abby realized she was falling. Then she was gripped around the waist by a strong arm. She forced herself to release her death grip on the gelding's mane in order to reach and lock her arms around Winston's waist.

Winston held her under her arms, half dragging her as they both struggled to get her mounted behind him as his big bay raced with the herd. Abby unsuccessfully attempted to get her leg over the bay's sweaty flank, feeling as if she was being beaten to death, caught between the horse and the pressing cattle.

"Hang on!" Winston shouted above the din, a command that was unnecessary as Abby clung tightly to his leather belt. She began to slip from Winston's grip and screamed louder, hardly realizing that the terrified sound came from her own lips. She was going to be killed, trampled under the merciless hooves. A sharp horn grazed her thigh, and she realized something wet and sticky was running down her leg.

"Don't drop me!" Abby screamed, tightening her hold. Her frantic plea seemed to give new strength to Winston, who tightened his grip also and hoisted her a little higher. "Please don't drop me!"

"We're almost out!" Winston yelled. Abby buried her face in his shirt and squeezed her eyes shut, knowing that any second she was going to find herself beneath the churning cattle. She didn't want to die! Dear God, she didn't want to die!

"Abby!" Elan's voice penetrated her terror just as she felt his arm encircle her waist in an iron grip. Winston released her and she was hauled across Elan's horse, painfully raking her ribs across the pommel. She opened her eyes and discovered Elan had them clear of the herd, though they still raced along with it.

By the time Winston and Elan reined in their horses, Abby had recovered some of her rattled senses. She was shaking uncontrollably, and her jaw was clenched so tightly it hurt, but she thought she was all right. She chanced a look at Elan's face and found it white beneath the sweaty grime. His eyes were like burning coals, and she unconsciously shrank beneath his furious glare.

Abby swallowed painfully past the choking lump in her throat. "I'm . . . okay," she said shakily as she struggled to sit up. Elan abruptly released her, almost tossing her off his saddle. She slid weakly to the ground, collapsing when pain shot up her thigh and her leg failed to hold her.

"You're hurt!" Elan's words were harsh as he quickly dismounted and dropped to one knee to flip her unceremoniously over on her stomach and examine the back of her leg.

"You act as if it's my fault," Abby wailed, giving in to the searing pain she had forgotten during her nightmarish ride through the stampeding herd. "Ouch!" she screamed when his fingers found the wound. "You're hurting me!"

"It *is* your fault," Elan was quick to point out. "You had no business trying to do the job of a man. It will not happen again!" Abby pushed herself up on her elbows and craned her neck to glare at him. If he thought a little scratch on her leg would keep her from her herd, he was sadly mistaken!

"You've been gored." Abby glanced up at the sound of Winston's grim voice and found him hovering over her, worriedly frowning. She'd all but forgotten him. He held his hat in his hand and swiped his shirt sleeve across his grimy face. Abby blushed hotly, realizing that she owed him her life, and also that she had dismissed him completely as soon as Elan got his hands on her.

"Thank you for rescuing me," Abby said to Winston. "I don't know what happened."

She winced as Elan's fingers probed her wound. "Ouch! I'm not one of those damn animals you love to skin, you know." Then she felt the cool blade of Elan's knife slide up her leg as he slit her jeans. "You're ruining my jeans!"

"How bad is it?" Winston asked, squatting down for a better look and nervously fingering his mustache. Abby clenched her hands together and bit her lip to keep from crying out again. She was really hurting, and she was suddenly scared. What if the wound got infected? She could die of an infection, since antibiotics hadn't been invented yet. God, what a horrible thought!

"Bad enough," Elan said soberly, sitting back on his haunches. "I have to get her to the cabin and sew it up." The wound, though not as deep as he had first feared, was a good six inches across the back of Abby's right thigh, and it was bleeding profusely. Elan used the material he cut from Abby's trousers to bind the gash. Working quickly, he was finished before Abby could put up too much of a fuss.

Abby buried her face in her hands, unable to stop shivering. Had Elan said he intended to sew up her leg? She was sure he had. The very idea made her sick to her stomach. Surely he didn't mean it. She fought down the bile that burned her throat, and drew a ragged breath. She hurt like hell.

"Do you need some help?" Winston asked. Abby moaned and clenched her hands tighter. The damn herd hadn't killed her, but the thought of Elan's doctoring was about to. And she had no more faith in Winston.

Abby heard Elan's low sigh and braced herself. "What about the herd?" Elan asked.

"To hell with the herd," Winston replied, dropping his hand to Elan's shoulder and giving him a reassuring squeeze. "Let's do it."

Abby rested on the bed, face down, her head buried in the pillow, her hands over her ears as she tried to shut out Winston's and Elan's discussion about how best to tend her leg. She hurt like unmitigated hell, and their conversation did nothing to relieve her anxiety. If anything, it made it much worse.

The ride to the cabin had been horrible. Elan had unsympathetically thrown her over his saddle like a sack of potatoes, making all her blood rush to her head. She had felt each bone-jarring step the horse made on the mile-long journey, which had seemed never-ending. But his hands had been gentle when he got her inside and undressed her. She lay now covered only by a sheet, and she had to admit he was probably doing the best he knew how.

Though she dreaded the idea of Elan taking her needle and thread to sew up her wound, he couldn't possibly do any worse than the quack she'd found tending Lori. At any rate, the doctor was too far away. She didn't think she could stand the ride over the mountains to Helena, and her leg would probably rot off before he could be found to come tend her.

"Here, Abby, drink this." She looked up to find Elan by her bedside, the whiskey bottle in one hand, a cup in the other. She wanted to cry. His voice was kind, but his face looked grave.

"Oh, God," she moaned. "It's going to be bad, isn't it?" She wasn't good with pain; in fact, she was sure she was allergic to it. What she wouldn't give for a shot of morphine!

Elan poured a generous amount of the amber liquid into the cup and squatted down without answering. He held it to her lips. She gasped when the fiery liquor burned a path down her throat and hit her queasy stomach. She pushed the cup away.

"You need to drink it all, Abby." Elan was insistent. She shook her head. Elan hesitated, then thrust the cup back to her lips.

"I can't," Abby protested weakly. "I'll throw up if you make me."

"I will hold you and pour it down your throat if I have to," Elan replied. Abby glared at him. His face looked as if it had been carved from stone. He'd do it. She knew he would. She opened her mouth and gulped the whiskey down, choking back tears. She'd be damned if she'd be a baby about it!

Elan stood and pulled the sheet from around her injured leg. She felt him cut away the bandage, then felt the warm water as he tenderly washed her upper thigh.

"What do you want me to do?" It was Winston's voice. Abby recognized the distinctive thud of his boots and jingling spurs as he made his way across the cabin. Then she heard the scrape of a chair being dragged up to the bed. She peeped over her shoulder to see Elan ease himself down. Winston held a basin that Abby realized contained the instruments of her impending torture.

"Give me the basin and hold Abby," Elan directed, taking the basin from Winston and setting it on another chair. Abby tensed, understanding what she was in for.

"Abby?" Elan said softly. She lifted her eyes to his

face. "This is going to hurt, but you must be sure to keep still."

"No kidding," she muttered, locking her teeth and dropping her head to her pillow. She felt Winston's hands on her, felt the pressure of his knee on her uninjured leg. She would have laughed if she hadn't hurt so badly. Winston was taking no chances on her kicking him senseless.

At Winston's direction, Elan poured some of the whiskey over the threaded needle he had placed in the basin. Then he poured a generous amount over Abby's wound. She screamed, jerking her leg reflexively. Elan steeled himself for what was to come.

He picked up the needle and took a steadying breath. He met Winston's eyes briefly, saw his own naked pain mirrored there, and quickly dropped his gaze to Abby's leg, realizing what he was about to do would be the hardest thing he had ever done in his life. He would sooner cut off his right arm than hurt Abby, yet there was nothing else he could do.

Elan worked quickly, plying the needle, shutting his ears to Abby's low, whimpering moans. She was wet with perspiration and trembling all over with the effort to keep still by the time he made the last stitch and tied off the thread. Elan looked up as Winston released Abby and shakily got to his feet. The man was as pale as she was, and Elan wondered for a moment if Winston was going to faint. Instead the rancher turned on his heel and almost raced from the cabin.

"It is done, Abby," Elan said as he bound her thigh with clean linen. "Rest now." He moved to wipe her face with a damp cloth, and dabbed at the blood trickling from her lip where she had bitten it through. Her eyes fluttered as she tried to focus on his face, but she was too tired to speak. She did find the strength to reach up and touch his drawn face. He cupped her hand, drawing it to his mouth and kissing her palm lightly before releasing it and placing it carefully on the pillow beside her head. She closed her eyes, wanting only to sleep.

When Elan pulled the quilt over her, Abby wondered vaguely why she hadn't passed out. The pain had been nearly unbearable, yet she had remained awake for each searing jab of the needle. In all the books she had read, people passed out at the least little pang. It wasn't fair, she decided miserably as she drifted into sleep. It wasn't fair at all.

It was well past midnight when Abby awoke. She was so cold that her teeth were chattering. She must have made some sound, for when she opened her eyes, she found Elan standing over her and holding up the lamp. "I'm cold," Abby complained, shifting beneath the heavy covers, involuntarily crying out as pain shot through her leg. "I need another quilt."

Elan set the lantern on a chest by the bed, then squatted down. He put his hand to her forehead. She was warm, but not burning up, as he had feared. "All the quilts are on the bed, Abby," he said. "Are you thirsty?"

"Yes." Her tongue was thick in her mouth, and she swallowed with difficulty. Elan got her a cup of water and held it to her dry lips, wiping her mouth with the edge of the sheet when some of the water trickled down her chin. She drank greedily. The cool water tasted good even though it sent her into another shivering fit. He made her take a sip of the whiskey, and she welcomed its warmth.

Elan hastily removed his buckskins and moccasins and climbed into bed with Abby. He gathered her into his arms, determined to give her some of his warmth. He carefully pulled her along his length, cupping around her spoon fashion, avoiding the bulk of the bandage on her wound.

Abby gratefully accepted Elan's warmth, allowing him to fold her within his arms. The thatch of thick black hair on his chest was like a warm, scratchy rug against her back, and she imagined he was wrapping her in a furry cocoon as he draped his arm around her and she allowed him to draw her against his hairy body and legs.

"This is nice," Abby murmured as warmth stole over her. She reached up to entwine her fingers in his and felt his comforting squeeze. "If I didn't feel so rotten, I'd let you in my pants."

Elan grinned, relieved she felt well enough to tease. "What pants?" he asked innocently, moving his hand down the curve of her bare hip, then back up past her waist to her ribs and then her breast.

"You'd better stop that. I'm not sure I'm up to it," Abby said as she placed her hand atop his and rubbed his knuckles with her thumb.

"I only want to hold you, Abby," Elan said. "I came close to losing you today. I will not take that chance again. You are to stay away from the cattle." He felt Abby stiffen, and he readied himself for the argument that was sure to follow. He had told Winston to take all the cattle with him up to the high country, but had relented when Winston insisted on cutting out Abby's herd and leaving it in the meadow. Winston was not willing to face Abby's wrath if he did otherwise, and when Elan calmed down enough to think about it, neither was he.

"You know how much that herd means to me," Abby said. "I'm sorry you don't like it, but that's just the way it is. It's not open for negotiation."

"I had not thought to parley with you, Abby," Elan replied seriously. "You will not go near the herd again, and that is my final word."

"It's my herd. I worked for it, and I intend to do what I think is necessary to build this ranch," Abby said stubbornly.

"You confuse me, Abby," Elan muttered, his lips brushing her neck.

"How?" she asked as another shiver shook her, this one having nothing to do with her fever.

"I do not understand why you insist on having the herd when you also insist on going to the Little Bighorn in the summer to look for the medicine bag. It makes no sense to me. If you plan to return to your own time, why bother with the herd?"

"What if we can't find the medicine bag?" Abby asked impatiently. "Don't you see? If I can't find the medicine bag and go back to my time, then at least I have to build the ranch. It's the future for my family."

Elan seized the opening she provided. It might just be possible to convince her to stay with him in this time. "If you return to your time, what will happen to the ranch, Abby? Who will build it for you?"

Abby thought for a minute. "Somebody did, obviously," she said. "How should I know?" His question worried her, posing a problem she hadn't considered. When *did* her great-great-grandparents come on the scene? All the family records showed the original homestead claim was filed in 1875. It was now 1876. Where were they? And if they did suddenly come along, what in the world would she do?

"But who?" Elan wondered aloud. "I know nothing about ranching, and I am not sure I want to know."

"God help us," Abby muttered. Elan was right. He

didn't know a damn thing about ranching. Perhaps Winston would take pity on Elan and take him under his wing if she had to leave without him.

Why was he being so obstinate? Couldn't he see that ranching was the future? Unless somehow he returned to his own time, he would have to learn cattle. Either that or work for wages for some other person, and he was too much his own man to do that for long. His trapping wouldn't last forever. Suddenly the thought of leaving Elan behind made her want to cry. Was she falling in love with the big lummox? She thought she'd been in love with Paul, and look where that had gotten her. But Elan wasn't Paul. He didn't slink off with his tail between his legs when she dug in with both heels. Not Elan. He just dug in right along with her.

Elan nibbled Abby's earlobe, and she cast aside all thoughts save those of the muscular body pressed to her bare skin. "Abby?"

"Mmmm?" Her heartbeat increased drastically when his hand slipped over her leg, and she forgot to breathe when his fingers began a gentle exploration. He was hard, insistent, against her bare bottom.

"I want you." Abby lifted her head to look over her shoulder, to look into his heavy-lidded eyes. His simple statement sent her blood surging, and she turned carefully in his arms, her hand seeking and finding the firm evidence of his need.

Elan sucked in his breath sharply when she touched him with her hand. She drew back her head to look at his face. "What do you want?" she teased, wanting to hear him say it again. "Tell me."

"I want this," Elan groaned, tightening his embrace. Her hand and lips grazed his chest, exploring the hard contours of his body. "Stop, woman," he rasped, folding her hand in his and lacing his fingers through hers. He dipped his head to trace her mouth, to slowly draw her bruised lip between his teeth, then to trace her small, even teeth before thrusting deeply with his tongue. She returned his kiss, pressing herself eagerly to him, making soft whimpering sounds.

"I will not hurt you, Abby," Elan promised, lowering his head to nuzzle between her breasts as his hand lifted her leg. They lay facing each other with Abby's wounded leg thrown over Elan. He positioned himself and pressed for entry, his hand cupping her bottom and pulling her to him.

"Ohhhh!" Abby gasped, releasing a shuddering breath, her nails digging into Elan's upper arm. Elan froze, then moved to release her.

"No!" she cried, tightening her hold. "Don't you dare stop now!" She didn't think she could bear it if he stopped. She moved against him, ignoring the throbbing pain in her leg. She was going to hurt no matter what she did, and what Elan was doing to her was decidedly better than suffering alone.

"I do not want to hurt you, Abby." Elan touched his lips to her closed eyes and cupped her face in his hand, his thumb stroking her chin.

Abby opened her eyes, overcome by the tenderness in his voice. "Make love to me, Elan," she begged softly, tangling her fingers in his hair and pulling his head down until he rested his scratchy cheek on her smooth one. "You won't hurt me."

He moved against her, slowly, carefully, building the cadence, until she thought she'd scream from the sheer pleasure of his rock-hard thighs slamming into her, until she begged him to fill her completely, until he took her with him in one final soul-shattering thrust.

They lay locked together, panting and sweaty, and together they drifted into sleep, content to be in each other's arms, to shut out the world and sleep in a lovers' embrace without thought of anything or anyone but the pure joy of the other's touch.

15

"I'm still so mad I could scream!" Abby said, dabbing her mouth with the blue-checked linen napkin she pulled from the picnic basket. She flopped down on the quilt with an exasperated sigh. Annie straightened a corner of the quilt and sprawled out beside her in the shade of the stand of quaking aspen. Abby had sent Lori and Sally back to the house for a nap after they'd all gorged themselves on Mrs. Johnson's fried chicken and fluffy buttermilk biscuits lathered with freshly churned butter. Abby still insisted that Lori nap every afternoon. The girl was steadily improving, but Abby feared she'd never regain her full strength.

"Elan only did what he thought was best, Abby," Annie said, seeking to mollify her nettled friend. "And wouldn't you rather be here with Lori than stuck all by yourself in the cabin? I know I would. I'd be scared to death to stay by myself up there for even one night, much less several weeks."

"It's just his way of making sure I don't go near my herd," Abby said. "He had no right to haul me over here against my wishes. He wouldn't even let me stay for the branding, and I'm not to return to the cabin until he gets back. I could cheerfully strangle him!"

"Now, Abby," Annie said reasonably as she reached to pat Abby's hand. "He's your husband, and it's your duty to obey him. Besides, I'm glad you're here so we can visit."

"My duty!" Abby cried. "What's wrong with you, Annie?" Abby pushed herself up on one elbow to study her friend's serene face. "You've been mistreated by men for so many years and now you have the gall to tell me to obey! I don't believe you!" Annie tightened her lips and stared at the fluffy clouds drifting across the big blue sky. Abby poked her in the ribs. "Look at me and tell me you really believe that nonsense!"

"I do," Annie said, cocking her head to look at Abby's flushed face. "You're safer here than you would be by yourself in the cabin, and Elan knows it even if you won't admit it."

"*Et tu, Brute*," Abby muttered, dropping back down on the quilt. She did enjoy giving Lori lessons, and now included Sally in the sessions. It was better than staying by herself, but she worried about her herd. Of course, there wasn't much she could do. The cattle would range all over, and would have to take their chances with wild animals, but she would certainly feel better if she weren't so far away. Several of her cows were ready to calve, if they hadn't already. She not only wanted to be home, she needed to be there!

"What did you say?" Annie inquired sleepily, stifling a yawn.

"Nothing, just forget it." It wasn't so much that she minded being at Winston's ranch. It was that Elan had made the decision to join Winston's drive and dump her at the ranch without consulting her. It was bad enough that he had commandeered the roan for the trip, but even worse was his insistence that she stay at the ranch until his return. He had made no such demands when he worked the spring roundup.

Of course, Abby knew she shouldn't be riding until her leg healed completely, and she also knew it wasn't really wise for her to be at the cabin for several weeks alone, but what chafed her was Elan's brazenness in making no effort to consider her wishes. Since her accident when the herd stampeded, he had treated her as if she didn't have an ounce of common sense, and had steadfastly refused to allow her near anything on four hooves. When he returned, he would have his hands full. That was for damn sure!

"Annie?" Abby asked. "Are you asleep?"

"Yes," Annie drowsily replied.

"Oh, for heaven's sake, Annie," Abby complained. "I thought we were having a conversation."

"All right," Annie said, rubbing her eyes and sitting up. "What is it?"

"Don't you think women should have the right to do as they please? I mean, what makes men think they're superior?" Abby demanded.

Annie rolled her eyes and reached to secure a loose hairpin. "I don't know, but it probably has something to do with the way they see themselves, or at least the way they want other men to see them."

Abby sat up and smoothed her dress. "I'm not sure I understand what you're getting at."

"Well . . ." Annie paused, frowning thoughtfully. "When I worked in the saloon, sometimes the men who acted the meanest around the other men were the ones who treated me the best when we were alone. It's an act, I think. They have to swagger around and act tough, because if they didn't, the other men wouldn't respect them."

"What about John Winston?" Abby asked. "Did he act that way?"

"No." Annie paused reflectively. "He wasn't mean, but the other men sure do respect him. Mr. Winston just acts real sure of himself. I think that has a lot to do with it, too."

Abby nodded. "It's the male ego thing. That's exactly how Elan acts. They all swagger around and scratch and spit. It's almost like dogs marking their territory."

"I don't know what a male ego is," Annie replied with a giggle, "but I do know that men like to think women are helpless. It makes a man feel good to be able to take care of a woman."

"What about you? Do you like being taken care of?" Abby asked.

"I like having my shop and making money in a respectable way. It's a lot better than being pawed by any miner or cowboy who has two bits to spend, and if that's what you call being taken care of, then yes, I like it very much." Annie lifted her wobbling chin and took a deep breath.

"Oh, Annie!" Abby hastened to make amends. "I'm sorry! I didn't mean to hurt your feelings. Please forgive me!" Annie gave a watery sniff and nodded. "It's just that I find it hard to accept any man telling me what to do," Abby went on. "And I hate being helpless!"

"Does Elan beat you when you disobey him?" Annie asked.

"Heavens, no!" Abby exclaimed, horrified at the very thought. "Whatever gave you such an idea?"

"I thought he was going to beat me once," Annie admitted, meeting Abby's wide eyes. "I don't ever want him mad at me again."

"Oh, God, Annie, when?" Abby's heart went into double time, and her mouth was suddenly bone dry. She wasn't sure she wanted to hear, but she was even more sure she had to find out what Annie was talking about. Elan and Annie? She felt sick.

"It was the night before Mr. Winston's party last October," Annie said quietly. "He came pounding on my door like a wild man. He was looking for you."

"He wasn't looking for me," Abby said. So that was how he had found out she'd been with Annie. But then, what the hell had he been doing there in the first place? The answer was all too obvious. It was the night she had told him she wasn't a virgin. He'd left her bed and ridden off into the night. Now she knew where.

Annie lowered her eyes and plucked at her dress, a blush staining her cheeks. "He was only there a few minutes, I swear. We didn't do anything. He left as soon as I told you weren't there. I thought he was going to hit me, but he didn't. That's why I thought he might have beaten you. I've never seen any man so mad."

"He might have wanted to," Abby said lightly, in an effort to dispel the gloominess of the conversation, "but he didn't. At any rate, now I know how he found out I was visiting you."

"I'm sorry," Annie said miserably.

Abby patted her hand. "Honey, it's not your fault. I don't blame you. Things weren't going so well with us then. I'm really not surprised Elan was knocking on your door."

Annie looked up. "He never came back."

"That's a relief!" Abby said with a chuckle. "Now let's pack up our picnic and find a deck of cards. I feel lucky today."

"What about the fitting?" Annie asked. "That's why I came out. Remember?"

"Okay," Abby agreed. "We'll do the fitting and then we'll play." Annie was making Abby a split-skirt riding habit and had come for the final fitting. Elan would probably turn inside out when he saw it, but Abby didn't care. He'd live to get over it. She would always believe he had deliberately destroyed her jeans, even though of course her leg injury had warranted it. But she knew he had hated to see her wear them because they revealed to others what he wanted only himself to be able to see.

"Riders coming," Elan said, pulling his roan mount up beside Winston's big bay and half turning in his saddle. Each man led a pack horse. They were making good time and were a couple of days at the most from the ranch. Elan was ready for the trip to end. He missed Abby, and knew if he stayed away too long, there was no telling what she might do. He had the uneasy feeling she would set out for the cabin in spite of his demands that she stay at Winston's ranch. She could be stubborn when he crossed her.

Winston had received a good price for his herd and had managed to sell most of his string of horses to Ford. Only Frank and one other hand were returning with them to the ranch, and they had been left far behind with the chuck wagon and the remaining horses. Ford had been quick to hire Winston's spare hands for the long drive north. Some of the men would return for the fall roundup, and Winston could easily replace those who did not.

"Anybody you recognize?" Winston asked, lifting his hat and running his fingers through his hair before replacing it.

The two riders were coming fast, churning dust in their wake through the tall grass.

"No," Elan replied as the riders neared. Winston dug in his pocket and removed a cheroot, which he put to his mouth. He took his time lighting it. He seemed unaffected by the appearance of the strangers, but Elan noticed Winston drop his right hand to rest it on one of his pistols. Elan moved his own hand to his waist and loosened his hatchet. He wished suddenly for his long rifle, but Abby had long ago warned him that the rifle was out of place in the time they were in. He had left it wrapped in a deer hide behind the trunks, along with some implements stored in the shed.

Winston was carrying a wad of money in his saddlebags, and anyone aware of the purpose of their trip would know that. Elan scanned the terrain. They were in the open, with no cover available in the undulating sea of grass surrounding them.

The riders slowed as they neared and stopped a few yards away. Both were young, not much older than twenty. They were dressed in drover's garb, complete with long coats and slouch hats. Their colorful shirts were grimy, their boots scuffed and worn.

"Afternoon, gentlemen. Mind if me and my partner ride along?" The high-pitched voice seemed out of place coming from the overweight round-faced saddle tramp. His tiny brown eyes, lost amid folds of fat, darted from Winston to Elan, who tilted his head at Winston and awaited his lead. The speaker's companion, lean and lank with pimply skin and a scar that began at the corner of his left eye and disappeared into his greasy blond hair, said nothing.

"Where you boys headed?" Winston asked conversationally.

"The Blackfoot Valley," the rider replied. "Me and Pete was planning to hire on with some outfit. I'm Harry

Petty, and this here's Pete Turner." Pete grinned, revealing a row of blackened teeth.

"We hadn't planned on company," Winston said. "Don't know of anyone hiring this time of year. You boys are too late for the roundup."

"Don't we know it!" Petty slapped his leg. "That's us, all right! Always a day late and a dollar short, yes, sir!"

Winston clenched his cheroot between his teeth. "I'd say your best bet would be to strike out for Helena and see if you can pick up a drive headed for Wyoming. Pickings are gonna be slim in the valley until the fall roundup."

Petty smiled crookedly, a mirthless slash that failed to reach his shifting eyes, which strayed from Winston to Elan. "We'll just do that." Elan and Winston watched the duo until they were out of sight. Petty paused once to look over his shoulder for a long moment before spurring his mount into a gallop.

Winston turned his bay, putting his back to the riders. "I don't like the looks of those two," he commented as he and Elan resumed their interrupted journey.

"They will be back," Elan said. "During the night, I'd guess."

"I think you're right, my friend," Winston agreed, squinting into the setting sun. "We'd better find a good place with plenty of cover to camp."

"The vest is too loose under the arms," Abby complained, twisting to look in the full-length mirror. "And I want the skirt shorter." She hiked the split skirt up to the tops of her boots. "This is where it needs to be." The skirt fell about three inches below her knees.

Annie stepped back and eyed her critically. "You're determined to make him pay, aren't you?"

"Why, Annie." Abby feigned innocence. "Whatever do you mean?"

Annie snorted. "You know very well what I mean. Elan will have apoplexy when he sees the length of your skirt. It's not ladylike, Abby."

"I don't care. This is where I want it," Abby said petulantly. "He can like it or not." She'd done all the compromising she intended to do by way of fashion. She'd allowed Annie to make her the accustomed undergarments of the day, but she positively hated the long drawers that tied at the waist and covered her to her knees, and the chemise, though prettily laced with pink ribbon, was even worse than a damn bra.

She'd drawn the line at a corset, refusing to wear one under any circumstances. As it was, she felt as if she'd suffocate. She pulled the skirt up higher and regarded the thick cotton stockings. They were mud-turkey ugly, she decided as she dropped her skirt. What she wouldn't give for a pair of Hanes and some silk panties! If dressing in all these layers was what it took to be a lady, then she'd just as soon pass, thank you very much!

Anyway, she didn't know why Elan had to be such a stickler when it came to her clothing. *He* didn't even wear underclothes. She suppressed a giggle as she thought of how he'd look in a pair of red wool long johns.

Annie knelt and began to pin the new hem. "Be still, Abby. It'll be lopsided if you keep fidgeting," she muttered, tugging impatiently at the blue twilled fabric. "I swear, sometimes I wonder about you!"

"Wonder what?" Abby asked distractedly, admiring the tiny rose Annie had embroidered on the lapel of the vest. Annie certainly had a way with a needle.

"Turn around and let me pin the other leg," Annie instructed. Abby did as she asked.

"Wonder what?" Abby repeated, looking over her shoulder, but seeing only the top of Annie's bent head. Annie finished pinning and stood.

"I wonder why you deliberately try to provoke Elan." She pulled at the vest. "Hold out your arms and I'll pin it."

Abby held out her arms. "I don't try to provoke Elan," she said. "It's just that we don't always agree, that's all. Besides, I've been thinking. . . ."

Annie groaned. "I don't think I'm going to like this," she said, stepping back and surveying her alterations. "You can take it off now. I'll take it back to the shop and have it ready in a day or two."

"Why don't you run me up to the cabin before you go back?" Abby asked, removing the vest and folding it before handing it to Annie. She unbuttoned the split skirt and stepped out of it. Annie took it and draped it over her arm, then reached for the blouse Abby unbuttoned and removed.

"I knew I wasn't going to like it," Annie said, tossing the clothing across the small cot and holding out Abby's black dress.

"As long as you've got the buggy anyway?" Abby cajoled. Roberts had taken to lending Annie his buggy whenever she wanted to visit the ranch. Abby figured Winston had something to do with the trader's generosity, but she didn't question it. She pulled the dress over her head and struggled into the long sleeves. "I really do want to go home," she persisted, buttoning the bodice. "Elan should be back in a few days. I'll be fine."

"I'm probably going to regret this," Annie said skeptically, planting her hands on her hips. "If Elan hasn't beaten you, he probably will now."

"I can handle Elan!" Abby said, giving her a fierce hug. "You won't be sorry, I promise!" She hastened to gather her things, not wanting to give Annie a chance to change her mind. She would deal with Elan. After all, what could he do? He would see that she was fine, perfectly capable of taking care of herself. She hummed a little tune as she gathered her things.

Elan sprawled with his back against the rocky outcrop that towered over his head, taking the first watch. He huddled within his bearskin coat, a welcome wrap in the brisk night air. A cup of coffee would have been good to wash down the cold canned beans he and Winston had eaten for supper, but Elan knew as well as Winston that a campfire would only make them better targets.

Winston slept, rolled in a blanket in the fireless camp they had pitched near the Blackfoot River. The quarter moon, when it wasn't hidden behind the clouds, provided fleeting light. Elan fingered one of Winston's pistols and wished again he had his long rifle. Winston cradled the other pistol beneath the blanket.

The night was still, the only sounds the quiet rustle of a slight breeze through the willows and the distant burble of the racing waters across the rocks, but Elan listened intently, knowingly. He gnawed a piece of jerky, chewing thoughtfully.

He was eager to see Abby, and could only hope she was over the fit she had thrown when he left. At least he did not have to worry about her. She was safe at Winston's ranch.

It had been almost a full year since the Indians had been at the cabin, but he still had an unsettled feeling about them. He and Winston had seen Indian signs on the trail, and Winston had speculated that a small band had left the reservation for a spring hunt. Winston had seemed unconcerned about it, but Elan could not put it out of his mind.

He was probably worrying for nothing. They were miles from the cabin, and who was to say it was the same Indians who had issued the warning so long ago? He thought back to that fateful day. How different his life would be if he had never found the old Indian with the medicine bag. But then, he would never have found Abby either, and he could not now imagine a life without her.

Would she continue to insist on going to the Little Bighorn in the summer to search for the medicine bag? He had told her he did not want to live in her time, and yet she still seemed determined to make the trip. Did she not feel for him as he did for her? Could she return to her time, if she had the opportunity to do so, and forget the year they had spent together?

Her feelings for him must run deep, otherwise she would not make love with him as she did. He thought of Abby's small hands on him, her sweet mouth, and the smoothness of her skin when she rubbed wantonly against him. Only sporting women did those things with men they did not love. But then, she had been with another man. She had told him so. He pushed the thought from his mind, for in truth, he did not like to think of it.

Abby stood in her chemise and drawers and warmed herself by the stove, holding out her hands to catch the heat. Annie had been unable to stay when she dropped her off at the cabin and had made a quick departure. Annie wanted to be back in the settlement before dark, and Abby hoped she had made it. Damn, a telephone would be nice, so she could call Annie to make sure she was safe. That was one of the things she missed most of all.

She had never realized how much she relied on the phone until she found herself without one.

Abby eyed the kettle of water she had put on to boil and had to admit that hot showers were another thing she definitely missed. It was damned inconvenient to haul water to bathe, and she had to be content with what her grandmother had called a "spit bath" when she was too lazy to get water from the creek, and that was most of the time. Elan handled that chore when he was home.

Abby used a kitchen towel to lift the kettle and pour the steaming water into a basin already half filled with cold creek water. She picked up the bar of soap and a washcloth and set to work. It would be nice to feel clean when she slept. A wolf howled somewhere near the cabin, and Abby jumped, sloshing the water over the edge of the basin onto the floor. She put down her soap and washcloth to check the door latch, then laughed at herself. She didn't really think the wolf would come knocking at the door!

The only wolf she had to worry about was Elan. She shivered deliciously, thinking of his tender lovemaking. She missed him so much she ached. Then she remembered that she had gone against his wishes, and she wondered about Annie's remark. Elan would certainly be angry, but he wouldn't dare beat her. No. He would never do that. The anguish on his face when he had sewn up her leg told her, more than words ever could, how he felt about causing her pain.

Abby pulled off her drawers and craned her neck to see the ugly scar on the back of her leg. She traced it with a fingertip. It might fade in time, but it would never disappear. Elan's skill as a plastic surgeon left much to be desired!

*   *   *

A faint rustle beyond the picket line where the horses were tied drew Elan's attention. One of the horses snorted and moved restlessly. Elan tossed aside the jerky. When the fight came, it would be good to have Winston by his side.

Elan's respect for Winston had grown considerably over the months he had known the rancher. Elan no longer distrusted him as he once had. It was obvious that Winston's interest lay strictly with Annie. And although Elan disliked the thought of Winston's friendship with Abby, he could understand it. Abby was the type of woman no man could ignore.

Five minutes passed, then ten. Elan waited patiently, noting Winston's tensed posture, his changed breathing. He forced himself to remain still, to breathe evenly. Elan had killed men, but it was never something he enjoyed. It always left him with a sense of sadness, a sense of loss. There should be a better way for a man to settle his differences. Tonight he and Winston were going to have to kill the two men they had met on the trail or be killed themselves. Elan wished that it were not so, but the men had made the choice for him.

Instead of taking Winston's advice, Petty and Turner had doubled back and followed Elan and Winston. Even if Elan had not caught a brief glimpse of them on a far rise an hour before dark, he still would have known the men would come. He had seen it in their eyes. Winston was no fool. He had seen it, too.

A twig snapped, and immediately Winston was on his feet and running toward Elan. Elan caught the bright flash before he registered the sound of the shot. He instinctively dived for the ground, rolled, and fired in the direction of the flash of light. A high-pitched scream rent the air.

"Goddamn sonofabitch!" Winston cursed soundly as he tumbled to a halt beside Elan. "The bastard shot me."

"I think I got the fat one," Elan said, scrambling in a belly crawl around the huge rock. Winston quickly followed, panting and cursing.

"You hurt bad?" Elan asked, removing his knife from its leg sheath and cutting a strip from the tail of Winston's shirt.

"Just winged, I think," Winston said grimly. "My left arm. I can still shoot." Elan explored along Winston's arm until he encountered the sticky blood. Then he tightly bound the wound.

"Stay put," Elan said. "I will find the other one." He clamped his knife between his teeth and, holding the pistol, crawled through the brush, inching his way along. He knew about where Petty had fallen and guessed Turner would be close by. Another shot rang out, and Elan heard the whine of the bullet as it passed his ear, then the distinctive ping as it ricocheted off the rock. Winston answered with a barrage of his own, leaving the smell of burned powder permeating the air.

"You done killed my partner and now you gonna die, big man." Elan froze at the sound of Turner's plaintive whine, determining the man to be behind him and to his left. "Toss out that gun, real slow like." Elan tightened his grip on the pistol and cautiously moved his arm away from his body. "Toss it!"

In one fluid movement, Elan tossed the pistol and rolled, snatching the knife from between his teeth and hurling it in the direction of the whining voice. He had only the time to register the flare of light and the searing burn across his temple before darkness engulfed him. He never heard the crack of the shot.

16

Abby fairly danced down the well-worn path to the stream, swinging her wooden buckets and humming a little tune. Rain had come during the night, and shimmering drops of water clung to the pines. She took a deep breath, inhaling the rich earthy smell that comes with a good soaking. The path was slippery and she slowed her pace, not wanting to slip and fall. She had plenty of linens and clothing to wash without adding the hated black dress she wore.

She was lighthearted in the face of the fresh new day. The sun had quickly dispelled the dense patches of fog she'd found upon awakening, and the sky promised to be bright and sunny. Even the prospect of a day of scrubbing linens and clothes on a rough washboard failed to dampen her spirits. She was home and Elan would soon return. Her cattle grazed in the beautiful natural meadow below the cabin, and all was right with the world!

"Dear God!" Abby gasped, reflexively tightening her

grip on the buckets and feeling her stomach seize in a cramp as she came to a abrupt halt. The Indian materialized from nowhere and barred her path. Just looking at him froze her blood and sent her heart slamming against her chest. He was hideously painted and naked except for a breechclout, leggings, and moccasins. A necklace of bear claws hung from his neck, and numerous earrings dangled from his ears. In his right hand he held the most wicked-looking blade she had ever seen. Elan's hunting knife paled in comparison. He grinned at her, an evil baring of large white teeth, and she inexplicably thought of Little Red Riding Hood and the Big Bad Wolf. In the next instant she recognized him. When she'd last seen him, she'd threatened to blow his ugly head from his shoulders. Would that she had!

He held out his left hand and motioned for her to come closer. Abby stepped back a pace. *In his dreams!* He beckoned again, piercing her with his poisonous black eyes. She took another step backward, never removing her eyes from the harsh planes of his painted face. Her pistol was strapped to her left leg. Her right leg was still too tender to bear the straps. If she could just get to it! She moistened her dry lips as her brain madly raced.

The Indian stood scarcely half a head taller than she, but he was wiry and muscled, without an ounce of fat. She had no doubt of his strength. She had to make her escape before he could grab her. He stepped toward her, and she swung her buckets with all her might, then snatched up her skirts and fled.

He caught her by her hair before she made two yards, jerking her up short and laying the knife at her neck. Abby's hands still clutched her skirt and she wondered wildly if she could hike the skirt and encumbering petticoats high enough to get to her pistol before he cut her throat. Her heart pounded frantically and her breath came in short, painful gasps as he snapped her head back and looked down into her face. Her eyes widened at the snarl he issued, the snarl that curled his upper lip over his teeth. She stared at him as she was afforded an upside-down view of his terrifying grimace. She swallowed convulsively, feeling the cruel blade rise and fall as it pressed into her exposed neck.

"What do you want?" Abby croaked, feeling herself dangerously close to tears. The knife pressed deeper, then he shifted it slightly, using the tip of the blade to nick her skin. She flinched, then felt the warm trickle of blood down her neck. She squeezed her eyes tightly shut, awaiting the inevitable, unable to believe his was the last face she would ever see.

To Abby's great surprise and immense relief, the awaited slash did not come. Instead, the Indian loosened his hold. She carefully raised her head when he removed the knife. Then he clamped an iron grip on her left wrist and cruelly twisted her arm behind her back. She screamed with the unexpected pain and instinctively brought her booted foot down hard on his toes. He released her and shoved her forward. She stumbled and fell face down in the wet grass.

And then he was on top of her, straddling her back. She was pinned to the ground. It took only a few moments for him to capture her flailing arms and twist them behind her waist to bind them with a leather thong. Abby writhed and kicked her legs, knowing it was useless, but unable to surrender. The leather bit into her wrists, and she realized dully that the circulation would soon be cut off. Her fingers were already growing numb.

"What do you want?" Her repeated question elicited

no more response than before, and she understood it really didn't matter whether he answered or not. She was in no position to stop him from getting anything he wanted. Slowly, her rage began to build. It washed over her in strengthening waves. He hadn't killed her, not yet. He must have something even worse planned.

She swallowed her fear, willing anger to take its place. He might kill her, but she wouldn't cower for him. She squirmed and cursed him soundly, calling him every vile name she could remember. He stood and lifted her by the leather binding her wrists. Abby screamed again as the agony shot up her arms, and as soon as she gained her feet she whirled and kicked him, feeling somewhat avenged when her boot made contact with his shin.

"Take that, you low-life bastard!" she screamed, turning to run again. He grabbed her by the arm and spun her around, backhanding her across the face as he did. Abby stumbled, tripping over her skirts, and would have fallen if he hadn't reached out to catch her by the throat and hurl her against a pine. She crumpled and slid down among the roots. He quickly removed her boots and bound her ankles in much the same manner he had her wrists.

She was so stunned she could only gape at him in confusion. He hauled her to her feet, keeping his hand at her throat while she fought for breath. Just when she felt herself on the verge of losing consciousness, he eased his grip. She took in great gulps of air as she stared into his expressionless face. Then, to her growing horror, he lifted the knife and slowly, methodically, began to cut the buttons from her bodice.

"No," Abby moaned, turning her head and squeezing shut her eyes. "Please, no." The last of the buttons popped free, and Abby felt the cool air on her heaving chest. Then she felt the blade of the knife run between her breasts, slitting her chemise to the waist.

Abby managed to force open her eyes and noted somewhat faintly that the Indian, far from regarding her lustily, instead seemed almost disinterested as he lifted the knife again to prick, reopening the wound on her neck. His calm detachment frightened her even more than hungry lust would have.

"Stop!" Abby screamed, feeling panic grip her with icy claws. "Please stop!" Did he mean to skin her alive? Her cries and pleas went unheeded as the stone-faced Indian relentlessly threatened her with his knife.

When she thought it would never end, when she felt surely he would act on his threats to skin her alive, he stepped back and slapped her full across the face. Abby's eyes sprang open in shock at the new hurt, and she moved her tongue gingerly across her swelling lip, tasting blood. The Indian raised his arm, and Abby involuntarily flinched. His facial features remained stoic, but Abby felt certain she noted an amused gleam in his hateful eyes. He pointed his finger and made a shooting motion as he barked a series of guttural grunts.

Abby shook her head slowly from side to side. "I don't know what you're saying," she said tiredly. He repeated the motion, making more signs with his hands, pointing to Abby, then making the shooting motion again and pointing at himself.

"I'd be glad to shoot you," Abby mumbled through her swollen lips, "but I still don't know what you're saying." The Indian backhanded her. Abby slid down the rough bark of the pine, then was caught by her hair and hauled upright. She whimpered as he continued to twist her hair and glare at her. Why didn't he just kill her and be done with it? Why was he torturing her so? Then it hit her with the force of a nuclear blast. He had come for her gun. He was enjoying torturing her because she had dared to threaten him, but he wanted her gun.

Abby quickly looked away, but not before the Indian saw the comprehension reflected in her eyes. She cursed herself for her stupidity. He grunted and released her. Then he repeated his hand movements. Abby shook her head. He was going to kill her eventually. She could gain nothing by relenting. It was possible he'd find the pistol at any rate, but she'd be damned if she'd help him. As long as she knew where it was and he didn't, there might be some hope of getting to it before he did, some hope of staying alive. And Abby wanted very much to live.

Bracing herself for the next blow, Abby was stunned to see the Indian drop his hand. He stared hard at her for several minutes, then took her by the arm, a bruising grip that would leave his fingerprints on her flesh. She couldn't really walk, trussed as she was, but she did manage to stay on her feet with a series of little hopping steps, knowing if she fell, he'd likely drag her by her hair. When he reached the cabin, he took another leather thong from his breechclout and looped it around her neck, then around the porch post. It dug tightly into her neck, allowing her just enough room to draw shallow breaths. She was light-headed from lack of oxygen, but fought to remain alert. If she passed out, she'd surely die.

The Indian's search of the cabin was brief but thorough. Through the open door from the porch Abby could see him plundering as he tossed aside the log cabin's contents as he had on his previous visit. She was sure now that he had been the one to pay the unwelcome visit the last time the cabin had been ransacked. He had to have stolen the medicine bag. Suddenly her heart leapt. But if he had it then, he did not have it now. Her spirits fell. What would he do when his search failed to turn up her gun? The not knowing was almost as bad as the physical torture he'd already subjected her to.

She flinched when he reappeared on the porch, certain he was going to abuse her more, but instead he strode past her without even a glance in her direction and made for the shed. Elan's rifle was in the shed! Abby attempted twisting her head so she could follow his progress, but gave up as darkness engulfed her.

And then he was before her, holding Elan's long rifle, a look of disgust on his heretofore unreadable face. He shook the rifle in her face. Abby carefully shook her head, feeling the rawhide choker cut deeper into her neck. The Indian tossed the gun aside, then took his knife and cut the bindings on her ankles. Before she could even think, he cut her loose from the porch post and wrapped the trailing end of the rawhide around his wrist. He jerked her off the porch, and she was forced to run along behind him as he made for the wooded ridge to the east of the cabin.

Elan swam into consciousness, blinking painfully in the glare of bright sunlight. Getting his bearings, he lurched up, only to fall back with a mighty groan. He lifted a heavy hand to examine his bandaged head, wincing as his fingers probed the tender spot along his hairline. *"Merde,"* he muttered. *"Qu'est-il passé?"*

"Don't speak that gibberish," Winston replied cheerfully, waving a steaming metal cup of coffee under Elan's nose. "But if you're wanting to know about last night, you were shot. Damn good thing your skull's thick as a slab of granite. Another damn good thing that pig sticker you carry found its mark."

Elan struggled to a sitting position, cradling his aching head in his hands. Nausea roiled in his stomach, but he risked reaching for the steaming cup, grasping it between shaking hands to lift it to his lips. The bullet that grazed his scalp might as well have cleaved his skull for all the misery he felt.

The last time he had found himself thus, he had been an untried boy of fifteen. He had reached his full height, but lacked the strength necessary to hold his own in a tavern brawl. He had joined the melee in defense of his father and had been soundly bested by a burly trapper, a man stronger and with decidedly more sense than he himself possessed at the time.

After a few gulps of the scalding coffee, he felt strong enough to attempt standing. He made it to his feet, but swayed alarmingly, prompting Winston to chuckle. "Man, you look like a poleaxed grizzly. Think you can ride?"

Elan considered the question. The horses were saddled, so he did not have that to contend with. He carefully nodded, gritting his teeth at the blinding pain the movement produced. Winston kicked dirt over the fire and took the coffeepot down to the river to rinse it. By the time he returned, Elan was in his saddle, not an easy feat considering his double vision. Winston had seen to the two saddle tramps. Two large mounds of rocks attested to their final resting place. Winston had their horses tied to his pack horse.

"I'll notify the sheriff in Helena as soon as I can," Winston said, answering Elan's unspoken question. "Let's ride."

It was late afternoon when they reached the ranch. Progress had been slow due to Elan's horse spraining a hock. Elan was forced to slow their pace after he relieved the horse of his saddle and transferred it to the gray gelding Petty had ridden. Elan gradually recovered, the pain in his head subsiding to a dull throb and the nausea disappearing. He had ravenously consumed the major portion of their noon meal, washing it down with at least a quart of black coffee before Winston jokingly asked how a blow to the head could stimulate such an appetite.

"Papa! Papa!" Lori squealed, waving from the shaded bench. Sally jumped to her feet and ran to meet the dusty travelers. Winston leapt from his horse to scoop her up, striding purposefully toward Lori. He lowered Sally to the ground and knelt to hug Lori, who flung her arms around his neck and plastered his face with kisses.

"And glad I am to see you too, Miss Priss," Winston said, removing his hat and dropping it atop Lori's short curls. "Sally, run to the house and fetch Mrs. Elan. I expect she'll be wanting to know we're back."

"She went home yesterday, Papa," Lori said solemnly. "Her cows are having babies."

"Are they now?" Winston said with some amusement, glancing over his shoulder at Elan, who had dismounted and walked into the shade in time to overhear Lori's pronouncement.

"Who took Abby home?" Elan inquired, maintaining a check on his temper. It was as he had feared all along. Abby had defied him, ignoring his effort to keep her safe. The little fool had no sense of danger. She was probably now out with her herd doing all the things he had forbidden. The last time she had done that she could have been trampled by the stampeding herd, could now be buried beneath the cold earth had he and Winston not been able to reach her in time. He should never have allowed her to keep the herd.

"Annie did," Sally piped up. Winston stood, gathering Lori up in his arms and reaching to take Sally's hand. Elan glanced over his shoulder to the horses, wanting to get to the cabin, and fast. His roan could not carry him. He ran a hand over the stubble on his face as he pondered his dilemma.

"Take a fresh horse and go," Winston said. "Consider it yours. It's little payment for the debt I owe you."

Elan declined. "You owe me nothing but the wages for the drive." He had done only what needed to be done. Winston would have done the same for him. There was no debt involved.

"Take a horse and go, man," Winston insisted. "Abby may need you." Elan frowned, then reached out his hand. Winston had voiced his own concerns, and he could not allow his pride to interfere with Abby's safety. Winston released Sally's small hand and shook Elan's firmly. "Don't be too rough on her, Elan," he cautioned, chuckling, as Elan strode toward the corral. "Get her dander up and there's no telling what she might do!"

In a matter of minutes Elan was riding hell-bent for the cabin. With each passing mile his unease grew. It was foolish, he knew, but he could not put Abby's accident from his mind. She was more fragile than she would admit, just a tiny slip of a woman. Albeit she was headstrong and determined, but the fact remained, she weighed scarcely a hundred pounds. She was no match for a maddened heifer or, God forbid, one of the bulls. But he knew she would not hesitate to take one on if she set her mind to it. What she needed was a good thrashing, though he knew he could never bring himself to raise a hand to her.

Elan's sense of impending disaster grew alarmingly when he rounded the bend in the trail to discover there was no smoke curling from the stovepipe of the cabin. He urged his mount into an even faster pace when he noted the open door and his rifle on the ground. He vaulted from the horse before it halted, snatching up the rifle, running across the porch and into the gloom of the ransacked cabin. He emerged in seconds with his rifle ready and crouched to examine the ground. What he found stopped his heart for a scant moment before it began to drum painfully in his chest.

"Abby!" Elan shouted, his deep voice booming across the empty land. "Abby!" Anyone hearing the terrible noise would have recognized the agonized yearning in the tortured call. It was a sound to pierce the soul and lift the fine neck hairs, the bellow of a man in the throes of anguish. And its only answer was the quiet rustle of wind through the pine boughs and the harsh panting of a winded horse.

It took less than five minutes for Elan to piece together the puzzle. The broken grass stalks, the drops of blood, Abby's blue satin ribbon with strands of fine black hair attached, the matted grass, the abandoned buckets, her boots. Then he found the buttons, picking them one by one from among the pine roots and grass, closing them in the palm of his hand as though they were priceless jewels. Elan threw back his head and roared. The new cry that issued from his throat became the snarl of a feral and wounded animal and would have struck sheer terror in the heart of anything alive, man or four-legged beast.

Elan rapidly retraced his steps to seize the trailing reins he had tossed aside when he leapt from the saddle. He tugged the winded horse behind him as he followed the trail left by Abby and the Indian who had taken her. He had made perhaps three miles through the dense forest of lodgepole pine when he came upon the horse droppings and cropped grass where the Indian's hobbled pony had grazed. The droppings were cold, several hours old. Elan swung into the saddle and turned his mount in an easterly direction. He leaned low over the saddle, never taking his eyes from the ground. He had no difficulty tracking as long as the light held. The rapidly approaching darkness would slow him, though, and when it came, Elan traveled instinctively, realizing the Indian's course never veered from its easterly direction. It was the smell of smoke that alerted him sometime after midnight that his quarry was near. He dismounted, looped the reins over a low-hanging limb, and followed his nose.

Elan cautiously approached the camp from the south, downwind. He crawled the last fifty yards, feeling his way through the underbrush and over the rocks, carrying his rifle in the crooks of his elbows. It was unlikely he would have need of it, but on the off chance the Indian was alone with Abby, he would use it rather than take the risk of hand-to-hand combat. There was always the chance Abby could be hurt if he failed to dispatch the brave from a distance.

Elan picked up the scent of the man standing watch before he spied him in the scant light of the waning moon. He would know that smell anywhere, the blend of wood smoke, body odor, and bear fat. He lowered his rifle to the carpet of pine needles and slowly gained his feet. Moving from pine to pine, he materialized behind the brave. In a single motion, he took the brave by his greased scalp lock and brought his knife across the man's neck, slitting it from ear to ear. He gently lowered the Indian to the ground, wiped his knife across the Indian's buckskin leggings to clean it, then clenched it between his teeth as he lowered himself once again to the cold dew-dampened ground and crawled to the top of the ridge to look down upon the camp.

It was perhaps thirty yards from his spot, and he searched it thoroughly, finding Abby tied to a tree before moving his eyes from west to east, taking in every detail. He forced himself to dismiss her while he concentrated on the formidable task of getting her out alive.

Elan swallowed the raw rage that had fueled his search and allowed him to dismiss his aching head. He forced himself to take deep, calming breaths and allowed cold reason to blanket the burning hatred in his heart. A man fired by fury made costly mistakes, and he could not afford a mistake. Abby's very life depended on his ability to think clearly.

The Indians were camped by a racing mountain stream, and, far from slumbering, all were up and about. He spotted six Indian ponies hobbled to graze in the small clearing and began a mental tally of braves to put with them. Four were in a semicircle around the blazing campfire. They sat cross-legged, smoking a pipe which they passed from one to the other, talking in low voices. Elan narrowed his eyes, searching through the smoke. He knew the man he hunted, and he was not in the group. He had killed the brave left to guard the camp, so one brave, the one he sought, the one who had warned them to leave the cabin, was unaccounted for.

For a brief instant Elan dared a glance at Abby. She was well away from the fire and deep in the shadows, but he could see that her arms were tied behind her to the tree. She was nude to the waist. From her stiff posture, he assumed she was bound by the neck as well. He dragged his gaze away, afraid of the wave of fury washing over him. He could not afford to lose his head. A movement caught his eye. The missing brave emerged from the trees and walked by Abby, ignoring her as he passed her by to join the others around the campfire.

Elan backed down the ridge and slithered around the camp to come up behind the tree where Abby was bound. It was a large pine and afforded some cover. "Abby!" Elan whispered. "Do not make a sound." He waited, then spoke again, praying she had heard him over the noise of the racing waters. "If you hear me, slowly shift your legs."

Abby thought at first she was dreaming. She opened her right eye; the left one was swollen shut. Had it really been Elan's voice? No, she decided, it was impossible. There was only the Indian and his hunting party. They had bound her to the tree and forgotten her. For that much, at least, she could be grateful.

She was a mass of cuts and bruises, and figured she was probably unrecognizable to anyone who knew her. Her unbound hair fell in a tangled mess around her face, obscuring what little vision she did have. If her arms were still attached to her shoulders, she didn't know it. They were long since numb, and she worried about her hands. She hadn't been able to feel them since she had been at the cabin. Her lips were cut and swollen. She tentatively touched them with the tip of her dry tongue. She had been given neither food nor drink, and although the thought of food nauseated her, she desperately craved water.

She was unable to stop shivering, being exposed to the cold night air. What was left of her dress began at her waist. The cut on her neck wasn't deep, but it stung nonetheless. She thought several of her ribs were cracked. When the Indian had delivered her to the camp he had pitched her off the horse, then dismounted and kicked her several times as she rolled in the dirt and listened to the harsh laughter from the other braves. Then, tiring of his sport, he had dragged her to the tree and tethered her, drawing her arms up and around the scraping bark that also bit painfully into her bare back. She could only hope the Indians would soon tire of her altogether and put an end to her suffering.

"Abby!" She tensed. It *was* Elan! She fought down the sob that choked her. Dear God, now they would kill him too! She shifted her legs.

"Go away before they kill you," she all but hissed out of the corner of her bruised mouth. There were too many for him to fight, and she couldn't stand the thought of losing him to their savage torture.

"Listen to me, Abby," Elan demanded. "I will not leave without you. You must do as I say." He breathed easier knowing she retained enough of her spirit to issue orders, but he had to make her understand she must bend to him now. He could cut her loose and they could run for it, but he doubted her ability to go far in her condition. He could easily carry her, but he could not carry her and outrun the five braves. He had no choice but to kill them. He could take one with his rifle, but could not reload in time to shoot the others. That would leave four. He was reasonably sure he could take one with his hatchet. That left three for hand-to-hand combat.

"Please, Elan," Abby begged. "I don't want to be responsible for your death."

"Then do as I tell you. I will not leave you!"

"All right," Abby agreed after a lengthy pause, "tell me what to do." It was useless to argue. She had to help him in any way she could. A tiny ray of hope sprang in her breast as he outlined his strategy. If he cut her loose and she could get the feeling back in her hands before the Indians discovered she was free, it was possible she could get to her gun and blow the damn bastards to the happy hunting ground before they killed him. She decided against telling Elan of her plan. She meekly agreed to run when the fight started.

17

Elan slit the rawhide bonds, cautioning Abby to keep her arms behind her as though she were still bound until his shot alerted her to flee. Then he disappeared into the darkness, leaving her to await his lead. She was immediately able to breathe better, and took great gulps of air into her starved lungs. It was several minutes before she felt the needlelike tingling signaling the return of feeling to her hands. She willed her fingers to move, but had no way of knowing if they complied with her command.

The Indian had neglected to retie her ankles when he had bound her to the tree, and she cautiously flexed her aching legs, hoping they would hold her when she made it to her feet. She had stumbled and fallen several times after her abductor dragged her from the cabin, and her feet and legs were a mess of cuts and bruises.

Elan sighted along the bore of his long rifle as he crouched in the shadows beneath a dew-laden pine bough. He knew he must keep the element of surprise if he expected to accomplish his goal. It was pure luck the Indians had not discovered his presence in the half hour since he had murdered the sentry. Their carelessness told him they had not expected anyone to look for Abby. Had they known he was away when they took her? It was an answer he would never have. He cocked the hammer, then pulled the trigger, tossing aside the gun as he released a banshee yell and scrambled down the ridge, taking loose stones with him.

It took Abby a few seconds to recover her senses in the midst of the terrible bedlam breaking loose around her, and had she not known it was Elan, the horrifying scream heralding his arrival would have surely paralyzed her on the spot. It had no such effect on the painted braves. They began a mad scramble toward their weapons, all but the Indian who had abducted her. Elan's bullet had found its mark.

"Ohmygod, ohmygod, ohmygod," Abby whimpered, bringing her leaden arms forward as she saw a brave sprinting toward her, arm upraised, a war club at the ready to split her skull.

The snarling man tumbled at her feet with Elan's hatchet between his shoulder blades, and the war club rolled out of his lifeless hands. Abby struggled to her feet, swaying dizzily, leaning against the pine for support while she tried to gain her equilibrium.

"Run, Abby, run!" Elan yelled as he raced to collide with a charging brave. Elan, his attention momentarily straying to Abby, went down in a tangled heap with his adversary. They rolled dangerously near the campfire, caught in a struggle to the death, Elan brandishing his knife, the Indian gripping a war hatchet. The two remaining braves stood to one side, watching the struggle closely and ignoring Abby, clearly perceiving her as no threat.

Elan found his back pressed to the rocky ground as the brave countered the thrust of his knife and rolled over atop him. Elan's fingers closed over the wrist of the hand gripping the war hatchet while the brave's steely grip stayed his knife; Elan's formidable strength and his grim determination were the only things keeping him alive. He realized his gamble had worked. The two other braves would await the outcome, would not shame their companion by entering the battle to steal his coup. Elan would have them to deal with when he bested the man he now fought.

Abby clawed at her skirt, fumbling awkwardly with the holster before forcing her fingers to close around the pistol. She raised her shaking arms to a shooting position, then drew several deep breaths. She had to shoot before Elan and the Indian rolled again and switched positions. She couldn't risk hitting Elan. She braced herself and counted to three before she squeezed the trigger. The brave crumpled and was immediately tossed aside as Elan rolled and crouched before uncoiling to prepare himself. She swung around and fired again to shoot the brave who now charged toward Elan. The remaining brave, younger than the others, a boy really, seemed rooted to the ground. His eyes widened as the last of his party fell, and he shifted them quickly from Elan to Abby. Then, without warning, he whirled and sprinted for the trees.

"Shoot, Abby!" Elan yelled in full stride. "Shoot!"

Abby pulled the trigger and watched the brave fling out his arms and fall. Her pistol fell from her fingers as she slumped to the ground and buried her face in her hands. The carnage was too much. She had followed

Elan's order and killed a mere boy. It was too much to comprehend. The hate she felt earlier was gone, replaced by a strange sense of enormous loss. She tried desperately to dredge up the hate, to use it as a protective armor, but it was gone in the wake of the awful bloodletting.

Elan ran to Abby's side, dropped to his knees, and gathered her close. He clasped her to his heaving chest, damp with sweat and blood, and pressed his lips to her disheveled hair. She sagged in his arms, unresponsive.

"It is over, Abby," Elan crooned, bringing up a blood-stained hand to cup her chin and tilt her head. He moved his lips and hands softly over her bruised face as though he could kiss away the hurts, and he tasted the salty tears slipping unchecked from beneath her swollen eyelids. He brushed back wisps of matted dark hair to examine more closely her battered face. Then he drew her up as he stood, supporting her with one arm behind her back, the other catching her behind her knees. He took her close to the fire, stepping contemptuously over the sprawled bodies of the dead. Just seeing the brutality inflicted on Abby made him wish he could resurrect each and every one of them just to kill them again.

Elan gently laid Abby by the fire, regretting there was nothing to cushion her from the damp, cold ground. He used his knife to cut strips from her petticoat, then removed his buckskin shirt and draped it over her to keep her warm while he took the strips of cloth to the stream to immerse them in the racing waters.

Abby was as pale and still as death when he returned to wash her wounds. She accepted a drink from the hide water bag Elan held to her mouth, swallowing as he instructed when he lifted her head, and she allowed him to slip his shirt over her head and arms. The sleeves fell past her wrists, and she watched impassively as he rolled them, hesitating briefly when he exposed the raw rope burns. If she was aware of the pain in his eyes, the grim lines of his face, she gave no sign, and Elan's unease grew with every passing minute.

"Abby!" Elan spoke urgently, seeking to penetrate the curtain she had drawn around herself. "It had to be done. There was no choice. I will not let you do this to yourself. You must put it behind you."

Abby blinked as she tried to focus, then lifted her head. She reached out a trembling hand to rest it against the stubble on his cheek. "He was just a boy," she murmured. "He was only a child." She felt no remorse for the others, but she knew shooting the young boy in the back would forever haunt her dreams. She should have ignored Elan and allowed him to escape.

"It had to be done," Elan repeated. "If you had not killed him, he would have returned to his people and reported what happened here. You see the revenge we faced. It would have come back tenfold if the boy had taken his message to the other braves of the village. You would never have been safe. As it is now," he continued, "they will never know what happened. When the scouts find the bodies, they will not be sure who did the killing. I will erase all evidence of our being here, and I will turn the ponies loose. We will return home by a different route. By the time the bodies are discovered, no trail will be found."

It was near dawn by the time they mounted the horse and put the Indian camp behind them. When the rain began to fall, Elan lifted his head and blessed the icy drops, refusing to consider seeking shelter even though he worried about Abby. The rain would wash away any trace of their trail, and he urged his mount to a faster pace after taking a blanket from his pack and tossing it around his shoulders.

Abby wore his buckskin shirt, and he had also wrapped her in his bearskin coat, but she continued to shiver, and he was more than a little concerned for her. It would be hours before he could get her warm and dry. In her extended state of shock, she was dangerously near collapse.

"Elan?" Abby's questioning voice startled him. She had not spoken in hours, and rode slumped against him, her head resting between his shoulder and chin. His arms were around her as he held the reins.

"What is it, Abby?" Elan inquired, brushing his lips across her soaked hair. Rain washed over them in torrents, falling so hard that it was often difficult to see.

"I want to go home," Abby said. "I can't take this anymore." She desperately wanted civilization if there was any way to find it. The dull shock of killing the Indians had finally worn off, and she was aware of how absolutely miserable she was. Not an inch of her bruised body was dry, not an inch was warm. Her bare feet couldn't have been colder if she had waded in a glacial stream, and she feared she would have pneumonia before her ordeal was over. It wasn't Elan's fault. He was doing everything he could, but the fact remained that she was getting sicker by the minute. Her throat was scratchy, and her head throbbed.

"We will be home soon, Abby," Elan promised. "Just a few more hours and you will be warm and dry."

"No," Abby answered, shivering violently as another hard chill hit. "I want to go to my home in my time. I'm not cut out for this. I want to wake up in my bed with my things around me. I want to go back where I belong!"

Elan tightened his arms around Abby and rested his chin atop her dripping head. She was right. He had to get her back to her time. He loved her as he had never loved another, and the thought of losing her was more than he could stand, but he recognized her needs and would force himself to put them before his own. He would do everything she asked.

"As soon as we return to the cabin and I have you well again, we will go to the Little Bighorn, as you wish," Elan said with a heavy heart. "Perhaps you are right and the Indians who will gather there will have the medicine bag with them. I searched the hunting party carefully, and they did not have it."

"Thank you, Elan," Abby said tiredly. "Thank you for coming after me. I really didn't expect to see you."

Elan stiffened at her admission. How could she think he would not come? She was as much a part of him as his beating heart. "How could you think that?" he admonished hoarsely. "You are my woman."

"So you came for a possession stolen?" Abby asked cautiously, tilting her head to read his face, feeling a pang upon seeing the hurt cloud his dark eyes.

"I came for my woman," Elan said softly, dropping his gaze to her upturned face. "No man can ever take my woman and keep her while I have breath left in my body."

Abby twisted around and wrapped her arms around Elan, pressing her face to his chest, feeling the soft cushion of his curly matted hair, and suddenly she was oblivious to the pouring rain, the freezing cold. She was safe in his arms. Nothing could harm her there. She loved him fiercely, this rough mountain man who had fought so bravely to free her. His huge size and gruff demeanor were but a facade to shield a warm and caring nature. "I am your woman, Elan," she said solemnly as she listened to the steady beat of his heart. "Whatever happens, I will always be your woman, and I will forever keep you in my heart."

It was late afternoon before they came to the homestead, and though the rain continued to fall, it had slackened to a fine mist. Fog swirled so thickly Elan was unable to see the cabin as the horse picked its way across the creek. The horse stumbled coming out of the water, giving Elan a jolt that brought him stiffly upright in the saddle. Abby, slumbering in his arms, stirred at his abrupt movement. "We are home, Abby," he said, dismounting and lifting her from the saddle. Her eyes fluttered, but she did not fully awaken. He ran the last few yards to the cabin, cradling her in his arms.

He lowered her gently to the bed and stripped her of her ruined clothing, tossing it carelessly aside and covering her with a quilt before returning to unsaddle the exhausted horse and put it out to graze. Finding the bottle of whiskey, he forced several swallows down her throat, ignoring her weak protest. It was more than an hour before he had the tub filled with steaming water and ready for her bath. He still wore his bloodstained buckskin breeches. They were plastered to him like a second skin. When he had Abby clean, he would then take the time to attend to his own needs.

Abby fully awakened when Elan lowered her into the steaming tub. She winced as the warm, soapy water made contact with her cuts, but allowed Elan to bathe her as if she were a baby. She realized she lacked the strength to do it herself, and far from being self-conscious, she welcomed his loving touch on the most intimate parts of her body. She opened her eyes at his sharp intake of breath, grateful the eye that had been swollen shut now opened, if only a bit. She had feared permanent blindness.

"*Merde!*" Elan muttered as he tenderly soaped and washed the woman he loved. The light of the campfire had not allowed him to see the full extent of the horror inflicted upon her. His face darkened as his anger grew. He moved the lamp closer for a better look. He knew Indians and their ways, but the extent of their cruelty could still shake him. He rocked back on his heels, taking inventory of Abby's injuries. The bruises on her swollen face were shades of green and blue, as were the ones on her rib cage. There seemed to be no permanent damage, and for that he gave thanks.

"I guess I look like something the cat dragged in," Abby said ruefully, noting the grim set of Elan's face. She wrapped her arms around her knees and rested her chin on them.

"The bruises will fade, Abby," Elan replied. "Soon you will never know they were there." He soaped her matted hair, then rinsed it with a pail of water he had set aside for that purpose. Watching the soapy water trail down Abby's curved backbone, Elan was reminded of her very strong spirit, for she was not strong physically. A less determined woman would have died under such harsh treatment. He could trace every fragile vertebra, and he longed to press his lips to her damp flesh and kiss away the hurts.

"I thought I would never be clean again," Abby said with a soft sigh, relaxing under Elan's strong hands. "You're spoiling me." Elan laughed and lifted her from the tub, wrapping her in a large linen towel he had warmed by the stove. She balanced on unsteady legs and swayed, allowing him to catch her and pull her against his rock-hard chest.

"Feeling better?" he asked, planting a kiss on the top of her head.

"Much better," she replied as the old familiar yearning washed over her. "Make love to me, Elan. I need you to hold me and love me." She wrapped her arms around his waist and lifted her head. He gazed down into her eyes, searching her face. She had never wanted anything so much in her life as she wanted him now. Perhaps it was because she had thought during those long hours of captivity that she would never see him again. Perhaps it was because she needed to reaffirm the fact that she was alive. But whatever the reasons, she felt her desire grow with each thud of his powerful heartbeat until she was weak from the wanting.

Elan scooped her up and strode rapidly to the bed, gently laying her down and covering her with the quilt. In a matter of minutes he had stripped and washed in the remains of her bath water and returned to the bed clean and fresh. He towered over her, his eyes moving across her as she tossed aside the quilt and lifted her arms. With a mighty groan he sank to his knees, and she drew his head to her so that he rested his face on her breasts. She was surprised to feel him tremble. She stroked his stubbled cheek, seeking to soothe, but her hand froze when it encountered moistness. Then Elan heaved a great shuddering sob, and it was she who now crooned and comforted him.

"It's all right," Abby said softly, clasping his head between her hands and forcing his dark eyes to meet hers. She kissed the tears spilling from his lids, her hands moving to tangle in his damp hair. At her urging, Elan eased into bed. The anguish reflected on his chiseled features tugged at her heart, pierced her soul, drove her into deeper depths of passion. He poised himself over her, resting his huge hands on either side of her shoulders. Then he lowered his lips to hers, gently searching her mouth, taking possession when she parted her lips and touched the tip of her tongue to his.

"Stop me if I hurt you," Elan whispered, releasing her lips to dip his head and nuzzle her breasts. Abby ran her hands over his rippling muscles, enjoying the feel of their play beneath her fingers, lost in sensual sensation. She arched her back, gasping when he abandoned her breast to trace a trail with his tongue to her belly button, then back up her rib cage to bury his face in the hollow of her neck. She opened her legs, responding to his gentle nudging, and moaned aloud when his lips nibbled her earlobe.

"I want you inside me," Abby begged impatiently, tugging Elan by his hair. He responded by moving over her body, then capturing her lips once again. She met his need when his tongue plundered her mouth. She ran her hands up and down his quivering arms, realizing he was deliberately holding himself away for fear of hurting her.

Elan struggled against his raging desire. He allowed her to push him over, and he lay on his back awaiting her next move. She trailed dainty little kisses across his chest. He balled his fingers into fists, reminding himself to be patient. When her fingers closed around him, he issued a mighty groan and called her name.

Abby lifted her head and stared into his heavy-lidded eyes. "What do you want, Elan?" she inquired playfully. "Can't you see I'm busy?" He took her then, rolling her carefully to her back and possessing her totally as she met him move for move until both were lost amid the needs that drove them.

Afterward, he gathered her into his arms, sated, spent. She nestled against him, resting her head on his shoulder, her hand on his heaving chest. His arm tightened around her, and she lifted her face to his. He gazed into her eyes, basking in the love shining from them. "You have drained me, woman," he growled, "but there is something we must discuss before another day passes."

"What is it?" Abby asked, content in the afterglow of lovemaking. She moved her fingers to trace his lips, those lips that awakened her to such bliss.

"You must not disobey me again," Elan said, sitting up and propping himself on one elbow to gaze down at her while his other hand stroked her hair away from her face. He had to convince her to yield to his judgment. Her belief that she could take care of herself was not only foolish but dangerous as well.

"I'm sorry," Abby said, and she meant it. She had never been so sorry in her life that she had gone against his wishes and returned to the cabin. He had been right to fear for her safety. But who would have guessed the Indian would pick that time to show up?

"I must have your word that it will never happen again," Elan said. His hand moved to grasp her chin so she could not look away. "Promise me!"

"I can't," Abby replied, her blue eyes clouding over. "You can't expect that we will always agree, and I refuse to make a promise I might break."

Elan's face darkened as his black brows shot together in a frown. "You must learn to obey, Abby," he said softly. "I need to know that you will do as I tell you."

"What do you plan to do if I don't?" she demanded. "Beat me?"

"Do you think that I should?" Elan asked.

"You wouldn't dare!" she gasped. This was her Elan speaking, the man who cared enough to risk his life against impossible odds. This was the same man whose tears of pain she had just kissed away, tears shed for the hurts she suffered. He would never harm her. She couldn't imagine him lifting a finger to hurt her no matter what she did. But she would not lie to appease him.

"Do not try me, Abby," Elan warned, dropping her chin and lying back, his fingers laced behind his head as he stared at the ceiling. Nothing else had worked to curb her impulsive nature, and he could only hope she would take his implied threat seriously, for he knew in his heart he could never touch her in anger.

Abby turned her back to Elan and rested her face on her hands. She didn't believe for one minute Elan would live up to his threat, but nonetheless, she couldn't help but worry.

18

It was more than a week before Abby's bruises faded and she was willing to appear in public. She and Elan spent the time preparing for the journey to the Little Bighorn. Elan refused to leave her even to hunt or fish near the cabin, and she found herself accompanying him as he went about his daily chores. He often paused in his tasks to take her in his arms, and on more than one occasion they rolled like love-struck teenagers amid the wildflowers blanketing the meadow. They understood their time together could be drawing to a close, and though neither could openly admit it, they each seemed driven, making love with passion and abandon, sealing forever their feelings for each other. Abby gradually regained her strength and confidence, blooming under Elan's constant attention.

It was with something akin to regret that Abby finally closed the cabin and climbed into the buckboard to make the journey with Elan down the mountain and into the valley. She twisted around in the hard seat and stared at the cabin until it was out of sight. She had spent so many wonderful nights there, first with her father as she grew up, then with Elan. She blinked back the tears filling her eyes, determined to look ahead rather than behind as she shifted her position, turning her back on the homestead.

"It is not too late to change your mind, Abby," Elan said, pulling on the reins and bringing the buckboard to a halt. He wiped a wayward tear from her damp cheek and gave her a crooked grin. "We can have a good life here together."

"No, Elan," Abby said, reaching out to touch his hand. "I have to find the medicine bag. I want to go home." Elan released the brake and slapped the reins. "Will you at least think about going with me if we find the medicine bag?" It took all of Abby's courage to ask. They had been over it time and time again. She had been racking her brain for days trying to think of a fresh argument, one that would convince him he could be happy in her world. But it was hopeless. And she hated herself for asking, because she knew how miserable he would be in the 1990s. She was only being selfish in wanting him there with her.

Elan could not answer for a long moment. Abby's plea tore at his heart, and he had to steel himself against it. He had questioned Abby extensively about her world. It was no place for him. As much as he wanted to be with her, as much as he loved her, he could not go with her to her time. She must make that part of the journey without him. He would do everything he could to find the medicine bag, but beyond that she must travel alone. But how could he ever let her go? He was not sure. It would be like losing a part of himself. He would never be whole again.

"I cannot go with you, Abby," Elan said, staring straight ahead, unable to look at her face. She moved closer to him and leaned her head on his shoulder. He put his arm around her and pulled her to him, giving comfort even as his heart was rent apart.

They had decided after much discussion to take John Winston into their confidence. It was as much a matter of necessity as it was a need to say good-bye to Winston and Lori if they did not return to the Blackfoot Valley. They could use another horse, for traveling in the buckboard would slow them considerably. It was already well into June, and if Abby remembered her history correctly, the Battle of the Little Bighorn took place in the last week of June, 1876. She wished repeatedly she had paid more attention in Mrs. Ridgeway's Montana History class her second year of high school, but unfortunately she had not. The exact date continued to elude her.

"How do I look?" Abby asked nervously, patting her hair, checking to see it hadn't escaped the ribbon catching it away from her face. The ribbon was the blue satin, carefully saved by Elan when he rescued her from the Indians. Her hair had grown a lot in the last year and now fell in soft black waves well past her shoulders. She wore her favorite blue dress and carried the matching bag she had sewn.

Elan smiled into Abby's worried eyes. "You are beautiful." He set the brake on the buckboard and paused to drop a light kiss on her lips before jumping down. He took her in his arms to help her to the ground, and as always she enjoyed the physical contact with his muscular body. She could never tire of the look and feel of him.

"Courage," Elan said, his hands lingering at her waist. "The worst that can happen is for him to think we are mad." Abby managed a faint smile as Elan stepped away.

She squared her shoulders and marched up the steps to rap on the door. It was answered almost immediately by Mrs. Johnson.

"Good afternoon, Mrs. Johnson," Abby said pleasantly. She failed, however, to dispel the woman's perpetual frown. "I wonder if Mr. Winston is at home." Mrs. Johnson stepped back, holding the door open for Abby and Elan to enter.

"He's working on the ledgers," Mrs. Johnson said, sending a nervous glance in the direction of Winston's office. "He left instructions not to be disturbed." At that moment Winston flung open the office door and stepped into the room.

"I thought I heard someone. By golly, it's good to see you," Winston said, striding forward to take Elan's hand. "Mrs. Johnson, find some refreshment for our guests." Mrs. Johnson acknowledged her employer's request and made her departure. "Come," Winston said, "sit and make yourselves comfortable."

"We prefer to speak in private," Elan said. "Perhaps the office?"

"Of course," Winston agreed, offering his arm to Abby and leading them into his office.

"How is Lori?" Abby asked as Winston seated her in one of his overstuffed chairs. Elan closed the door and took a straight chair near the stove while Winston seated himself behind his desk.

"Lori's doing fine. Every day she seems to be a little stronger. She's eager to resume her lessons."

Abby laughed at the twinkle in Winston's eye, unsure if he was teasing. "That's unusual. Most children are happy to put their lessons behind them!"

"Ah, here are our refreshments." Winston closed his ledger and pushed it aside as Mrs. Johnson knocked and entered. She served slices of spiced apple cake with brown-sugar frosting and steaming black coffee before reluctantly withdrawing. Abby made a polite effort to eat, but gave up, her nervousness so great that the bite she swallowed lodged in her throat. She noted Elan seemed to suffer no such apprehension. He rapidly disposed of his cake and, with her permission, made short work of hers as well.

"Now," Winston said, putting aside his china plate and tossing his crumpled linen napkin over it. "What can I do for you?" Abby glanced at Elan, who lifted an inquiring brow, neatly tossing the ball back into her court. She was sorely tempted to do something childish like sticking out her tongue, but managed to curb the impulse.

"Elan and I are planning a trip," Abby began, thinking it best to draw Winston in gradually. Her fingers played with the drawstring on her purse, and she found herself wrapping and unwrapping the blue ribbons around her knuckles.

"Oh?" Winston inquired, his brows knitting with interest as he leaned forward in his chair and propped his elbows on the desk blotter. "Where are you going?"

"To the Little Bighorn," Abby replied.

Winston sat bolt upright, the color draining from his tanned face. Abby was so taken aback by his reaction that she sloshed some of her unwanted coffee over the rim of the china cup and into her lap. Winston half stood to come to her aid, but she waved him away as she reached to set the cup on the edge of his cluttered desk. "No! No! I'm quite all right!" She used her napkin to blot the stain. Something wasn't right, but she couldn't quite put her finger on it. She couldn't imagine why Winston should have such a response to her statement.

"I don't believe that's a good idea," Winston said as he slowly eased himself down and stared at Elan. "Forgive my interest, but what is the purpose of the trip?" Elan again arched a brow at Abby. She seemed to be doing fine so far, and he was content to let her do the talking. After all, it was her idea to inform Winston of their plans. He had felt they should only request the loan of a horse.

"We have lost something we believe we can find there later this month," Abby said as she lifted her chin and directed a murderous glare at Elan. Fat lot of help he was. And what in the world was wrong with Winston? He looked as if he'd seen a ghost. Was he ill? If he'd paled at her first statement, he'd now turned positively ashen.

"That something wouldn't happen to be an Indian medicine bag?" Winston asked through clenched teeth. Abby gaped at Winston, then exchanged glances with Elan. Well, at least something had the force to move Elan, she noted with some satisfaction as he shot to his feet.

"Do you have it?" Elan roared, taking a step toward the desk. He felt himself losing his temper at the same time as he wondered incredulously what the rancher knew of the medicine bag. What purpose would he have in ransacking the cabin and stealing it? Had it been at the ranch all along while he and Abby worried over it?

Winston held up a restraining palm that served to stop Elan's advance. "No, I don't have it."

"How did you know?" Abby asked, reaching out to tug at Elan's arm. She caught buckskin and yanked sharply. He retraced his steps to sprawl in his chair, stretching out his long legs and crossing them at the ankles. His effort to convey a relaxed appearance didn't fool Abby for one second, and she was sure it didn't fool

Winston either. Beneath Elan's calm exterior was a finely strung wealth of taut muscle, as deadly as a coiled rattler and poised to strike at the least provocation.

"I found the medicine bag eleven years ago at the Custer Battlefield," Winston replied. Abby's hand flew to her mouth, muffling her gasp. She sought Elan's attention, but it was focused on Winston. She may as well have been invisible. "I wandered off the marked paths and discovered a white teepee pitched among the willows along the river. Being curious, I lifted the flap and went inside. The medicine bag was the only object on the dirt floor. Naturally I picked it up."

"The year?" Abby asked. "What was the year?" It was impossible. Her brain seemed to shut down, refusing to cooperate. All she could do was stare wide-eyed as Winston continued his monologue.

"It was 1984," Winston said, rubbing his hand over his face. "I was a career officer in the army and I had always wanted to explore the Custer Battlefield. Seems as if I explored a bit too much."

Abby blanched, twisting the ribbons tighter around her fingers. "You knew." She felt suddenly vulnerable, exposed. She had assumed she and Elan had blended with the sparse population of the valley, that they had been accepted in the small community. Had others secretly harbored doubts as well?

"That you were from the future?" Winston inquired. "Certainly I knew. I suspected as much from your sudden appearance in the valley, and from your feminist attitude, but your watch confirmed it. You must not have realized that wristwatches aren't worn in this time. And then there was the aspirin when Lori was sick. I was never so glad to see anything in my life. But what I can't understand is Elan. He can't possibly be from the twentieth century."

Abby laughed, a hysterical little trill that served to release at least some of the tension in the small room. "Not on your life. You are looking at a real live adventurer and trapper who traveled with Lewis and Clark from 1804 until 1806."

"At your service," Elan interjected dryly, prompting a wry chuckle from Winston and a dirty look from Abby.

"Anyway," Winston continued, "when I came around, it was pitch dark. I fumbled about until I got out of the teepee. I had no idea I had been sent back in time to 1865. I wandered around in a stupor for days before a couple of buffalo hunters found me. Even then I didn't have the sense to go back for the medicine bag. By the time I realized what had happened and gotten together the means to return, the teepee was gone, and with it the medicine bag. I made my way north to the gold strikes and made the money to put together this ranch. And you know the rest."

Unable to sit still another minute, Abby rose and began to pace the office, desperate to find an outlet for her restless energy. Winston's story, incredible as it seemed, paralleled Elan's too closely. She was certain she was on the right track. The medicine bag would be waiting for her along the Little Bighorn. She just knew it. Abby paused at the window and impatiently flung aside the heavy gold velvet drapes to view the distant snow-covered mountains. Before her was a beautiful vista, and she pulled the drapes wide, allowing bright sunlight to stream through the windowpanes. Perhaps the golden light could clear her thoughts.

"Would you like to come with us?" Abby inquired, soaking in the warmth provided by the sun. "Wouldn't you like to see your loved ones again?"

"You are welcome to join us," Elan added, watching conflicting emotions break the careful control Winston strove to maintain. Two men would certainly have a better chance of accomplishing the mission, and he trusted Winston's judgment. Winston had strong feelings for Abby. He would never let harm come to her. But could he stand aside and send Abby and Winston into the future together? He pushed the thought from his mind, unable to deal with it.

"No," Winston said, leaning back in his chair and staring at the ceiling. "I can't go back. When I didn't return to my base, I would have been labeled a deserter. I can't just reappear after eleven years without an explanation. And—" He chuckled without humor. "—I'm afraid they wouldn't believe the real reason for my disappearance."

Elan considered Winston's explanation. Winston was right. His sudden reappearance after such a long time would be hard to explain. But what about Abby? He wondered if she had given it any thought. How could she just return to her former life and resume where she had left off? There were certain to be questions.

"Did you have a family?" Abby asked, breaking the strained silence following Winston's words.

"A pregnant wife and a widowed mother," Winston said, turning in his chair to affix Abby with a hard stare. "And no, I do not wish to see them again," he said as she opened her mouth to speak. "I've put that part of my life behind me. Can you imagine what it would do to them to have me turn up after eleven years? My place is here with Lori. Have you thought of Lori?" he continued before Abby could dredge up any semblance of a reply. "How could I subject her to such an uncertain future? This is her home."

"But modern medicine," Abby faltered. Lori was still ill, and Winston had surely considered that she could be cured more easily in the future. He must have agonized over his decision. And she realized he was right. How could he take the chance of removing her from everything familiar? How would a young child cope with something as intangible as time travel?

"Modern medicine?" Winston waved his hand, dismissing Abby's suggestion. "Modern medicine failed to cure my father's cancer. It couldn't save him. So much for a hundred years of medical knowledge!"

Abby unwrapped her new outfit from the brown paper in which Annie had tied it and dressed quickly by the flickering light of the lamp. Elan was long up and gone, seeing to saddling their horses and loading their things on the two pack horses Winston had provided. Winston had insisted on helping provision them for the journey, though he strenuously disapproved of the trip. When he found he could not dissuade Abby, he proved to be a valuable ally.

Winston had accompanied Elan to the settlement the previous afternoon. Elan had wanted to settle their account with Roberts, and Abby requested he pick up her things from Annie while he was there. Abby had decided not to accompany the men, but rather to stay with Lori and Sally. She had explained to the children that she and Elan were going on a long trip and might not be able to return. The girls were confused, and made Abby promise to come back if she could. In the late afternoon she had been surprised to find that Annie returned with the men. Abby had been glad to see her friend even though saying good-bye was difficult.

Abby strapped her holster over the split skirt and checked her appearance in the full-length mirror. It was as she feared. She did look like Annie Oakley, but there was no way to wear the holster under the skirt. The leather flap would hide the pistol from view, and if she found she had need of it, whoever saw it wouldn't live to tell about it. Winston had provided Elan with a repeating rifle and pistols. They would be well armed for the trip.

Abby put on her leather jacket and zipped it up to her neck. She combed her fingers through her hair, then tied it back with the blue ribbon. Taking a last look around, she breathed in deeply to calm herself and then left the room.

The sun was just brightening the eastern mountains with soft rosy hues when Abby walked down the steps and across the yard to meet Elan by the carved bench. Winston led two horses from the barn. It was cold, and she could see her breath and the horses' breath as well. The horses, a black one Winston had given Elan and a beautiful chestnut mare with a blazed face for her, were snorting and stamping their feet. Winston wordlessly handed her the chestnut's reins and returned to the barn to get the pack horses.

Abby stroked the mare's nose, murmuring softly as Elan and Winston went over the route they would take. Winston thought they should ride south to Three Forks and then southeast to the Little Bighorn. Elan was familiar with the country to the forks of the rivers from his journey with Lewis and Clark, and readily agreed with Winston. If they rode hard and met no resistance, they should be able to intercept Custer before the battle. Abby was mildly surprised to find Elan offering no objection to her mode of dress. A brief tightening of his lips had been his only reaction. Perhaps he realized how foolish it would be for her to try to ride several hundred miles in a cumbersome dress and petticoats.

"I won't say good-bye," Winston said as he held out his hand to Elan, who grasped it tightly. After a moment

Winston turned to Abby. He hesitated, glancing at Elan. Then he took Abby in his arms for a hug. "Till we meet again," he said softly, releasing her and stepping back.

"Till we meet again," Abby repeated, finding herself perilously close to tears. John Winston had proved to be a close and reliable friend. She would miss him. "You will explain everything to Annie and see to my herd?" Abby asked as she grasped the pommel and placed her left foot in the stirrup. Winston handed her the reins after she was settled in the saddle.

"I'll tell Annie when the time is right. And don't worry about the herd or the cabin. I'll keep an eye on them." Winston tipped his hat and stepped away. Elan took the reins of the lead pack horse and mounted the black one that Winston had given him. A quarter of a mile across the pasture, Abby looked over her shoulder and found Winston still watching. She lifted her hand in farewell before riding over a hill and losing sight of him.

Within an hour they were fording the racing waters of the Blackfoot. Elan rode along the bank for several hundred yards before he found a suitable place to cross. Abby, close behind, lifted her feet from the stirrups to keep them out of the icy waters, but failed to stay completely dry. Even her skirt got splattered as her horse climbed out on the south side of the turbulent river, and she realized this was only a taste of what was to come. On this trip, there would be many streams and rivers to cross. She pulled her mare up next to Elan's horse, eager for conversation. Elan hadn't spoken more than a word or two all morning.

"By going over Stemple Pass we should make Helena by nightfall," Abby said. "Maybe we can find a place to spend the night," she added hopefully.

"We will camp," Elan replied. "I want to avoid people

as much as possible. We do not need to draw attention to ourselves." He had been thinking about their conversation with Winston the day before. If Winston had realized soon after meeting them that he and Abby were from a different time, then others might also question them. Of course Winston had the advantage of being a traveler through time himself, but Elan wanted to take no undue chances. He had his long rifle with him in addition to the weapons Winston provided, and Abby had her pistol. The weapons alone would cause curiosity. He would not take the chance of having to explain himself.

There was also the matter of Abby's skirt and his buckskins. He had seen no other women in such a short skirt, and he believed her clothing would draw attention. Abby couldn't very well wear her dresses and ride comfortably, but he had been shocked nonetheless. As for his buckskins, they were not as out of place as Abby's short skirt, but they were different enough to arouse interest. He could not with good conscience complain about what Abby found comfortable when he could not be forced to wear the stiff cotton trousers Abby called jeans.

"How long do you think it'll take to make the Little Bighorn?" Abby asked, casting a sidelong look at Elan's profile. He was so handsome it sometimes took her breath away. He had taken the time to shave, and her eyes lingered on the smoothness of his jaw before moving to the wide expanse of his fur-covered shoulders. His thick black hair was pulled back with a leather thong, and the ebony waves glistened, still damp from his early-morning bath.

"If you keep looking at me like that," Elan replied with a grin, "longer than it should!" He urged his mount into a faster pace, and Abby spurred her chestnut into a trot in order to keep up.

When they began the climb over Stemple Pass, Abby was forced to admit she missed her old pickup and the much-cursed gravel road. At times she found her horse almost vertical as the surefooted mare seemed to claw her way up, scattering loose rocks and dirt that bounced down the mountain. She refused to look down, and instead kept her eyes trained on the rumps of the pack horses. Elan seemed unfazed by the hair-raising ascent, glancing over his shoulder only occasionally to make sure she was still with him. She gritted her teeth and hung on. If he could do it, so could she!

It was late afternoon by the time they reached the rolling hills and stopped for a rest. They had ridden hard, pausing only briefly to eat the meal packed by Mrs. Johnson once the mountains were behind them. Elan had shed his bearskin coat and Abby had removed her leather jacket, though Elan knew they would need them again as soon as the sun dipped behind the western peaks.

Elan squatted along the bank of the small fast-running creek and filled the canteens. Abby, a few yards downstream, drank deeply from her palm, then cupped her hands in the stream and splashed cold water on her face. Elan paused, caught by the display of sparkling water and the lithe dark-haired form splashing in it. She tipped her face to the sun, allowing the cooling moisture to drip down her neck, then pulled a piece of linen from her pocket and patted herself dry.

Abby stretched and placed her hands on her hips, arching her back. Then she very gingerly rubbed her bottom. Elan grinned at the sight. She had kept up with him all day, never complaining, but she had to be saddle-sore. When they made camp, he would lay odds she would forget about anything but sleep.

Elan hooked the canteens over his pommel and

reached in the saddlebags to dig out the map Winston
had provided. They should be able to camp near Helena
by nightfall. He intended to skirt the town to the east and
camp well away from its inhabitants. He was not foolish
enough to believe he could avoid any contact with others,
but he was determined to keep his distance as much as
possible. Abby was the type of woman to draw a man's
eye, and he wanted to avoid any hint of trouble.
Winston's description of the rough-and-tumble mining
town left him with little choice.

He wondered if he had made the right decision in
bringing Abby to search for the medicine bag. It was a
dangerous undertaking in the best of circumstances, and
the Indians were moving in the same direction. They
should be relatively safe for another day or so, but each
mile south increased their chances of running into a tribe
or a hunting party on the move. They would soon be
traveling through buffalo country, and there were sure to
be Indians following the herds.

"Mount up, woman," Elan called cheerfully, rolling up
the map and stuffing it in the saddlebag. "Two good
hours of daylight left." He gathered the reins of the pack
horses and mounted. Abby stiffly hobbled to her chestnut mare and hoisted herself into the saddle, releasing a
weary groan when her bottom came into contact with the
hard leather. Elan threw back his head and laughed,
prompting Abby to stick out her tongue at his back as he
splashed across the creek, leaving her to follow behind
the pack horses.

19

"What are you doing?" Elan asked, observing with perplexed interest as Abby uncoiled the braided rope and painstakingly placed it in a circle around their bedrolls. He had a length of canvas Winston had given him but he preferred to sleep under the stars if the weather permitted, and the night thus far was clear, not a cloud in the sky. Seeing the familiar stars overhead never failed to give him a feeling of security in this new time. Whatever men might do, he was certain they could never breach the heavens. He would always remain firmly convinced of that, even though Abby claimed men walked on the moon in the year 1969. Not that he believed her to be mistaken, but he often wondered if all the amazing things she told him were true or if she enjoyed teasing him to see how gullible he could be. Sometimes he suspected the latter.

Abby glanced up to find Elan inspecting her, his hands on his hips, an amused frown narrowing his brows. "I'm guarding against snakes," she said as she continued to unroll the rope and place it on the ground. She had read somewhere or seen a movie or something about snakes not crossing a rope. It was probably just a bunch of bull, but she wasn't taking any chances. She stamped her foot. "Don't look at me like that!"

"Like what?" Elan asked mildly, his lips twitching, his dimples deepening. *Mon Dieu,* but she was beautiful in the moonlight with her flushed face and her flashing blue eyes. She impatiently brushed a stray lock from her face, a useless gesture, for it fell once again against her cheek. Abby stepped inside the circle of rope and dusted off her hands, well satisfied with her snake barrier.

"Like I'm crazy," Abby replied, exasperated by his amused grin, refusing to be taken in by his gorgeous dimples. "I don't want to take any chances on finding a snake in my bedroll, and if you had any sense, neither would you."

"That," Elan asked skeptically, pointing to the rope, "will keep them away?"

"I'm not sure, but I think it might," Abby muttered, dropping to her knees and straightening out the blankets. It was going to be a miserable night. She was certain of it. The cold ground was practically sprouting rocks, and though she had spent the better part of an hour tossing aside loose pebbles, she hadn't seemed to make a dent. A campfire would have been heavenly, but Elan had forbidden it. The sun had long set, and the glorious warmth it had provided during the afternoon was completely gone. Her only hope for heat lay with Elan. He was almost as good as a wood-burning stove and she was impatient for him to join her.

"Well?" Abby asked as she finished her task and settled back on her heels. Darn him. He hadn't made a move to prepare for sleeping, and stood watching thoughtfully with his head cocked to one side.

"Well, what?" he answered, striding past the bedrolls in the direction of the hobbled horses, his long rifle in his hand. Abby squinted after him in the darkness, able to see only the faint outline of his broad shoulders in the scant light provided by the moon and stars.

"Aren't you coming to bed?" She looked longingly at the nest she had made, unwilling to settle in without him. She shivered, shoving her cold hands into the pockets of her leather jacket.

"I want to check the horses," Elan called. Then he was gone, melting into the darkness. Abby muttered a curse under her breath, then crawled under her blanket fully dressed, unwilling to sacrifice a single scrap for the sake of comfort in the sharp night air. She did however rid herself of the holster and pistol. As for Elan, he seemed perfectly happy and unaffected by the chill, and Abby wondered, not for the first time, at his stamina. In all the months she'd known him, he'd never voiced a hint of complaint, regardless of the weather, and he acted as if riding more than fifty miles astride a horse was no more trouble than a leisurely automobile ride in a Lincoln. At the thought of that incongruous picture, Abby smiled. She could no more see Elan behind the wheel of a Lincoln than she could picture herself astride a rodeo bull at the Calgary Stampede.

How long Abby waited, she wasn't sure, but it seemed forever. The longer she waited, the more agitated she became. She locked her chattering teeth, willing herself to ignore the bone-chilling cold and failing miserably. She shifted uncomfortably, moving her tailbone off the uneven edge of a rock that seemed to appear from nowhere, only to encounter another stone even larger than the first. For every rock she removed there was always another to take its place. She rolled to her side and opened her eyes, giving up on sleep. Not three feet away, she spied the pile of wood she'd gathered for the campfire before Elan had forbidden it. She drew her hand from under the blanket to touch her nose. It was as cold as an ice cube. "That does it," she mumbled, resolutely flinging back the blanket and crawling over the rope on her hands and knees.

One tiny fire couldn't possibly hurt a thing. Elan was being overly cautious, and she'd be damned if she'd freeze to death to humor him. She fumbled in her pockets for the matches, congratulating herself on having the sense to keep them handy. In a few minutes she had a blazing fire and did everything but crawl in it.

Elan couldn't possibly expect her to spend more than a week on the trail without any amenities at all. He was just being stubborn. She knew he really didn't want to make the trip, and this was his way of making his point to her. Maybe he thought that if he made her uncomfortable enough, she'd beg to return to the cabin. Sometimes she wanted to scream in vexation at his mulishness. After all, she wasn't helpless, dependent on him for her every need. And that was really the crux of the matter. Elan still viewed her in that light. He wanted her to be a fragile female so he could boost his ego caring for her.

Certainly she'd gotten herself into a horrible mess with the Indians, but then when he came to save her, hadn't she saved him as well? Elan, as big and strong as he was, couldn't possibly have fought off the entire band of Indians at one time, though it was clear he thought he could. After she'd recovered from the ordeal, he'd given her a tongue-lashing for not doing as he told her and running away when the melee started. Though she'd been tempted to, she'd carefully avoided pointing out that she'd actually saved his hide.

*   *   *

Elan patted the mare on the rump and cocked his head, sniffing the wind. The smell of wood smoke drifted past his nose in the brisk night air. He spun around, tensing as he realized the direction from which it came. "*Merde!*" he spat, charging toward the camp. The little fool was determined to do as she pleased, even at the risk of endangering them unnecessarily. The blaze of a fire could be seen for miles on the open prairie, and the scent of smoke was just as dangerous. Anyone in the area could fix their position. It was true that he did not feel they would be in any great danger camped along the Missouri this early in the trip, but he was a cautious man, unwilling to place Abby in any more peril than he had to.

The more he thought about their undertaking the more he regretted allowing Abby to convince him to bring her. They would be fortunate to escape with their lives, and were he not a man of his word, he would turn the horses north and forget he had ever heard of Custer or the Little Bighorn.

Abby shrieked when she felt the two strong hands clamp under her arms and was hauled to her feet and tossed to one side as though she were a sack of goods. "Elan!" she cried, scrambling over her bedroll. "Stop it! Stop it now!" He vigorously kicked dirt over her fire, ignoring her protests, smothering all but a few glowing embers, then whirled to face her. Abby drew herself to her full height, shaking with rage tinged with a growing sense of unease. He'd snuck up on her, scaring her half out of her mind when he grabbed her and flung her out of his way. She pressed a fist between her breasts as though she could slow her galloping heart, and her breath came in shallow little pants. "You scared me!"

she cried, crossing her arms over her chest, forgetting that discretion is the better part of valor and immediately taking the offensive. She'd known he'd be angry with her, but she'd never actually feared him after their first encounter almost a year past. She refused to fear him now.

He towered over her, six and a half feet of muscle and sinew, well over two hundred pounds of hard flesh and brawn, and she lifted her chin and glowered when he took a casual step in her direction. "I said we would have no fire," he growled, advancing another pace. She dug in with both heels and refused to retreat.

"I was cold, and there's no reason why we have to freeze to death. There isn't anyone else around for miles!" She found her voice breaking despite her best effort to remain as calm as Elan appeared, and Abby knew him well enough to know he was far from calm. He was in control, but was far from calm. It angered her, brought tears of frustration to her eyes.

"Will you never learn?" Elan asked, his hand shooting out with lightning speed to snare her wrist and yank her to him. Abby gasped, finding herself molded to the hardness of his chest and thighs as he used his free arm to crush her against him, and then she relaxed, melting into his embrace. She raised her face, certain he would kiss her, convinced he had forgiven her, as he always did. He had only to hold her in his arms and he was as lost as she. She lifted herself on tiptoe and offered him her lips. "Not this time, Abby," Elan murmured, his black eyes glittering dangerously in the dim light of the moon.

"I'm sorry," she said, lowering her voice to a seductive whisper even as she lowered her eyes. "Come lie with me and make me warm." She shifted against him, feeling her blood begin to pump and sing through her veins, marveling at his ability to send her spiraling into heated desire with the simplicity of his touch.

"It will not work this time, Abby," Elan said, a note of regret deepening his voice. "You have disobeyed me once too often. I thought you learned better after I rescued you from the Indians."

Abby's heart skipped a beat, then sprinted into double time. A nagging little voice told her she was treading dangerous ground, but the words escaped her mouth before she could stop them. "Saved me?" she cried as her anger flared. "If I had run like you said instead of shooting those braves, we'd both be dead meat and you know it! Whether you want to admit it or not, I saved your ass!" She twisted away, attempting to remove herself from his grip, suddenly frightened more than she wanted to admit at the cool anger reflected in his dark eyes.

When Abby failed to break Elan's iron grip, she used the only option available. She kicked him in the shin. His only response was a low grunt as he slipped his arms around her and pinned her arms to her sides. She attempted another kick, but he sidestepped, and before she could mount a second attack, Elan spun her around and hoisted her over his shoulder. He quickly removed her boots from her kicking feet, tossing them aside as Abby screamed and pounded his back with her fists. "I knew you really didn't want to come. You're just trying to make me as miserable as possible. You can't do this! You wouldn't dare! I'll hate you forever! I swear I will! If you lay one hand on me, I swear I'll shoot you dead!" Her threats soon dissolved into sobs as she braced for the blows sure to come. She'd never felt so humiliated in her life. She was glad she was on the way to returning home! She was! She'd be well rid of Elan and his hopelessly dated chauvinistic attitude!

Elan curbed his growing temper as Abby threw her fit, and he realized as she pounded his back with her small fists that she actually thought he was going to beat her. If she only knew that he would sooner die than hurt her, she could save her breath.

Perhaps this was best. Having her hate him would make it easier for them both when they parted. And if the words rolling off her tongue were any indication of her feelings, she would hate him for all eternity and then some. He strode purposefully to her bedroll, stepping over her rope, grinning as he did so. If the rope comforted her, then so be it. He considered relenting and bedding down with her, then thought better of it. She might be uncomfortable, but she would not freeze, and truth to tell, he did not trust himself to sleep anywhere near her. He was too accustomed to reaching for her in his sleep. He dumped her unceremoniously to the ground, chuckling at her shocked stare as he gathered up his bedroll and strolled off into the darkness of the night.

"Wh–where're you going?" Abby stammered, scooting off the jagged point of a rock and rubbing her tender bottom, still not believing she'd escaped punishment from him. Saddle-sore as she was, she couldn't have hurt any worse if Elan had beaten her. She immediately regretted the fit she'd thrown as she contemplated a sleepless night in the freezing dark. She started when Elan materialized by her side, certain he'd changed his mind about letting her off the hook. In a defensive gesture, she tugged her blanket around her shoulders and braced for combat.

"Give me the matches," Elan said as he knelt to Abby's level and reached out his huge hand, prepared for the scuffle sure to come. He should have searched her before he released her, but his thoughts had been elsewhere at the time. He did not want to have to worry about her building another fire as soon as he was conveniently out of sight, and knowing Abby, she was sure to do so.

Abby lifted her chin, glowering mutinously, and for a full minute Elan examined her tear-streaked face, fighting his longing to kiss away the hurt, to feel the soft flutter of her long lashes caress his own roughened cheeks, to feel her lips swell beneath his, to feel the delicate sigh of her breath warm the hollow of his neck.

But it was not to be. Abby grudgingly thrust the matches into his hand, and he closed his fingers around them. "I will sleep by the horses, Abby," he said, and, kicking dirt over the remaining glowing embers, he was gone, leaving Abby dispirited and all alone.

Abby scrunched under the blanket and curled into a tight, wretched little ball, cramming her cold hands between her thighs, seeking warmth. She told herself she didn't care, but the truth was, she cared a lot, and her temper was rapidly replaced with remorse. The hateful words she'd hurled at Elan had been meant to hurt, and she was sure she'd accomplished her goal, but instead of feeling vindicated she could only summon forth melancholy, and of that she found a good healthy dose.

It had to be near dawn, Abby thought groggily, burrowing deeper within her blanket and rolling to her back, then shifting to her right side. She had suffered the tortures of the damned since she had bedded down on the hard, unforgiving ground. Camping without a tent and inflatable mattress was for the hardy or the foolhardy, and Abby now understood just how spoiled she was. A firm hand clamped over Abby's mouth, sending her eyes flying open, her pulse racing. She stared wide-eyed into

Elan's drawn face, scant inches from her own, feeling his
warm breath brush her cheek.

She realized it actually wasn't anywhere close to
dawn, for the night was as black as pitch except for the
faint glitter of the distant stars and the moonlight peeping through scattered clouds. Elan put a finger to his lips
and Abby nodded mutely, half her face covered by his
large paw, which smelled faintly like copper. She noted
that Elan's hair was dripping wet. She couldn't imagine
why he had felt the need to bathe in the freezing waters.

Elan cautiously removed his hand from Abby's mouth
and helped her to her feet. When she reached for her
boots, he stopped her and scooped her up, carrying her
several yards before depositing her in a stand of cottonwoods and willows by the riverbank.

"Stay put and do not make a sound," he mouthed into
her ear. He waited for her acquiescent nod before quickly
and efficiently breaking camp.

He had sensed the approach of the brave when the
Indian came for the horses, long before the animals
began their restless movements and snorts. The brave
was young and probably inexperienced in the game of
horse thievery. Elan had no difficulty dispatching him,
but he worried that more of his party would be in the
area. He had briefly considered waking Abby but
promptly discarded the notion. He could not chance taking her with him, and all things considered, she was safer
left alone. Should other braves appear during his
absence, they would be after the horses, and Abby was
well away from where the animals were hobbled and
grazing in the tall grass of the valley.

Scouting north along the river, Elan had traveled
scarcely three miles before coming upon a large encamp-
ment boasting more than a dozen teepees and over fifty

head of horses. He realized he and Abby had nearly blun-
dered into a small tribe off their reservation and on the
move to their summer hunting grounds. He had not
crossed the Indians' trail; backtracking, Elan discovered
the tribe came from the north and was traveling south.
He wanted to be well out of their reach when they broke
camp, especially when they discovered the missing brave.

He figured they had two or three good hours of darkness before the sun made its appearance, and he planned
to be miles away when it did. The body of the brave was
well hidden, weighted down with rocks beneath an abandoned beaver lodge in the swift-moving waters. If his
luck held, it would not be discovered. He would have
tossed it into the river to let it drift away, but there was
always the chance someone in the camp would see it as it
passed by, or it could snag on any number of objects and
be found.

He hated the thought of traveling on the open prairie,
for they could be seen for miles once the sun rose. The
rolling grass-covered hills afforded no cover such as
could be found in the thickly forested mountains or along
the riverbank.

Hoping to disguise their trail as much as possible, he
knew they would have to chance riding in the icy stream
for at least a few miles. It flowed to the northeast, and
though they would be traveling upstream, fording it to the
south, he had little choice. It was possible the ruse would
buy him the time he so desperately needed until he could
find a place to come ashore and strike out for the east. He
decided to abandon his plan to remain in the sheltered
valley until he reached Three Forks. Instead, he would
make for the east, then travel south to cross the
Yellowstone and find the Rosebud Valley.

Elan carried Abby's boots in one hand and with the

other gathered the reins of the horses, leading them along the edge of the stream as he plotted their new route. He had not expected to encounter Indians so early in their journey, and if tonight was any indication of the coming days, they were in for an arduous trek.

Abby trembled, hugging her arms around her, afraid to move, afraid to breathe. Her feet were not only cold, but were wet as well. Sinking in the spongy ground, she was at least ankle deep in the freezing water, with her stomach tied in knots and her heart in her throat. She wondered what had happened. Her legs began to shake, and she was afraid she would collapse from cold and exhaustion before Elan returned. *Where was he?* Was someone or something lurking in the darkness into which he had disappeared, or was he overreacting again? The more she thought about it, the more convinced she became that the latter was closer to the truth.

Abby cocked her head at the sound of the snapping twig. At last! So Elan was losing some of his stealth, or maybe her senses were improving. He wouldn't sneak up on her this time! If her teeth hadn't been chattering so hard, she would have laughed, for she imagined he enjoyed being able to move undetected through the night. Well, she had his number now.

"Elan," she whispered. "Over here!" He not only had lost his ability to move quietly, but had lost her as well, and she was ready to be found and moved to higher ground. She'd had about enough of his high-handed theatrics!

The muscled body that slammed into her with a resounding smack was not Elan, Abby realized belatedly, losing her footing and tumbling to the boggy ground beneath taut naked flesh, the scream she would have released stayed by the smelly hand clamped over her mouth and the knife blade at her throat. She dug her hands into the spongy ground, tearing at the mud and grass, searching for a rock, a limb, anything to use against the Indian atop her. She wouldn't go through it again. She couldn't. This time she would fight to the death before being hauled off. A hand snaked its way up the leg of her skirt, and Abby whimpered, writhing ineffectively. For the brave to have rape on his mind, he must have killed Elan, for surely he would understand that a woman wouldn't be alone out in the middle of nowhere. Hot tears scalded her face as Abby abandoned her clawing search and raised her fists to pound and scratch the brave's face. Let him slit her throat. She'd rather die fighting than live and be used as brutally as she'd been used before. He released her mouth to catch her wrist, and when he did, Abby screeched at the top of her lungs, tearing at his braided hair with her free hand, the sound of her voice in the still night air giving her renewed strength even as the blade pressed deeper into her throat.

"Abby!" Her name involuntarily escaped Elan's lips as her shrill scream disrupted the quiet night, and he abandoned the horses, cursing himself for a fool to have left her when he knew that other braves could be about. He moved cautiously but quickly, sacrificing stealth for speed, and could have found her easily even if he had not known where to look. The loud thrashing in the willows was unmistakable, and Elan plowed through the thick growth, heedless of danger, his blood drumming in his ears, his bone-handled hunting knife gripped tightly in his hand.

The brave swung his head around and slashed with his

knife a fraction of a second before Elan crashed into his lithe silhouette, knocking him off Abby and rolling with him into the edge of the river. Elan felt the blade graze his arm as they tumbled into the icy waters, but he was oblivious to anything except the straining grunts made by the brave and his own harsh breathing before the icy waters sucked him under.

Abby dragged herself to her knees, then pulled herself upright by clinging to the branch of a willow as if it were a lifeline. She swayed unsteadily, drawing in deep breaths of the sharp night air as she fought to clear her head. She strained her eyes, but failed to see anything other than the shadowed outlines of Elan and the Indian. She fell to her knees and scrambled around, feeling her way through the soggy grass and tangled roots. She had no way of knowing how the combat was going, and her only hope of helping Elan was in finding something to smash the Indian's skull. She had no earthly idea where to find the horses or her pistol.

Her numbed fingers scraped against a large, rough rock, and she frantically clawed it from the damp earth. Lifting it with shaking arms, she staggered into the swift current, slipping over the slick surface of submerged stones and falling hard on her rump, dropping the heavy stone across her thighs. With a strangled sob, she struggled to her feet and sloshed through the racing waters, her skirt dragging at her legs, threatening to unbalance her once again. Closing her eyes and muttering a prayer, she brought the rock crashing down on the head of the Indian brave.

20

"*Please,*" *Abby cried,* stiffly arching her throbbing back as she sat upright from the prone position she had assumed sometime before daybreak, staying in the saddle only by wrapping her arms around the chestnut's neck and resting her face in its coarse mane. "I've got to rest!" They were in the river, making better time since dawn broke but traveling slowly all the same, and Abby was soaking wet. She hadn't had a chance to dry out before Elan tossed her on her horse and struck out, and following in Elan's wake, Abby and the chestnut had been thoroughly splashed for hours. She shivered uncomfortably, fearing she would never know warmth again. Her sopping skirt clung damply to her legs, and her wet stockings were beginning to make her legs itch.

Elan held the chestnut's reins, not trusting Abby to keep up without him pulling her along, and he had tied the pack horses to the chestnut. By doing so, he was assured they would all stay together. He drew his mount up short and half turned in his saddle at Abby's plea, his mouth drawing into a taut line as he evaluated her bedraggled condition. Muddy smears blemished her pale face and matted her tangled hair. Her reddened hands were scraped and scratched, and she had broken several nails. Her clothing had suffered as well, looking as if she had spent the morning scuffling in a thorny bog.

Elan sighed, lifting his hand to shade his eyes as he scanned the rolling hills through which they traveled. The only trees on the barren prairie grew along the creeks and streams, and there were precious few of them. However few they were, at least they did afford some measure of cover. As much as he hated the thought, it was time to leave the river. It was taking them farther and farther off course. They had traveled it for miles, but he knew if the Indians followed, his ruse would not work for long. He could only hope he had effectively hidden the bodies of the two braves where they would never be found. There was nothing to do but leave the river and push as fast as he could for as long as Abby and the horses could hold out.

Elan urged his horse out of the water, tugging on the reins. He dismounted on the dry rocks along the riverbed and lifted Abby from the saddle. "We will rest the horses while you freshen up," he said. "Then we go." Abby nodded wearily, too tired to answer, then trudged through the willows to find a secluded spot.

Elan flexed his stiff shoulder, feeling it loosen. The slash from the brave's knife was not deep and had required little attention, but he feared his shoulder would have been broken if the boulder Abby had hurled had not bounced off the brave's head before striking him. As it was, he had a bruise the size of a melon, and he felt as if he had been trampled by a buffalo. He was chilled to the bone as well. It was getting harder and harder to save Abby from marauders. Perhaps, he thought with wry amusement, he should allow the next ones to keep her and let them do the suffering.

He checked the hooves of each horse, scraping off mud with his knife and searching for stones they might have picked up in the riverbed. He removed the few he found, then performed his own morning ablutions while he impatiently awaited Abby's return. The morning sun burned down, chasing away the last vestiges of the early-morning fog and drying his buckskins. Abby would soon feel better when her clothing dried and he got some food in her. He realized she was just about done in, but he could not afford to stop. Not yet. She would have to hold on a while longer. He dug into the saddlebag to find their meager meal.

"What's for breakfast?" Abby inquired, emerging from the willows, picking her way over the rocks to Elan and the horses. Elan wordlessly handed her a strip of elk jerky and a cold biscuit. Abby sank down on the trunk of a small pine, no doubt uprooted and transported downstream in the spring floods. She had dabbled in the river, cleaning her face and hands as best she could, but mud and bits of grass still clung to her hair and stained her clothing. Her face glowed damply in the warming sun, and Elan was relieved to see some color return to her cheeks.

"Some coffee would be wonderful," Abby said, allowing her eyes to challenge Elan's penetrating gaze, her fingers unconsciously raking her tangled hair. In fact, she would gladly sell her soul for a cup of steaming coffee. She could almost taste it, strong and liberally sweetened, hitting her stomach and giving her strength, releasing a jolt of caffeine to jump-start her aching muscles.

"We cannot build a fire, Abby." Elan gnawed another bite of jerky. "We will travel fast and rest as we must, but you must understand, there will be no fire. A fire," he continued, "is like a beacon, and if we are to live to see the end of this journey, we will not be able to have a fire."

"How long before we get to Three Forks?" Abby mumbled dispiritedly, flicking dried mud from her skirt. According to Winston, there was a sizable settlement near the forks of the rivers. If she could live to make it, she would insist Elan stop there to rest. She was still annoyed with him for sweeping so wide around Helena. He was being overly cautious. There was no logical reason to avoid the mining towns.

"We will not be going to the forks," Elan said, finishing his meal and brushing crumbs from his hands. He took a metal cup and dipped grain from a cloth sack wrapped in oilcloth and slung over one of the pack horses, then dumped the grain in a metal plate and proceeded to feed the animals. "We are turning east. I think it best."

"There's nothing to the east but unsettled plains!" Abby said, aghast. "You're talking about traveling several hundred miles into nothingness!"

"If our luck holds," Elan agreed, dipping more grain. "We will cross the Yellowstone, then make for the Rosebud. If our timing is right, we can find Custer before the battle begins. As it is, we have more than a week of hard riding ahead of us."

Abby struggled to her feet and went to mount the chestnut. With a resigned sigh, she grabbed the pommel and shoved her booted foot in the stirrup, hoisting herself into the saddle. "Then let's do it," she said, taking the reins and turning the mare into the eastern sun. Elan finished feeding the pack horses and put away the plate. He mounted the black gelding and quickly caught up with Abby as she cleared the willows and made for the open prairie.

*   *   *

Abby crossed her arms over the pommel and waited for Elan to return from the nearby hillside. They were in the valley of the Rosebud and had struck the Indians' trail the previous evening just before nightfall. Elan told her the trail was several days old, but he remained wary nonetheless. Today, only hours earlier, they had found evidence of numerous shod horses following the trail, and Elan was convinced they were near the end of their journey. It had to be Custer and the Seventh Cavalry just ahead of them.

The sun beat down mercilessly, hot and punishing, as it had since they had left the cool mountains, and Abby could feel not the slightest hint of a breeze. She had long given up any hope of comfort, and concentrated instead on mere survival, determined to keep up without complaint as she swatted mosquitoes and flies. If she looked as wretched as she felt, then she was a sorry sight indeed, for she hadn't had a real bath since the journey began, and though she had a change of undergarments with her, she still wore the split skirt and blouse with its matching vest. She had changed her undergarments regularly, washing them in the creeks and streams, but her outer clothing looked as if she'd lived, eaten, and slept in it for days, as indeed she had. It was no wonder Elan showed not the slightest interest in her.

Elan had become more and more distant as their journey progressed, forgoing conversation, judiciously avoiding her when they did stop for brief rests, and she realized she'd hurt him deeply, more deeply than she'd imagined when she'd thrown her screaming fit over the building of the campfire. She had soon realized he was right and had only been concerned for her safety.

She often found his brooding eyes settling on her, but when she made eye contact, he looked away or found some chore needing attention. He gave her no opening for apology, nor did he seem inclined to offer one to her for his own behavior. The close bond they'd shared seemed forever broken, leaving Abby with an enormous sense of loss for what might have been.

Abby suddenly sat straighter, her attention captured by two riders rapidly approaching from the southwest and kicking up a plume of dust. Elan scrambled down the hill, apparently spotting them as she did. She pulled her pistol, then reached across Elan's horse to take Winston's repeating rifle from the leather scabbard attached to his saddle. She tossed the rifle to Elan.

The riders were definitely Indians, but were dressed in a mishmash of cavalry blue trousers and printed shirts. One wore moccasins, the other black knee-length cavalry boots. Beneath dusty soldier's hats their hair flowed loosely down their backs, streaming almost straight out behind them, so fast were they riding. As they neared Abby wondered uneasily if the battle was over and if the Indians were dressed in some of the spoils of war.

Elan guardedly viewed the approach of the riders, weighing their demeanor, studying every detail of their appearance. There was nowhere to run, caught in the open as they were, and he gauged it best to hold his ground, but he prudently remounted in case he and Abby should have to run for it. Something troubled him about the riders as they grew near enough for him to inspect their dress and the saddles on their horses. These were not braves astride Indian ponies, and suddenly it came to him. The men must be cavalry scouts sent out by the large patrol he was tracking.

The two riders reined in their horses, halting in a cloud of dust just yards from Abby and Elan. "Are you with Custer?" Elan called, urging his mount around the chestnut and pulling the pack horses with him, placing himself between Abby and the Indians. The two men exchanged glances, and the half-breed riding the big buckskin spoke.

"Who wants to know?" he asked suspiciously, peering around Elan at Abby, who moved her chestnut up beside Elan, her pistol in her hand. "You ain't planning on shooting, are you?" he asked her.

"Depends," she replied coolly, meeting his stare as she ignored Elan's stiffening posture. She knew very well what Elan was thinking. He expected her to remain silent while he did the talking. Well, he should know after all the time they had been together that it was against her nature to be the retiring female he desired.

The second man chuckled, and the first one managed a slight grin. "We're with Custer," he affirmed, nodding at Elan. "Now, what the hell are you doing out here? Don't you know there's an Indian war about to commence?"

"That's exactly why we're here," Abby said. "We need to find Custer. We have important information for him about the Indians."

"I am Elan and this is my woman, Abby," Elan interjected. "We have ridden far to give our information to Custer."

"Yes!" Abby eagerly interrupted, smiling sweetly. "We've got to find Custer! Can you take us to him?" Elan sighed and curbed his tongue. Abby was playing the helpless female well. She would soon have the two men willing to do anything for her. As if he needed them to find Custer! Any fool could follow a path as large as the one Custer left behind. It was impossible to cover the trail of several hundred horses. Elan noted, however, that the cavalry traveled light, and he wondered about the lack of wagon or artillery tracks. Either Custer was inept, or he was unaware of the large number of Indians camped along the Little Bighorn. Perhaps he and Abby could be of some assistance after all. But could they change history? It was a perplexing question.

"Well, ma'am," the half-breed said, shifting in his saddle, then removing his hat and wiping his brow on his shirt sleeve, "the general's sorta busy right now. Why don't you tell me and Bloody Knife what's on your mind?"

Abby's spirits fell, the disappointment evident in her voice. "I really must see General Custer. It's a matter of life and death!" she added, widening her eyes for effect, pleased to see Bloody Knife show some interest in her speech. He leaned over to say something in the half-breed's ear, speaking in a guttural tongue Abby couldn't understand. He spoke for nearly a full minute, occasionally pausing to point in the direction from which they had ridden. When Bloody Knife finished his say, he straightened in his saddle and looked directly at Elan.

The half-breed nodded, then edged his mount closer to Elan, reaching out his hand. "Name's Mitch Bouyer," he said. "Scout to Custer and the Seventh Cavalry. Pleased to make your acquaintance, Elan. We'll take you to Custer, but I warn you, he won't be pleased."

Elan took the offered hand, catching Abby's eye, observing her self-satisfied smile. "Lead the way."

They could see the camp several miles out, lighted as it was by numerous fires, and from Bouyer's muttered curses, Abby realized the scout was as disturbed by the fires as she knew Elan would be. What must Custer be

thinking to announce his presence in such a manner? If
Elan knew better than to build fires in enemy territory,
surely a seasoned Indian fighter such as Custer pro-
claimed himself to be would know better. Abby followed
the men, riding behind Elan, who rode with Bouyer.
Bloody Knife scouted more than a mile ahead of their
small party. She urged her chestnut to a faster pace and
caught up with the men. "He's got fires burning!" she
exclaimed worriedly, casting her eyes at Elan as she came
alongside his horse.

"So it seems," Elan replied dryly. Custer was a fool,
and Elan immediately lost any respect he might have had
for the renowned Indian fighter. After nearly two weeks
on the trail without a fire, now he was dragging Abby
into the middle of a camp lit up like the Fourth of July.
They might as well send out engraved invitations. What
the hell had he gotten into?

"Bloody Knife's tried to tell him," Bouyer said tiredly,
pushing his mount up a hill, "but he won't listen. Custer
has stars in his eyes."

"I don't understand," Abby said, gripping her saddle
tightly with her knees as they climbed the rise. "What do
you mean by that?"

"You'll see soon enough," Bouyer said. "It's his way or
no way. All he wants is a star, and damn the conse-
quences."

"But I thought he was a general," Abby said, Bouyer's
meaning suddenly dawning on her. "Everything I've ever
read about him calls him General Custer."

"That's the rank he had when the Civil War ended,
but he's a colonel now, ma'am. And it shore rankles him.
It rankles him something fierce."

Apparently Bloody Knife had prepared the camp for
their arrival, for when they passed the sentries, they

received no challenge. It was as though they were expected. Abby rode with Elan, keeping her chestnut near his horse, appreciative of his presence in the milling crowds of soldiers as she searched for Custer.

She would have known Custer anywhere, even if he hadn't been crouched before a fire conferring with Bloody Knife, for he was a man to stand out in a crowd. When she spied him, his back was to her, and then he stood, tossing the remains of his coffee from a tin cup into the fire. He slowly turned to face the three of them, Abby, Elan, and Bouyer, with his hands on his hips. His rumpled navy-blue shirt showed evidence of much travel, and his trousers were stained and dirty. Around his neck was a long bright red scarf, one end thrown over his shoulder. His dusty black troop boots reached his knees. He had wavy golden hair on his head and also on his upper lip, trimmed into a thick mustache. His face was ruddy from sunburn where it had not been shaded by the broad felt hat he wore.

Abby stared unabashed, completely mesmerized and speechless, pinned by deeply set clear blue eyes fairly glowing with fanatical zeal. Custer impatiently tossed aside the stick he had been using to draw in the dirt, causing Abby to flinch as he dismissed her outright and directed his attention to Bouyer. "What's this nonsense Bloody Knife's been telling me?"

"These folks claim to know where the Indians are," Bouyer said, calmly dismounting and handing his reins to Bloody Knife, who rose to take them.

Custer swung his head and addressed Elan. "What do you know?"

"The Indians camp along the Little Bighorn southwest of the Little Wolf Mountains," Elan said. "But you need more men if you intend to make war with them."

Custer whirled around almost before the words left Elan's mouth, and he strode toward a group of officers, barking orders as he made his way through the camp.

Abby hesitated only briefly, then dismounted and picked up the cup Custer had discarded. She held it out to Bloody Knife, who filled it with steaming coffee from the gallon pot resting in the coals. From the general's own rations, he dipped her a generous amount of sugar. Abby gulped the scalding brew, burning her tongue and the roof of her mouth, but reveling in the instant warmth and jolt of caffeine. She accepted another cup, which she sipped more slowly as she wandered through the camp.

There were no tents, and the men were gathered in small groups around tiny campfires. Some were munching their rations of hardtack, but most were resting, sleeping soundly on the hard ground, their saddles used as pillows, their blankets drawn around them to ward off the chill night air. A few glanced in her direction, nodding as she passed, murmuring cursory greetings, and as Abby stared into their faces a horrible sense of foreboding swept her.

She was among the living dead, and their faces haunted her, touched her very soul. Young faces, fresh into manhood with smoothly shaven cheeks, and old faces with grizzled beards, veterans of many campaigns, all destined to find their final rest on the hill that would be known as Custer's Last Stand. A gangly youth looked up from the harness he was repairing and flashed her a wide grin. A strangled sob escaped her throat, and she stumbled, sloshing the dregs from her cup onto the ground. Elan's hand caught her elbow, steadying her, and she glanced over her shoulder, unaware until then that he had followed her. It was the first time he'd touched her since the first night on the trail, when they'd had such an awful row, and when she would have swayed into his embrace, he set her aside with a measured look, his features hard, his mouth a tight line.

Her step took on a new purpose, and she found herself no longer wandering aimlessly among the men. She would make Custer listen to her. Let him think what he would, but she couldn't let his men go blindly to their deaths without at least trying to stop the gruesome massacre that history said they faced.

"General Custer!" Abby's voice rang out, interrupting Custer's officers' call, and she hurried toward the huddled men, who viewed her approach with puzzled frowns. The general paused, half turning to face her as she neared. Elan was a step behind. A young orderly stepped in front of her, impeding her advance, but hastily removed himself when Custer ordered him aside. "May we speak in private?" Abby inquired somewhat breathlessly as she halted a scant yard from Custer.

"We move out in fifteen minutes." After issuing the curt order Custer dismissed his officers, who exchanged worried scowls.

"But sir," came an apprehensive protest from a trail-weary dark-haired officer wearing the insignia of a major, "the men are exhausted!"

"Fifteen minutes, Major Reno. That will be all!" Custer shot the words through gritted teeth, his recessed blue eyes flashing as he drew himself up to his full height of just under six feet.

"Yes, sir!" Reno growled, spinning on his booted heel and striding away, taking the other officers with him to spread the word of their departure. Abby waited impatiently until she had Custer's full attention, glancing around to be sure no other ears were listening. She and Elan seemed to be the last thing on the soldiers' minds as they rapidly began to break camp.

"General, I must tell you that if you engage in battle tomorrow, you and all your men will die. You have to wait for reinforcements." Abby paused for Custer's reaction, but was completely unprepared when it came. She expected Custer to doubt her, and she had her arguments ready, but she never expected the harsh roar exploding from his lips. His maniacal laughter shook her, making her forget her carefully prepared case, and she took a step back, bumping into the solidness of Elan, even as Custer took a menacing step in her direction.

"Madam, do you think I wage my campaigns on the whimsies of females?"

"But you have to listen!" Abby blurted out, abandoning her meticulously prepared case. "I know what I'm talking about! If you wait for General Terry and Colonel Gibbon, you can win the battle, and I can find the Indian medicine bag! I have to find the medicine bag!"

"Bloody Knife," Custer called across the camp as the scout rode by. "Take these two with you and the other scouts. Don't let them out of your sight!" Custer directed a cold stare in her direction. "When we have brought the hostiles to their knees, madam, you may collect all the medicine bags you desire." He left them in the care of Bloody Knife and took the reins of his mount from an orderly, mounting to gallop off and lead the column, his back stiff, his eyes looking neither left nor right.

"Do you see it?" Bouyer asked, hunched down by Elan on a bluff overlooking the Little Bighorn. Elan adjusted the binoculars, training them on a spot between the thick growths of willows and cottonwoods as he searched for the village Bouyer claimed was there. Movement akin to squiggling worms caught his attention. The pony herd.

Thousands of horses. Elan nodded silently, then brought the binoculars from his eyes, pausing to wipe sweat from his brow with his sleeve before relinquishing the field glasses.

"It is there," Elan agreed, searching the cloudless sky for some hint of a breeze. "Just as Abby said it would be." He backed his way down the bluff, an inch at a time, Bouyer at his side. Abby waited at the camp with Custer and more than two hundred and fifty of his men; the remaining troops were divided between Captain Benteen and Major Reno, each officer sent out separately to sweep the area.

"I'm sending for Custer," Bouyer said when they reached the two scouts holding their horses. "Maybe when he sees the size of the village, he'll listen to reason."

Elan loosened the laces of his shirt, seeking relief from the relentless heat, his eyes again searching the sky and finding nothing but a soaring red-tailed hawk. It was nearly noon, the sun a huge orange ball directly overhead, baking the prairie grasses and the men alike.

While they waited, Elan contemplated taking Abby. and fleeing, something he should have done during the forced march the previous night. Why Custer demanded he and Abby ride along with the troops was a mystery, unless Custer distrusted him and Abby and believed they might somehow forewarn the Indians of Custer's advance. As if the Indians needed warning, Elan thought with disgust. Custer had done all but herald his arrival; Elan knew, and figured Bouyer knew as well, that the Indians expected them. For all Custer's talk of catching the Indians before they discovered his troops and scattered, Elan still wondered if the man really believed his own words.

Elan observed the growing cloud of dust with concentrated interest. Custer, half dressed and riding bareback, approached in a thundering of hooves, throwing himself dramatically from his mount and scrambling up the bluff. Elan followed Bouyer and Custer at a more leisurely pace and crawled next to the general as he squinted into the binoculars.

"I don't see a thing!" Custer exclaimed, lowering the field glasses and glaring accusingly at Bouyer. Bouyer took the glasses and lifted them to his eyes, pointing as he did.

"They're there, General. More damn Indians than you ever saw together." Custer snatched the binoculars from Bouyer and peered through them again, snaking forward on his belly until his torso overhung the bluff.

"Well, I've got eyes as good as anybody and I don't see any damned Indian village or anything else!" Custer inched backward and leapt to his feet, readjusting the glasses before clamping them again to his eyes. "You see them, Elan?"

"Send for reinforcements, General," Elan said, standing and brushing off his buckskins. "You will need them."

"Let's go, Bouyer," Custer barked, thrusting the binoculars at the scout and scampering down the bluff, leaving Elan to wonder if the general would take his advice.

21

"*Oh, God, it's started.*" Abby sank to her knees in the dry grass beneath the blazing sun, clamping her hands over her ears, shivering even as she felt the trickle of sweat slip between her breasts and roll down her abdomen. It had begun, and though she and Elan were far too removed to hear the terrible screams of the dying men and horses, occasionally she could distinguish the sound of gunfire. By holding her hands to her ears, she could shut it out, could almost pretend the smoke and dust came from something as ordinary as a whirlwind instead of from charging cavalry and firing guns.

Custer had been determined to lead his men into certain death, and no amount of pleading on Abby's part could deter him. Against the advice of his scouts and junior officers, he had made his advance on the premise that the tribes would scatter if he waited until the following morning, when the troops could be reassembled and reinforcements brought up. But after less than twenty-four hours in Custer's company, Abby knew better. Custer was frantic for victory and the glory coming with it, and he meant to share it with no other commander. Today he would make his wife a widow and take his place in history. Her only regret was the men he took with him, and they did not go unknowingly to meet their fate. It was written in their eyes as they rode out, and it was something Abby would never forget.

Elan's heavy hand touched Abby's shoulder, and she looked up through eyes blurred with tears to find him standing beside her, watching even as she watched. He dropped his gaze to her tear-streaked face, then sank to one knee as he gave her shoulder a squeeze. She placed a timid hand atop his long callused fingers, feeling her heart soar when he laced them through her much smaller ones.

Elan was tired, and it showed in his hooded eyes, in his drawn face covered with two weeks' growth of coarse black hair, in the slight droop of his broad shoulders. He had gone virtually without sleep for most of the trip, prowling at night while she slept like the dead. Abby had learned to drop off at a moment's notice, and had often slept the few minutes several times each day when Elan stopped to rest the horses. Even so, after the sleepless night of forced marching, she was exhausted, and practically hysterical with fatigue. Nearly two weeks of hard riding across punishing prairies and fording countless treacherous rivers and streams had finally caught up with her. She used her free hand to swipe at her tears, succeeding only in smearing the grime on her face.

Elan took the wide hem of Abby's skirt and dabbed at her damp face, attempting to repair the damage. "It is time to go, Abby." He pulled her to her feet, then dropped his arms to his sides, forcing himself to keep his distance. "There is nothing more to be done."

"Go where?" Abby asked dully, surveying the open terrain. "How are we ever going to get out of this mess?" Fresh tears spilled as Abby thought of the thousands of Indians around them, Indians hyped up on blood lust who wouldn't hesitate to kill any white available. Her stubbornness in searching for the medicine bag had done exactly what Elan feared all along; it had placed them in grave danger. She was no closer to finding her way back to her time than she had been before leaving the Blackfoot Valley. She should have realized she couldn't change history. She should also have realized Custer would have no patience for humoring a woman in the midst of an Indian campaign, regardless of what she wanted or the information she had to offer.

Elan considered Abby's question, and his own good sense told him to take Abby and ride as fast as they could go; however, something held him back. Abby would never be truly content until she was sure the medicine bag could not be found, and her reasoning for searching for it in the valley of the Little Bighorn was sound, for surely there had never been such a gathering of tribes as that camped along the river. It was possible that after the battle ended they could still find it, and however slim the chance, he was determined to see it through.

"How long does the battle last?" Elan asked, slapping at a mosquito buzzing around his head. *Merde,* but it was hot, the day airless without any hint of a breeze and not a cloud in the sky. It would be much cooler in the shade along the river, but he dared not chance entering the valley.

"An hour or two, but the Indians won't move out until tomorrow evening," Abby replied. "At least that's what Winston said. Major Reno and Captain Benteen will be trapped on a hill tonight with some of their men. Many of them will survive."

"We will stay here until the Indians are gone," Elan said, turning his back on the distant battle, though it was hard for him to ignore it. "Then we will explore the battlefield and the abandoned village."

Abby nodded, settling down to wait, accepting his decision though she knew she for one had no intention of exploring the battlefield. Elan could go if he wished, but he could count her out. The very thought of wandering through the carnage sickened her. If she had to scavenge among the dead for the medicine bag, she would just as soon forget about it. She sprawled in the grass, throwing her arm over her eyes to shade them from the relentless sun. Then she dozed.

Abby opened her eyes, blinking in the sudden glare of the setting sun, trying to decide what had awakened her. "Do not move." Elan's calm voice stilled her very breath. She had learned to trust his instincts, and when he spoke in the low tone he now used, he was very serious indeed. She carefully glanced around and found him off to her left standing statue-still on the balls of his feet, holding his bone-handled hunting knife in his hand. Then, in a flash of movement, he hurled the blade and hauled her to her feet, scooping her up in his arms, fiercely crushing her to his chest.

"You forgot the rope," Elan growled, forcing his arms to release Abby. He settled her on her feet, then reached up to unwrap her arms from around his neck. She was white despite her sunburned face. She scanned the ground, and he chuckled at her belated concern.

"Thank you, Elan," Abby said shakily, watching the headless rattler flop about in the throes of death, suddenly thinking of the soldiers on the battlefield. A little cry escaped her throat, and without thinking she threw herself into Elan's arms, seeking to confirm his unfailing strength, his ability to protect her and keep her safe.

"I'm sorry, Elan," Abby sobbed, releasing in a flood of tears and hiccuped words all the pent-up emotions she had been suppressing for days. "I've been acting like a spoiled brat, and I've hurt you. You've been right all along, and I've made things so much harder by not listening to you. Can you ever forgive me?" She rested her cheek on his stained buckskin shirt, inhaling his rich masculine scent.

Perhaps it was the knowledge of death all around that made Abby burn to reaffirm life, or perhaps it was the way Elan's arms cradled her as his hands stroked her back, but she wanted him, needed him. She ached to have him take possession and brand her once more as his own. Her arms lifted to encircle his neck, to sift her fingers through his thick black hair, to slowly run her hands over his muscled shoulders and dig her fingers into his hardened biceps. She heard him groan, and, growing more excited, she lifted herself on tiptoe to nibble at his neck.

Elan wanted to take her, desired her more than life itself, but he had vowed to return her to her time if he possibly could, and if he took her now, he knew he would never let her go. Only by keeping himself distant and by encouraging her anger could he steel himself to her soft touch. "I am filthy from the trail." He removed her arms from around his neck and took a step back.

Abby faltered as he moved her aside, and she longingly searched for any indication, any suggestion of forgiveness. She found none in his set features. "I asked for forgiveness," she said slowly, lifting a hand to place it on his chest, feeling a spark of promise in the drumming of his heart.

"Words once spoken can never be recalled," Elan said steadily, glancing down at her small hand resting over his heart. She waited hesitantly, uncertainty flushing her soft features. Elan thumbed a wayward tear from her eye. "No more tears, Abby." She lifted her chin to meet his gaze, her eyes deepening in color to the familiar midnight hue that never failed to touch his soul, and with a small sigh she turned to walk away. He caught her arm and she paused, glancing over her shoulder, her chin quivering. It was almost his undoing, but he held fast to his conviction, knowing he would otherwise be forever lost. "Watch for snakes," he said gruffly, releasing her. She nodded, then stiffened her spine and left him to seek a comfortable spot near the packs he had taken from the horses. He was not surprised to see her take her sliver of soap from her saddlebag.

Elan held his tongue when Abby poured a few drops of precious water from her canteen over a scrap of cloth and washed her face and hands. A woman needed some comforts, and truth to tell, he could use a good washing himself. She dug deeper into her saddlebag and came up with a comb, which she used to rake through her tangled hair, then tied the freshly combed locks with a scrap of ribbon. Watching her perform her womanly tasks was always a pleasure.

For the duration of their journey Abby had kept herself as clean and fresh as she possibly could, bathing in the icy streams, scrubbing her hair frequently, washing her underclothing regularly. But since joining Custer's troops the previous day, Abby had not had the opportunity to perform her simple ablutions.

Elan hoped that Abby's interest in her appearance would help keep her mind off the events surrounding them, events he could not push from his mind. It was difficult for him to stand aside and not join the fray, and had he not had Abby with him, he would have stood with Bouyer. He wondered about the man whose background was so like his own, son of a French-Canadian and an Indian squaw, and felt that if they had been given the chance, he and Bouyer could have been good friends. Would Bouyer survive? Not very likely if he rode with Custer, and he had been with Custer when the troops rode out. Bloody Knife had been sent with Reno. It was a senseless loss for both the whites and the Indians, and Elan could only hope each would learn the lesson well.

It was just past dawn on the morning of June 27 when Abby and Elan made their way through the sun-baked grass and sagebrush and into the cool shade of timber in the Little Bighorn Valley. Elan, returning from his scouting the evening before, had reported the Indians were breaking camp and moving slowly in the direction of the Bighorn Mountains. He and Abby spent another night in the open to make sure the Indians were long gone before they descended into the valley to conduct their search.

"I don't know why we can't go and find Reno and Benteen," Abby complained as her horse crossed the Little Bighorn. "We can at least tell them the Indians have gone."

"They know," Elan replied, pulling on the lead of the pack horses, urging them across the stream. "I have no wish to become entangled with the cavalry again. When the investigation into this mess begins, I want no part of it." Elan worried about having to explain his and Abby's participation in the affair. Too many questions would be asked about their timely arrival and about their knowledge of events. It would be difficult to explain how he and Abby came to be involved. Perhaps if they could leave without reminding Reno and Benteen of their presence, the two officers would forget about them altogether, or at least place no importance on them.

"You can leave me here," Abby said, pulling the chestnut to a halt in the shade of a towering cottonwood. "I don't think I've got the stomach to go up that hill." Elan pulled his horse about and rode to Abby's side to hand her the lead for the pack horses.

"You are right," he agreed. "It is no place for you. But you must promise to remain in this place until I return. I will not be long."

"I promise," Abby said, dismounting and stretching her back. She dropped the reins and allowed the horses to crop the sweet green grass growing near the river. With a curt nod, Elan left her.

He smelled the bloated carcasses of the men and horses before he spied them, and he paused to tie a strip of cloth over his nose. The bodies of the men had been stripped, and most were mutilated. But Custer, except for his wounds, was virtually untouched. A cavalry horse, wounded but on its feet, shied away as Elan approached, and he decided to leave it to graze. The Indians had taken their dead with them, and Elan realized he had known all along that they would. The medicine bag was not on the hill with Custer. Perhaps it had been left behind when the Indians broke camp. That was the only place left to look, and the camp had stretched for three miles along the river. He would take Abby and they would search every inch of the terrain.

Elan had often heard his father speak of the horrible ways of war, but this was the first time he had experienced it firsthand, and it weighed heavily upon him. The dead littered the ground from the river to the top of the hill, where most lay, beneath the grueling sun. It was difficult to walk away without doing something for them, but he knew he should not interfere. The army would bury its dead.

"It was bad, wasn't it?" Abby asked softly as Elan approached. She rose to meet him, rushing across the small pebbles and through the grass. She could see the anger in the tightness of his jaw and the sadness reflected in his eyes. She reached out to touch his hardened thigh, seeking to offer some reassurance, some comfort after what he had witnessed, and her breath caught in her throat as she made contact with his muscled flesh.

"It was," Elan said abruptly, finding it hard to speak of what he'd seen and offering no details. "But there is no sign of the medicine bag. The Indians have taken their dead with them." He dismounted, his movement causing Abby to drop her hand self-consciously to her side. "Nothing lives on that hill but one horse. You and Winston were right. Custer led them all to their deaths."

Elan strode purposefully to the river and hastily began to strip off his buckskins. When he pulled his shirt over his head and tossed it to one side, Abby stared in speechless amazement. Of all the reactions to the slaughter, this was the last thing she expected. When he removed his moccasins, she hardly noticed, so intent was she on the rippling play of sinew in his wide shoulders, and so fascinated was she by the way his back narrowed as it tapered into his waist. But when he stripped off his buckskin trousers, giving her a full view of his hard, muscled buttocks and thighs, she found her tongue.

"Are you crazy?" she cried, becoming more and more agitated as turbulent thoughts raced through her head. That he should have the nerve to strut about bare-ass naked in front of her in broad daylight without any shred of modesty was more than she could take! She wanted to turn her back, to ignore his blatant display, but he held her mesmerized as he wadded his trousers into a ball and hurled them aside. "You'll catch your death!" she spluttered as he waded into the stream and lowered himself into the icy waters, submerging himself to the waist.

"Will you toss me the soap, or do I have to come get it?" Elan asked, arching a brow, biting back a grin as he observed Abby's discomfort. That she could still react like a blushing virgin amused him greatly, and he loved nothing more than to see the color stain her cheeks and bring sparks to her eyes.

His question spurred her to action, and he splashed water over his back as he waited for her to dig her hoarded bar from the saddlebag. She tentatively approached and held the small bar out to him, acting for all the world as if it burned her hand. "Are you so determined to watch that I have to stand and walk over to get it?" Elan teased, making as if to rise. Abby hurled the soap, then backed up several steps, her eyes firmly focused on his face.

"Perhaps you would like to join me?" Elan casually inquired, catching the bar and rubbing it over his arm. "The water is brisk and will stir your blood." He moved the bar to soap his chest, seemingly unaffected by Abby's suspicious glare as he vigorously scrubbed.

"I don't think so," Abby replied guardedly. "I bathed while you were gone." She couldn't imagine how he stayed in the freezing water, but there was no way she would join him to find out. She had to grit her teeth and force herself to wash with a small cloth dipped in the stream. She knew she would die from shock if she plunged in, and here Elan was, leisurely washing as though he were immersed in a natural hot spring!

Elan enjoyed the cleansing despite the temperature of the water. Not only was he eager to wash away the smell of death that seemed to cling to him, invading every pore, but he wanted to rid himself of two weeks' worth of dirt and grime picked up on the trail. Abby's efforts to civilize him had apparently worked, for never before had he worried about such things.

Abby stood transfixed, watching Elan bob like a duck to wet his hair and beard. He washed both thoroughly, then went under to rinse, coming up shaking his head, slinging icy droplets in all directions. Then he rose, and before Abby could avert her eyes they drank in the sight of him, following the streams of water as they ran down his chest and through the thick curly hair of his groin to drip in silvery droplets down his legs. He was truly magnificent, emerging from the shallow waters like Neptune from the sea, and just looking at him filled Abby's heart to overflowing and sent heated desire spiraling through her.

She dragged her gaze away and turned her back, stumbling through the willows, unwilling to have him see the naked longing etched in her face. He didn't want her. She was nothing but a burden he wanted to discard, for why else would he continue to insist on finding the medicine bag? She wasn't sure finding it was the answer anymore. If he asked her to stay with him, she would, and gladly, for she realized as pain enveloped her heart that she loved him. She knew in her soul that if he wouldn't go with her, she would stay with him. He had sacrificed so much and she had given nothing. She would spend the remainder of her life loving him if only he would allow it. But she wouldn't beg. She had apologized and he hadn't accepted her apology. She could only be happy with him if he wanted her, if he loved her as she loved him, for without mutual caring and understanding, what would she have? Nothing more than she had already, and that was not good enough.

Elan shook like a wet dog, then used his hands to brush the excess water from his torso as he waded from the river. He was refreshed, renewed, ready to face whatever the day would bring, and as soon as he dressed in the clean buckskins he had packed away, he would find Abby and together they would meet their destiny. It was important to him that he present a civilized appearance.

Before he met Abby he had been as one with the animals in the woods, hardly caring how he looked or how he smelled as he went about his trapping or exploring. Civilization and the comforts associated with it had meant little to him, and though he could hold his own in civilized company, he rarely sought it out. Women were something else altogether. He had realized as he was educated at the mission schools that half-breeds were considered something less than human, and when he was questioned about his lineage, he had quickly learned to claim his father's French-Canadian bloodline, conveniently omitting his mother's Indian blood. He had been unwilling to seriously consider taking a wife without revealing his full family history, and he had known no respectable female would have him when she learned of it.

But today he would tell Abby, and the thought of sharing his most closely guarded thoughts with her lifted his spirits. If they did not find the medicine bag, he would tell her of his lineage and ask her to marry him, for he loved her more than he had ever thought it possible to love another. If she found the medicine bag and insisted on returning to her time, he would still tell her, for he wanted her to take with her the full truth of who he was and where he came from. Somehow their fates were linked, if not here in this time, then somewhere in another time. He knew this as well as he knew his own name, a name he had not been called since he left the mission schools. He would tell her that also, for it was important that she know him fully.

When Abby looked up to find Elan standing over her, she wished she had joined him in the river and repaired her own disheveled appearance, for he had never been more handsome. He had taken the time to trim his hair and had shaved his beard as well, leaving his smooth cheeks and chin a shade lighter than the rest of his face. He flashed her a crooked grin that deepened his dimples and reached his dark eyes, and she couldn't help but return his smile, wondering as she did what had put him in such a humor. "You look like the cat that ate the canary," she quipped, noting that his grin broadened considerably. "Are you frozen solid?"

"Not frozen, but I will not complain of the heat anytime soon," he replied with a chuckle. "I fear you might have spoiled me with your warm water and your bathing tub."

"If you liked the tub, you'd love a hot shower," Abby said as she strolled with Elan to find the horses. "Modern bathrooms are one of the things I miss the most. There's just nothing like steaming up the mirror and stepping from under a pulsing stream of hot water to dig your toes into a plush rug in a heated bathroom."

"What else do you miss?" Elan asked, holding back a branch as she walked through the willows. She paused to wait for him, and he dropped his arm comfortably around her shoulders as they resumed their pace. Abby relaxed against him and put her arm around his waist as he adjusted his step to hers, glad he was at least now willing to be friends again. She had truly missed the comfort of his arms.

"Books, I think, more than anything," Abby said thoughtfully. "I love to read, and I haven't read a book in almost a year. If anyone had told me I could survive this long without one, I wouldn't have believed it." She tipped her head to see his face. "What about you? What do you miss the most from your time?"

"I do not know if I can explain it to you," Elan said worriedly, slowing his step as he searched for the right words. "It is not something you can touch or even see, but a feeling deep inside."

"Tell me," Abby encouraged. Elan paused, then leaned against a large cottonwood, pulling Abby to him. She rested her face against his chest and listened to the steady beat of his heart as he wrapped her in his arms.

"When I stood on the east bank of the mouth of the Missouri and talked my way into the trip that brought me here, there was such excitement running through my blood that I thought my heart would burst. And that excitement grew with each mountain we crossed, with every new thing I saw. I felt the same when my father took me on my first hunting trip when I was but a boy, and then the first time we trapped along the Missouri. Do you understand what I am trying to say?"

"I think so," Abby said, plucking at his shirt. "It's the adventure you miss." Elan laughed, prompting Abby to scowl and toss her head, but he rested his chin atop her head and she could see only the corded muscles of his neck.

"Since I found you I have had many adventures," Elan said dryly. "It is not the adventure."

"Then what?" Abby frowned and punched him playfully in the ribs, realizing she was being teased.

"Do you remember the map Winston gave to us?" Elan lifted his chin, allowing Abby to peruse his face as his tone grew serious once more.

"Yes," she answered hesitantly. "But what does the map have to do with it?"

"In my time, this land was not mapped. A man did not know what lay beyond the next hill, the next river. That is what I miss, and even if I should go back to my time that would be forever lost to me, for now I know." He took her by the hand then and led her toward the horses.

22

"Elan! Wait for me!" Abby sprinted, stretching her legs in an effort to catch up. Elan had spotted the two white teepees pitched well away from the river as they walked the horses while searching for the Indians' camps. He had taken off, leaving her and the animals behind. They had crossed travois tracks, deep parallel grooves digging up the grass and cutting into the hard soil, marking the trail the Indians had taken to the Bighorn Mountains, but the teepees were the first hard evidence they'd found. Abby's excitement grew as they neared the hide-covered structures. Hadn't Winston described such a place when he'd told them of his encounter with the medicine bag?

Abby wondered how Winston and Annie were, hoping that the two of them could find a way to make a life together. Annie was working diligently to become respectable, and Abby had faith Annie would succeed in bringing Winston around. As for Lori, she loved Annie

dearly, for how could she not? Annie's winsome personality had quickly captivated the child. Abby found herself
missing the three of them acutely, for they had all been a
large part of her life over the last year. Sometimes Abby
found it hard to believe all that had happened in the span
of twelve short months, and had someone else told her
such a fantastic tale of time travel and adventure, she
would have escorted the poor soul to the nearest mental
hospital, just as anyone in her time would do for her if
she came home relating such events.

It was still almost too incredible, and Abby had long
since given up trying to make sense of it. She could
accept it, and she could deal with it, but there was simply
no way she could understand it.

When she saw the poles outside the lodges with fresh
scalps hanging from them, Abby stopped in her tracks,
fighting nausea as she waved away the buzzing flies.
Interspersed among the scalps were other spoils of war—
metal belt buckles and shell casings, brass buttons and
remnants of army-blue cloth, horse tack, and other
scraps of metal and leather. Hung by rawhide strips, the
ornaments swayed in the faint breeze, occasionally
releasing a clinking sound when pieces of metal struck
together. It was a horrifying sight, wind chimes made of
bits and pieces of the Seventh Cavalry, and once Abby
mastered her fright, anger surged to take its place.

"Filthy savages," she cried, digging her nails into the
palms of her hands in impotent rage. "Nothing but murderous savages!" She turned her back on the ghastly
sight, swallowing bitter bile as her stomach rolled threat-
eningly.

"It is their way of honoring their dead, Abby," Elan
said gently, appearing silently at her side. "You must not
let it frighten you."

"Why can't they at least leave the dead alone? Why do they have to desecrate the bodies? How can they be so cold and insensitive?" Abby's questions tumbled out, one after the other as she tried to come to terms with the massacre. Knowing the fate of the Seventh Cavalry and being unable to do anything to change it weighed heavily upon her, and she had played her conversations with Custer over and over again in her mind, certain she could have stopped him had she found the right words. She never considered telling him the truth, for he wouldn't have believed her, but surely there should have been something she could have said.

"It is their way, Abby, and you cannot be expected to understand it any more than they can understand the ways of the whites," Elan said soothingly as he stroked Abby's hair. She trembled beneath his touch as he placed an arm around her.

Buds from the shedding cottonwoods filled the air, clinging to their clothing and littering the ground, reminding Abby of cleansing snow. She wished they could fall thickly enough to cover the horror of the last two days, but realized no amount of cleansing could ever erase it from her mind, and only by attempting to detach herself from it could she hold on to her sanity.

"I'll be fine," Abby said, brushing ineffectively at her hair and clothing. "I think I'm over my hysterics."

"Then we will explore the lodges." Elan took her hand and tugged her along behind him to the nearest teepee, his long strides countering her deliberately slow steps. She hung back while he lifted the flap, and he released her hand to enter the gloom. Abby briefly considered striking out for tall timber, where she could hide and try to forget, but instead took a deep breath and hesitantly followed his stooped back.

The interior was dark, the only light coming from the open flap through which they entered, and by remaining in the entrance, Abby blocked most of that. It was hot inside the lodge, the air thick with the sickeningly sweet smell of death. Abby peered around Elan, then shrank behind him, her hand covering her nose and mouth in a futile effort to block the odor. She weakly rested her forehead against his back, and breathed through her mouth. One quick glance was all she needed to know she wasn't interested in searching further. She closed her eyes when he moved away from her, unwilling to look again upon the faces of the decomposing Indians.

Six dead braves, finely dressed and generously bedecked with ornaments, populated the teepee. Each was bound standing to a vertical pole. Numerous rawhide strips hung from the poles and from the top of the teepee, and tied to the leather thongs were more of the same ornaments decorating the poles outside the lodge. Animal hides covered the dirt beneath their feet, and several woven grass bowls were placed about, all filled with various kinds of roots and berries.

"It is not here," Elan said, taking Abby by the arm and leading her through the open flap of the teepee. Abby all but raced into the open, opening her eyes and breathing deeply in the fresh air. "We will try the next one."

"Oh, no!" Abby shook off Elan's hand. "Not me! I'll wait right here. Hurry," she called after him as he strode off. "I want to get out of here!"

The place gave her the heebie-jeebies, and she wanted nothing more than to leave and never look back. She'd seen enough death and dying to last a lifetime. She'd been living a fantasy, believing she could find the medicine bag when it could be anywhere in the world, not to mention in any time period. Elan hadn't been anywhere near the Custer Battlefield when he'd come across it, and neither had she. Just because Winston had found it along the Little Bighorn didn't mean it would pop up again in the same spot. Just because it was logical to look for the medicine bag at the greatest gathering of Indians ever known didn't mean it would be conveniently awaiting her arrival. After all, what had logic to do with it? There was absolutely nothing logical about time travel!

Elan paused just inside the teepee, blinking to adjust his eyes. It was another burial lodge, much the same as the first one he and Abby had entered, but this one contained the bodies of five braves, not six. The center pole of the tent did not have a body lashed to it. Instead, hung among a quiver of arrows and below a painted leather shield was a finely quilled medicine bag.

He cautiously advanced a step and peered closely, his blood drumming in his ears, his hands prudently clasped together behind his back. It was the bag he sought. He staggered back, tripping over the bleached skull of a buffalo, hardly feeling the sharp bones beneath his feet.

The time had come, and he was not ready. He had known it would be difficult, but he was unprepared for the searing pain that tightened his chest and made breathing next to impossible. If he were a lesser man, he could walk back outside and tell Abby the medicine bag was not to be found. She would not question his word, but then he would never know true inner peace. He wanted Abby only if she wanted him, and though he knew she enjoyed bedding him, he wanted her love. And he wanted it unconditionally.

"What is it?" Abby ran to Elan as he emerged from the lodge, panic-stricken at his ashen color and his apparent disorientation. He shook his head, lurching past

her, catching her wrist and pulling her back when she
ducked her head to peer into the fetid-smelling teepee.

"Do not go in there." Elan's voice brooked no argument,
and Abby allowed him to drag her away from the open flap,
gulping fresh air to replace the foul odor she'd inhaled.

"The medicine bag is in the teepee," he said. Abby
stared at him, opening and closing her mouth, unable to
find the words she needed.

"Are you sure?" The question, barely whispered, was
all she could manage as a myriad of emotions vied for
control, and none of them the ones she expected.
Shouldn't she feel jubilation that their journey had been
successful, or satisfaction that she was right in coming?
And where was the excitement? Shouldn't she be fairly
dancing in anticipation of the possibility of returning to
her time?

But all she felt, amid the fear and uncertainty, was
pain—breathtaking, heart-wrenching pain. She doubled
over with the force of it, wrapping her arms around her
waist. It was time to go, but she wasn't ready to leave
him. But what choice did she have? Elan had risked his
life to bring her, and he seemed determined to see her go.
Really, wasn't that what she wanted? It was just the
shock of actually finding the medicine bag that had her
confused. Of course, that was it. She was suffering from
shock. After all she'd been through during the last few
months, it was no wonder. She straightened her spine
and lifted her chin.

"Wait!" Elan's deep voice boomed, halting Abby as
she stooped to enter the lodge. She hesitated for a
moment, then stepped resolutely through the opening
before she could change her mind.

It took her a few seconds to adjust her eyes to the darkened interior of the lodge, but when she could distinguish

the contents, she knew Elan was right. There was no mistaking the beautifully quilled medicine bag with the two intertwined jagged lightning bolts, one black, the other bright red. She concentrated on the medicine bag, willing herself to ignore the macabre sentries guarding it. It was waiting for her, just as she'd known it would be. It would take her home, and somehow everything would be all right. She closed her eyes and took an uncertain step, her hand outstretched.

"Noooo!" Abby sprawled face down among the hides, flattened as if by the force of a freight train, squeezing her eyes tightly shut as she fought for breath beneath the crushing weight. She gradually became aware of harsh rasping in her ear and cracked open one eye, finding Elan atop her. She squirmed beneath him and pushed herself up on her elbows, not an easy effort under his considerable weight.

"What are you doing?" she cried. "Get off! I can't breathe!" He rolled off her, then lurched to his feet, bending to take her hand. She allowed him to pull her to a standing position, then found herself pushed ahead of him through the opening of the lodge.

"There are things I must tell you before you leave!" he said urgently. He released her and walked away a few steps. She nervously pulled at her clothing, straightening her blouse and skirt as she waited for him to regain his composure. Finally he spun to face her, and she realized she had seen such raw emotion beset his features only once before, and that had been the night they'd returned to the cabin after he rescued her from the Indians.

"I'm listening," Abby said worriedly, feeling jittery and uneasy knowing the medicine bag was so near. She'd worked up her courage, but Elan had stopped her. What if she couldn't get it back? She crossed her arms under her breasts and took a deep, shaky breath.

Elan's eyes swept over her from her head to her feet as he sought to stamp her features forever into his mind. She had never been lovelier, and he wanted to remember her as she was now, with her shiny black hair falling in lustrous waves past her shoulders, her flushed cheeks suffused with color, her blue eyes wide beneath their dark lashes. He let his gaze drift down the body he knew so well.

Jerking his attention back to his purpose, Elan gathered his nerve and spoke. "I believe we have been brought together for a reason. When we came together to this time, it was not a thing of chance, and now that you are leaving, I want you to take a part of me I have shared with no other person."

Abby took a step in Elan's direction, but Elan held up a restraining palm, halting her in midstride as he continued. "When I was but a boy, my father took me from the village where I was born. My mother and many other members of her tribe had sickened and died with the smallpox, a disease brought by the whites. It was a terrible summer and I remember it well. For some reason unknown, I was spared. He took me to a school run by missionaries, and there I learned to put away my Indian ways. I eagerly took the knowledge they offered, learning to read and write because they said it would make my father proud. I learned to dress like the whites and to talk like them. I also learned to deny my mother's people, for half-breed Indian boys were not acceptable in polite society, not then, and— as I realized when I came to this time—not now."

Abby took another step toward Elan, her heart aching for the lonely little boy removed from everything familiar and sent to a place where he felt himself to be an outcast, but something in his face stopped her, told her he wanted her to keep her distance.

"Do not pity me, Abby," he said softly. "It is not your pity I want." Abby drew an unsteady breath, resisting the urge to hurl herself into his arms and kiss away the hurts he'd kept locked inside his soul. To think she'd made such an unfeeling comment about trappers and their squaws! Her face burned with the memory, and she could only hope he could forgive her ignorance.

"My father came for me when I was a young man. He was angry the missionaries had not completely erased the French tongue I spoke and replaced it with English. I did not understand at the time, because it was the language he spoke and the language spoken by many of my mother's people. But I came to realize he was right, and I tried to put my French away."

Abby laced her fingers tightly together, nervously dampening her dry lips. She ached to go to him, to stroke his hair and draw his face to her breasts and tell him she understood his pain, understood his need. She yearned to hold him in her arms and make everything all right. How could he believe his Indian blood would repel her? Indian blood was part of her own heritage and she had recognized that he was a half-breed the first time she'd laid eyes on him. Didn't he realize how obvious his bloodline was?

"So today, I, André De Coux, only son of Jean De Coux, a French-Canadian trapper, and his squaw, Sweet Summer Rain of the Menominee tribe, tell you these things so that you will know me for who I am." Elan drew himself up proudly. "Elan was the name my mother called me, and when I left the mission school I took my name back to honor her memory."

Abby gave an involuntary little cry, bringing her fingers to her mouth.

Elan paused, steadying himself to meet Abby's pain at his betrayal. Had he been the man he wanted to be, he would have told her of his blood before taking her to his bed. Now he could only hope she could forgive him, that she would not hate him. "I tell you these things because I can no longer deny the love I have for you."

Abby felt the color drain from her face, saw the confused concern in Elan's eyes. André De Coux! Her great-great-grandfather? She swayed, suddenly light-headed as she groped to absorb and make sense of this bewildering enlightenment. She was in love with her great-great-grandfather, and he loved her. *He loved her!* The phrase sang through her mind. *He loved her!*

And then it came to her, the knowledge that left her with an overwhelming sense of peace, the acceptance of the absolute rightness of it all. *She was Sara Abigail De Coux.* All the pieces began to fall into place, and Abby was at last able to solve the puzzle.

She, Sara Abigail De Coux, was exactly where she was meant to be. She had been sent to this time for a specific purpose. She knew that now. Not only was Elan her great-great-grandfather, but she, Abby, was her own great-great-grandmother. She had been sent to marry Elan and to begin the legacy of the De Coux ranch. The conflicting claim the government used to seize the ranch made sense now. Her attorneys had contested the record of a prior claim to the land, but the government insisted it was there, a barely legible scrawl they all thought read Sparne. All she needed to do was remove the Spooner name from the homestead records, and the government would lose its advantage when it tried to take the ranch. The De Coux ranch would now stay in her family. She couldn't believe it hadn't occurred to her before that Sparne was actually Spooner.

Abby launched herself into Elan's arms, sobbing as she clung to the buckskin covering his chest. "Hold me, please hold me. Keep me close as long as we live and never let me go." Elan lifted her in his strong arms, dipping his head to press his mouth on her trembling lips as her arms encircled his neck and drew his head down. "Tell me again," Abby breathed into Elan's ear when he released her lips to nuzzle her neck. "Tell me you love me!"

"I love you, woman," he growled playfully, kissing the tip of her nose as his hands slid up her ribcage. "Now you have wrung it from me and I shall never know another minute of peace!" Abby laughed delightedly, wanting to sing, to dance with her new-found joy. "And if I can get you out of these clothes, I will show you how much! That is, if you do not mind bedding a half-breed," he added on a more serious note. Abby stayed his hands, then teasingly danced away.

"I'll take off my blouse, but first you have to take off your shirt!" Abby said, darting near and tugging at the buckskin before stepping lightly out of his reach. Elan unlaced the rawhide ties, then pulled his shirt over his head. He stood holding it in his hands.

"Done!" he called, lifting a dark brow suggestively. Abby shucked her vest, tossing it carelessly to the ground. She slowly unfastened the tiny cloth-covered buttons of her blouse, pulling it out of the waistband of her skirt to undo the last two. She shrugged it off, then held it out in one hand. Elan reached to take it, and she tugged it away, whirling in a circle. He caught her by the waist, stopping her spin. She laughed, breathlessly, dizzily, when his hands found the ribbon ties of her chemise. "What must I trade to remove this?" he inquired, rubbing the ribbons between his fingers and his thumb before lazily stroking her erect nipples beneath the thin material.

"Your name?" Abby asked softly, trembling beneath his touch. At his sharp intake of breath Abby's hands stilled their exploration of his muscled back.

"Done!" Elan lowered her to the lush green grass, pillowing her head with his arm. Abby sighed contentedly, her eyes wandering over Elan's shoulder to scan the big blue sky overhead. She had never imagined she could know such peace, such happiness. "Come back to me," he whispered in her ear. "Stay with me now and forever."

She smiled, hugging her newly acquired knowledge. When the time was right, she would tell him that their fates had joined for a purpose, just as he believed, and she would tell him who they were and why they had been sent to Montana Territory in the year 1875. It was their time, and they would make the most of it.

"I am with you, Elan. I am with you forever and always, even into our next life."

Major Stone Daniels dismounted, pulling off his gloves and slapping them impatiently against a hardened thigh while he allowed his horse to drink from the creek. His men were busy on a nearby hill, hastily burying the remains of Custer's Seventh. The scout, Walks Big, scrambled a ways down the bluff, motioning that he should come, then rushed back to the top.

The major hurried up the rise, leaving his mount behind in his excitement. Walks Big was rarely in a hurry, and if he was moving faster than molasses, something important was up. The major looped his gloves through his belt and took the field glasses from the scout, bringing them to his eyes to search the rolling hills of yellowed grass and sage.

Then he spotted the objects of Walks Big's interest.

Riding unhurriedly to the northwest and leading two pack horses were a big man dressed in buckskins and a woman wearing some sort of split skirt. They were moving slowly, kicking up little dust.

"What the hell?" the major asked, lowering the glasses and wiping his brow with his sleeve. It was hotter than hell out in the open, and his shirt was plastered to his back, making him itch. But even so, he was better off than the poor wretches burying the dead. He'd vow they would forgo their rations this day.

"Don't know," Walks Big grunted, reaching for the binoculars and peering through them. "Woman is white."

"What about the man?" The major took the binoculars from Walks Big and looked through them again as he asked his question.

"Can't say." The Indian shrugged indifferently. "Maybe. Maybe not."

"That's not a hell of a lot of help, Walks Big." The major shoved the field glasses at the scout and made his way down the rise. "You think we need to catch up with them?"

"What for?" Walks Big asked, coming down behind him.

"They might know something about what happened here," the major replied tiredly. Damn! It was like pulling teeth to get anything out of the Indian. Sometimes he thought the scout deliberately baited him.

"Big battle. Custer dead. Indians gone. What more to know?" Walks Big asked philosophically.

"Let's ride," the major said, not arguing the point as he gathered up his reins and mounted his horse. "I want to look through those burial lodges we passed a ways back."

"Bad medicine." Walks Big turned his mount in the opposite direction. "Ain't going."

"Suit yourself," the major replied, spurring his mount, pulling on his gloves as he rode.

The grass where he stopped and dismounted from his horse was matted, and the major fell to one knee as he examined the small boot prints. The woman. Larger moccasin prints belonging to the man. The tracks were fresh, only an hour or so old, and from the look of the broken grass stalks, it wasn't difficult to determine what the two had been doing in the shade of the cottonwood. The major grinned. Had he arrived a bit sooner, he'd have caught them at it.

He rose and strode toward the teepees, grimacing at the fresh scalps hanging obscenely on the poles. Thank God he had ridden with Gibbon and not Custer. His scalp was still firmly attached, and he wanted to keep it that way. He was a month out of Fort Lincoln, and feeling every weary day of it. He wondered when he'd see the fort again. He had a sinking feeling the Indian campaign was only just beginning.

The fetid air inside the lodge grabbed at his lungs, and he hurriedly untied his neckkerchief and used it to cover his nose. He didn't usually collect spoils of war, but his eye was drawn to a finely quilled medicine bag hanging on the center pole of the teepee. It would be an eye-catching ornament to hang from his saddle horn and to show the ladies on his next leave. Ladies back East in the States were always fascinated by the savage ways of the West. The bag was sure to gain him entry to many a young maid's bed. He reached for the bag.

Epilogue

August 15, 1877

Abby reclined on a quilt, her back propped against a towering pine on the rise overlooking her meadow, her hands resting comfortably atop the great mound of her belly as she watched Elan's approach from the creek. The birth of their child was only days away.

"How do you feel?" Elan set his buckets in the grass and dropped to one knee beside Abby on the quilt, his eyes quickly scanning her face for any sign of distress. Her pregnancy had been uneventful, but Elan guarded his charges most diligently, refusing to allow her to ride from the day she had told him of her condition and waiting on her to the point that she sometimes wanted to stamp her foot in vexation.

"I'm perfectly fine," Abby said. "I'm pregnant, Elan, not sick. You really shouldn't worry so much." He grinned at her, the lopsided grin she knew so well. It served to deepen his dimples and crinkle his eyes, and her heart melted, overflowing with love for the gentle giant who sheltered her so securely, shielding her from any hurt, any worry.

"Your time is near, and I think I should go to Helena and bring the doctor." Abby quickly shook her head, and Elan's grin vanished, replaced by a frown.

"You know I don't trust him," Abby said. "I thought we agreed." The baby kicked, and Abby smiled. He was going to be as strong as his father if his prenatal antics were any indication. She knew the baby would be a boy. She took Elan's hand and placed it on her belly, enjoying the look of wonder stealing across his face as he bent and placed his cheek on the mound. From the first time the baby moved and Abby shared it with him, Elan had been fascinated. A lock of dark hair fell across his forehead, obscuring his face, and Abby tenderly brushed it back, leaning to leave a kiss in its place.

"At least let me go for Annie." Elan lifted his head. "She will want to be with you."

"Annie can come later," Abby said, fingering the heavy gold chain and nugget hanging around his neck—the necklace she'd traded to Roberts, now back in her family, where it belonged. Elan had given it to her the day of their wedding, placing it around her neck to drape over the white lace and satin of the gown Annie had lovingly sewn for her. Abby had worn it until she conceived their child. Then she had taken Elan's gift to her and made it a gift to him, a gift to be handed down through the De Coux men from father to son, just as it was meant to be.

"I do not know if I can do this thing you ask," Elan said heavily, taking Abby's small hands in his much larger ones as he searched her serene face and found none of the fears he harbored. Instead, Abby's face was radiant, shining with an inner glow.

"We will do it together," Abby said. "There is no one I trust as I trust you. You will bring our children into this world, and they will grow and have children of their own who will populate and settle this land. This is the way it is meant to be."

Elan bowed his great head as he listened to Abby's confident words, taking strength from her convictions, for he knew her small size was no indication of her immense will. If she said it would be so, then it would be so. Lowering their hands to her belly, hands still locked together, his over hers, he made a vow. "Together, Abby, forever and always."

And so they were.

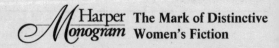

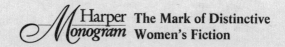

Echoes and Illusions
by Kathy Lynn Emerson

Lauren Ryder has everything she wants, but then
the dreams start—dreams so real she fears she's
losing her mind. Something happened to Lauren
in the not-so-distant past that she can't remember.
As she desperately tries to piece together the
missing years of her life, a shocking picture
emerges. Who is Lauren Ryder, really?

The Night Orchid by Patricia Simpson

In Seattle Marissa Quinn encounters a doctor
conducting ancient Druid time-travel rituals and
meets Alek, a glorious pre-Roman warrior trapped in
the modern world. Marissa and Alek discover that
though two millennia separate their lives, nothing
can sever the bond forged between their hearts.

Destiny Awaits by Suzanne Elizabeth

Tess Harper found herself in Kansas in the year
1885, face-to-face with the most captivating,
stubborn man she'd ever met—and two precious
little girls who needed a mother. Could this man,
and this family, be her true destiny?